UNDERCURRENTS

SUSIE NAPIER

ISBN 978-0-244-92468-3

"Oh what a tangled web we weave, when first we practise to deceive!"

Sir Walter Scott

Slipping the anchor

Fiona Lindsay hears its protest before she sees it in its bucket prison but she knows what must be there; a live crab hitting the sides in vain frustration. Though its pincer weapons are decommissioned by tightly wound rubber bands and its tenacious grip disabled, it still has enough weight to throw around and rattle its setting. Finding it thus surprises her, not because of its size or vigour but because she's never known her sister use anything but a cooked crab from the fishmonger to make her famous mousse. But Fiona has dispatched live crabs many times before now - yet something about this one makes her feel like an executioner. She stands there watching, hesitating, almost feeling sorry for it but it must be done. So, with her well placed piercing its protestations stop.

She picks up *The Scotsman* from the door mat and takes it to her room where she sprawls across her bed running a pencil down the listings of flats to let. Dundas Street; Great King Street; Cumberland Street. Nothing is suitable, those Edinburgh flats are too big for one girl on her own and there is nobody she wants to share with.

Rolling over she lies on her back aimlessly tapping her foot on the floor and thinking, not for the first time either, that it would be more sensible to find a job in London as all her closest friends have gone there. It's just that it feels such a big step. Then with a weary sigh she sits up and sees her reflection in the mirror. An image about which she can be confident but isn't. She presses her palms against her head of fluffed-up hair. It's so annoying to have loose blonde waves when the new decade's hairstyles are neat and sleek with flicks at the ends. Fiona Lindsay, undeniably so fair of face, so slim, so lithe of limb, tends like most women to wish for what she doesn't have.

'Fiona,' her sister Amy shouts from the bottom of the stairs, 'have you got the paper? Graham wants it.' It's her faintly irritated tone of voice again.

'Sorry, I'll bring it down.'

'Well make sure you do,' ricochets off the staircase wall.

And under her breath Fiona says, 'anyone would think I made a habit of it. It's Saturday morning, nobody's in a rush are they?' while tugging a brush through her hair. Then picking up the newspaper she picks up her thoughts again too. It isn't that she doesn't like her teaching job at Miss Bethune's Cookery School, she likes her brother-in-law Graham Burnet too, she certainly doesn't dislike her sister Amy, and she loves her small niece and nephew. Then there's her room at the Burnet's house in Caroline Street, she's grown quite fond of it since moving there three years ago in 1957. But she can't help what she feels and she feels she has outstayed her welcome. She knows a job in London makes sense and it would mean she could leave with the maximum of grace and the minimum of enquiry. All she has to do is get used to the idea.

Apologising to Graham when she hands him the paper, he replies that he hadn't known she had it and it doesn't matter, then he asks what she's doing today. Only lunch with Mary and the cinema afterwards. He's stopped from saying anything else when his children, Mathew and Petrina, giggle into the room, crash on his lap and he tickles them until they shriek.

'Don't encourage them, Graham,' Amy says while snapping on her leather gloves then cramming a flat hat on the back of her head. 'I'm taking the car and your lunch is under the pyrex dish. Fiona, make me a big apple pie for tomorrow's lunch will you? Graham, you haven't forgotten your brother's ship is back in Rosyth and he's coming for lunch tomorrow?' said while she's applying lipstick without benefit of a mirror. 'So is Nigel MacMuckle - you haven't forgotten that have you?'

He has forgotten, about his brother that is, his mind is more on the painting Nigel's bringing for the next art sale. 'That Wilkie he has on the Victorian landing at Glenduir.'

'Honestly, Graham!' Amy's exasperation out of proportion to the offence, but that's the way it is. And off she goes, herding the children and herself sideways out of the door in a welter of instructions to, 'do as you're told; don't forget your mittens; put your hats on the right way round - because it isn't funny like that.' And, 'Fiona, you haven't forgotten about the crab have you, make it into a mousse won't you.' There's no question mark though.

'I'm going out, Amy...'

And the disembodied voice calls, 'but *you* can make a mousse and an apple pie standing on your head and in record time can't you?'

'You didn't let me finish. I've done it, I'm waiting for it to cool.'

And when the hall echoes with the slammed door's full stop, Graham, shaking his head, says, 'happy families eh, Fiona?'

Motherhood and apple pie, Fiona wonders who said that when later she walks up the hill to The Clipe Coffee House. She's pleased with her new camel coat even if it had been too expensive. Then she stops to tuck her independent waves back under her silk head scarf and check her watch - it's one o'clock. And from the Castle's battlements the cannon fires once telling Edinburgh the time too. Looking north across the Firth of Forth she can't see much, the invading sea mist is too heavy. They call it the haar and Fiona Lindsay hates it.

Foghorns in the Firth of Forth estuary boom their mournful notes and are so familiar to her that she hardly ever notices but today she can't ignore them. It's like hearing a requiem for an interrupted life, an early abandonment of all she'd wanted and loved, for her childhood home across that same stretch of water in Fife. The Grange they call it. That fine, old house with its south-facing fields dropping away into the distance of golden sands. The place where she played as a child and from where on a summer's day you could see the Island of May in the sparkling Forth. The house, the farm, everything is owned by a stranger now but the beach belongs to everyone and she's been back there over the past three years, always with the children and Amy. Whichever sister is driving, and without a word spoken, they always avoid that junction. The one which claimed their parents' lives one haar-hung night on this same date three years ago. The hated haar that tricks your eyes into mistaking your speed and the direction of others' veiled headlights... She sniffs sharply, brushes away a fugitive tear and plunging her hands into her pockets she's almost at the Coffee House.

Mary says she look down in the dumps, so that's blamed on the weather. But once they settle at a corner table to gossip it isn't really a surprise when Mary says she's got the job in Paris as an au pair.

'Very soon I'm going to be the only person I know left in Edinburgh,' Fiona says. 'I'm thinking of going to London but I like teaching at Bella Bethune's, though sometimes I feel I'm still a student there. She takes me under her wing you know. I think she sees me as some poor, orphan child - but I shouldn't mock, she's very kind.'

'Well then, go to London, you should. You haven't got anyone at the moment have you, there's no-one to keep you here is there? Unless you're keeping quiet about that farmer,' Mary laughs. 'The one at your twenty-first birthday party and the other one. Your brother-in-law's friend, you know - the painter?'

Fiona puffs her cheeks out and puts her fork down, 'oh, the farmer, yes, pity about him,' and cocks her head when she says, 'would anyone really want graphic descriptions of Aberdeen Angus bulls and artificial insemination techniques while trying to eat a steak? It put me right off.' As for the painter - well, he wanted to paint me in the nude.'

'I should think so, most men would.'

'That's it, most men. But he wasn't most men, if you see what I mean.'

'Oo, how exotic - so you can pose for him without worrying,' Mary means it.

'A shame really because he was interesting and attractive, damn it.' Fiona means it too.

62 Caroline Street is deserted when Fiona gets home that evening. No children's chatter and noises, no Home Service voices from the radio in the kitchen, no opera playing on Graham's old gramophone. She makes the apple pie in silence thinking how she'll miss the elegant Georgian house she's had no choice but to call home. But home is as much a state of mind as place and that unwanted, bleak thought tries to settle but is interrupted by a sound like a clapper board as the front door opens. There's Amy's sheep dog manoeuvres to keep the children on track and the usual familiar sounds. Calls to put the kettle on; coats to be taken off; eggs to be boiled; toast to be made. There's Graham's waft of Gauloise tobacco as he nods absently at instructions not to over-excite the little ones at tea-time. The bustle of family life. Yes, Fiona will miss that whether she's in London or only a matter of streets away. But this is Amy's, this is her home, her husband, her children, she has certainty, security, not the bereft void Fiona feels

- like one uncherished, one dispossessed. Then Graham halts those gathering reminders with what appears to be a highly original thought, yet it isn't for the first time. He suggests they have tea with the children and Amy's protestation is poorly staged. Unconvinced by her performance Fiona knows the real reason is that they want to watch the new television set. And she, not in guilty thrall of the new house entertainment, baths the children and puts them to bed then reads them a story too, something she enjoys. Yet when she joins the adults they've watched *Dixon of Dock Green* and the television is turned off. Their restraint is not quite yet eroded. Amy's knitting needles click and Graham sits staring at the half-hearted fire snapping and smoking in the grate.

Then looking at her as she sits on the piano stool he says, 'why don't you play something for us, Fiona? Play something gentle, play *Liebestraum*, you always do it so well, so expressively...'

'Something else she's so good at?' Amy's mouth smiles a little but she doesn't look up from her needles. 'But wait a minute, you haven't told me what you did today, Fiona?' and with that the knitting is laid aside.

'Me? lunch, the film - you know. I think I'll buy myself a new dress for the Christmas Ball.'

'So, you weren't looking at a flat?' Amy says ignoring Graham's obvious glare.

'I... How did you know?' but Graham saves her.

'Amy?' he says slowly but turns to look at Fiona. 'She spotted it in the paper, you'd marked the column.'

'Well, no I wasn't,' Fiona says looking down at her hands splayed on her knees.

And Amy cranes to catch her sister's eye when she asks, 'were you going to tell us?'

'I was - but I think I've made up my mind to go to London, you know I could share - and well,' she says, expecting an interruption. 'I mean - you don't mind?'

'Why would we?' Amy shrugs. 'I can understand that, I mean I can understand your wanting to be more independent. You can too, can't you, Graham?' He agrees yet with some discernible reluctance. And, apart from asking Fiona when she thinks she might move out and is she hoping to find a similar job in London, the subject closes quickly and nothing more is said. That Amy has let go so easily astonishes Fiona, it's what she wanted but finds she resents and those abandoned comparisons at tea-time muster again. Unconsciously she flicks her hand as if to bat them back into her hinterland of gagged grief. Fiona's fractured life has yet to heal and how, with all its comfortable compensations, can Amy's loss equal hers? Though knitting needles tick-tick and the fire spits there's another void left hanging in that room and nothing with which to fill it - *Liebestraum* won't do now. So checking on the apple pie and crab mousse gives Fiona a reason to leave the very married Burnets to their silent, domestic coupledom by a struggling fire and blank television screen.

Got away with it! No discussion - she doesn't mind!!! My fate is sealed. Bought My Fair Lady LP - Saw Thirty-nine Steps. Mary going to work in Paris. <u>Eddie Burnet</u> tomorrow.

The page in Fiona's diary lies open with last night's entry written up in her neat handwriting. While she puts it back under the lining paper in her dressing table drawer she hears Eddie arrive. She's pleased he's coming. And, as she usually does, Amy will perk up too when he's around. Probably because there are always parties on board his ship, *HMS Continent*. But Nigel MacMuckle is late, Graham looks at the clock when Eddie says he's looking forward to seeing him, it's been a while. Then Eddie plays with the image, chuckling over, 'The MacMuckle of MacMuckle, Clan Chief in all his finery, who could forget that?' And Fiona looks at the Burnet brothers both out of the same mould but so different, she's never noticed or thought about it before. Eddie the traditionalist, the trained leader and as tall and narrow as Graham is short and round. Graham, the chairman of the family Fine Art Auction House. Graham with his softness, his fairish hair nearly reaching his collar, his fresh complexion, his comfortable bulk and wearing his stylish clothes unselfconsciously like the aesthete he is. He doesn't look as if he should pair with his conventional brother any more than he should with Amy. She's slim and straight, conventionally dressed too, dark hair off her brow, flicked at the ends and framing a sallow, androgynous face of planes and angles. What Graham likes to describe as a stylized art deco portrait. Looking at those three people she's known all her life Fiona thinks how much one takes for granted if you've grown up with them. Almost as if you don't see them or what they really are, as if familiarity breeds a kind of blindness. Graham asked Amy to marry him as soon as she was old enough to like the idea, now Fiona thinks she married the wrong brother.

And she hears Nigel MacMuckle's voice before she sees him. He sounds like her father and it makes her think of the best chocolate, deep and smooth. And she's curious to see the man she's never met yet has always known something about. The man with the mad name and a feudal, Lairdly life.

'Hope I haven't held you up, Amy,' he says as he bends to kiss her while casually handing Graham a dusty painting. Of course she says he hasn't and passes him on to Fiona whom he's always managed to miss since she's been living at Caroline Street. 'At last, Fiona, and how d'you do,' he says smiling and holding her hand in both of his, but Eddie has to be greeted and reminisced with. So Fiona looks more closely at Nigel MacMuckle, broad shouldered and tall with his open smile and very, blue eyes. His wild, wavy, dark, red hair and lots of it too. Yes, she supposes he would be thought imposing, but finery? Old, worn corduroys, leather-patched tweed jacket, Argyll and Sutherland Highlanders' tie - but his brogues are polished to a high shine. So he is *The* MacMuckle of MacMuckle, he couldn't be anything else but the definite article she thinks just as he turns round and smiles at her again.

'No I made lunch, Fiona only made the mousse and this apple pie,' Amy replies to Eddie's question as she mashes the pudding up for Mathew. But apple pie is a favourite of Eddie's especially with custard and Fiona's isn't out of a packet either. Nigel agrees with him but includes a compliment on Amy's roast beef.

'Did *The Thirty-nine Steps* film do John Buchan credit, Fiona?' Graham asks. She thinks so and is sure he'd like it. 'Would you like to see it again then?' he says.

'Why would she?' Amy's eyes widen to match her vowels and Nigel jerks his head as if he's been cuffed about the ear. 'I mean once you've seen it, you've seen it,' she goes on, 'and anyway nothing is ever as good as the original book, don't you think?' and she looks at her two guests for affirmation only to be teased by her husband about her lofty tastes.

'Well, I'm something of a Buchan fan,' Nigel sounds apologetic about this. 'So I would be critical too, Amy, but I'd like to see it anyway.'

At this Graham claps his hands together and with some literary pretension says, 'and why doesn't that surprise me, you are a natural Buchan hero with your inclination to tramp the heather and sleep under the stars on damp bog-myrtle.' Then with some feeling, 'I'll never forget the hundreds of midge bites I had to put up with. Irritatingly, they appear to know not to bite the Laird.'

'Nah, come on, you know I've grown out of that,' Nigel says, leaning back in his chair. 'I got it out of my system during National Service, now I go cross country ski-ing in Norway, in fact I'm off there soon,' and he catches Fiona's eye. But she's more interested in Eddie now asking if they are all coming to the party on board the ship - of course they are. Though there's regret that Nigel lives so far away otherwise he'd have an invitation. He regrets living so far away too because getting to the back of beyond takes a long time and he should be on his way.

'You'll come back next week to see your painting go under the hammer, won't you?' Graham presumes. 'I'm taking the sale myself.'

'I wasn't planning to,' he says, then glancing at Fiona. 'Can I let you know?'

'And you'll stay here won't you?' Amy says.'

So getting up from the table, he quietly says to Fiona, 'might see you again at the end of the week.'

When he's gone they talk about Nigel MacMuckle, the years he lived in Edinburgh. About the flat in Heriot Row he'd shared with his cousin Charlie Scott. How Charlie went to South Africa and Nigel back to his rundown castle in Glenduir and they agree that couldn't have been a particularly welcome prospect.

'Why, what did he do when he lived here?' Fiona asks.

'He learned the wine trade. He knew what was planned for him so he didn't need a career path. But I think he'd rather be here than there,' says Graham.

'Why?'

'His mother had lost almost everything after his father died. The land and moorland I mean, and there is only one hill farm left and it's tenanted. She wouldn't take advice from anyone. Anyway, I want to take another look at this Wilkie picture he's selling. Poor bugger, selling paintings for much needed funds is becoming a

10

regular habit these days. He should do more painting himself, he's good. But Jean, that mother of his, never encouraged it and I suspect she's made him feel it's not quite comme il faut, as she'd probably put it.'

'Not married either, like me,' says Eddie.

'Surprisingly not. He's had lots of girlfriends, some pretty keen, but he's never sealed the deal,' Graham says as he wipes dust from the canvas.

It surprises Fiona that someone like Nigel should be artistic. To her he seems to be so typical of what he is in life. Yet it surprises her more that so many girls had been keen on such a shambolic figure - quietly charming though he is.

Underway

'Which one should I wear, Amy?' Fiona at her bedroom door holds a blue patterned cocktail dress in one hand and a black one in the other, but Graham chooses the one with the tight skirt before his wife can answer. Happy with his choice, Fiona then spends more time than usual doing her hair and make-up, choosing the right shoes and making sure the seams of her stockings are straight. Two sprays of Chanel No 5 and a couple more on her hair then she's ready to be seen at the cocktail party on board *HMS Continent.*

The Officers' Wardroom is full of people, too full, but Eddie quickly finds them only for Amy to attempt some kind of confidential exchange with him. Fiona, glass in hand, sees a friend but Amy grabs her before she can say anything to anyone.

'Fiona, Fiona, that's Tim Robinson, watch out,' she says under her breath and would have winked if it hadn't been bred out of her. Naturally Fiona wants to know why. With a slight air of agitation Amy nods in his direction, 'I must have told you about him - he's the navigator, he's the one who... I must have done.'

'No you haven't,' but another young officer with a braying laugh corners Fiona for an introduction. She gives him as little mannerly attention as she can get away with while she looks over his shoulder at the one she is supposed to have known about. The one in the chalk stripe suit, neat, brushed, the confident, good looking one, the one with dark, shiny, floppy hair, dark brows and blue, very blue, eyes. The one with the teasing, easy smile - Tim Robinson. Watch out is what she's been told to do and watch him she does. She listens too while Amy chats quietly about him to a politely reluctant Eddie. Straining to hear what they have to say against the other man's unwanted prating, she catches only fragments.

'... a love 'em and leave 'em type...' questions Amy and Eddie shakes his head.

'...charming and amusing,' he replies and Fiona thinks there's a note of admiration in his voice.

Then Amy, quite loudly this time, lets out, 'one-night stand type,' and definitely with far too much relish Fiona thinks. But the young man with her, who is rapidly becoming an unwanted limpet, asks a question and she misses the next exchange. When he draws breath and gulps his pink gin she hears Amy again and quite clearly too.

'I've already met Tim Robinson briefly - the last time you were here, you know he's bruised a number of girls by his liaisons with them, and, do you know there's a rumour he even has a little black book!' Sharply, Fiona turns to look at her sister and sees Eddie's raised eyebrows too.

'Well,' he says, 'there's never a shortage of willing lambs queuing up for Tim Robinson's kind of slaughter, Amy.' Fiona hears that quite distinctly and the silence with which it's met.

As if revived by his gin, the socially challenged one declares he is *HMS Continent's* Supply Officer and tells of how the cases of water biscuits have been smashed by careless handling and what a bore it is for him and his careful calculations. But he finds it funny too, so in the midst of his guffaws Fiona doesn't hear Eddie say that she's grown up very pretty and is going to be able to take her pick. She doesn't see Amy's expression either. But it is Eddie who rescues her from stories of shattered biscuits. With a quickness of step and thought she takes another gin and tonic and is steered back to Amy. But she's in deep conversation now with a plump, fussing friend.

'I nearly had a fit when we arrived - he couldn't be avoided and neither could I,' she harrumphs.

'Are you sure he recognised you?'

'Well he's seen me often enough, Amy, he was never out of our flat, for goodness sake.'

And beginning to take notice, Graham says, 'who are you talking about, it sounds intriguing?'

'Tim Robinson - that's who,' Amy whispers.

And like a conspirator he whispers back, 'oh I see, what's he done?'

'For your information, Graham, he took advantage of my flat-mate, that's what he did - and far too often as well,' says Amy's friend with a nod and a sniff. 'Then it was on to some other poor girl with hardly so much as a by your leave. That's what he does, and, she's still upset.'

'Oh heaven forfend, breaks hearts for a hobby does he? What a cad, tut tut, what's the officer class coming to?' Graham sucks his teeth. 'It must be the times we live in, 1960 - but no, hang on, this is Scotland so up with Calvin and down with free love.' He laughs at his own joke, adding, 'come to think of it, we don't do free much of anything,' and splashes his drink over the fussy friend.

'Shh, here he comes,' Amy says through a fixed smile but her friend, blotting her bosom, turns to the loitering Supply Officer.

Tim Robinson had noticed Fiona and it's Eddie who's to introduce him. As if she knows, she looks at him as he crosses the room with a lop-sided almost half smile, as if he's holding something back. Putting out his hand to Fiona he introduces himself.

'He's our navigator,' Eddie says, 'I don't think you've met before have you?'

'No we haven't,' they reply as one and laugh at it like two ham actors. Amy manages to combine a warm reminder that they've briefly met before with a glassy-eyed look but Graham takes her away. It isn't an awkward silence but the social cues do fail and looking up at the young man with the attractive smile makes Fiona smile about his rumoured little black book.

'So, you're the navigator, does that mean you're good at keeping on the straight and narrow?' she blurts. 'Sorry no, I didn't mean that, I mean you keep everyone else - the ship - on the straight and narrow.'

'Well I try to,' he laughs, quite naturally now. 'But sometimes you can't take a straight course, surely you don't want to hear about that do you? What do you do, Fiona, I'm sure it's a great deal more interesting than charts and compass?'

'Me? I teach girls to cook for a Cordon Bleu certificate and that's not interesting either.'

'Not at all, I like good food but you have to go to France to get it. Take lamb, the Navy cooks it for too long. I like mine pink, just the other side of slaughter. I should get you to show the ship's chefs how to do it properly.'

'You like lamb?' she chokes.

'Ah ha, so you haven't had one of our gins before - strong aren't they?' he laughs. 'Do you want me to give you a pat on the back?' his hand raised and ready but she's alright. 'Have you been on board any of HM ships before?'

'My father was in the Navy, but I was too young for cocktail parties then. If we ever went on board a sailor would look after us, they were good fun,' and she looks round quickly. 'You know, even without your uniforms, in mufti you all look...'

'The same?' Tim laughs. But she dries up because she's seen the suede, desert boots on his feet. Was that a strike of individuality against all the other polished black leather shoes? 'You're right though. You see it's an easy option,' and he pats his lapels. 'The problem comes when we try to dress casually, my brother's a Royal

Marine and he says it's too creative for military types you see. So swarms of us turn up ashore in matching dark suits, or at a pinch flannels and sports coats and in the end it's just another uniform. I like your dress.' That makes her feel better, but she blushes anyway. Then touching her arm he says, 'you didn't get lectured on any victualling problems by our Supply Officer I hope.'

'Oh yes I did,' and they both look at him on his own and she feels a bit mean.

'He could tell the chefs to roast the lamb pink if you said he should.'

Fiona looks down and shakes her head. 'Now Tim, that wouldn't do, would it?' she says, surprised at how challenging she sounds.

'No I suppose it wouldn't, but I can think of something that I hope would. Will you let me take you out to dinner, somewhere up to your standards, how about Friday night? We aren't in harbour for very long before we're off again.'

'Friday? I mean yes please, thank you very much,' she says, thinking she doesn't much care if he only takes her out for a bag of chips.

Amy watches, Graham watches, Eddie watches, but Fiona and Tim don't notice and for the rest of that short evening they talk only to each other. He makes it easy. She likes his teasing expression, he's funny too with a rumbling laugh gathering into a suppressed explosion and infecting her by its unexpectedness. Too soon though Amy is ordering them to leave, they've stayed long enough. Fiona looks at her watch, the time has gone so quickly but in the hub-bub of departure Tim touches her arm.

'See you Friday, seven thirty? I'll get your address and number from Eddie.'

In the car on the journey home, Graham ribs Fiona saying he thinks she's made an impression, chuckling that she has a choice between the noisy Supply Officer or the smooth Navigator. He scoffs at Tim's supposed reputation, at what Amy calls him; 'a sex maniac'. He says it must be an exaggeration. But Amy won't have it, she cites those broken-hearted girls so there has to be truth in it. Leaning sideways towards her he taunts with, 'maybe they threw themselves at him. It does happen you know, Amy. He's handsome and entertaining isn't he, isn't that supposed to be irresistible in a man?'

'Why ask me?' a slight scowl in her tone, but Graham just grins straight ahead at the road.

So Fiona says brightly, 'well I'll be able to tell you, he's asked me out to dinner on Friday.'

'You what?' and Amy turns round to look at her in the dark.

'Dinner - going out to dinner with Tim Robinson.' Fiona's cat's cream smile briefly lit by a street lamp. In the sudden silence, for the first time ever, Fiona hears her sister lost for words, and in the rear mirror she can see Graham smirk. Then suddenly Amy takes a noisy gulp of breath.

'Did you see what he had on his feet? she says. He's supposed to be an officer for heaven's sake...'

'Oh well, that's that then isn't it?' Graham says trying not to laugh and failing. 'Fiona, you can't possibly go out with a man who wears *brothel creepers*.' Then he sucks his teeth, 'he probably wears his socks in bed too. No, Fiona, it just won't do, you can't risk it.' And she tucks her head down trying to smother her giggles while Amy huffs and calls them both immature.

But her little sister trills, '*I* think he's what you'd call dashing, Amy, and I happen to like his brothel creepers - and him too, he's nice,' and she tosses her head though they can't see that.

'Dashing, dashing?' The best Amy can come up with for that, then it's, 'as for nice well *I* know his reputation and it is *not* nice.

And isn't that part of the reason Fiona wants to know more?

Mary comes for supper on Wednesday and Nigel MacMuckle turns up too. He's tidier this time though his hair is as wild as it was before but Fiona is now thinking it suits his fine head. He arrives with a bottle of single malt whisky for Graham and chocolates for Amy. Then he fishes in the pocket of his big, tweed coat, saying he hopes she'll like it and hands Fiona a copy of Elizabeth David's *French Provincial Cooking*. For a moment she doesn't know what to say, too embarrassed by his unexpected present, but thanks stumble out as she holds it up against her. He hopes she hasn't got it already.

'No, no I haven't, I really wanted this I was going to buy it.' She is delighted but he looks delighted too. She almost wants to kiss him as she would anyone else who'd given her a present, but never before has someone on so slight an acquaintance done such a thing and she stands awkwardly wondering what to do or say next. So Mary takes the book from her and flicking the pages looks up at Nigel to tell him Fiona is cooking tonight and did he know?

Of course he didn't and anyway he's sure Elizabeth David can't teach Fiona anything. Fiona thinks him a flatterer. But she's embarrassed by his compliment too and apologises that they're not going to be eating anything French tonight just venison casserole, as Scottish as can be. Nigel rubs his hands together.

'Oh good, that's a favourite of mine,' he says and then she thinks he's a shameless flatterer. But potatoes waiting to be boiled need her attention and while she puts the pan on the hob she can't help feeling touched by his thoughtfulness.

Mary still has the book when she comes into the kitchen opens it and reads out, *To dear Fiona, with love, Nigel. November 1960.* Looking at Mary standing in front of her with a silly grin on her face, Fiona puts a hand on her hip with, 'isn't that a bit much, I mean - with love? I've only met him once.'

'Well, he obviously has it in mind that you are going to be meeting a lot more, hasn't he?'

'D'you think so?'

'Of course, I think he's quite dishy.'

'What?'

'Yes, can't you see it?'

'No, not really.' Then she remembers. 'But Graham did say he'd had lots of keen girlfriends, so maybe I am missing something. Honestly, it's like that thing people say about buses all coming at the same time...'

'Why, who else is there? You've kept that quiet.'

'No, I've just met someone that I *did* think was quite dishy...'

'And?'

'I don't know if there's going to be an 'and' but I hope so. He's taking me out to dinner on Friday night - we'll see.'

'Come on then,' Mary says, 'turn the tatties down and join the party next door, see if you can see what I see with Mr MacMuckle.'

'Want this,' Graham asks and holds up Nigel's present of twenty-five year old Driech Single Malt. Mary does, she wants to try it, then she sits down on the small sofa next to Nigel. Fiona notices that as she asks for her usual gin and tonic - and come to think of it she's never known Mary drink whisky before - or ask anyone about paintings and very quickly her friend and Nigel look as if they are chatting like old friends. What does Mary know about his valuable piece of Scottish art going under the hammer tomorrow? Mary isn't interested in paintings, Scottish or otherwise. But then Fiona remembers the potatoes and drags herself away muttering she should mash the tatties. Nobody pays attention except Nigel, he likes mashing potatoes, he says he's good at it and he's told the truth.

Draining them with a flourish, mashing them with vigour, back on the ring, adding butter and milk, stirring to stop them catching then adding salt and pepper. Keen to know if they are good enough he offers her the pan and spoon. Fiona is impressed. They taste perfect and with no lumps either.

'You know what you're doing,' she says.

'Hm, well I think so,' and he dollops them into a vegetable dish asking if there is anything else he can do to help.

'Do you cook, Nigel? I'm surprised.'

'No, not really, well not at all,' and he scrapes the pan. 'You see my mother has a cook- housekeeper but she's never been very good at the cooking bit and I'm afraid my mother is clueless, so I've had to learn to do some basic stuff like scrambled eggs. As for mashed tatties, someone else showed me how she did hers because you can't imagine they could possibly be so dire until you've had them at my mother's table. It doesn't help that she never eats the things.'

Fiona, leaning against the kitchen table with her arms folded, smiles at his honesty but feels sorry for him despite the humour in his telling. 'Nigel, thank you so much for the book it really was very thoughtful of you,' she says as he lifts the casserole out of the oven for her. 'I was so surprised, you see - and it was so unexpected too - and thanks for your very nice inscription, I didn't notice it at first. He puts his hand on her arm as if to stop her running on.

'My pleasure, Fiona. I'm glad I got it right.'

Most of them talk about red deer and stalking while they eat the venison. Nigel's time in the wine trade as they drink the Chateauneuf du Pape and the coincidence of Mary's brother renting the same flat in Heriot Row that Nigel shared with his cousin in the mid 1950s. And yet another coincidence, that when it was put in front of him the lemon mousse happens to be a particular favourite of his. But this time Fiona doesn't think Nigel MacMuckle is a flatterer. She likes him. Clearly, her friend does too.

And when Mary leaves, Fiona stands at the door to see her off, it is raining heavily so Nigel grabs an umbrella and accompanies

Mary down the steps and to the waiting taxi, he's even asked her address and passes it on to the driver. He waits there until she goes while Fiona watches from the shelter of the doorway. He did such a simple thing, something taken for granted yet open to another interpretation in a way Fiona's never thought of before. She thinks that's probably how Mary understood it.

The house is still at 7 o'clock on Thursday morning except for Fiona creeping down the stairs trying not to wake anyone. Then she hears a familiar voice call her name and with a jolt she looks up to see Nigel leaning over the banister rail above her. 'Sorry Fiona, didn't mean to startle you...'

'Nigel! No you didn't,' shaking her head, pressing her fingers to her brow.

'It doesn't look like it,' and he makes to join her below.

'No it's alright, it's just that - your voice, you sound like my father,' and waves her hand as if to stop him in his tracks.

'Perhaps we went to the same school?' he teases. And that's attractive, then she sees him properly. The smile, the eyes, the hair, tamed from its first and probably only brushing of the day. Without pyjamas covering those well formed calves or triangle of chest, it is clear the only garment he wears is a Paisley silk dressing gown, tied tightly at the waist. She's going to Perth and it's on his way home, he wants to drive her there.

'Thank you but I'm driving there to collect some big cooking pots and wouldn't be able to take the train back.'

'Easy, I'll bring you back again too.'

'It will take up too much of your time, you have to be at the auction this morning.'

He doesn't give up. 'Well, what about tea, anything later in the day, the picture will be sold by then?' But that can't be done either, she has someone to see and then her grandmother on the way back.

This is true but she knows it sounds like an excuse and she feels as if she's disappointing an affectionate child.

'What about some other time?' she says as consolation.

'Promise?' he says, turning into an eager and affectionate child. So she promises but she really does have to go. She leaves him with wishes for luck, lots of money for the painting and more thanks for the cookery book.

'Safe journey, Fiona. I'll be in touch.'

So Mary was right, he does plan to meet up again. The idea isn't unappealing but she can't help feeling cornered. Yet now there's the intriguing image of him stripped of all his thrown together clothes, revealing enough athletic attraction to keep her interest. Something pleasant and new to her flutters in her stomach as she thinks about it.

'That'll put some lead on his roof,' is how Graham puts Nigel's profit from his dusty, grimy picture. It sold for well over the estimate and he's gone home to Glenduir with the prospect of very handsome cheque. Fiona is pleased for him but is his place really as bad as they make out? Worse, she's told but the MacMuckles probably don't see how bad it is and it's so big they probably forget about how much needs doing in all the rooms and places they don't use. But Amy says it's a very romantic place and that Fiona would probably like it except that it's so far away - and she's very keen to know if Fiona likes Nigel.

'Yes, why wouldn't I, but I think Mary did more.'

'She always was a flirt, I think he was just being polite,' and Fiona knows she's right. Nigel's politeness and relaxed good humour annoyingly ticks another box for her.

'Where is Glenduir?' she asks.

'Up a remote glen an hour away from Inverness, why?' Amy smiles.

'Just wondered.'

Tim had booked a table at The Skeely Skipper overlooking the Firth of Forth and as they step through the doors he stops in surprise at the burst of lights, mirrors and brassy gold. But Fiona knows it and has been there before, everyone has, it's been around for decades and is the place to go. Ushered to a table in one of the bays, Tim eyes the mirrored walls, which don't let anyone escape images of themselves at all angles including ones never even seen before. Sitting side by side on a red, plush banquette she points at their many reflected selves like pieces in a kaleidoscope and he admits to thinking it is a bit off-putting that you can't turn your back on it and does she mind. Of course she says she doesn't.

With all the aplomb she knows he will have, he orders oysters once he's sure she likes them. It isn't that she doesn't, it's their clichéd symbolism which bothers her. It's impossible for him at twenty-nine and with worldly ways not to know it either. But their next course, his lamb cutlets - and of course he wants them pink - and her Dover sole hold no erotic messages as far as she knows. Settling back and angling himself towards her he takes her hand and fixes those blue, blue eyes on her.

'You know we sail again soon don't you?' he says, 'so if it's alright with you can I suggest that until then we do this a lot and often?' with a twitch of a squeeze on her hand. She nods. 'Good, well in other places too and you can show me some of the sights. I want to go along the Fife coast and I'd sail to The Island of May if the weather was alright, which it isn't - do you sail?'

'Yes, and my childhood home looks out to the island. My father took us girls out there in the boat - in the summertime, I liked that. Pity we can't now, but we can go to the beach near my old house, I think you'd like that but we'll have to choose a good day otherwise you won't see a thing in the haar.'

And he looks pleased with himself, 'ah, the haar, I know what that is. D'you like that - impressive for a Sassenach wouldn't you say?'

And she laughs at it, 'no it isn't Tim, you know because you're a sailor and you've been told.'

'Well it was worth a try. Any chance we could do your beach tomorrow?'

'Tomorrow?'

'If you're free why not? Remember we aren't here for long. How about it, eh?'

'Well... why not,' and she wonders why she feels she should have hesitated.

'Jolly good and here's our oysters,' he says and sits back.

Laid before them in a silver dish, twelve fleshy invitations glisten in their shells. Fat lemon wedges perch round the edges and a sauce boat of something for dressing sits in the middle. Tim's request for Tabasco is put in front of him and without words he picks a shell up in his fingers and turns to her.

'Naked or dressed?' he asks straight-faced and nods at the condiments.

Did he really say that? 'Erm... Naked I think?'

'Open,' he says and moves the oyster close to her lips. 'Head back a bit - that's it. Good?'

Everywhere in the mirrors she sees endless clones of themselves from different points of view. It adds to her embarrassment, and she always chews oysters too. He looks at her, that half smile playing, his head cocked as if he's waiting for something. 'If you swallow it in one you can't really taste the sea, or d'you think that's being a philistine?' she explains and drinks some water.

'Don't be ridiculous, you could never be a philistine, Fiona, you do what you like. Want another one?' he makes to pick it up.

'No, it's your turn,' and she has no intention of feeding it to him.

24

'Well I like mine spiced up, you should try it on the next one.' Sprinkling a dash of Tabasco first then the lemon and with a deft hand he pours the shell's loose contents into his mouth without a drip. 'These *are* good, 'he says. 'Go on have another,' but she pounces on one before he's stopped talking. She would try it his way this time then realises she'll have to put it down. But as if he's read her thoughts he applies the extras then watches with a teasing smile as she tips his preference into her mouth - and dribbles. Could it get more embarrassing than her chin being dabbed by a handsome man in a chalk-striped suit with dark, floppy hair and blue, very blue eyes? Yes it could when she is her own unavoidable observer in all the mirrors and the object of other people's attention too. She whispers that she's making a dog's dinner of everything while she wipes away the spicy brine dripping down her open neckline. 'No you're not,' he says and hands her another oyster. As he does she feels his thigh settle alongside hers but she doesn't move an inch. Neither does she during her Dover sole or Peach Melba.

Much giving and taking passes between them while they concentrate close-up on their physical selves both finding their mirrored multiples disconcerting. His interest confirmed with those steady blue eyes of his and the little taps and touches of finger tips. She feels when the coffee cups are empty that she is too and as if she's known him much longer. Then she looks ahead forgetting she'll meet her face's inevitable reflection, Tim is still turned to face her and she points to their reflection repeated into infinity. She says, 'look, d'you see? It goes on forever, we can't get away.'

And so he looks too, saying, 'don't think I want to, Fiona.'

It is such a perfect ending that she knows she shouldn't speak even though the same sentiment is poised in her head.

The taxi takes too short a time to reach Caroline Street, she asks him in but he won't. He takes her to the door and she puts her hand on the handle but he holds it there. They have The Grange beach tomorrow to look forward to 'even if it rains frogs and blows a hoolie.' Then he lets her hand go to hold her face and kisses her very gently on the lips - and then again.

Falling in...

Tim likes her red Mini though Fiona doesn't quite believe him once she knows he's left a MGB at home in Hampshire. And for her, once in Fife, the further east they drive the more she likes that. They pass through Seatoun, a village lining the beach and she points out the hotel by the harbour, that's where they should have lunch.

Standing on the track overlooking the sea she points back to The Grange in the misty distance across a long field dotted with pigeons and gulls picking at the rich earth. She describes the house and how much she'd loved the place and wants to believe him when he says he would have liked to live there too. He takes her word for it that the house gave a good view of the May Island, its foghorn's persistent voice is almost the only evidence that anything is there in the haar.

'I think you miss your parents very much don't you?' he says. 'My father isn't too well, he's convalescing in Madeira... Anyway, how about the beach now?'

'Hm, sorry I was somewhere else... Well not exactly,' she says. 'You see, I stood here on this very spot with my father, he told me that when he was a little boy, during the first World War, he and his brother watched the lines of battle cruisers and destroyers steam out into the North Sea - to make their grand sweeps like luring sirens - was how he put it and I've never forgotten that. He said the sea glittered but then it fogged like a shroud because of the ships' black smoke and it had scared him. I think I've remembered it because he made it sound so poetic, yet it was such a destructive image.'

'But not enough to stop him from joining the Navy, and, he liked poetry too, good man. Do you like poetry?'

'He taught me Scots ballads, Sir Patrick Spens was his favourite...'

'Go on then,' he says.

Not wanting to disappoint but with some reluctance. *'The king sits in Dunfermline toun, drinkin' the blude-reid wine. Whaur will I get a skeely skipper tae sail this ship o mine? O up and spak an eldern knight, sat at the king's richt knee; Sir Patrick Spens is the best sailor that ever sailt the sea...'*

'And?'

'We'll be here forever if I go on.'

'Alright, so what happens then?'

'His ship sinks in a storm,' she says and points out to the fogged North Sea, *'tis fifty fathoms deep; an there lies Sir Patrick Spens, wi' the lords at his feet.* Wasn't a good choice after all. For a sailor, I mean.'

'Oh, don't worry about that. Well delivered, like the lingo too,' and he's takes her hand to scramble down off the track.

Gulls wheel and mew high above, waves crash and dump, sucking back again to the same exact beat. With heads down each with an arm across the other they crunch along the shingle. Fifteen minutes of hard going underfoot and he points at a cave, they should have a break, but she stops to quickly pick something up. He leads the way she already knows, up over the sand and the torn edge of the path, through the wet grass to the big outcrop of rock pierced by the elements. And, inside one of its refuges they sit on a boulder close together.

Pressing his forehead against hers and opening her hand he asks what's in it.

'It's a bit of sea glass, I used to collect it. I've always wondered how long it takes the sea to turn a jagged piece of smashed bottle into a smooth piece of emerald. Well, that's what I thought when I was eight! Look how beautiful they are when you hold them up to the light,' and she drops it when she tastes the salt kiss of his lips.

Then he says, 'you know we are sailing soon don't you, but I'll be back in early June? You'll be here when I get back won't you?'

'Actually... I don't think I will.'

'You won't?' and his arm drops down her back as he looks at her.

'No, what I mean is I'm hoping to find a job in London, I've lots of friends there and I'm going to have a look round for something early in the New Year. So by June I really don't think I'll still be here.'

'That's alright,' he says brightly and puts his arm back around her shoulders.

'Is it?'

'Yes - because we won't be back for very long before I go to my next appointment.'

'Oh - I didn't know. Where is it?'

'Portsmouth and I'll have leave of course,' he murmurs and takes her right hand then lifts it up to look at the ruby and diamond ring she wears.'

'It was my mother's,' she says.

'It's beautiful. And what was your mother's name?'

'Dorothea.'

And slowly he smiles, 'Dorothea? My mother's was Dorothy, she died three years ago.'

'I'm sorry, I didn't know. Three years ago, two coincidences...'

'Perhaps; perhaps not. You know their name means gift, do you?'

'No I didn't. '

Still holding her hand he runs his thumb across her knuckles and says, 'do you like rubies?'

'Hm, never really thought about it, I like blue, sapphires are...'

'The colour of your eyes.'

'No yours, mine are greener.'

'Like this?' He picks up the piece of dropped sea-glass. 'Can I keep it? It'll be a talisman, I'll keep it in my pocket when I'm away,' and she curls his fingers round it and kisses his cheek. But he doesn't let her go and holds her face to kiss her so keenly that she thinks she might stifle, but it's the most desirable stifling and worth all the breath she's got.

'You're wonderful you know, I think everything about you is...' and he shakes his head as if he can't find the word - he can't - then sags a bit when he sighs and opens his palm to look at the scuffed pebble of pale glass, dried of its wet lustre. 'I'm sorry there's so little time,' he says to it and then kisses her again.

'Tim, I am going to miss you,' said into his neck.

'And I'm going to miss you,' breathed into hers. Then looking at his watch he's surprised it's nearly lunchtime. They should go back to that hotel, get something to eat and a warm-up too.

The foghorn warns and on the beach the thrust of the in-coming tide sends wisps of sea-foam scudding along the shore. Too enticing not to chase she pulls at his hand leading him across the wet sand then on to the rocks of black, knotty fingers stretching into the Forth. She knows them well, they were her playground years ago, the place where rock pools collect treasures with each tide. Every step is slippery but he holds on to her and she takes him further out where the swell batters the rocks and he holds her even more tightly. But as she never could resist a rock pool and sees another piece of emerald glass she bends down. Her red scarf falls off. She reaches...

'Fiona, leave it - don't,' he shouts as a sudden huge wave slaps them both - he loses his grip on her. Over, engulfed, she goes under. Nose, ears, eyes, throat invaded in a benign gurgle while 'Fiona, wait - grab something,' is only a muffled hum meaning nothing to her. But a survival reflex rights her, gasping and gulping her head rises up into the hissing air as he gets hold of her arm. Everything blurs but she can see enough. He's up to his chest in the water, she hangs on to him but another surge fells them. Her tweed coat drags, dragging her back and underwater again deadening her ears with its dishonest, lulling sound. Strops of untethered kelp tangle with her legs and she can't see anything in the sand-clouded water. She's kicking against the fetters. The foghorn booms. Tim's voice tunes in and out and in and out. He's grabbing her under her arms, gripping so hard it hurts and she grasps up at the air. Moving backwards in the smacking waves he pulls her with him, she hears the chorus of herring gulls' raucous repetition above, she hears and feels his exerted breathing close to her head but he's reached the rocks. Heaving himself and her on to them she lies flat with wide, stinging eyes, catching breath, open-mouthed like a landed fish. 'Fiona, listen to me, you have to get up and go now,' he wheezes, pulling at her resisting body. 'Fiona, come on - please try, that swell could hit again.' But mouthfuls and inhalation of sea water have all but muted her. He doesn't wait, he man-handles her upright, steering her sagging, breathless self back across the slippery rocks, stumbling and stopping with each wave's strike, but none is as vicious as that first one which caught her. Yet back on the firm safety of the wet sand the hiss and suck of the waves keep up their relentless beat. Those gulls cluster above, screaming and laughing as if it all serves her right. But she's safe with him holding on to her. And she's so cold, she wants to stop to get her breath, paroxysms of coughing make her legs weak, but he's telling her to keep going, they'll be at the car soon. So she leans, she presses closer to him yet she can't voice any thanks. But the bass call from the May Island warns again and now, as if answering, there's the note from the other foghorn further up the Forth. He glances over his shoulder to where she'd fallen and she looks too. The rocks are submerged in eddies of cresting spume and on each shore-bound wave her scarf floats in. A red tell-tail on the tide's flow and soon to be dumped on the shingle.

Suspicious eyes in the street watch the car come to a halt with a jolt at The Seatoun Hotel. Whispered remarks start at the sight of them, of Tim dripping wet and supporting an equally soaking girl as he pushes the hotel door open. In the dim, brown reception area the owner looks up from her paper work.

'Dearie me, so what happened then?' she says.

'The sea did,' he snaps back as he lowers Fiona on to an out-of-place velvet chair. 'Can I have a room please, with a bathroom, lots of towels and a couple of bathrobes. And tea, sandwiches and a bottle of brandy too.' The owner glances with some distaste at her newly upholstered chair being drenched. He says he'll pay for the damage and gestures she should hurry up with his request and all the while Fiona shivers.

'We have nae rooms with bathrooms, so you'll hav'tae use the one at the end of the corridor just like a'body else,' she says and there's a hint of hostility there, then like an afterthought she adds, 'I can get you extra towels but we have nae bathrobes...'

And there's a hint of sarcasm in Tim's voice when he says, 'can't you see she's completely soaked? Any chance of a dressing gown then - she needs something dry,' and like a staged photograph rests his hand on Fiona's shoulder as a Victorian paterfamilias would.

The owner tucks her chin into her neck and through pursed lips comes, 'aye, I can see that - and you're wet yoursel.' I'll hae a wee look roond and see what I can find you.' Then she bends to look closely at Fiona. 'She's drookit,' stating the obvious but incomprehensible to an Englishman's ear. 'Are you sure you're nae wantin' tae get a doctor tae her,' and her hostility has gone. No, that isn't what he wants, he can take care of things himself but he wants the tea as soon as possible.

In that cold bedroom and before Tim takes off his soaking duffle coat he begins to remove Fiona's outer garments. Now he's lost his command voice when he gently tells her to sit down and switches on the inadequate electric fire set in the wall. 'I'll run a bath for you, you need to warm up, you take the rest off. There's a couple of towels.'

'What about you, you must be freezing,' her voice quavering with cold.

'Don't worry about me, I'm fine, I'll have that bath after you,' but the waitress knocks on the door with a tray full of all the things he'd asked for. Putting down the pile of extra towels the owner hands Fiona a dressing gown.

'Here you are then, you can hae a loan of mine,' and turning to Tim she smiles, 'I can get my man's for you, if you're wantin' it?'

'Anything, thank you,' encouraging the pair to leave. 'Fiona, have a swig of that brandy, look, I'll put it in your tea, put plenty of sugar in it too - and eat something, I'm going to run that bath.' Probably because of the effects of shock she finds it easier to follow instructions rather than think for herself so does as she's told.

There is little difference in size between the bath and hand towels and though her hands shake she dries herself as best she can. Damp, clammy and trying to control her shivers she puts on the borrowed dressing gown. With a tap on the door his voice calls that the bath is ready. Everything seems to be executed at speed and grabbing some towels and her too he leaves her in the steamy bathroom without another word. She doesn't want to take long, she shouldn't keep Tim waiting for his turn, just enough time to feel warmed through. Lying there in hot water, the steam misting the window and running down the glass like tears, she still shivers. Closing her eyes she slides down further into the water covering her shoulders, but that sensation and roaring imagery floods her head... With a gasp she sits up in a wash splashing over and on to the floor just as the May Island foghorn wails its warning. This trembling runs deeper than mere chill and she scrambles out of the bath, slipping, shaking, and drying herself in the bathroom's chilly haze with small, hard towels. Putting that slightly sticky dressing gown on again is a struggle of sleeves resisting her damp arms and buttons refusing to engage. All she wants is to get back to the bedroom, where it's safe, where Tim will be.

She should have warned him, as he had done her, when she lets herself into the bedroom but he's still in most of his wet clothes and tossing back his brandy. 'Better?' he says without waiting for an answer and leaving her there. While she waits she doesn't dare close her eyes but can't avoid hearing the foghorn so she stands at the window grateful that it faces the street below and not the famed view across the Forth that guests would want. But Tim doesn't take long in her bath water, he is back, clad in one undersized bath towel round his waist and another round his neck. And it's as if that sight of his almost naked physique steaming slightly has shifted her focus. As he dries his hair, her attention is fixed and she can't look away. As if he knows he stops and looks at her, the teasing smile and cocked head giving her something like encouragement - or so she likes to think. But then he breaks the piquancy by asking if she feels better and sits beside her putting his arm round her shoulders and stretching his legs. There's black hair in damp, slicked streaks down his shins, he even has tufts of it on his toes. And that on his chest makes a rasping sound against her nylon dressing gown. She'd melt into him if she could. They say nothing, anyway her

34

throat is rough from salt water and coughing but she knows she'd feel better if he held her tight, preferably on this bed. Then he clicks his tongue impatiently wondering out loud when the woman is going to come with the dressing gown for him. Noble words she thinks as he stands up again to carry on drying his hair.

'I'm sorry, Tim - I put us both in danger, I should have known better,' she offers, and he looks at her hard.

'You're sorry? I shouldn't have let you go so far out on those rocks, I shouldn't have let you go on those rocks at all ...'

She cuts across him with a sudden anxiety, 'Tim, what are we going to do?' and he becomes the trained, military planner again. His impatience at being stranded without a dressing gown has to be beyond his control but when it does arrive he will go downstairs and phone Graham who will drive over with clothes for her and let Tim borrow some of his own. There is no alternative is there? They can't stay there overnight while their own dry, even if they would in a place like this. And she can see he is right and it's reassuring. She looks down at her cold, bare feet on the greasy, swirly carpet and with a shrug of resignation says, 'good old, reliable Graham - yes of course he'll come to the rescue.'

'Don't you want him to?' Tim says. 'You've had quite a shock you know and I feel very responsible. I don't think your sister thinks very much of me and now I've let you nearly drown isn't going to endear me to her, is it?'

'I didn't nearly drown.'

'Believe me you very well might have done,' and he's back sitting with her on the bed. He takes her hand and now there is no tease in his smile as he drops to his knees and holds her close to him. 'You don't see how difficult this is, do you?' pulling back enough to look into her eyes. 'I don't imagine in your twenty-one years that you've had much experience of the ways of the flesh, have you?' She shakes her head and looks down but he lifts her face up again.

'No, not much,' which is her unfortunate truth and he nods once at that. Wanting him back and close to her again her fingers brush the small of his back and travel up to his neck. His expression questions and she lets her lips answer as he gently lays her flat on the bed. His foot runs down her shin, his hand copies it on her thigh and she copies that on his. Then those words of Graham's, 'maybe they threw themselves at him' come back to her and she questions if this what she is doing. If it is then she can't blame them, how could anyone resist him?

And so she doesn't expect or want to hear, 'no, this isn't how it should be, you're too vulnerable, and, not snatched in a third rate hotel either,' said quietly against her ear. But a knock on the door interrupts, the dressingown has arrived and his terse thanks ask that it be left there. Does she have him back to herself again? She's happy to make it difficult for him to be honourable, but he props himself up on an elbow, his blue eyes unsmiling and serious.

'Fiona, I'm not rejecting you. You've had a bad experience. Look, just let me get that bloody dressing gown ...' One sob erupts from her and she presses her forehead hard into his chest. Then as if someone scolded her she tries to swallow back the rest and turns away. But he doesn't let her, moving with her, keeping her gently curved against him. He soothes, 'it's shock - you're shivering again,' and encloses her in the eiderdown. Curling up against him she feels both shame and his concerned hands patting and smoothing at the feather-leaking cocoon he's made for her. He says nothing else but it's safe up against the steady rhythm of his breathing and his heartbeat so much slower than her own. And, she breathes deeply, again, then once more. The tremor stops and so do his hands. All she can summon to say is she's sorry. 'Don't be, there's nothing to be sorry for,' he says, stroking her brow with his fingers, 'keep warm - have more tea - I'll get that dressing gown then I'd better make that telephone call, don't you think?' Watching him put it on - a garment of such grossness that it makes them laugh - she notices that he doesn't try to hide a brief glimpse of his nakedness while he struggles with fastening it. 'Graham will be here as soon as possible so we'll have to stay for as long as it takes won't we?' Tim says when he comes back in his ridiculous garb. 'I made sure he knew you were alright and told him to reassure Amy... You are alright aren't you, you would tell me if you weren't, wouldn't you?' She isn't but that's not what she says. There is something of the same polite efficiency in their previous comings and goings from bedroom to bathroom. His military reflex saved her and set her right again, but though she is now buttoned in a frilled and quilted shortie dressing gown, patterned with poodles and Eiffel towers, she feels it might as well be a nun's habit.

'Tim?'

'I know, what are we going to do while we wait? Well, there's bound to be a Gideon Bible in that drawer, we can take turns of reading it to each other,' said with a straight face and a nod at the bedside cabinet.

'What?' she turns to look at the piece of scratched furniture and he's laughing.

'Fiona, come here,' he says and sits beside her. 'I shouldn't tease you, should I? 'Why don't you try to sleep for a bit. You are very vulnerable aren't you? I'll stay here beside you, it'll be alright.'

'You're very paternal,' she says as she settles down against him.

'Am I?... Well that's not really the role I wanted for myself...'

To admit she wants him to play his envisaged role is beyond her experience. She's never seduced anyone and no-one had ever seduced her but she knows he will another time soon and she isn't going to stop him.

'You look like a hermit,' Graham grins when he sees Tim in the dun coloured robe, frayed sleeves and tied with an Army webbing belt. And when Fiona shows off her pink quilting with mock pride he calls her a souvenir from Paris. His arrival on his own is a relief. To be found by Amy in a bedroom with Tim and in a state of semi-undress regardless of the circumstances would confirm all Amy believes about Lieutenant Tim Robinson Royal Navy, officer and not a gentleman.

Left to dress on her own, she hurries into her dry clothes and discards the dressing gown in a neatly folded bundle. Looking down at Tim's shoes neatly sitting side by side, she sees he's filled one with his loose change, his wallet, keys, pen, the nugget of sea glass and - a little black book. With a gasp and step backwards as if it might rise up and bite she stares at it. Nobody will come in without knocking first...

Who will know? She will...

Does she want to know? Does she not.

Snatching it before she can change her mind she opens the wet pages, her heart bumping with guilt then relief that he uses waterproof ink. Written in his tidy, legible hand she reads nothing but brief comments on books he's read, each with a date, a star rating and the occasional literary quote. But there are names with telephone numbers too - none of the female ones has any tick or cross or star or number. Peeling the sticking pages apart the little book gives up more of the same - and it isn't even black - it's navy blue. Ashamed of herself she throws it back into the shoe and turns away from it. But both satisfaction and laughter come over her when she thinks how, if she ever feels the need, she'll be able to put her sister right on Tim Robinson's fabled, little, black book.

Now everything feels better for Fiona, as if she has found new confidence through Tim's interest in her. He phones her twice on

Sunday and early on Monday morning too. She fields Amy's disapproval and objections so well that Graham winks, nods or puts his thumbs up when he thinks his wife can't see him. The decision to work in London is easy now and after New Year Fiona has arranged to stay with her old friend Susie and look for a job. But Bella Bethune's face falls when she's told of Fiona's plans, she puts up objections but they are of fond concern and once reassured that Fiona has lots of friends there, she puts a brave face on the loss to herself and the school. She gives the names of agencies and assumes Fiona will give notice only when she had found something. That is sensible but, though she keeps it to herself, Fiona wants more flexibility. How long would it take to find the right thing, months possibly, and she wants to go soon, settle in and look to the future. Portsmouth is only an hour and a half away from London by train and not much more by car. But it would perhaps be tempting fate to even think about that let alone admit it to anyone.

Planning of another sort doesn't make it easy for Tim to see Fiona. There's a busy week ahead with the ship preparing for their imminent departure. Her thoughts drift to him whether she wants them to or not. She tries thinking about Christmas but the pleasure of that is bound up with disappointment that he will be gone by then. He'll have to take her present with him and on her way home she stops at Jenner's window. It glitters with a display of reindeer, snow and sacks of unwrapped presents. Children's toys lie tumbled about and she sees a lamb, woolly coated and glassy eyed. With a larky chuckle at her own inventiveness she buys it.

Amy wants to know what she has been doing when Fiona gets home. Amy always wants to know.

'Oh just some Christmas shopping, I saw another dress I might buy for the Christmas Ball - can't make up my mind - and I saw something for Tim in Jenner's window and I got some more presents while I was there.' And of course Amy wants to know what's been bought for him.

'A lamb.'

'What do you mean a lamb?'

'A toy lamb, it's just a little joke, Amy,' and she doesn't offer to show it.

And Amy looks at her sister smiling to herself, sits down opposite her, knees tight together, hands clutching a glass of sherry and leans towards her. 'Fiona, I have something I feel I must say.'

'What's happened?'

'I'm worried about this business with Tim.'

'Oh not that again, look I'm alright, I fell in the water and he pulled me out, I'm fine.'

'That's bad enough but it's not what I mean...' and Fiona puts her hand up and her head down.

'Here we go,' she says. 'You were going on about it in the car on the way home from the party as if I wasn't there. Who are these girls who've been so badly treated by Tim, sex maniac? It's ridiculous Amy. I know he isn't.'

And coming into the room Graham asks, 'what's all this I can hear, or can I guess?' he looks at his wife then her sister.

'You probably can,' Fiona says, stretching back in the chair.

But towering in hers, Amy puts her drink to one side and lifts a finger. 'Listen to me, you were seen at The Skeely Skipper, Di Reid was there and saw you and Tim behaving like...'

'Like what, Amy?' Fiona says.

'Well, she said he was feeding you oysters and you were letting him. What were you thinking of, you know better than that. He might think - in fact he probably does - that he can carry on like that, making an exhibition of himself and a fool of you... Was he really pawing at your face?'

'Oh for God's sake, Amy.' Fiona stands, her shopping bags falling over on the floor. 'It was one oyster and I didn't know he was going to do it. He was being playful, he didn't make any sort of exhibition and I dribbled a bit so he...'

'Sit down please, Fiona,' Graham soothes. 'That Reid woman really should learn to keep her trap shut, Amy. I don't like her and never have, don't listen to her. She's the one who passed on all this stuff about Tim and his conquests and who poured poison in your ear at the *Continent* party, wasn't she?' but his question goes unanswered. 'Let Fiona be the judge.' Amy, sitting in the same tight position visibly bridles and Fiona, gathering up her bags in silence, grabs the toy lamb as it falls out on the floor.

'That lamb,' Amy points and gabbles, 'why has she bought a toy lamb for a grown man? It's a code, I know it is. It means something.' Graham's look at his wife is of alarm.

'Yes you're right,' snaps Fiona, 'it does and I'm going to dye it pink too, work that out if you can.'

'A pink lamb, pink lamb, what's that supposed to mean?' Amy demands.

Picking it up Fiona mutters, 'that's for me to know and you...' and stumbles over the other bags in her rush to remove herself from a sister who appears to be losing her sense of reason and proportion.

Their father would have said that even in the best regulated families things can be knocked off course but never complain, never explain, though Fiona has never been a devoted follower of his advice. But she in her bedroom and Amy in her self-belief, will carry on as if nothing has happened. Fiona, in the middle of thinking it might be time to break that habit is interrupted by Graham's shout that she's wanted on the telephone. But he's gone by the time she gets there and she picks up the receiver hoping.

'Oh, Nigel it's you,' a hint of disappointment colours her words.

'Ah yes, my doppelganger voice, throw you again did it?'

'Sorry, no it wasn't that,' this time embarrassment adds shading and she hears him draw a long breath. 'I can't hear you very well,' she says.

'I'm in Norway...'

'Norway? Oh yes you said you were going didn't you. Gosh, I'm honoured you've phoned.'

'So, how are you, so did you get all the big pots in Perth - for boiling missionaries were they?'

'Oh very droll,' she says hardly disguising the sarcasm yet disliking herself for it too, but her voice softens, 'in fact they were almost that big. Did you get home safely, Nigel?'

'Yeah I did - but Fio...'

'Oh and I'm pleased for you that your painting sold so well.'

'Mm - Listen, Fiona, can I come down sometime and take you out to dinner or whatever you'd like to do?'

'Well, I know I promised didn't I?'

'You did,' he says. 'I get back...' The line clicks then buzzes but it doesn't matter, she knows whenever he does get back he is going to be in touch and where's the harm.

It's the Midshipman from *HMS Continent* who knocks at 62 Caroline Street's door that Wednesday evening. Shyly, he announces he has a letter from Lieutenant Robinson for Miss Lindsay and hands it over to Amy. He refuses her invitation to come in, he has to get back to the ship, but he had the most spare time and his own car to ferry the message.

Taking the envelope from her sister who's examining it too carefully, Fiona wonders out loud why Tim has written when she expects to see him that evening. Ignoring Amy's inquisitive look she takes it to her room and sits at her dressing table where she feels something small but bulky inside it. But she reads the letter first.

Fiona dearest,

I am <u>so</u> sorry but I won't be able to see you this evening. By the time you read this I will be on my way to Madeira on compassionate leave. My father is gravely ill and the outlook doesn't look at all good.

Realistically I don't think I'm going to get back to Rosyth before we sail and nobody could be more sorry about that than I am. I hope to rejoin Continent at Gibraltar. Sadly that also means I haven't had time to get your Christmas present or be able to give it to you myself. So, I have enclosed the best I can do for the moment - it will make sense when you open it! Forgive the presentation, I have no access to any sort of festive wrappings!

Sorry I couldn't deliver this myself but a taxi is waiting to take me to the airport.

Yours until hell freezes over,

Tim. X

The idea that she might not see him again until June had never crossed Fiona's mind, her plans for the few remaining times they'd see one another lie discarded. She shakes the envelope and a small package rolls out. Something wrapped in a piece of writing paper and tied with string. How can she wait until Christmas? She can't. And pulling off the paper, two oyster shells put together to make one spring apart and sit side by side on the paper with a written message on it.

The shinier one of these was the first oyster you ate and the other was mine. They didn't contain any pearls but I promise there will be others for your pretty neck... T x

It is the most romantic thing she's ever known or read or heard of in her life. How can Amy, how can anyone doubt him now? But how much sweeter it would be to keep it all to herself, to imagine the future when he's back. Her independence, her pleasure and his face when she gives him lamb done pink - twice over.

She writes him her 'delighted' thanks for his 'imaginative present', her sadness that she hasn't seen him before he left and her hope that his father might get better soon. She finishes with some family trivia, signs it with all her love and takes it to the post box straight away.

Amy's curiosity remains more or less intact, all Fiona allows is the reason for Tim's hasty departure and of course she notices the look of relief on Amy's face. Why the envelope had felt lumpy Fiona keeps to herself, a secret has never been more precious.

HMS Continent sails without Eddie Maxwell, who's already left the ship, but more importantly without Tim Robinson. Whenever the telephone rings Fiona looks up, it just might be him if the ship is in port, but she knows it is very unlikely. Gibraltar, Malta and Aden are on the ship's programme where her letter would be delivered and the ship's mail posted too. She looks every day on the hall table always to be disappointed when she doesn't find an envelope in the handwriting she wants to see. She consoles herself in the privacy of her room where she takes Tim's only letter out from under the lining paper in her dressing table drawer. She reads it every evening, the oyster shells in her hand while she does. And when Graham spots her hesitating at the empty hall table he puts his arm round her suggesting it must be because Tim's family circumstances are more difficult than he knew or was able to say. She appreciates his efforts, especially when he says he can't believe she won't hear from Tim.

But the waiting becomes too much and she writes to Tim again. One side of a page making a gentle and genuine enquiry as to his father's health and the formulaic one about his own that everyone includes in letters. Her first attempts thrown into the waste paper basket in crunched up balls of increasingly edited truth and hurt until what she writes doesn't even begin to convey what she really feels. She looks at the page and thinks there is no point, he will write when he can and she just has to wait. And that page joins the rest.

As days pass and she hears nothing from him she tries to hide her disappointment, sleeps badly and her spirits lower. Without anyone she feels she can confide in and a gathering loss of that new found confidence, she takes to going out on long walks alone in all weathers. Then flu sends her to bed.

'My life is turning into a Victorian novelette,' she says when Graham brings her a hot water bottle.

And following him with a hot toddy Amy adds, 'more of an opera isn't it?'

'Is it?' Fiona says, looking at Graham, the opera buff.

'She means *Madam Butterfly*,' he says quietly. 'Unfortunately that other Lieutenant sailed off into the wide, blue yonder too.' Fiona doesn't respond, she slips further down the pillow and turns her face away. Graham beckons Amy with his eyes and when they are on the stairs he says, 'what are you doing for God's sake? She's down and she's ill too - that was a cheap crack.'

'Well it's true, don't encourage her, she won't hear from him again.'

'You don't know that, Amy...'

'Oh really? I wouldn't put money on it.'

Yet Amy has always been a good nurse, she likes ministering to people and the next day she sits on Fiona's bed. 'Poor old you, eh?' she says and takes her sister's hand.

'I'm on the mend, I think.'

'Hm - try not to think about him,' though that isn't what Fiona means and she senses Amy's, 'I told you so', straining to be let out of her arsenal.

'It's just that I thought he'd be in touch,' and unconsciously she nods at her dressing table. 'Graham says it might be because his family...'

'I know what Graham says, that's just men sticking together, Fiona, they don't see things the same way as we do. Listen, there's plenty more fish in the sea, put it down to experience, that's the best thing to do.'

'Amy... I wrote, I replied to his letter,' and she glances at the dressing table again.'

And Amy sees that, 'did you indeed?' she says. 'Well don't do it again, you know he'll think you're chasing him.' Fiona knows that to be the received wisdom but is too weary to debate it. Hesitating at the door Amy turns to her, 'I think Tim Robinson can get away with it because he's never in one place long enough...'

'Amy, please listen to me, Tim never said or did anything, fast - as you would call it. He really didn't.'

'Well he didn't know he was going to run out of time, did he? He's a wolf, Fiona. Or maybe he's playing a long game. Anyway I think we should stop talking about him, put it all out of your head. But I am truly sorry you've been hurt like this. You should try to sleep, you'll feel better in the morning.' Quietly she closes the door.

Sinking back on the pillows Fiona knows that's a received wisdom too, even Tim suggested sleep as a salve to her shock. In the past she'd noticed it to be true, it worked after her parents were killed. But now, though she knows she's lost faith in him, that ache which hits within a second of waking hangs about like a shadowing gloat. Then a shiver of anxiety passes over her when she thinks about moving out. The Burnets haven't really talked to her about it since she told them and much as she thinks she still wants to leave she feels a small hurt that by ignoring it they seem not to care. She longs for her mother's sympathetic ear, her understanding, her comfort. All she has is Amy's un-nuanced take on life and her unquestioning acceptance that unpleasant things should not be talked about. To her grief is a private situation and kept to oneself, and, it's something like grief that Fiona feels about Tim's loss. Yes, that's what it is, recognisable, undeniable grief. Even if she could talk to Amy about it she knows it would be thought outrageous to liken what she felt for her parents death with what she feels about the brothel creeper-shod wolf, Tim Robinson. After all he's only done what Fiona was warned to expect. Her sister would call her self-indulgent to her face and more of the same to Graham while they lie close at night, warm, safe, comforted...

'That telephone call was for you, Fiona. It was Nigel, but I told him you were laid up,' Graham says as he puts his head round the door.

'I didn't hear the phone. Thanks, I thought he'd be in touch when he got back.'

'Well, he's had some sort of an accident it seems.'

'That must have spoiled his holiday. Poor, old Nigel. What's wrong?' she splutters through her cough.'

'He fell going downhill fast and says though it was nothing dramatic he's pulled muscles in his groin and thigh according to a Viking medical man, as he called him. Anyway I suspect he's in some pain one way or another, difficult to walk. So I wouldn't expect to see him immediately, but he says he'll try. He doesn't want to jeopardise being back in working order for the Ball - and they've had a ceiling collapse at the castle - a water tank burst,' and he rolls his eyes.

'I forgot he's coming to the Ball,' she frowns.

'Anyway he's sorry and may I say he really did sound it. Can I get you anything?'

No, he can't, she just wants to lie down again and sleep. And as she closes her eyes she does feel for Nigel, but the idea of the big man, so confident and self-possessed, suffering the indignity of

pain in the groin, wasn't without humour. Maybe she could enjoy
more of him.

Past, Present

Well enough to go back to work for the last day of term Fiona has recovered her strength but she's recovered some of her will too. It hurts like hell that she's heard nothing from Tim but she's made up her mind she isn't going to dwell on the past, she will think about Christmas and the holidays, the parties and friends home again. Beyond that the future is sketched out and will fall into place, small steps are all that she should attempt for now. But despite her resolution she still scans the hall table for what she wants to see but only other people's Christmas cards and letters offer themselves. She sits at her dressing table to read them then looks at herself in the mirror, her lips are chapped and need a slick of lip salve. Opening the drawer it sticks halfway, she's never known it do that before and pushes her hand in. She can feel her face powder, it has spilled out of its box, not that she ever uses it much. A lipstick has rolled under the lining paper and from the back she pulls away her diary and random bits and pieces which caused the jam. She finds what she wants but sneaks her hand under the paper and touches Tim's envelope resisting the desire to read it. 'Don't' she says aloud and obeys her own instruction, pushing the drawer shut. 'Think about Christmas, think about everyone coming home, think about the Christmas Ball - and that evening dress.'

And that evening dress fits perfectly. Packed in tissue and into a box she carries it home thinking about how sophisticated it is compared with the girlish one she has in her wardrobe. And there's pleasure in imagining how she would do her hair and what shoes she'd wear with it, that almost puts a skip in her step. Then she turns the corner into Caroline Street and stops at the sight of the dropped sun in a gold and rosy sky. At the wheeling starlings finding their roosts in the musky scented air of brewing hops. The windows of number sixty-two with the curtains open and the lights within giving the house warm eyes. But, a terrible surge of sadness rises in her again yet she doesn't give in to it. And neither does she when she sees there isn't an envelope from Tim amongst the others. With a shout that she's home she takes the new dress upstairs without showing it to Amy because she's going to send Tim a Christmas card, what harm could there be in that. A cheery card illustrated with a fat, red robin in the snow and she writes Tim's name at the top and signs hers with unquantified love. Carrying her new dress over her arm, she takes the card downstairs to add to the top of Amy's pile for posting - and the telephone rings.

'Nigel, it's you, oh... How are you? Sorry to hear about the accident.'

'It's a mess, water everywhere but the worst is over now.'

'Sorry?'

'Oh, I see, no I'm fine now thanks - sorry we got cut off last time we spoke. Anyway, so, Graham said you were ill. Better now?'

'I am, thank you...'

'Look, I'm sorry it's been this long since I got back, I just wanted to ask you what would you like to do when I come down? Dinner, theatre, concert?'

'You mean before the Ball on the 22nd? Nigel, today is the 17th and isn't it a long way to come when we'll see each other then?'

'Well, Fiona, when I think of taking a girl out it is usually on her own not with a ballroom full of people,' he mocks, but it's gentle.

'Where would you stay if you did, a hotel?' And there's a pause.

'Maybe Amy would put me up? And another pause. 'Alright, as I am staying for the Ball perhaps that's enough. I do have other friends and there's always The Highland Line Club. But you can let me know, find out what's on and I'll see to it?' and he pauses again, 'but maybe you aren't feeling up to going out quite yet?'

'I'm sorry, Nigel, what must you think of me, I did promise didn't I?'

'You did, but I would hate you to think you had to - just to humour me. You should probably save your strength for all the dances and I'm sure you'll give me some of them. How's that?'

Fiona sitting at the bottom of the stairs, feeling wretched again and swamped by yards of pink taffeta and tulle, says in a very small voice, 'that's fine... Of course I'll dance with you, Nigel,' ignoring a tear.

And gently he says, 'well, I think I should let you go now, I expect you've got something to watch on that television set Graham pretends he only bought for the children,' and that makes her laugh.

'Oh - you've noticed?'

'Oh yes, I notice, Fiona.'

She puts the telephone down, she pushes her dress aside, she's ashamed of being so cavalier with his feelings. Nigel MacMuckle, that decent, good-natured man is only making clear his interest in her - and with a light touch he'd allowed her an honourable back down too when she'd been graceless. She likes his sense of humour, even offering to stay at The Highland Line Club is probably meant as a joke. After all, don't all its members tend to be decrepit Presbyterian ministers and washed-up land owners from The Grampians to the Outer Hebrides? So, she sits there hugging her knees and what she recognises in herself is anger and knows she is directing it at the wrong man. Fiona Lindsay feels sorry for Nigel MacMuckle and herself.

Second post on the twenty-second of December, the night of the Christmas Ball, and on the hall table Amy's usual neat pile of post for Fiona. It amounts to three envelopes none of which is from Tim and she leaves them there. Graham has stopped giving his occasional explanations for Tim's apparent dereliction and Fiona has begun to feel more anger, but now it's towards herself. How could she have misjudged so much and that's serious but suddenly she has a flippant thought when she hears Nigel arrive. What were the chances of English Tim Robinson knowing how to dance anything more complicated than The Gay Gordons and Fiona likes dancing reels. But surely you can't be called The MacMuckle of MacMuckle and live in a castle up a glen for nothing, Nigel is bound to know how to do all of them.

And when he sees her it's, 'oh hello, I didn't see you there, I didn't expect it to be so long but what with one thing and another - anyway it's good to see you again,' and he lands a kiss on her cheek.

'But you're quite better now aren't you? Did the ceiling really cave in that badly?'

'I'm fine thanks...'

'I expect you've underplayed the damage and it's much worse than you let on,' says Graham as he takes his friend's coat.

'Water does a great deal of damage, gets everywhere - that's the worst part, but we don't want to talk about that, do we?' then Amy calls his name and distracts him with the offer of tea and chocolate cake, which he correctly presumes Fiona baked.

'And I expect that's a favourite of yours isn't it?' she replies, unable to resist.

He says, 'how did you guess?' and looks surprised, 'oh you're ragging me, Fiona.'

Without thinking she lightly pokes him in the shoulder, 'well I've never met a man who didn't like chocolate cake - call it a safe bet,' and chuckling he opens his mouth as if to say something, then doesn't.

Whisky and gin quickly follows tea and cake, Amy doing most of the talking and Fiona wondering why she's taken liberties with Nigel's shoulder. There is something about him which makes her want to be cheeky. Of course nobody mentions his groin strain but she supposes the inappropriateness of it has something to do with her unexpected familiarity. And as if he's read her thoughts, he looks at her.

'So Fiona, you're fighting fit again too,' he says, 'and up to a few reels then? Graham tells me you're keen and the best partner too, so...'

'Me - am I?' and he nods. But she wonders what else he'd been told, not that it really matters, she just doesn't want to be thought a fool.

'You know, I was thinking as I drove down that we must have met at Graham and Amy's wedding?'

'Don't think so, I was only fourteen at the time...'

'Fiona was my bridesmaid,' Amy adds.

'Yes, and I wasn't even allowed one measly glass of champagne.'

'Ah well, we'll have to make sure that doesn't happen again, Fiona, won't we?'

That surprises and pleases her and her glance is met by him as if he's waiting for it, though his gaze is so intense that she looks away again. Amy, suddenly aware of the time, gives instructions as to when they should gather again before the Ball. But she turns back to look at Nigel, she hopes he doesn't mind but he'll have to share the bathroom Fiona uses. Of course he doesn't mind.

Amy knows Nigel is interested in Fiona, she's even a little excited about it, she's tugging at Graham's sleeve and whispering even though they are alone. Graham has noticed it too but he warns and reminds her that Fiona is still bruised by Tim. She shouldn't forget that they've met lots of Nigel's girlfriends over the years and some of them had been very keen yet he never sealed the deal. His track record isn't any better than Tim's. Amy protests at that, she insists the two men shouldn't be compared, Tim Robinson is a wolf, not to be trusted and Nigel is reliable, solid, and after a moment's consideration, Scotch. Graham sticks up for his friend whom he thinks she's made sound very dull. He knows Nigel has a very nicely tuned sense of humour and very popular with the girls despite a rundown castle and no real money. He grins at her when he says she should be a better judge of Nigel MacMuckle's appeal than he is though it is returned with a blank look. But Amy will have the last word; she is quite certain he isn't the love 'em and leave 'em type like Tim Robinson and that's that. Yet Graham doesn't let her draw the line, he says if past performance is considered he wouldn't put money on it.

And Fiona, happily getting herself ready for the evening, hears Nigel's faint, tuneless singing coming from the bathroom. It amuses her and she wonders if he knows just how flat and sharp he is. Then she looks at herself in the mirror once more. Her blonde hair up, lightly sprayed with Chanel No 5, her make-up done and she puts on her mother's best necklace and matching earrings. And with a stab of regret she remembers Tim's promise of pearls and it makes her stop for a moment. But the dress lures and in a rustle of pale, pink taffeta she steps into it and loves it all over again. The fitted, strapless bodice embroidered with crystal and pearl beads holds her comfortingly tight and with her hands smoothing her small waist, the full skirt drops down and into place. Pleased with what she sees, she picks up all her things and runs downstairs.

54

Graham, poking the fire to get it going and having little success, almost drops the poker when he sees her, saying she looks beautiful and her new, pink dress very fetching. The fire refuses to oblige and he gives it another half-hearted poke. So she's teasing him about his feeble fire making skills while Nigel, with his empty glass, quietly lets himself in.

'Ah, come in there, what will you have, Nigel?' says Graham. 'I can't get this damn fire to go. Another whisky and soda is it?'

But Nigel stalls and the single syllable 'yes,' sounds vague, distracted, so much that he doesn't hand over his glass. His attention is solely at Fiona's disposal and astonishingly so is hers towards him though she says nothing and looks down at her hands. Then she dares to look up and straight at the man in front of her who had never looked anything other than unkempt, except once when he was clad in very little.

His dark, red waves are brushed and he wears the finest Highland dress she has ever seen. The kilt has never been so perfectly worn. Its plaid of fair and faded red to rust, tightly pleated to swing with every step. From his silver-buckled belt hangs a long, jewelled dirk its hilt surmounted by a huge, yellow cairngorm and is like none other she's ever seen. His high-necked doublet of finest velvet flaunts silver buttons of wolf-like masks down the front and at the cuffs. Around his neck is tied a jabot of old lace the colour of parchment and pinned with a large Scottish pearl. There is a romantic aura about him - a wildly, romantic aura, he radiates it and it holds the scent of soap and wood smoke and moss and cedar and... She steps back to see him better - she can't help herself - and his elaborate, silver-mounted sporran directs her downwards to splendid checkered hose, each gartered with a red band on those equally splendid calves. Tucked against one, a sgian dhu, this time with an amethyst in its hilt. And on his feet his silver-buckled shoes shine. He looks down following her gaze, a look of concern on his face. 'Do they need more buffing d'you think?'

'No, sorry - I wasn't thinking that at all. I think you look magnificent, if you don't mind me saying so.'

'Oh - *you* think that, do you?' said with a note of surprised embarrassment. 'Well, Fiona, I hope you won't mind my saying I think you look lovely.' Ravishing is what he wants to say but it is a word he's only ever heard or read. He's never before had the need to use it. Nigel MacMuckle, The MacMuckle of MacMuckle, despite the hyperbole of his name and style is not practised in the use of superlatives.

But the sudden bustle of Amy dressed in green satin intrudes with mocking at Graham that he can't make the fire to go properly. Taking the poker from him, Nigel adroitly stabs at the coals.

'You look like a Highland hero finishing the enemy off.' Fiona says just as the flames flare into serious fire and light up the room.

'Oh would that it were true! But that should do it,' he says as he slaps his palms across one another like the finish of business done.

Amy Burnet greets and herds all her other guests into the Assembly Rooms. More people stop to chat and Fiona looks over to her friends wishing she was with them, then surprises herself when she thinks perhaps not. But Nigel falls behind catching up with his friends and when he joins the others at their table he glances at the bottles of wine then goes off to find a waiter. Then he keeps her apart while he marks both their dance cards, he wants at least the first and last dances then asks her what reels she'll give him. She wants the Eightsome and the Foursome, then Hamilton House, she's eager but asks if she's being too greedy. Of course he doesn't think so and presses her for more waltzes and quicksteps until Graham with mock concern tells him he's being the greedy one.

With perfect timing the waiter arrives with a bottle of champagne, shows it to Nigel and he signals it to be opened, samples the glass, then once filled hands it to Fiona. 'There, for you, you've got some catching up to do, I think,' he says in an confidential way.

'I have?' she says and raises the glass to him hoping he doesn't notice her rising blush too.

And Amy's head turns, 'what d'you mean by that, Nigel, you aren't trying to get my little sister drunk are you?' she laughs.

'Certainly not, would I ever? Fiona knows what I mean, don't you?' and there is that intense, blue-eyed smile again and she stays with it. How marvellous it feels to have a shared secret and he isn't going to give it away, not even to Amy. And once all attention is turned away from them she mouths, thank you, and drinks from his glass.

When the band strikes up for the first dance they take to the floor, people look at her but she sees they look as much at him. There are many kilted men, dinner jackets too of course, but she has to admit that compared to every other man in the room he has the greatest presence - Nigel MacMuckle makes them all look unfinished.

'Shall we?' he says and takes her hand placing his other on her back, his thumb resting lightly on her skin below her shoulder blade. She wonders if he will drop it an inch - he doesn't.

'I hope I don't step on your toes, they wouldn't stand a chance,' he says as they waltz and she feels his breath on her forehead.

Hoping she doesn't sound surprised she tells him he dances beautifully and she feels the slight tremor of his silent laugh, he doesn't look as if he would be particularly light on his feet.

'I'm told I don't have a musical note in my head,' he says, 'which I suppose is right because I can't tell, but I do recognise the beat. That's the trick.' And this time he spins her in a reverse turn.

She looks down at his feet keeping in time with the music and notices her pink silk crushed against his kilt, 'I don't think we match though, look, my dress clashes with your tartan,' how gauche she thinks she sounds.

'Only one little mismatch, and it doesn't matter does it?' he says and gives her hand a light squeeze.

And every reel he dances he does so with the laid-back ease of one who can't even remember learning them. He is the best dance partner Fiona has ever known and when they chat together while waiting their turn, with good humour, the rest of the set barrack or prod them into paying attention.

Others have been paying attention too. The whisking rush of taffeta heralds Susie and Emma, two of Fiona's oldest friends, following her into the Ladies cloakroom.

'Who is he?' says Emma even before the door swings shut, 'Mary's not giving anything away, where did you find him, Fiona? He's... Well he's...'

'Amazing,' says Susie, not known to gush.

'D'you think so?' Fiona says combing her hair back in place. 'He's a friend of Graham's...'

'Oh come on, Fiona, he's magnificent isn't he?' and that makes Fiona smile.

'Funny - that's what I said too, but it's the get-up isn't it? You haven't seen his usual look!'

'No, you dope, it wouldn't matter what he had on, he's a hunk - are you blind? Come on, what's his name?' Emma insists.

'Nigel MacMuckle,' she laughs. 'Have you finished, can I go now? This is getting just like school all over again.'

'Well you'd better, *I* wouldn't leave him lying around, somebody else is bound to pick him up and Mary keeps eye-ing him you know.' Susie's tap is now full on.

And there is Fiona's place at the dinner table, the chair next to Nigel, Amy made sure of that. He breaks off from dutifully chatting to a celebrated Edinburgh bore to see her into her seat. But the bore hasn't finished banging on about his wartime exploits; he's 'caught in the beam, the flak's rising with bandits at ten to two.' Fiona has heard it before. So, she sits there watching Nigel, he can't bale out and his eyes don't even stray to her. Everyone, even Nigel, knows Biggles actually flew a desk but of course Nigel won't challenge him, she can tell he'd never expose this man's little conceit. She imagines he'd pass it off later with, 'toujours la politesse,' like her father would have done. And then she thinks about the impression he's made on all her friends without even trying. She knows she has his attention, she knows he is interested and that she was dazzled by the glamorous image he presented earlier. But quietly watching him now she sees beyond the dressing, he's naturally modest and unaffected, clearly attentive and unaware of his own quiet charm. And the girls are right, he is what they liked to call a hunk. But she asks herself if his attributes are just a tally of calm admiration. Yet still she watches him and a heavy strand of hair falls over his forehead. As he pushes it back he looks at her and she catches her breath with a jolt. It's as if he's heard her thoughts again and tilts his head, as clear a question as words would be. But her answer is just an embarrassed shake of her head.

Too soon the lights dim for the last waltz with Nigel guiding her to the floor, a light hand, this time squarely placed between her shoulder blades. 'So have you enjoyed yourself?' he asks and holds her a little closer.

'I've loved every minute of it and thank you so much for the champagne it was such a lovely surprise - and that you remembered what I'd said.'

'Of course I'd remember.' Her hair glances against his chin as he draws her in even closer.

And there is that wonderful mixed scent again rising with every gentle lift of his chest and she hears herself say, 'listen, there's a message in the music they're playing, do you know it? It's, *I Could Have Danced All Night* from that new musical, *My Fair Lady* - I've got the LP.' Again she wishes that she hadn't, she thinks she's the one who's being school-girlish now.

'Sorry, but I wouldn't know what I was listening to - remember? But I'll try very hard with this one. Shall we have a go at me taking you out - on our own - alone - somewhere tomorrow? I don't have to go back until the following morning.'

'Alright why not. Where?'

'Let me surprise you,' and he squeezes her hand.

And he takes that same hand when they sit in the back of Graham's car for the short journey back to Caroline Street, she lets him keep it there. Graham, on a second wind, offers nightcaps when they arrive but is the only one who doesn't climb the stairs to bed and sits by the bright fire where he falls asleep.

Goodnights given and quietly they shut their doors. But the fates have it - or do they - that within minutes Fiona, in her Vyella nightclothes and Nigel only in his Paisley, silk dressingown, meet again as they both open their bedroom doors to go to their shared bathroom.

She half whispers, 'oops who goes first?' laughing into her hand.

'Go on it's yours, I can wait,' he whispers back and the floorboards creak as he moves. 'I'll go back to my room, I'll cough and make a noise otherwise Amy might get the wrong idea - corridor creeping,' said under his breath while he points at the floor.

She won't take long but when she opens the bathroom door to come out he is still there and puts his finger up to his lips, he wants to say goodnight again and bends down to kiss her cheek. 'Good

60

night, dear Fiona, thank you for putting up with me all evening. So, until tomorrow. Bonne nuit et fais de beaux rêves,' and now he kisses her hand.

'Merci - toi aussi,' she says and she doesn't feel awkward with him, but barefoot, face washed and hair fluffed up from brushing she feels at a disadvantage.

He doesn't care.

Nigel, in his bed, turns off the lamp, closes his eyes and smiles to himself that there is only a wall between them. He imagines her in her bed, blonde hair fluffed up on the pillow, her soap scented face, her knees pulled up against the cold and naturally he wishes he could keep her warm, if nothing else. It's a provoking image. He turns his light on again and reaches out for a book from the pile on the bedside table. Any book to divert his thoughts, but *Little Women* doesn't do it and he tries to settle down a second time. Would it be too much to hope that she might marry him? For that is what he wants, he's never been so certain about anything in his life. And he's never expected to feel so much or so quickly. Of course he'd expected to marry some good-natured girl at some point but he never expected to feel anything more than the fondness he feels for his dog - though that is quite an extreme fondness. This girl has stirred emotions and feelings he didn't know existed and that's a complete revelation to him.

While Nigel MacMuckle conjures his future Fiona Lindsay lies in her bed, her eyes open in the dark, her blonde hair fluffed on the pillow, her knees pulled up against the cold and daring to do something of the same. She thinks of the approval and admiration from three girls she has always trusted and wonders what would it be like to share a bed with him. That self-possessed yet uncontrived - and yes - attractive man who has paid her so much attention. The startling thought of him waiting for her outside his door with only flimsy dressing gowns between her and his body is an exciting thought. The memory of not so long ago, of other dressing gowns, one of pink quilting the other like hermit's tatters, doesn't play back with any urgency. But she turns her light on again too and stares blankly at the dressing table where Tim's letter hides undercover. Then lying back she looks at her alarm clock but counts two hours gone before she falls asleep.

Valiant attempts to hum the opening bars of *I Could Have Danced All Night* wake Fiona. The noise from the bathroom is just as Nigel said; only the rhythm is identifiable. Smiling at his perseverance she waits until she hears him go downstairs, she won't let him see her again until she is properly dressed it would spoil the charm of their unmasked goodnights.

Coffee percolates, toast pops out of the toaster, Amy feeds one child while the au pair helps the other, Graham reads *The Scotsman* and fills the air with his French tobacco. And Nigel, when he appears, pulls a funny face at the children then their solemn little expressions crumple into giggles. Petrina aged five and Mathew of three and a half are told who the funny man is but all they want is for him to keep entertaining them. Fiona hears their screams of delight at the puppet he's made from his napkin but he drops it to stand up and kiss her good morning. She just smiles and without thinking pours him more coffee as if it were something she has always done. Amy with Mathew's toast in her hand misses his plate.

'If you don't think it unfriendly of us to desert you all, Amy, do you mind if we go out for the day?' Nigel asks.

'No not at all, you two please yourselves,' she says while Mathew picks the toast up off the floor and into his mouth.

A chilly, damp Edinburgh day and Nigel says he hopes his choice of the Botanical Gardens will please Fiona, which it does. He points at an unlikely mud- spattered yet shiny Daimler, his mother's car. His Land Rover was too dirty and uncomfortable for possible ferrying to dances, he explains. So she sinks into the passenger seat and pulls the collar of her sheepskin coat up round her chin, but she's forgotten her gloves. She mustn't worry, he says he'll keep her hands warm and anyway they are going to the Tropical House and it won't be cold there.

She doesn't look out of the car window much on their short journey. While they talk she looks at his profile and the rather long hair curling on his neck, she sees his elegant but strong hands on the steering wheel, she looks at his thighs too. And that doesn't feel brazen but perfectly natural, perhaps he hasn't noticed. But when they arrive he firmly puts his arm round her while they walk to the huge greenhouse.

Damp heat surrounds them as soon as he opens the door. Nobody else is there and the only sound is the faint but insistent drip of condensation hitting the stone floor. Above them soars a giant palm and tiny droplets fall on their faces as they look up. Appearing to be genuinely interested, he points out two orchids high in the canopy, but she knows that this warm, embracing atmosphere is only a setting for his intentions.

A fat baptismal drop of tepid moisture falls on her brow and runs down her nose, her burst of surprise makes him smile. Then with a finger he gently follows its course down to her lips where he traces their outline and fixes it with a kiss so intense that she looks up and into his blue, very blue eyes and he does it again. This time she matches it as if again it's the most natural thing to do.

He pulls her closer, 'I live so far away,' he says while resting his chin lightly on the top of her head. 'It's been difficult lately hasn't it? But I can't go home tomorrow without knowing if there's any real chance for me ...'

'Mm, I know - I will be far away,' she says slowly with her arms still round his waist.

'Well - is there?'

'Weekends, you mean?'

'It has to be really...'

'Yes it would, but...'

'There's people and places I can stay,' uncertainty creeping into his voice and he lifts her chin to look at her, but with a slight shake of her head she looks down again. 'Sorry, I think I must have got it wrong,' he says and she feels his grasp of her loosen but she doesn't let go of him.

'No, you haven't, not really. It's just that I'd planned to...'

'You don't have to explain you know, I'll take whatever you'd like to give - even left-overs, Fiona.' She might have expected to pick up sensations of humour with that last remark, but there's none, just the uninterrupted measure of his breath and a tentative hand running up and down her back.

And now she looks up at him to say, 'would you - is that fair?'

'Fair? Well, faint heart never won fair lady, let's say that instead. So I'll ask again, can I see you here, there, or for that matter anywhere else you'd like to choose?'

'No - I don't imagine you could possibly ever be faint-hearted could you, Nigel?' and his weight changes from one foot to the other - maybe that signals impatience. 'Yes, why not, let's...' Her answer cut by his kiss, lingering, loitering, like a well placed lure.

Then landed she rests her head against his tweed jacket and there's nothing she wants to say, it would be superfluous. But he says he has an idea and looks at his watch.

'How about going to The Skeely Skipper for lunch in about half an hour?' and she smiles a little lop-sided smile while tidying his tie back against his shirt.

'Actually, Nigel, I would very much like a bag of chips.'

'You what - you want a bag of chips?' he laughs.

'Yes please, that's what I'd like - a bag of chips from the chip shop in Fettes Row, thank you very much.'

'Very well then - that is what you shall have! I like chips too as it happens.'

'And why doesn't that surprise me, Nigel?'

'You like teasing me don't you - well I like it too. Anyway there's something else I want to ask you. What are you doing at Hogmanay we always have a party at home, could you come up for that? My mother's there so it would be respectable, ' and she feels his suppressed laugh against her. 'It would really please me if you could.'

But she sees he looks anxious, 'Yes, I'd love to come.'

'Oh good, that's that then. I'll collect you from Inverness. Stay for a few days won't you, when can you come, 30th, 29th?'

'30th until the second of January? I'll have to get back then because that's when I'm going to...'

'That's tremendous - terrific.' At last Nigel MacMuckle has found easy use for superlatives.

And he sleeps well that night in the novelty of deep contentment. Fiona doesn't, she lies awake sighing, turning over and back again, prodded by what feels like guilt. There's still the echo of Tim even though she knows if she saw him again in June there can't honestly be a reasonable excuse to compensate for the way he let her down. Yet knowing the theory doesn't seem to quite cancel out the lurking emotion she still feels for him. Despite keeping him at the back of her mind the desire for the unfulfilled promise still has energy - if she lets it. She likes Nigel, she likes his unaffected courtliness, she likes how he kisses her, smiling that the only word to honestly describe it is, divinely, corny though that is. His physicality is more earthy yet sensitive too - and who would have thought that - she can't even pretend to herself that he is Tim. In fact, by the time she's thought those thoughts she thinks she doesn't want to. But then she chides herself for making comparisons. She would go to Nigel's castle for Hogmanay, just let things happen and enjoy him. After all she's planning to move to London soon, isn't she?

The warning of bad weather on the A9 the following morning finally sends Nigel on his way. It's the kisses whenever they find themselves alone that's keeping him. And once he's gone Fiona comes back into the house and finds Graham and Amy standing exactly where she left them.

'What?' she says to their amused faces.

'Oh nothing, nothing at all,' says Graham, 'come on, let's finish that coffee, I'll give you the low-down on the fiefdom that is Nigel's Glenduir and Jean the grande dame that is Nigel's mother. We'd better prepare you.'

'Don't scare me, I might not go!'

'No you must - you should,' Amy says but pokes Graham in the back.

'He said his mother had been widowed for years, so what happened to his father? I didn't like to ask.'

'The poor chap fell out of a tree and broke his neck a week after Nigel was born,' Graham says as if it were nothing exceptional. 'Dad knew him, always said he was a good egg and eggs were his downfall. He was a very keen bird watcher and he thought there was an osprey's nest up the tree, but there wasn't. Must have slipped and that was that.'

'That's terrible, so Nigel never knew him then?' Graham shakes his head and lights his Gauloise. 'Nigel's very like him to look at and in manner too, according to Dad, and that's no bad thing is it, Fiona?'

'Don't tease her, Graham,' Amy says. 'You're right, it is sad and it's sad that Jean has made such a pig's ear of the Glenduir estate. Muckle must be spinning in his grave...'

'Muckle - who's Muckle?'

'His father was called Muckle they all were, Nigel's the first not to have the name. She must have decided that, Muckle couldn't exactly object could he?' Graham says.

'What's she like?' Fiona asks.

'Jean? She's very grand, but nothing you can't cope with.' Amy says. 'She's some sort of sideways descendant of Sir Walter Scott and I don't think she can quite forget it.'

'Amy's right, she likes to be addressed by her formal handle. It's, Madam MacMuckle, thank you very much, so bear that in mind when you meet her, won't you.'

Fiona wrinkles her nose. 'Why would anyone want to make themselves sound like a brothel keeper?' which appeals to the Burnets. 'I'm bound to get it all wrong, Graham.'

'No you won't, Nigel has no airs, you've seen that. He'll look after you, don't worry.'

'But take warm clothes,' Amy warns, 'and a hot water bottle, the castle's big and very cold unless you're standing right by the fire. It's a romantic place but sorely needs money thrown at it.'

'He says he has a herd of Highland cattle, but it didn't sound as if he really farms?'

'No he doesn't,' Graham says. 'Jean sacked the estate's factor less than a year after Muckle died and she was hopeless at running it herself. Wouldn't take advice and lost almost all the land, the grouse moors and there's only one hill farm now and that's tenanted. So Nigel took over a reduced Glenduir. You'll see his paintings I expect. He did clever cartoons of us all when we did National Service. I still have mine somewhere. You'll see some of his father's watercolours too, exquisite in that accomplished Victorian way. I believe he made many bird studies but I've never seen them.'

'I wouldn't have imagined Nigel painting somehow, he comes over as - well, what he is.'

'Do you think so? What about that shock of hair and the artless dressing, don't you pick up the Bohemian about him? Anyway I think he tries his best with what he inherited but where the income comes from I do not know, no business sense you see.'

'Oh, a trust, I expect there's money, bound to be.' Amy cuts across Graham's discouragement, as she would see it, and gives him a hard look.

Fiona stares into the fire, a smile slowly crossing her face. 'He did look marvellous last night, didn't he?'

Glancing at Graham again Amy sits back in her chair like a contented cat. 'Yes he certainly did, even I could see that.'

It's Christmas Eve and it doesn't bring Fiona the final chance of a card from Tim and she almost didn't look for it after Nigel left. But later that day there is a delivery in the form of a bouquet. Red chrysanthemums with a little card from Nigel. Her laugh is a slightly embarrassed one as she reads it out to Graham and Amy. 'Please forgive the utilitarian nature of these flowers - apparently they can't get red roses at this time of year - sorry! A very Happy Christmas and looking forward to seeing you soon. With much love, Nigel.' Then with the conditioned reflex women have with any flowers, she sticks her nose into the blooms despite knowing they won't have a sweet scent. But it's sweet of him to send them and that evening she telephones Glenduir Castle for the first time. The nicotined drawl of a female voice answers.

'Yes, Glenduir Castle, who's that?'

'Hello, this is Fiona Lindsay speaking...'

'Oh, is it? This is Jean MacMuckle here, I expect you want to talk to Nigel, not me - do you?'

'Ah - yes - hello Mrs - Madam MacMuckle, is he there please?'

'Somewhere, we had a flood you know, we didn't find out until we couldn't run any hot water. Made a fearful mess of everything, it's what's called a pain in the neck. Hold the line will you, I'll ring the gong. No, down, sit, Diabalo, sit for Mumma.'

A small dog's yap and scuffle accompanies retreating footsteps on what sounds like a stone floor, then the sonorous ringing of what has to be a large dinner gong and his mother's shout of Nigel in two articulated, extended syllables. Fiona can hear the footsteps and yaps retreat into silence and while she waits her heart thumps in spite of finding her imagined scene at Glenduir so funny.

'MacMuckle here?'

'Nigel it's me - Fiona.'

'Oh Fiona, what a pleasant surprise, sorry I took so long to get to the telephone.'

'Nigel, thank you so much for the lovely flowers, they arrived at lunch time...'

'No, they're not lovely, Fiona! Christmas Eve and there isn't much to choose from I'm afraid. Should have got on with it sooner. You're probably going out this evening?'

'No, we will be here, 'I'm cooking a special supper for us then it's - well you know the sort of thing - sherry and a carrot to be put out for Santa and Rudolph then an early bed for us because the children will be up at the crack of dawn to see what's in their stockings.' She stops her detailed ramble with, 'anyway, what are you doing?'

'Wishing I was still at 62 Caroline Street, it sounds charming... No, I'm picking up plaster, the ceiling keeps dropping more of the stuff since the tank burst. It was one of the best plaster ceilings here too. Otherwise nothing.'

'Don't you have a special dinner tonight?'

'Not likely, my mother's cook has flu, though she doesn't believe her, so that means it will probably be iron rations and possibly Instant Whip if we're lucky. But a kind person handed in a Christmas cake so I won't starve,' he says airily.

Fiona wants to commiserate but he doesn't sound miserable yet to her it undeniably is. So she says, 'poor you, I wish you were with us here too,' and she means it.

'Well that's good, I'm pleased about that, Fiona.' The yapping dog and the murmur of his mother's distant voice interrupts him. 'I'm sorry, Fiona, I have to go, now I am being told the water coming out of the bath taps is red, not brown, what a home-coming.'

'Brown?'

'Yes, it's the peat that does it, soon you'll see for yourself. Better go and see there isn't a stabbed body in the new tank. I'll talk to you again, but I'm looking forward to seeing you very much at Hogmanay, my dear Fiona. Happy Christmas tomorrow.'

'And to you too, Nigel,' she says but thinks, you dear man.

Those red chrysanthemums are arranged for the Christmas dining table. Then Fiona goes to her room to finish wrapping her presents and when all are done she looks at the bag in her wardrobe, the one with the toy lamb in it, the one waiting present without a destination. She could give it to one of the children but the idea of seeing it around the house is going to be too much of a reminder. She doesn't know what to do with it and instead gathers her parcels into a pile then looks out into the street from behind the curtains. It's snowing, she looks up at the picture of flakes falling slowly and caught in the cool light of the street lamps, the sky dark and scattered with bright stars, the cars moving slowly over the rumbling cobbles, their headlights making warm beams to show them the way. Then suddenly she flicks the curtains closed again and kicks the bagged lamb further back into the wardrobe where she can't see it.

Christmas Day and snow is thick on the ground. Inside 62 Caroline Street the children play with their new presents under the tree, sometimes quietly, mostly with great gales of excitement. Graham has managed to make and keep in a good fire and Amy red-faced, fusses with the roast potatoes while Fiona makes bread sauce. Nothing about the day is any different from any other Christmas Day Fiona has known, give or take small children or late parents. But as she thinks about the next year to come she knows she will be a visitor to Caroline Street next Christmas and a pang of anxiety catches her.

Crackers snap, paper hats find heads and silly jokes are laughed at, the food is delicious and Fiona gets the silver sixpence in her Christmas pudding.

'Well that's good luck then,' Graham says. 'Good luck for your new adventure in London, you'll be off before we know it,' and he raises his glass to her. 'Amy, let's drink a toast to Fiona's future success in everything she does. And ladies, lunch was extra good this year, I shall miss your Cordon Bleu additions to our fare, Fiona. Lucky chap who gets you, I say. Now who would like a glass of port, or what about that Driech Single Malt that Nigel brought?'

Fiona tries the whisky and is surprised to find she likes it. She's thinking about Nigel anyway, thinking about what he had for lunch and hopes for his sake that the cook turned up. She looks down at her lap to hide her amusement. If the poor woman was still in her sick bed Nigel would have had to make scrambled eggs and mashed potato with his Christmas cake to follow.

'Penny for them,' Amy says. 'Miles away - in the Inverness direction perhaps?'

'Yes I was, I was thinking about Nigel's Christmas lunch. The cook was ill yesterday.'

This amuses Graham greatly. 'Well I don't imagine Her Majesty Madam MacMuckle can turn her hand to much, so for Nigel's sake I hope the cook got better.' And he picks up one of the mottoes from a discarded cracker and laughs. 'Hey, very appropriate for Madam, listen to this. Why did the oyster blush?' and both women shrug. 'Because he saw Queen Mary's bottom. That's a good one for the old girl, though I expect she'd never admit to having such a vulgar thing as a bottom.' But Fiona is still with the oyster... reluctantly.

Future

With a thump and click of slamming carriage doors, the guard's whistle pierces, then a wrenching squeal, an exaggerated hiss and the Inverness train moves slowly out of Edinburgh. Polite nods and smiles dispensed as the four people in the carriage settle down to their chosen exiles. Fiona at a window seat takes out her book but it sits unopened on her lap, instead she idly watches the northern fringes of Edinburgh thin out. Then on to the great, red, spanning bridge over the Firth of Forth. From high up there she looks down and eastward to the headlands of Fife though she's too far west to see where The Grange would be. But on the left she sees the warships docked at Rosyth and squeezes her eyes shut as if they hurt.

How long is it since she was sure and Amy was wrong? And wasn't it all a contradiction? Tim the incontinent; Tim the restrained; Tim the rescuer; Tim the deserter, and the words match the metre of train on track. Then it picks up speed and taunts, what d' y'want what d' y'want what d' y'want what d' y'want?

What do I want? She nearly says it out loud. Not another mistake, to be happy again, to belong, to be wanted, not to be lonely anymore... And a gentle voice from the seat opposite asks if she's alright. She thanks the kind face but it looks unconvinced so Fiona opens her book but the print blurs as she loses focus from a lack of will to read. Closing her eyes again she sinks back into her seat and with the train's rhythm she drifts in and out of less than sleep but more than day dreams. Sun and sand, water returning to shore. It washes over her in warm, hushing waves, stroking, rolling, back and forth, lulling. But there's an indistinct presence against the light, it tries to turn away but doesn't, someone she doesn't want to let go, whom she can't hear properly, someone whose offered hand she wants to take yet it is too insubstantial. Who is it? Is it Tim, her rescuer, whom she's so deliberately trying to dismiss? But the exclamation of squealing brakes brings her back with a physical jolt at the train's halt. To Fiona's enquiring glance at the platform the kind woman opposite tells her they've arrived at Perth, but the time has gone so quickly and she closes her eyes again. She understands her reverie - it isn't difficult - and all she wants to do is chase and catch up with it. But it's gone.

She opens her book again, words, a chicken drumstick and a slab of fruitcake will fill her appetite instead. But once the train passes into the high moors of north Perthshire the landscape and temperature change. She pulls her coat round her shoulders while the backs of her calves bake in the heat from under the seat. Outside rushes past in battering cadences as miles and miles of bleak December lour over the landscape. Snow covers moors, treeless and desolate where there is no line between sky and land. Watching its sameness with curiously morbid fascination she feels a small knot of rising fear as snow blasts past the window banking the track edges and beyond. She might get stuck in Glenduir, she has to go to London and she fears she might not be able to get back in time.

And it's the kind woman again who tells her they are coming into Inverness. As the train slows down Fiona glimpses Nigel on the platform, hands in pockets dressed in that long, belted, tweed overcoat, wellington boots and yellow scarf wound round and round his neck. She waves as her carriage passes him, he catches up with it, opens the compartment door and she doesn't even have time to gather her luggage together. His quick kiss and grab at her case before she can say much makes her and her fellow travellers smile.

'Climb in,' he opens the door of a muddy Land Rover and throws her luggage into the back. 'There's a rug and hot water bottle for you on the seat, you'll need them, there isn't a heater in this thing,' and he brings a rush of cold air in with him as he closes his door. 'Warm enough?' and he tucks in the loose ends of the rug.

'What a lovely thing to do, Nigel,' she kisses his cold cheek; he kisses her lips. A heart-stoppingly, tender kiss.

She tells him about her journey, the snow and how she couldn't see the horizon. And he's so pleased she's there but there will be more snow, possibly drifts and the roads in the glens are twisty. With her hot bottle clutched against her under the rug, Fiona lets him talk and watches him with the same interest she had when he took her to the Botanical Gardens. What blue eyes he has, his hair tousled and wet from the snow and that coat - something his father wore, she thinks. Then she asks him why he isn't called Muckle, wasn't his father and all the other clan chiefs before him? She's glad he isn't, she thinks Muckle is an terrible encumbrance for anyone, but she'd never say so.

'Ah that, some fancy of my mother's I'm told, it would never have been allowed if my father had been alive. Did you know he had an accident falling out of a tree when I was just 8 days old?' and as she does it spares him from having to go into detail. 'Well, she had free rein then didn't she? People like to believe it was because she thought the name Muckle MacMuckle, The MacMuckle of MacMuckle was yet again over-egging an already saturated pudding. And why not? Reasonable to think that. But that sort of thing doesn't bother her, she doesn't think it extravagant. The truth of it was her enchantment with her ancestor Sir Walter Scott and all that romanticised Caledonia...'

'I don't get it,' Fiona gives him a puzzled look.

'Well, I might have been *Ivanhoe*, God forbid.'

'Too Saxon,' she says.

'Or *Guy Mannering*?'

'And that sounds too English. *Rob Roy,* wasn't that on the list?'

'There's a Robert already.'

'Ah, got it - *The Fortunes of Nigel*. A good portent though,' she says.

'I don't know about that! Anyway my father forbade it, he said she could use for any dog she might have. The poor man had no say as it turned out. Caused quite a stir at my baptism though.'

And she laughs at that saying, 'come on, you can't possibly remember!'

'No, but I've been told the story often enough. My piper's father...'

'Your piper?'

'Yeah - the Chief has his own piper, not that he's any use at it, though I can't tell and that's a blessing I'm told. Anyway, he's the Robert. Robbie MacMuckle...'

'MacMuckle?'

'Almost everyone in Glenduir is a MacMuckle, we're very cut off you know. A small gene pool too, I suppose. It's his family's hereditary position, but *his* father, George... Well that's another story, he was a championship class piper but my father never appreciated that either I'm told, like me he had a tin ear. Are you still with me?' She touches his arm. 'Well, George liked to tell how the minister said the name Nigel like a question when he held me over the font and my mother had to tell him to get on with it. Apparently the name shocked the congregation, I can imagine it well - mass shuffling of Sunday shoes and all that. Nobody expected anything so - foreign. If Muckle was good enough for all my predecessors then it was good enough for me and people thought my mother must have lost her wits. Then after the actual baptism it seems the minister made it worse, blundering on trying to mollify the general dismay. He said it was a fine name, and its root was Latin, but it would be more familiar to them in its Scottish form of Neil - and it meant black. Well, and wasn't that a misnomer if there ever was one? I presume my mother didn't know, I was as redheaded as all the MacMuckles are, but too late, the deed was done,' and he laughs at the thought of it. 'So George said everyone collared him on the way home.' And affecting an accurate if exaggerated local accent, Nigel quotes him. 'What does Madam MacMuckle think she is doing, herself and her Lowland ways right enough? So it is being a Latin name - a Church of Rome name? And poor, old George fighting them off with protestations that it was English and of course that was thought even worse, much worse. But, as they say, revenge is best served cold and once I started to look as if I was going to be tall, which was expected anyway - a grand, muckle laddie, y'know - everyone started calling me muckle Nigel. Everyone except Ma. It pleases her not one jot. So that's it, that's the story.'

'You tell it so well,' she says and ruffles his dark, red hair, 'and I like Nigel.'

'I'm glad to hear it, I like you too, quite a lot actually.' Then rounding one of the final bends she sees it, his castle on higher ground.

'Nigel, it looks as if it's made of iced gingerbread.' And that is a good description. Icicles hang off the turret's conical roofs in long spikes and snow sits in neat confectionary slabs on the crenellations. 'It's so romantic,' she says almost wide-eyed with wonderment.

'I hope so,' he says. 'Nearly there - and - and - here we are.'

Straight ahead tall stone gate posts grow closer. A carved, wolf-like, heraldic beast sits on each but top-knots of snow on their heads have turned them into passive poodles. Fiona's amusement at their reduced dignity prompts thoughts that his mother Jean's dignity wouldn't be if their brief telephone introduction and all she'd been told is true. She reaches out to clutch Nigel's knee. So, placing his hand over hers he drives in too high a gear and judders to a halt at the door.

'Oh God,' he mutters, and when he turns the ignition off she understands his petition. A tall, red-haired man in the kilt, of the MacMuckle tartan too, is standing at the castle door and he's making a noise on the pipes, a wailing, reedy noise. Fiona struggles to contain her mirth though she thinks it is being made worse by her nerves.

'Ready to face this?' Nigel says and squeezes her hand. 'I don't know whose idea this Highland welcome is, but I reckon it's a bad one, still mustn't put him down. That's Robbie by the way.'

'I guessed as much,' and she stands by the Land Rover with Nigel until Robbie removes the mouthpiece with a banshee's howl from the deflating bag.

'Thank you very much Robbie, we weren't expecting that, were we Fiona?' and Nigel turns to her with a wink.

'Ach away with you, you know fine well it is being tradition, muckle Nigel, so you do,' Robbie protests. 'I was just thinking to myself it is time to be reviving some of them, right enough.' Then he looks at Fiona, a kind smile spreads over his fine face as Nigel introduces them.

'Pleased to meet you, Miss Lindsay,' he says.

'And it's good to meet you too, Robbie, what were you playing?'

'What was I playing? Well now that was being *Mony a mickle mak's a muckle* composed by my father, so it was. He was playing it during the D-day landings, giving that piper of Lord Lovat's something to think about, right enough. But there is being not a hope for me these days. Not unless this Cold War is turning hot and nobody is wanting that, sure enough.' So I was thinking it is time to be giving it another airing.'

She looks at Nigel. 'Mony a mickle...?'

And with the carelessness of habit he says, 'the battle cry of the MacMuckles, the motto too as it happens. Anyway thanks again Robbie, Fiona must be getting cold and I must take her in to meet Ma now.' And with that Robbie, for all his easy friendliness, makes a very discreet and quick neck bow, which Fiona notices and Nigel probably doesn't.

Jean MacMuckle waits, she watched from behind a curtain when she'd heard Robbie's cacophony heralding their arrival, that way she could prepare herself. Careful not to overstate Fiona's importance to her, Nigel has kept his hopes to himself. Of course there were other girls as house guests over the years but he's kept everything except the minimum of details to himself about this one. Though Jean has told her friends she thinks Fiona sounds alright on the telephone.

Seeing Fiona standing there in the snow she sees a pretty and well turned out girl. Her camel coat, Aquascutum by the look of it, and sheepskin lined boots please Jean; it means the girl is sensible. And as the pair take their leave of Robbie and his best efforts the mother stands where she will be the first thing Fiona sees when she comes through the door, climbs the narrow curve of stone steps and into the Great Hall of Jean MacMuckle's home.

'Ah there you are, Fiona, what a pleasure it is to meet you in the flesh,' she drawls, a voice carefully kept apart from any early overexposure to a Scottish brogue. She moves towards Fiona, both hands outstretched.

'And it is for me to meet you, Madam MacMuckle,' whose hands are cold though the smile is warm enough.

While Jean takes in the details of Fiona; the pale, blue polo neck jersey, the pleated, tweed skirt and the unsurprising good manners, Fiona does the same. Nigel's mother looks nothing like him; she isn't particularly tall and is dark haired and brown eyed. She wears pearls with her twin set, elegantly tailored tweed suit and barely hidden scrutiny.

'I expect you would like to go to your room and have a rest after your journey, Nigel will show you where it is. Perhaps you would like a tea tray brought up to you? Nigel will do that too, won't you, Darling? We can have a nice, little chat later and you can tell me all about yourself then. I must go and rescue Diabolo – that's my little dog, you know. I put him out just before you arrived and the dear, little mite is still there shivering in the snow. I'll see you both before dinner.' Madam MacMuckle of MacMuckle turns away with a sharp, confident step of her well-shod foot.

For Fiona, in that moment, Jean's grandness is confirmed and so is her own mother's description of that type of woman; charming but ruthless. Now she's able to look at her surroundings and there's so much to take in. The Christmas tree is the biggest she's ever seen inside a house, ablaze with mis-matched lights and pre-war glass baubles, some of which are broken. But it is the theatricality of The Great Hall that enchants her. It looks like a Hollywood set for some silver-screened Brigadoon. Antique weapons make geometric patterns on the walls, monumental stags' heads look blankly ahead as if they've accidentally penetrated the plaster and couldn't care less. Then there's the furniture, good furniture taken for granted and neglected, whose surfaces are crowded with glass boxes containing more taxidermist's art. The smell in the place is the dirty sweetness of decay, of dust and centuries of huge wood fires' tar in the equally huge fireplaces. Fiona's exposure has only ever been to tame, old interiors of Lowland houses not the wild carelessness she finds here. Then she sees a portrait and points to it.

'Your father - it has to be hasn't it? You are so like him, Nigel.'

'That's what everyone says,' and they both move closer to it, she bends to see the signature, Jamie Napier, and says she knows he always caught a true likeness. 'Well done, obviously living in Graham Burnet's house has had an effect on you. Jamie was a friend of my father's - we're lucky to have one of his.'

'That big one's a Raeburn isn't it?' and she stands back to take it in.

'And well done again. That's Colonel MacMuckle of Glenduir, marvellous swagger don't you think?' and she nods slowly.

'The thing is,' she says tilting her head from side to side, 'you all look alike and it's not just the red hair and the height, even Robbie has the look.'

'Suppose so - must be that small gene pool I was telling you about. And the clan's progenitor must have been big to get the Muckle tag. Well I know he was, it's fact, a huge warrior of a man. All mainly oral history but documented enough. You'll have to ask the sennachie.'

'What's the sennachie?'

'The Clan archivist, that's what you'd call him nowadays. Anyway let's take you up to your room, we can do a tour later.' So he takes her case and her hand then passing the huge gong she heard his mother assault, he leads her up the grand Victorian staircase breaching the Great Hall's ancient wall and along the galleried landing. But she stops to look at a canvas not quite big enough to cover the unfaded patch of wall where another picture has been removed.

She stops, saying, 'this is interesting, not like anything else so far, is it one of the Scottish Colourists? I really like it,' and she tilts her head again.

He's slow to answer and with an embarrassed twitch of his mouth he says, 'a MacMuckle actually, it replaces the Wilkie I sold before Christmas, remember?'

'*You* did it?' and she goes up closer to admire it and that's easy. 'Graham said you painted, he said you were good too. Where is it, it's so full of light and colour?' and she steps back to stand with him taking hold of his arm.

'Loch Duir, we passed it on our way and we can get to it through the woods from here. One of my favourite places, I've loved it all my life. I'll take you down there and I can see I'll have to take you to a few galleries too. I'll look forward to that. The arts haven't quite passed me by, may not have a note in my head but I think I can draw alright. My father was very good, he did marvellous studies of birds, though they're very detailed and exact and you can see I like to use a broader technique. Though Robbie seems to have taken over his mantle in that respect, his wildlife watercolours are very similar.'

She looks at him, happy and relaxed, clearly pleased that she notices and knows. If Graham was right about Jean taking a dim view of his artistic endeavours then it must indeed be pleasing to hear praise. But he's modest and he waves a hand in the direction of one Victorian wing and explains that is where his mother has made a small apartment for herself since he returned in 1957. Then he leads her into the dimly lit corridor where all the doors look the same. But they all have nameplates and in his late father's elegant handwriting each holds a card inscribed with the name of a bird. But he doesn't sleep in this part, since he came back he sleeps in what was his father's room, his mother's adjoined it but she and Nigel both agreed it wasn't the right arrangement to have an interconnecting door between mother and an adult son. He drops her case to show her. Was that the established conjugal arrangement for married MacMuckles Fiona wonders as he opens his door, but she doesn't ask.

A soft, warm glow from the wood fire in the grate lights the room and it is as if she's stepped into another time. Nigel's wolfhound, Luath, rises from the rug to greet his master and makes a nuzzling enquiry of Fiona. But the animal takes second place to the eye-stopping bed standing like an island in the middle of the floor.

'All I seem to be doing is asking questions but do you sleep in this, Nigel?' and she approaches it almost reverentially, the firelight flickering on the great oak and red damask-hung piece. Lightly touching the worn drapery where glittering gold threads escape from the elaborate weave, she turns to hear his answer. He stays where he is, apparently enjoying her childlike surprise.

Then he beckons her and takes her face in his hands. 'Yes I do - and so did Bonnie Prince Charlie, once... But it does have a new mattress.'

'That's so romantic,' she says, 'Bonnie Prince Charlie I mean, not the mattress,' but he takes her hand to take her to her room, it's not far away. And when he opens the door of the bedroom named Dove the same warm firelight lights it too. She says nothing, covering her open mouth with her hand.

'You need fires here,' he says, putting on another log, 'better than an electric one. I lit it this morning so it would be warm for you,' and he helps her off with her coat.

And she kisses him her gratitude, which he holds on to and turns into a depth of desire new to her. He doesn't mean them to overbalance in their enthusiasm but the edge of the bed catches the back of her knees and topples her with him across her. And it all seems so natural to her, the whole length of her body close against his. The quickness of his breath and the sensations he stirs.

'Sorry - couldn't help it, I'm not trying to take advantage.' He turns to look at her, 'but you don't know what you do to me, you do it as soon as I see you.'

'You'd never take advantage,' she says, reluctantly remembering a similar script.

'Ah but I've been around nearly ten years longer than you and sometimes things aren't quite what you think they are.'

'Hm, well I do know that,' she says quietly.

But he isn't going to remind her of infatuation, he can't imagine she hasn't experienced that at some time. And he certainly isn't going to introduce her to the tyranny of lust, he's had enough experience of that. He kisses her again, this time with an urgent intensity that unlocks all the guard she's ever been taught to value. But too soon he stops and she opens her eyes to his looking down at her.

'So beautiful - you steal the sight from my eyes,' he says then strokes her hair back into place and quietly laughs. 'Huh, look at us, dishevelled, all corduroy, tweed and hair, I've made yours fluff up, Fiona Fluff - sweet,' and he sits on the edge of the bed as if waiting for something. She touches his back but he stands up.

The only removed garment, her coat, lies cast across the floor like a pale, shed pelt and he picks it up, silently she watches him. Then pushing his loosened shirt back into place he asks if she would like him to bring her some tea, she nods - anything to bring him back. Unselfconsciously he tidies himself, it fascinates her and finally he straightens his tie and rakes his fingers through his hair. Being included in something so commonplace yet personal seems to her as intimate as anything he's said or she's felt.

He doesn't stay when he brings the tea, a Highland cow needs attention but he will be back as soon as he can. So, Fiona takes off her boots and sits by the fire with her cup. The shabbiness of the small room is unexceptional to her. It only differs from what she's used to by the quality of the paintings on the walls and that two legs of her armchair have been replaced with books. Of course no-one would expect to see fitted carpets, the floorboards are wide and dark with age and threadbare, oriental rugs make a patchwork on them. She looks at the bed, its covers so recently disturbed by that flash of passion, and is pleased to see it is like hers at home in The Grange. A bed-and-a-half it was called. Four feet wide, Scottish and old fashioned, just enough for two bodies and indulgence for one. But a cracked bell rings outside in five dull strikes and at the small window, in the falling light, she sees the source. There over the turret roofs is a stable clock and it is lying about the time, almost, she imagines, as if it's a metaphor for the place. She likes that and that hers is a tower room in part of the original castle. Amy was right, it is all very romantic.

With the teapot empty and a slice of Nigel's Christmas cake eaten, she unpacks. The suitcase had belonged to her father, his name, *Lieutenant J P Lindsay RN* stamped on the leather. She lands it on the bed in amongst the disrupted eiderdown and suddenly feels what she's heard people describe as someone walking over their grave. She rubs her finger along the word lieutenant as if she wants to erase it and says, 'damn you Tim, wherever you are, don't you dare make me feel bad.'

A knock on the door and with a start she stubs her toe. 'Ow, ow, oh - come in,' and hops towards Nigel. Laughing, he catches her hand and asks her what she's done. 'Serves me right, had an angry thought and stubbed my stupid toe for it,' then she laughs but the threat of tears is close and not because the toe hurts that much.

And he sits in the armchair pulling her on to his lap asking, 'what were you angry about, am I allowed to know?'

'Doesn't matter, just a mistake I made once, that's all,' and she pushes her fingers through his hair and off his brow while he fumbles for his pocket.

'Here, this is for you. Happy belated Christmas,' he hands her an oblong box and with the quick, soft crack of its hinge she opens it with every cliché of surprise in her reaction.

'Pearls?' and she puts her hand up to her mouth. 'No, *you* can't give... Nigel I can't...' And she'd stand up but he gently keeps her there.

And he's frowning as he says, 'oh, sorry - why can't I? I thought you'd like them.' Then it's, 'they're Tay river pearls,' he makes it sound as if such a rare treasure needs an apology. 'Look, I didn't mean to upset you, but if you don't like them we can get...'

'No, it's a beautiful necklace,' and now he lets her stand up. 'I love it, it's just...' Just what? 'It's just that I think it's too much.' What else can she say?

And he stands too, reaching for her hand. 'Well, I don't think it's too much, I want you to have them,' and she turns away. 'Look at me, Fiona. Dear girl, has nobody ever given you a present before?' and she looks down again, ashamed.

'Not like this...' She takes the necklace out of its box and hangs it from her finger admiring the ten perfect pearls the size of fat mistletoe berries linked together by an impressive weight of gold chain. There on the clasp is engraved, from NM with love. She swallows hard before she looks at him again.

'Let me put it on for you,' he says it so kindly. 'Look in that mirror,' and as she does she sees him behind her, he looks pleased but there's a shadow there too.

'It's lovely, really lovely,' she says to his image. 'Please don't think I was being ungrateful - but pearls? I didn't expect anything like this or that you would have put so much thought into it. 'Thank you, thank you so much,' she says and gives him the kiss he wants. 'I have something for you too, nothing so grand,' then regrets her apology, but he has overwhelmed her and she opens her case, tossing her clothes aside in her embarrassed hurry. She gives him a leather photograph album stamped with his initials, N.M. in gold. Of course he thanks her and asks for her photograph to put in it. But the huge gong downstairs interrupts the start of something promising on the bed. The bed where Nigel had kicked her case on to the floor and where they lie amongst the strewn tissue paper and her clothes. The summons, he explains, means he's needed on the telephone and what they've started will have to wait until he's dealt with it. She sees herself in the mirror surrounded by her skirts, dresses and underwear and puts her hand up to the necklace. 'Pearls, he gave me pearls,' she whispers, wishing she could replay his giving and wipe out the hurt she knows she's caused him.

At half past seven, Jean MacMuckle waits in her drawing room with her Pug, Diabolo, on her lap. In one hand, a large Dreich single malt with a splash of soda to liven it up and in the other, a lighted Sobranie Black Russian cigarette. Immaculately turned out she wears a green velvet dress with a shawl of MacMuckle tartan at her shoulders. As Amy had said, the room is only warm near the fire and Jean's chair gives the best chance of being evenly heated all over. Diabolo looks up as he hears the sounds of four paws and two people laughing.

Calling out to Fiona, Jean hopes her room is comfortable and warm enough for her and she says it is. 'Now what would you like to drink? I think we have most things,' and gin is what she wants, that and something suitable to keep her warm, which she hasn't brought with her.

'Fiona, I think you're cold,' Nigel says as he hands her the drink.

And she lies, 'no, I'm fine thanks.'

'I'll get something from your room if you tell me where to find it.' And he waits, and Jean glances at Fiona and she sees that glance. Although she wears a suitable dress for dinner she had never expected to see Nigel wearing black tie and a smoking jacket.

So should she ask him to bring her a cardigan and make an error of etiquette to be noted by his formal mother or freeze in the interests of good form?

'I didn't bring a wrap with me I'm afraid, but it's alright,' is what she decides.

However, Nigel sees the goose bumps on her neck and arms. 'Ma, you must have something Fiona can have, can I get it?'

'Mmm, pretty necklace, Fiona, they are Scottish pearls aren't they?' Jean says and Fiona would answer but Jean is too quick. 'What's that you say, a wrap?' as she lifts the gold filter cigarette to her red lips. 'Here take this, Fiona, I can spare it.' Accompanied by a haze of smoke she hands Nigel her shawl. 'Nigel's father had that specially woven for me just before we were married, it is deliciously warm and soft I always think.' And Nigel drapes it over Fiona's shoulders.

'That's terribly kind of you, but I couldn't possibly.' And she attempts to take it off but Jean insists she can manage very well without it.

Mother and son look at Fiona; the mother's regard is of patronage and Nigel's of proud possession. But swathed in Jean MacMuckle's mantle, like an unwilling exhibit, Fiona feels awkward. Certainly it is both warm and soft but the waft of Jean's exotic Shalimar scent clings to the fabric like an indelible stamp of true ownership. Then with a real volte face Jean's expression changes into something like pity as she tries her hand at condolence.

'I am so sorry you lost your parents like that, Fiona, it must have been very trying for you, and of course for your sister, too. Two, three years ago now is it?' But Fiona doesn't want to answer. 'I expect Nigel told you I knew your father many moons ago - not well, but I do remember him. Anyway, I am sure it must have been a dreadful shock.'

Under the folds of the tartan shawl Nigel takes Fiona's hand while his mother establishes her small part in Fiona's history; smiling a little she thanks Jean and doesn't ask for more details. But Jean has more to say.

'I've met your sister, she's married to Nigel's friend Graham Burnet, isn't she? Everyone of Nigel's generation is married aren't they?' She asks questions but Fiona wonders if she's really talking to herself, then... 'I always thought Nigel would marry Georgina MacIntosh's sister, Elizabeth, so did her mother you know. Such a good match and the girl had money, pots of it, the grandfather was a marmalade millionaire, but she went off and married a very, dull stockbroker in the City of London. Never could understand that myself, she seemed quite set on Nigel and she would have been ideal.'

'I'm sure Fiona doesn't want to know this Ma.' Nigel's grip on Fiona's arm in proportion to his fear of her possible desertion.

'Nonsense, she's going to meet the MacIntoshes, anyway what woman doesn't like a bit of gossip? Then there was the Brewster girl, she had money too. She would have had Nigel, I know she would, the father was a dreadful man though, nothing more than a jumped-up fraudster, gave himself great airs and bought himself a tin-pot title,' and she stops to consider it. 'I suppose one could have put up with it though, the cash would have...'

'Please Ma, this is gossip at my expense I think, and you are embarrassing me, it really cannot be of any interest to Fiona, she doesn't know any of these people,' and Fiona, herself very embarrassed by Jean's outpourings, smiles meekly saying she doesn't mind.

'There, you see you're wrong, Nigel. However, there we are, Fiona. So, how do you occupy your days in Edinburgh? Nigel said you did the bride's course at that new Cordon Bleu place in Queen Street.'

'Yes, I went to Miss Bethune's but I didn't do the bride's course, I did the professional diploma,' then she stops, thinking she sounds boastful but Jean interrupts.

'But you don't have to work do you, not somebody's cook, or in a commercial kitchen?'

Nigel, now pressing Fiona's arm under the shawl. 'No Ma, of course Fiona is not going to be a domestic cook or anything else like that. She teaches at the school since she got her diploma.'

'Do you? And this is what you want, Fiona? Your family doesn't mind?'

Fiona is happy to answer for herself, but Nigel takes control again. 'Ma-*ma*, it's now the nineteen sixties and girls have jobs, you know that, I know you do. And remember, sadly as Fiona only has Amy and Graham' and turning to her, 'your grandmother too of course - she can make up her own mind about these things.'

'Grandmother, but you don't live with her?' surprise in Jean's voice. 'Is that your father's mother?'

'No, my mother's, Hope MacAdam. She lives with her older sister in St Andrews and I'm afraid her memory isn't what it was.'

'Ah, I see, a MacAdam, which... '

'Anyway, Ma, that's it isn't it, Fiona?' Nigel picks up her hand and kisses it and a small lull settles while Jean appears to consider what she's heard and seen. Then suddenly she smiles.

'Dinner tonight is a poor affair I am afraid. We've been fending for ourselves, you see, Fiona.' Jean holds out her empty glass to Nigel. 'Effie, who cooks for me says she's ill - a very great bore - people give in far too easily these days. She says she'll be back to do dinner for Hogmanay, I shall personally go and pull her out of her bed if she isn't,' she laughs. 'She only left a small cooked ham and other bits - and on Christmas Day Nigel attempted a roast chicken so we made do with that and a mince pie each with some strawberry Instant Whip on top - he even found some old

Christmas crackers in a cupboard. So it's more or less a cold collation tonight but this morning I did manage to put together a mould from a raspberry jelly made with Carnation Milk, I must say it looks quite pretty,' and she lights up another cigarette. 'Well, Fiona, I'm glad I didn't have to think about such things as work, it's very independent of you - brave too. But I expect it fills your day for you?' Jean smiles and taps the ash off her cigarette and Fiona suspects this is a question for which an answer isn't really wanted, but she does anyway.

'I can't twiddle my thumbs or live with Amy and Graham forever. 'I'm probably going to find a job in London...'

'When?' Nigel asks, his hand gripping her arm tight under the shawl.

'I don't know, but first I'm supposed to be going for a look round after I leave here,' he stares at her. 'Didn't I say?'

'No, I would have remembered.'

'I thought I mentioned it when we were at the Botanics, I'm sure I did, sorry.'

'I would have remembered,' and he squeezes her arm, but his mother is there and listening too.

Fiona feels his hand sliding away and bows her head. How could he have not known, she is sure she mentioned it - but then she hasn't thought much about it herself lately. So she is grateful when she remembers she's forgotten to bring downstairs her present for Jean. Excusing herself she leaves them and goes to gather herself and it.

Pouring himself a double whisky on top of what is already in his glass, mother and son then sit in silence expecting the other to say something and it's Jean who gives in first. 'The grandmother, which MacAdams are they?'

'I really wouldn't know, probably the MacAdams of Tar,' Nigel looks at his watch.

'Don't be such a smart Alec, it's a perfectly reasonable question, Nigel. Does she have to work, didn't her people leave her any money?' Jean MacMuckle wouldn't think that's an unreasonable question either and there's still a tone of resentment in Nigel's answer.

'I really wouldn't know that either, Ma, but if that's what she wants... And I guess she must have been left something, Jock Lindsay did have that place in Fife.'

'Ah yes, so he did, I remember now. Jock was a very popular young man, a contemporary of my brother Walter, but a bit of a toper you know. Wasn't he tight when they had the car crash which killed them?' Nigel doesn't answer. 'And they said he never wanted that farm in Fife - and he was no good at farming either. I expect he wanted to stay in the Navy but who was to know that older brother of his was going to come to such a sticky end.'

She's too keen to describe the sticky end and Nigel ignores her, neither can he sit there any longer.

He takes the stairs at a run, two at a time and finds Fiona in the corridor. 'Come on, back in here,' he says pushing her door open. He stands with his back against it as if he thinks she's going to run for it and taking Jean's present out of her hand throws it on the bed. The sudden urgent force of his arms around her makes her catch her breath and his kiss so insistent that it feels like another sort of drowning. Her head close against his shoulder and she feels him give out a great sigh. 'It doesn't matter whether you told me or not, I know now. Please Fiona, do you have to go to London? I don't want you to,' and his grip loosens as he looks at her waiting for an answer. A glance at his face and, appropriately, his eyes mirror the flames in the grate.

'It's not final, I haven't given it much thought over Christmas... I really thought I'd told you.'

'I said that didn't matter, look will you reconsider, reconsider for my sake,' pulling her back tightly against him again and then with something like an exasperated choke. 'Oh for Christ's sake - this is not how I meant it to be. Look - the last thing I want is for you to think I'm pushing you, I don't want to scare you off, but I love you and I don't want you to go anywhere.' Like a torrent stopped, his hold on her relaxes. She with her face still against the soft velvet of his jacket and he with his eyes closed waiting for her reaction.

'I don't know what to say, Nigel, I really don't...'

'Say you won't and say you will,' he breathes into her hair.

'You hardly know me,' and she looks up at him, his eyes still closed.

'I want what I do know and it's enough. Maybe it's too much to expect someone like you to want someone like me, after all what am I offering that's so desirable? I know it...'

'Don't say that, what you offer *is* desirable, dear, dear Nigel MacMuckle...'

'So - do you want it?' and her smile slowly opens while she places her hands on either side of his solemn face.

'How do I resist that?' and he takes those hands of hers and kisses each.

Jean MacMuckle doesn't ask what kept them and they probably don't realise how long they've left her on her own. But she's impressed with Fiona's present of the petit fours even if they are now tossed about in their box.

Nigel's mood is as bright as it was dark half an hour before and Fiona warmer than she's been all evening. But there is no time to sit, it's time to eat. But for Fiona it's as if she isn't quite there as the three formally dressed people sit at a table easily big enough to seat two dozen - not that she really notices that. Two of them with no appetite except for each other and the third with no appetite at all.

But it's difficult not to see that Jean had been honest when she'd said dinner would be a poor affair, it is. And all of this comedy set in a ridiculously grandiose room only adds to Fiona's sense of unreality. It's almost as if she's found herself at an attempted Mad Hatter's tea party. So, in rare 18th century china proletarian Heinz tomato soup tepidly sits and takes little time to consume. The gap between each course is as long as it takes Jean to smoke a cigarette, which without a glimmer of irony, she calls intercourse smoking. Fiona doesn't dare catch Nigel's eye. On more fine porcelain, chipped this time, slices of cold chicken lie. Lying about their origin because they look like and are as dry as cuttlefish bones in a budgie's cage. The vegetable dishes reveal tinned peas and big boiled potatoes without benefit of salt or butter. Conversation doesn't quite take off, all Nigel wants to say is for Fiona's ears alone and she is still too dazed to think of anything to say. Another gold-tipped, black cigarette is lit and with it fixed in her mouth Jean brings in the milk jelly which wobbles on its serving plate like a frightened, skinned rabbit, horribly and realistically pink. Nigel sits back laughing and pointing as it settles into a drunken lurch. He remembers the rabbit mould from his childhood but it was a white blancmange then - a white rabbit. And that confirms Fiona in her Wonderland head and she lets herself laugh at that. And then again when Jean says, 'off with his head' as she cuts into the pudding's neck. Hardly is the pink rabbit eaten and Jean lights up again. Breathing out on a streamer of smoke, she says, 'I'm going to bed, dinner always takes so long, doesn't it? Effie is back tomorrow, she'll clear away so leave everything.' She refuses her shawl when Fiona tries to hand it back telling her to keep it for the moment - and stretching her top lip, Fiona tries not to laugh as she watches Jean's Red Queen leave.

'Something funny?' Nigel says.

'Sorry, I think it's nerves,' she says but thinks the whole evening has been touched by surreal distortion. 'My head's in a muddle, I don't think I'm thinking straight.'

'As long as what you said to me earlier is clear, because I'm quite clear about it. You're tired that's all,' he says and kisses the back of her neck. 'I'll take you back to your room and check the fire too,' but she says she isn't tired, well - not that much.

And of course he doesn't leave her at her bedroom door; the fire needs more logs to keep it going overnight. Then longing stops him from carrying out the task quickly and she sits on her hands at the edge of the bed waiting and watching him. But he says he should go - he must go - the fire will stay in - it is getting late, and everything seems to finish with a question mark, even his kisses do. Afraid she'll misjudge or misunderstand, she can't find any way to answer.

'Bonne nuit et beaux rêves, ma cherie, sleep well,' he says with a light caress of his hand down the length of her arm to her fingers. Then lifting her hand he turns it and kisses her palm.

The erotic charge in that gesture feels like heaven and hell all at once and her lips part to form the words, 'don't go', but they fail. Only her faint 'goodnight' expires on a single breath as he closes the door behind him.

And he lies on his great bed with the scent of her perfumed neck still on him and it keeps him awake. Her vulnerability appeals to him. She matters too much for him to push her, he has to inspire confidence somehow. Tomorrow she will see what he has, he will tell her that life looks more opulent than it really is - that's only fair and if she doesn't take fright at the poverty of his offerings he will make his feelings clearer. His forefathers' bed suddenly feels very cold and empty but he doesn't own a pair of pyjamas so calls his willing dog to jump up where the animal happily settles down against him.

New Year's Resolutions

'I don't know why I keep her on, she's malingering, I know she is. What am I expected to do? Twenty two people will be sitting round that table for dinner tonight and look at all this food. I ask you, what am I supposed to do with it? And I am going out to luncheon today, I can't possibly cancel that.' Jean stands at the kitchen table, her hands up at her face looking at the ingredients.

'Get Jessie?' Nigel offers between mouthfuls of porridge.

'Jessie? She can't cook this kind of thing, anyway she's supposed to have this so-called flu as well. Everybody has the damn thing. It's a common cold for heaven's sake.'

Jean pokes at the huge joint of beef as if making sure it's dead. 'And how do you make a salmon mousse? I don't know.' She lights another Black Russian cigarette.

Fiona hesitates at the kitchen door and sees Jean prodding and muttering at fish and flesh. 'Sorry I'm late,' she says and Nigel, with a hug, tells her she isn't. Without looking up from her culinary nemesis Jean says she hopes Fiona slept well but it's only words.

'Ma, why don't you sit down and have some breakfast,' Nigel says, 'I'm getting quite good at porridge,' but Jean doesn't answer, she dismisses him with a tut and disappears into a huge larder. And to Fiona he whispers, 'Effie's flu has taken a turn for the worse and she's not coming in.'

'Do you think I can I help - would your mother mind?' Fiona shakes the spoon of the most solid porridge she's ever eaten.

'Well, she certainly wouldn't expect you to, but would you?'

Fiona would say yes if she could swallow more easily, but a nod of the head has to do instead. And of course Jean MacMuckle is happy for Fiona to help though she acts her reluctance very well. Then finally she sits down to her black coffee, another Black Russian and muses on what time she will have to leave to get to the hairdresser then to her friend's lunch table. So very inconvenient - as she says - but it doesn't really leave her any time to do much if anything in the kitchen. Nigel's knee makes contact with Fiona's.

But dogs need walking and girlfriends need familiarisation so this comes first before any kitchen duties, he takes Fiona by the hand and suggests a stroll to the loch and back.

The last day of 1960 and it sparkles, there's a winter sun and the fresh fall of snow lies like a crisp crust on the ground. It lines dark branches too, making them look glittered like cheap Christmas cards. Everything is muffled and still except the squash crush of their footsteps as they follow Luath's track of paw prints. Puffs of breath push out ahead of them as they talk and laugh down the hill through the stark birches, ancient oaks and pines. Go carefully, the mossy stones are lost under the blanket of white, but Nigel has her hand, he knows where and how to go. Luath puts up a cock pheasant and with its harem of hens they take flight, wings beating the air and a staccato of alarmed rasps. To Fiona that matches the eeriness she feels around her. Then Nigel stops to look at the loch.

'There it is,' he says with pride, 'Loch Duir, my place, the sun always shone.' He sounds so pleased with what he sees. 'So what do you think?' and tightens his arm round her. His pleased voice might expect a positive answer but Fiona can see nothing in the surroundings worthy of admiration only a place as dour as its name sounds and as dead as the flattened, rusty bracken all around them. The loch ahead of her in a long sheet of ice, sneaking away like an anaemic serpent surrounded by blackish trees. The drooping larches should be golden, orange in this sun, but they are obstinately not. On the shore random groups of big boulders, softened by their covering of snow, make inlets and between them tree roots are anchored in the ice. They make her think of talons.

But she finds, 'well yes, when the sun shines.' Then she points at something sticking up in the ice some distance away. 'What's that over there?'

'Ah ha, maybe it's the monster.'

'No, it has to be a tree trunk, Nigel.'

'Yes of course it is, but some people believe the folklore, that there's a sinister presence around here. They call it the Fuath, it's a shape-shifting manifestation and it makes bad things happen - you see the distillery over there? Well then, for generations it's been spotted by the workers and as they're surrounded by whisky I think you can draw your own conclusion,' he laughs. 'You'll find a lot of superstition in the glens, even in people who should know better. You don't believe in bogles and beasties do you?'

'No, I don't think so...'

'Anyway, Robbie used to row me about on summer afternoons when I was a very, wee boy.' But in fact she is thinking about bogles and beasties in particular and people's perceptions in general.

'Oh right, so how old was Robbie then?' she asks still looking at the humped and jagged black tree trunk.

'In his teens, he's ten years older than I am. We played pirate games in newspaper hats,' and he's lost to memory for a moment. 'They doubled as target ships on the water if we wanted to fire our cannons,' and he picks up a stone and lobs it on to the ice.

'So you had a toy cannon?'

'No, we had great imaginations. Just catapults armed with horse chestnuts,' and he bites his lip. 'Used to fish for trout too, you wouldn't find any now, God knows where they've all gone. But it was Robbie who showed me how with an old split-cane rod and I caught my first trout, it was and still is the best I've ever tasted. He gave me my first dog too, comical, ugly little thing it was, but I thought it was the greatest thing ever,' and she wants to know what breed it was. 'His father's Spaniel bitch had an unplanned litter and there was no doubt that my mother's Pug had to be the father. Anyway, I called the puppy, Pigling, and he used to come with us too. I used to sneak him under my blankets at night as well, easy to hide you see.' He's amused at that memory and he picks up another stone to skim it across the ice.

And she smiles at his sweet bedtime picture in her head. 'How did you get away with it, didn't your mother notice the dog?'.

'Nah, she only blew kisses from the bedroom door and I'd trained him to keep quiet. I reckon Chrissie, my nanny, pretended not to notice him when she tucked me in and read me stories.'

'And could that have been *The Tale of Pigling Bland*?' she says and squeezes his hand.

'Amongst others, until I discovered *Biggles...*'

'And John Buchan,' she says sounding a little pleased with herself.

'You've remembered! he laughs. Well, I could read that for myself and she'd gone by then. And very inappropriate for Chrissie to be hanging about my bed at that stage. She was very pretty and had her heart set on Robbie's father George.'

'Did George's wife know he had an admirer?' she says at the unexpected twist in his innocent tale.

'No, he was a widower. She died when Robbie was born and George was devoted to her memory, so when poor, old Chrissie left, she left with a broken heart.' He sounds sad as he sighs out a pall of breath. 'You're cold,' he says as he pulls her closer. She isn't but it's good to be close against him and she doesn't have to lie about finding his loch as fascinating as he would clearly like her to.

His mouth finds hers and there's a tender kiss but she can't help thinking about the little boy in bed whose mother only ever blew them. He looks at her and smiles. 'Your nose is cold,' and he touches it with his gloved hand.

'And, so is yours.'

'Maybe, but believe me nothing else is! Look it's starting to snow again, seen enough of my loch? We'll go back now.' He calls for Luath rooting in the bracken after something small and quick. And she's glad to leave such a desolate place, too colourless, too still, too oppressive, but of course it is winter and that's probably why it doesn't look anything like it does in Nigel's painting.

That they are playing house together that afternoon probably doesn't occur to them. She prepares and cooks in the kitchen and he in the cold, cavernous dining room, lays the table, decants the wine, and as keeper of the hearth, manages the fire. He also takes three telephone calls, each caller reciting from the same script; apologies but... and can't come to dinner after all.

In her dazed and disbelieving state Fiona hadn't taken in all the splendour of the dining room the night before. She stands in the doorway looking at the table laid with silver, porcelain and glass. As if he senses it he puts his arm around her shoulders to tell her that what she sees is misleading. He knows it looks grand but that's all they have and so they use it. He calls it relics of more solvent times and he expects it will go the way of all the rest before long. Money for the roof is more use than those possessions doing nothing but making a false impression. He shrugs as he looks about him and admits it's too easy to forget about the state of some of the rooms as there are so many but they'll need attention sooner than later. It's become a real drain on the resources. He gives a self-mocking laugh at his inability to make money.

'I look back and think why on earth did I go to Oxford; I should have gone to Agricultural College or even learned about forestry,' he says. 'A fat lot of use a third in Geography has done me. But it was the expected thing and we just did as we were told.'

'But you enjoyed it didn't you?' she says.

'Yes, but I spent most of my time rowing, that explains the third class degree - well I hope it does.'

'Of course, rowing - you would,' but he looks at his watch.

'Look, it's nearly time for another kiss,' he says.

'Silly boy,' she whispers and closes her eyes.

Scrabbling, yapping, and Diabolo signals Jean is back and she calls out to ask what the lovely smell is coming from the kitchen. Then she sees her son and his girlfriend kissing in the sort of way she's only ever seen on the dust jackets of cheap romances. She asks the question again and they finally split apart as she gives up and summons her dog.

'A moment Ma, we've had some people cry off,' Nigel calls after her.

'What - who's cried off, tell me?'

'The old MacLummies, Hector's laid up with flu and Grace thinks she's coming down with it too, but Glay's still coming - with his girlfriend.'

'Flu, what's the matter with everyone? I've never heard such nonsense. So anyone else?'

'Lottie and James Lennox, their bitch is about to whelp - they don't want to risk getting snowed in or stuck in a drift.'

'Ah well, that's understandable. Is that it?'

'No, the Campbells are *not* coming, they're worried about the weather too.'

'Well, you can't trust a Campbell anyway, can you? My grandmother was a MacDonald, Fiona. I'm going to have a rest,' she announces and snaps her fingers for Diabalo.

And Nigel wants to know if they have time to go upstairs for a rest but Fiona takes off, making a run for the stairs and mocking that he'll have to catch her first. He warns that he can and will, see if he won't and he's going to demand a forfeit too. Of course she isn't fast enough and he catches her round the waist before she reaches the middle of the stairs.

'See? You can't win. Your room or mine? I'll have the biggest kiss you can do, thank you very much.'

And it's in her room, and on her bed where he presses his face against her neck muffling his laughter. But she stops that with a perfectly placed and paced kiss and he wants seconds. And sinking against him into the warmth of his arms everything is so easy, so natural, all of it. She loves what he says to her, his humour, his modesty, his body. And she strokes his neck with a finger and he opens his eyes.

'I love your beautiful blue eyes,' she says.

'Do you? Well you know I love all of you, every single, tiny bit of you from the top of your beautiful head to the tips of your pretty toes.' And she thinks how all those corny love stories in women's magazines are not corny after all.

Perhaps because of their isolation the glens of Duir and Driech celebrate New Year more enthusiastically than even the rest of Scotland. Certainly Christmas remains a minor festivity compared to the serious enjoyment of Hogmanay and its customs.

On either side of the castle's oak door the ancient iron torchères are lit sending up curling, orange flames and cracking sparks in the air. Next, Robbie sets up the record player in the Great Hall for reels after dinner. He has never been asked to play the music but it doesn't matter because he likes to dance himself, especially The Sword Dance, a tradition which Muckle MacMuckle had started. Robbie is proud that the old Laird had taught him and he in turn had taught Nigel - as he knew he should. And since Nigel was old enough to stay up to see in the New Year, together the two MacMuckles entertained the guests. It's a performance looked forward to and someone will bring his own bagpipes and play the music for it - as it should be played.

Fiona, in her dressing gown, oversees the dinner she's cooked and gives instructions to Kirsty and Shona, almost the only people from Glenduir village who have managed not to catch flu. There is no sign of Jean anywhere and the sight of this young woman, Miss Lindsay, downstairs in her dressing gown makes them giggle. They both agree that Madam MacMuckle would disapprove of that. And, they've both heard The MacMuckle call Miss Lindsay, Darling, tell her she'd done enough and to let them get on with it. In fact he's taken her by the hand and sent her up the stairs to get dressed where she sits by the fire in her room and smiles. She seems to be smiling all the time even as she imagines Jean MacMuckle's dinner party and how formal it is bound to be. But provided Kirsty and Shona do what she's told them, she can relax. She hasn't met anyone who is coming. Nigel has told her about his old friend Archie MacIntosh, though he refers to him as Flashers, and his wife Georgina. The new, young Doctor Livingstone sounds fun even if the Minister, Willie MacVicar, doesn't.

She puts her feet up smiling at her pretty toes and that makes her think whether she'll put the hair on her beautiful head up or not and decides against it. The dress she's to wear hangs outside the wardrobe, blue velvet with a lace bodice and sleeves. She so wants to please Nigel and for him to be proud of her. It matters.

Ready to go downstairs, she picks up Nigel's necklace, it wasn't what she planned to wear with the dress but it's impossible that she would wear anything else. But this time she can't fix the clasp. Nigel can do it for her. Why she should feel so embarrassed to find him bare chested and dressed in nothing but his kilt doesn't last long. His new use of superlatives is put to good use at the sight of her as he manages the necklace with a caress of her neck. And he wants her to wait for him.

Watching the ritual of turning himself into something of a magnificent anachronism, Fiona revisits that same sense of inclusion and intimacy she did when she watched him tidy himself before. With the lace jabot tied and the pearl pinned she gathers up the velvet doublet and holds it for him to put on. And he does that thing again, shrug his shoulders, stretch his neck then draw a brush through his hair.

'Will I do?' he says and bows.

'Oh yes - you'll do very well,' and flicks a hair off his shoulder. I like watching you dress, funny isn't it?'

'Very - a Lowland thing is it?' he grins. 'I'll have to re-educate you, won't I?'

And Jean stands in her proprietal place near the fire in The Great Hall drinking her whisky and smoking another cigarette. Dressed in a column of black silk the burst of serious diamonds pinned to her bodice sparkles in the firelight. Seeing her son and Fiona together on the Victorian staircase she turns away at Nigel's light kiss of Fiona's hand. And the sudden noise of Robbie's piping outside makes Fiona jump but Nigel promises he'll stop when he's piped all the guests in.

'You look very pretty, Fiona, and that necklace again... It looks very well with that dress,' Jean says and touches a pearl.

'Thank you, I think it's lovely too, Nigel gave it to me for Christmas.'

'Did he indeed? He has good taste,' Jean looks at her son.

'I know,' he says and looks at Fiona.

'That noise is Robbie again,' Jean says. 'Tradition you understand, Fiona. 'If only he was as good as his father, George. *He* was a champion, you see. But one can't say anything and Nigel can't tell the difference anyway, poor boy, neither could his father. Not a single note in their heads between them, have you, Darling?' she says, looking at him. Fiona would like to say, she doesn't care, she likes Nigel's magnificent, unmusical head how it is.

The faint whiff of mothballs increases as people arrive and a man says, 'haven't the foggiest, Mucky,' to Nigel in answer to a question Fiona didn't hear. A man of Nigel's age but old fashioned with it and by his schoolboy chumminess she guesses he has to be Archie MacIntosh out of another castle in the neighbouring glen. Archie isn't a Clan Chief, Archie isn't a Laird either, Archie owns the distillery which makes Driech Single Malt Whisky and Archie is rich. His groomed military moustache, aquiline features and patinated hair make him look like an illustration from a 1920's issue of *Punch*. He's followed by his wife and both greet Jean even though their eyes rest on Fiona. 'So this is she, I'm Archie MacIntosh, I know your brother-in-law, you don't look like your sister, do you?'

'Fiona, and this is Georgina, Archie's wife,' Nigel says.

'Yes I'm his wife,' she says with a sigh and points at Archie as if there could be some mistake or perhaps to remind herself.

'Nigel's told me about you, it's good to meet you,' Fiona says as the uncomfortable feeling of being an exhibit visits again, but Georgina looks friendly and quite wrong for her husband. Her dark hair carelessly pushed back in a band and wearing an unfashionable but expensive dress, which needs ironing. Then a hectic merry-go-round of people come all at once, names and questions circle Fiona. When the last couple arrive even more mismatched than the MacIntoshes, Fiona looks at Jean for her reaction. But she's talking to and blowing smoke at an ancient man, Ossian Stravaig, whose kilt might have fitted him once but now hangs on him like a generous bath towel on a cadaver. Then Jean freezes mid-sentence and the old man turns to see what she sees.

106

'Who is that young Glaykit's brought, Jean?' he asks, his dead eyes lighting up.

'I was told it would be his girlfriend, can it be?' she says as Glaykit greets friends and the girlfriend stands looking slightly stunned. She isn't alone, it is reciprocated in the expressions of everyone else in the room. Introduced as Joyce, she is very blonde and very made-up with blue eye shadow and pink, shiny, snail's trail lipstick. She wears a very tight- skirted dress with a plunging, neck-line where her cleavage offers itself like an over-ripe peach. And some, mainly of the male sort, linger to inspect the fruit.

Fiona, now relieved of her curiosity status, feels sorry for Joyce standing alone surrounded by a cordon sanitaire now formed by the female sort. Young - but old enough to know better - Glaykit appears not to notice while he catches up with friends. But Nigel spots his mother's intention heading in Joyce's direction.

Jean puts out her hand, 'I am Jean MacMuckle and you have come with Glaykit?'

'Oh hi there, I'm Joyce,' she says. 'This is your castle then? I've never been in one before. It's like the Walt Disney one except this is ever so run-down. Must be old.'

'Well there's always a first time for everything isn't there?' Jean looks around her as if she's never noticed the disrepair before. 'So, Joyce, where do you come from?'

'London.'

Jean laughs, 'London's a big place, where?'

'SE1.'

'Ah...I don't know it. That must be Kennington, Lambeth I suppose? Very nice if you like cricket or military history I imagine,' Joyce looks blank.

'My mother means The Oval and The Imperial War Museum,' Nigel says.

'Oh OK, I've never been to the museum and I don't like cricket.'

107

'Ah well, so what do you do in SE1 then?' Jean asks and blows smoke at her, but she's used to that.

'Me? I'm a croupier up West, that's how I met Glay,' she nods at him helping himself to more whisky. 'He's lucky at the tables...'

'Yes I can see he'd have to be,' says Jean, glancing at Joyce's pneumatic super structure. 'And I expect you must be a good calculator,' she adds and leaves the girl to her son and Fiona. Swinging round, Glaykit waddles over to them, his corned beef complexion lit up with a squint-eyed grin.

'Mucky, me old matey, how's life eh, and where's Flashers Mac? Haven't seen him yet. Oh, and hello there - who might this be, eh?' Glaykit looks at Fiona, or she thinks he does.

'This is Fiona Lindsay, Glay,' Nigel says, tightening his arm around her. 'Flashers and Georgina are over there talking to Findlay Livingstone, the new doctor.'

'Bugger me! Were his parents having a joke giving him a name like that, eh?' says Glaykit Dunsinane MacLummie The Younger of Reeks, looking at the young man.

'They didn't expect him to become a doctor... I presume!' replies The MacMuckle of MacMuckle, quite pleased with his wit. 'Anyway, Glay, Joyce has been telling us about herself but we mustn't keep her to ourselves must we? And I haven't introduced Fiona to Snitcher and Mrs Snitcher yet. So, why don't you get Joyce another drink, her glass is nearly empty.' With Fiona firmly attached he steers her away but Archie MacIntosh lifts his glass to them as they pass.

'The scenery's quite interesting tonight, Mucky,' he says and looks over at abandoned Joyce bending to pat Luath. 'You'd think Glay would have told her what the right get-up was to wear here, wouldn't you?' Archie might admire that girl's natural assets but he sounds personally put out. His laid back reputation rarely fails and he is never anything less than neat, careful and correct in attire himself, but a gentleman's lack of grooming and sartorial errors insult him. The length of Nigel's hair has exercised him for years, made worse by Georgina calling it a glorious thatch.

'Come on, Flashers, Glay's showing us what he can get, isn't he?' Nigel laughs and squeezes Fiona's waist but she can't look, she's controlling her rising laughter at the men's mass reversion to type. She doesn't have to be told they've all grown up together. Their nick-names and blind accommodation of each other's foibles unite them in their exclusive tribe. Clearly none of them has the slightest idea of how ridiculously mad they sound and in many cases look.

The dining table is ablaze with candles flickering in the unavoidable draught but the effect flatters complexions even Glay MacLummie's. Jean sits at one end and Nigel at the other. Fiona on Nigel's right has Archie MacIntosh on the other side of her. Somewhere nearby, but not quite far enough, Robbie tunes up and practises as everyone eats Fiona's salmon mousse.

'You know the piper do you - or are they killing a cat in the kitchen for the main course?' Archie asks her.

'Or is it a haggis being dispatched? Hang on it can't be, there isn't a 'z' in the month,' she says and he likes that. But neither fillet of feline nor haunch of haggis appear. A baron of beef does, piped in by Robbie and carried high on a targe by Nigel. The same targe used by his ancestor to protect himself from Hanoverian swords at the Battle of Culloden. Standing up, the diners clap in time to Robbie's slow rhythm as the beef is marched all round the table once, then Nigel puts it down at his place. And with military precision Robbie removes his pipes' mouthpiece with the usual expiring squawk.

'So the cat lives to die another day,' Archie doesn't even bother to whisper.

But Fiona does. 'The sooner the better, it's in agony,' she says. But Nigel is the centre of attention, with joking verve he pulls the long ancestral dirk out of its jewelled scabbard at his waist and reaches for the sgian dhu down the side of his stocking.

'Mony a mickle maks a muckle,' he roars and plunges the knives into the meat and carves.

'What did he say?' Joyce asks Archie.

'The battle cry of the MacMuckle clan, it means many small things make something big, which now I come to think of it in plain English does make sense in a battle charge.'

Joyce doesn't, she sits down with her elbow on the table, her chin in her hand, gazing at Nigel being masterful.

Archie turns to her. 'So where did Glay find you?'

'London. What about you, where do you come from?'

'Driech, across the loch...'

'Pardon?' she giggles.

'I said Driech - it's on the other side of the loch.'

'Oh pardon me, I thought something was stuck in your throat,' and she's laughing more but Archie remains stony-faced. So now she's serious when she tries, 'have you lived there long?'

Turning his brilliantined head towards her and with an unforgiving look, Archie says, 'about seven hundred years, give or take a century. Otherwise expressed as lost in the mists of antiquity but not to be confused with the clan MacGregor, they're known as the children of the mist.'

'And the clan MacIntosh must be the children of the raincoat?' Too good a reply not to use for re-setting her sail with more humour.

'No.'

And Nigel's generosity with his wine is making everyone very noisy, except for Archie, who has relentless Joyce prattling away emboldened by too much drink. When pudding is placed in front of her she bursts into a torrent of words and even if Archie wants to chat he doesn't have a chance. She takes another gulp of wine.

'This place is like a film set isn't it?' she slurs slightly. 'Nigel looks like a Scottish hero from central casting.' Then she leans towards Archie with a confiding voice, 'mind you, I don't go for all those deer's heads on the walls next door - poor things. But I've never been to the Highlands before.'

Archie remains unmoved by her confession so she tries a direct question. 'Do the men up here wear those kilts all the time? They look fab - OK some of them do, but it's cool.' Archie finally gives her a glance, uncomprehending though it is. 'Oops, maybe I shouldn't have said that. But it's great, so romantic. I think I've had too much to drink, I'm such a lightweight - aren't I Glay?' He is too far down the table and doesn't hear her. 'Glaykie, Glay-kee, I'm saying I'm a lightweight,' and she pushes forward and slightly off her chair to attract his attention. The chair falls backwards and she whips round trying to catch it. Her very large glass of claret falls across the table and splashes Archie's heirloom, lace jabot ending in a pool on his Victorian sporran.

'Oh Hell, look what I've gone an' done.' Bending over him she starts wiping his lace with her napkin and he fixes his unavoidable gaze on her undulating neckline. But he winces when she tries to rub at his lap and sits like a statue while the puddle of claret from the table trickles down the side of his leg. Flapping her hands she pleads, 'Glay - anyone, I've spilled wine all over, Mr - what's your name again?'

'MacIntosh.'

'I've spilled wine all over Mr MacIntosh.'

'Pity I wasn't wearing one,' he drawls and continues to eat his pudding. She dares to look at the damage she'd inflicted on the dignified personage next to her. 'It will wash out I think, a good soak should do it,' and he doesn't reply.

And amidst the noise and lack of any other obvious interest only Glaykit MacLummie eventually looks down the table, rolls his eyes and dismisses her to sit down.

'Everything alright over there?' Nigel asks as Joyce, still standing, mops the wine off the table with the napkin which sends her remaining cutlery in different directions.

'Attempted GBH is what I think you might call it, Mucky,' Archie replies with a glimmer of a smile and something very like schoolboy sniggering breaks out round him.

But quietly Nigel gets up, 'here, let me,' he says as he lifts and rights Joyce's chair holding it for her to sit down again. 'I'll get you some more wine,' briefly resting his hand on her shoulder and taking the sopping napkin from her.

'No - don't give me any more!' and she hangs her head. 'I'm very sorry, I'm making a fool of myself and I've drunk too much. You must think I'm terrible,' and a tear drops on to her bosom.

'Don't give it another thought, it doesn't matter' and he hands her his handkerchief. Then gesturing to Shona, he points at the rest of his spilt best claret to be dealt with.

Fiona has seen and heard it all and when he sits down again she leans over and, without a word, kisses his cheek.

'Seen the time, Mucky?' Archie MacIntosh says and points at his watch. 'If you and Robbie are going to get your battle dance in before midnight you'd better get going with it now hadn't you?' People know what to do, this is part of a well worn ritual and they rise from their seats. Until this moment Fiona hasn't really believed Nigel was going to do The Sword Dance, she thought he was joking. But there is Robbie taking swords off the wall, unsheathing them, setting them in crosses on the floor and Archie MacIntosh picking up his pipes and inflating the bag. The others, except Fiona and Joyce, begin to clap the same beat and something of Fiona's sense of foreignness touches her again. But nobody is looking at her now.

The MacMuckle and Robert MacMuckle take position at their swords. The pair matched in height with backs straight, shoulders square, heads proud, arms akimbo and together they make low bows. Archie's fluting notes and stressed beat fills the Great Hall as the Chief's and his clansman's arms rise, elbows curve, fingers cock and one, two, one, two with the beat they enter the naked blades' quarters in steps circling the square, then it's high cuts, double cuts, swaying kilts, until a change of tempo, faster now in wide-legged leaps, yelps, throaty whoops. Lively, strong, bold. Tartan pleats fan left, right, left, right, lift and up, bare thighs flash, 'yeuch, yeuch, yeee-uch,' and it's over with another full bow. Applause and Fiona sees Joyce looking as appreciatively awe-struck as she feels herself. And while the two MacMuckles and Archie are handed drams Jean finds Fiona to ask what she thought of it.

'I'm lost for words,' she says. Though that's not true, she has lots but she can't tell his mother she found Nigel terrifically, stunningly, barbarically desirable.'

'Well, Fiona, I can tell you he does that as well as his father,' but she is barely listening, her eyes are following Nigel's every move and when he comes back to her she throws her arms round him.

'I didn't believe you were going to do it, you were magnificent - you *are* magnificent,' and she doesn't care if Jean hears that.

'What? Are you not knowing, my wee, Lowland lass, that no self-respecting Highland warrior is not knowing how to do the Sword Dance, right enough?' and he lifts her off her feet. 'Come on, it's nearly midnight and I'm having the first dance with you after Big Ben?'

Fiona, giggling at his send-up, straightens her dress and hears Joyce ask Glaykit MacLummie if he can do the sword dance like Nigel. Glaykit cannot, but Glaykit tells lies.

Now Robbie turns on a battered portable radio crackling out its broadcast as midnight approaches. With everyone's glasses charged, and halfway up the stairs, he counts down the seconds to midnight and as Big Ben strikes the shout of Happy New Year goes up with kisses, hands shaken and backs slapped. No-one except Fiona and Joyce look alarmed when Robbie then hands Nigel his rifle.

Pushing Glay's hands and face away Joyce says, 'Jeez, he's got a gun, what's he going to shoot?' At the open door and into the night Nigel fires one shot up into the air and she grips MacLummie's arm.

'Only the old year; he's chased off 1960, that's all,' he tells her as if she should have known. 'Come on, get on with it, finish what you were doing,' and grabs at her.

Fiona hears his explanation too and pulling Jean's shawl round her shoulders she goes to Nigel looking out into the night of heavily falling snow. With his arm round her, he closes the door behind them blocking out the others singing *Auld Lang Syne.*

'Shh, listen,' he says as the air fills with more single shots like a series of faint, random pops. 'I love that, you can hear all the other guns sending the old year on its way. Happy New Year my Darling...'

'Kiss me again,' she says.

'You don't have to ask...'

'Don't stop,' she hangs on to him.

'Hey - what is it?'

'I love you.'

'You do?'

'Promise I do.'

114

'You Darling girl, that's bloody marvellous. So that's it - you'll marry me then?'

'Yes - yes please.'

He holds her very tight, snow falling on them through the torchères' warm light and he says, 'this isn't how it was supposed to be, it was supposed to be romantic, not like this.'

'I think it's very romantic...'

'But you're getting wet.'

'I've been much wetter.'

The door opening interrupts and Robbie's head pokes out, ignoring their embrace he looks up at the falling snow. He says he thinks Nigel should tell the guests to go home, he knows the snow is going to get heavier and they'll be snowed in if they don't. But then he worries that Fiona must be cold standing there with only Madam MacMuckle's shawl for extra warmth.

'No, Robbie, I'm not,' she says, 'I'm feeling very, very warm, thank you.'

'Robbie's right, we'd better go in and tell them,' Nigel says, 'they'll be sorry they won't get some dancing - I'm sorry too that I won't get to dance with you...'

'Me too, I love dancing with you...'

'Well that's a good thing - you know what they say?' and she doesn't. 'It's the vertical expression of a horizontal desire?' And holding her against him again, he whispers, 'to be continued and that's forever after too. For now we'd better go in.'

Disappointed guests but with well practised skill wrap up, change their footwear and crunch across the snow. First the MacIntoshes, one stained pink in places, then the Snitchers - whose real name Fiona has never been told. Findlay Livingstone comes next, insisting he should be called Fin as Dr Findlay and Dr Livingstone jokes wear a bit thin. Slowly, he helps Lady Stravaig bent over with age and hanging on to her husband, Ossian. He, the cadaver brought to life by neglected Joyce's pneumatic charms. He's followed by their son, 'young' Stravaig, though he's sixty and his wife four years older. Then the MacVicars, the minister with his galoshes on the wrong feet and who's improved in drink and a MacLummie the Younger of Reeks who hasn't. And lastly Joyce picking her way across the snow in stilettos, her hand held high by Nigel as if they're trying out a minuet. One by one car engines turn then all that is left is exhaust smoke hanging over the snow.

'Went well I'd say, even if the cowards didn't try to make it,' says Jean as they warm themselves by the fire. 'You do realise you may well be snowed in here, Fiona, don't you? And the snow ploughs don't favour us either, one feels it must be something one said. Maybe it's a good thing that all the food wasn't eaten tonight, we'll have some to keep us going, perhaps we can rechauffé it. You must be tired, I really do thank you for dealing with all the cooking and it was delicious too.'

'I'm glad you enjoyed it, I enjoyed doing it,' Fiona replies. 'Thanks for this too.' She pulls off the shawl.

'No my dear, I don't need it... In fact I think you should have it - keep it, Fiona.'

'I can't...' But Jean doesn't turn round and carries on up the stairs.

'You can, she wants you to have it and so do I,' Nigel gently puts it back round her shoulders. But he has things he has to do before he goes to bed and when he has he'll come to her room to say goodnight properly. He won't be long.

'Promise?' I don't want to fall asleep and wake up tomorrow and find it's all been a dream.'

'Never.'

By Hogmanay standards it isn't late, only just after half past midnight. Nigel settles Luath by the fire in his room then takes off his weapons, sporran, doublet and jabot. From his window he watches the snow falling knowing they would almost certainly be snowed in by the morning. But what did it matter Fiona doesn't have to go anywhere now and turning to the bed he thinks how much he wants her. And that makes him wonder how many MacMuckles have been conceived there. He sits on it to unbuckle his shoes then gives out a low sigh as he drops back, his head hitting the pillow and that makes an unyielding crackle. It's a folded piece of paper on which his mother has written two words; marry her. He laughs out loud at the idea of Jean thinking she's arranged it when he tells her. But it augurs well, Jean had never before been quite so obvious.

'Can I come in?' he asks as he knocks lightly on Fiona's door.

'I don't think you have to ask any more do you, not now?' she says and he puts his arms round her. 'You were very kind to Joyce - you are kind.'

'Am I... You don't mean soft do you? I wouldn't want that thought of me.'

'No, it's not the same thing.'

'Oh well, toujours la politesse and all that. I don't doubt she likes his money but Glay's always been a meat-head and can be guaranteed to behave badly, but he should have been taking care of her. He knows Archie takes no hostages.'

'I thought they were your friends.'

'They are, we all grew up together, went to the same schools, National Service too - but, as you will find, this is a small pool and we all have to live here - make allowances, get on. I shouldn't be putting you off should I?' he says.

'You aren't, and it's good you can see things for what they are, I've only just realised that you don't always see people you've known all your life as clearly as you might.'

'That sounds profound, but for another time perhaps? There are much more important things for now aren't there? You did mean it didn't you, you will marry me, Fiona?' and his face is very close to hers.

'Yes, I meant it, I really do mean it. You look so worried, don't be... I love you.'

'Say it again,' and she does, over and over until he stops it with the longest, most lingering kiss yet. 'Are you very tired?' he says into her hair.

'No, not particularly, not too tired for you anyway. I'll never be too tired for you.'

'My sentiments too, come here,' he says as he sits on the armchair by the fire, pulling her on to his lap.'

'I can think of nothing nicer,' and she lays her head against him.

'Really - are you sure?'

'Stop teasing, Nigel, you know what I mean.'

'Do I?'

'Stop it, I can feel you're laughing.'

As if she weighed nothing he lifts her up and carries her to the bed, 'No, this is better. I won't do anything you don't want.' He isn't laughing now.

'I found your war dance very erotic - I think I'd let you do anything.'

'Would you?' but he doesn't wait for her answer, her mouth has a better use.

She stretches, her shoes tip off her feet and on to the floor, then they lie looking at one another, he clasping her thigh and pulling her close into him. She, fumbling at the button of his shirt, but he stops her hand and she understands the question in his eyes. 'I've never felt like this before, I don't want it to stop but I...'

'I know.'

'Nigel, I haven't...'

'Shh - do you want to?'

'Have you...?'

'Yes, is that alright?' and there's a smile in his voice.

'A lot?' she asks and feels his silent laugh.

'You might say that.'

'You know what to do, I don't...'

'You don't have to do anything.'

'Are you sure?'

'Darling Fiona, just stop asking questions and leave it to me.'

Piece by piece he undresses her and drops the clothes on the floor almost in slow motion until all that is left on her is his necklace. His own clothes, a shirt and kilt, he throws off and nothing before compares with the frisson of pleasure his skin gives against hers. Everything falls back into slow time again when his touch drowns her and instinct replies with that desperate longing turned into deep physical demand. He was right, she doesn't have to do anything, it just happens. He makes it happen. Noises come out of her mouth she's never heard before. And with a glancing touch of his weight, the curve of his neck for a moment coves her face in that scent of smoke and cedar. She'd touch him but he stops her hand again. His hands - confident hands - move her limbs and clutch her against him. Her back arches and her breath catches in her throat, her fingers press and he waits until she breathes it's alright.

It feels like flying,

rising,

soaring,

cresting... cresting...

A spent and in a loose-limbed slide, his weight half-settles on her and she can feel his heart, his noisy breathing in her ear then a long, deep sigh.

'You alright?' comes out as one slurring sound into the pillow, but she understands.

'Can't you tell?' she whispers. 'I want it again.'

That makes him laugh and he moves to face her. 'I love you my Darling Fiona.'

'And I love you too my muckle, bonny lad, I really do, Nigel. You won't go back to your own bed, will you?'

'Not if you don't want me to, I can practise holding you close to me all night and get used to seeing your lovely face when I wake up. I'll never tire of it.'

'And you say the most lovely things, I'll never tire of that... You make me want to cry.'

'Oh, don't - you'll get used to it.'

Then the bitten bites back

'You'll get used to it' and of course Fiona MacMuckle did, an apt ending for the tale of a girl who found her prince and for ever after lived in a fairy-tale castle. But Nigel isn't a prince despite a heritable status and property. The castle might literally look the part, if from a distance, or figuratively if from lack of real knowledge. But now in 1964 and over the past three years Fiona's increasing awareness of the crumbling fabric of her matrimonial home is something she has not got used to. Neither has she got used to vacant month after vacant month passing and no sign of an heir to pass the place on to. Nigel had become reluctant to talk about it and so the subject dwindled but so has his interest in the castle. Now he can hardly bother to replace light bulbs let alone have the roof patched or the alarming cracks in the walls surveyed - even if he could find the funds to pay for it. Yet Fiona never questions his lack of stewardship. She is afraid of his answer.

His burst of enthusiasm for painting has dwindled too. And when he does paint the subject matter has changed from landscapes full of light and economic brush strokes into intense, dark canvases, each smaller in size than the previous one. She keeps her opinion to herself but it puzzles her, even frightens her, if she looks at them for too long. Recently she suggested he might try a portrait, perhaps he could try his hand at following Napier's technique in the painting of his father as he admires it so much. But Nigel's finished picture is nothing like the Napier. Now there is something more like Munch's *The Scream* on his easel. The head certainly has red hair and she reasonably supposes that it might be his idea of a self-portrait but she kept her opinion to herself when she first saw it.

She also wishes her mother-in-law would learn from her how to keep her opinions to herself. Unlike her son, she has no qualms in talking about blood-lines. Almost as soon as Fiona and Nigel came back from their honeymoon she'd praised the local paragon of productivity in Georgina MacIntosh, 'a girl who simply pops them out, one a year.' And at breakfast from behind her newspaper shield she turns to what she calls the hatched column in *The Times* and there will be a breakfast litany of all the latest births to any family she knows no matter how remotely. Then when she's finished her phony interest she purses her lips with a sniff and rearranges her crumpled newspaper with angry battings of her hand. Fiona knows it for what it is - and it hurts, but Nigel dismisses his mother's disclosures. Isn't she just passing the information on? And he does nothing about it. Neither has he reminded her that the agreement was that she *lived* in her little flat and they live in the rest of the house. The only joint meet-up was to have been supper or invitation. But by cunning, which became custom, Jean then appeared for lunch then breakfast too and it hadn't taken long to slip herself into their daily life.

Fiona's nesting instinct had also played out in new domestic arrangements as Nigel made it quite clear that she was in charge, it is her home and she must do what she thinks fit. And this year what she thinks fit is to take the curtains down to be cleaned, if they'll stand it, wash all the loose covers and throw away age flattened cushions which fill the place with dust. She's put away the excess of ornaments each generation of wives added to the previous ones' collections. With mounting irritation Jean tackles this desecration, as she calls it, when she comes across Robbie moving furniture from room to room.

122

'What in heaven's name are you doing now, why are you moving that? Put it back at once,' she says to him as he carries a very heavy, very tatty wing chair.

And he puffs, 'Fiona is telling me to move it, right enough,' then dumps it down only for one leg to break off.

'I don't doubt that she has, but you mustn't,' and Fiona comes to see what the fuss is about though she can make a fair guess. 'Fiona, this chair has always been in the drawing room, this is the chair Dr Johnson used when he and Boswell were here during their tour of the Western Isles, it isn't for you to change things. And look, because you've moved it, it's now broken,' and she tuts as she picks up the leg.

Fiona, keeping her annoyance in check, says, 'it's full of worm, Jean, that's why the leg's broken off. It should be treated, it can go outside into the stable and I will do it myself.'

'No it will not, it goes back where it belongs, it will be perfectly alright. Put books in place of the leg, Robbie.' Fiona, annoyed though she is, thinks Jean has probably frightened the woodworm and they will defect anyway. 'It really is too bad you know, things are fine as they are in this house. If it was good enough for generations of MacMuckles then it is certainly good enough for you, Fiona. There is no need to do anything, I think it very presumptuous of you.' Fiona now doesn't hide her frustration and sighs loudly. Robbie, who has been examining his feet, looks up.

'So what am I to be doing with the chair then? Muckle Nigel is saying I am to be taking my orders from Madam...'

'There you are, that's conclusive,' sniffs Jean, puffing up her chest.

'No, he was meaning - Mrs - Fiona, so he was,' and Robbie nods at her.

'*I* am Madam MacMuckle,' Jean snaps and Robbie shoots bewildered glances back and forth between the two women.

'It's alright, Robbie, Nigel did mean me.' Fiona looks at Jean whose victorious expression must be for her retained status, Nigel's order can't have hit her yet so she quickly asserts herself. 'Please take the chair out to the stable, Robbie, then we can get on with the rest.'

Jean opens her mouth and lifts her arm in retreating Robbie's direction, but Fiona has turned away to the drawing room. The silence is broken by Jean's salvo echoing through the Great Hall.

'And, Fiona, don't you dare touch Nigel's bed, Bonnie Prince Charlie slept in it.'

Fiona turns round, 'I know that,' she barks. 'Perhaps you should make an inventory of everything that had a famous user, Jean. Perhaps Rudolph Hess slept in *your* bed - and Butcher Cumberland used the kitchen knives? Can I throw away the big chopping board or did Mary Queen of Scots practise putting her neck on it?' Fiona by then back in the drawing room doesn't see Jean's look of silent astonishment but it's only when she reaches the landing does she think of something to shout back.

'Well then, there are artefacts belonging to Sir Walter Scott and he was my ancestor, I am of that blood - and so is Nigel - and your own children will be too. That is *if* you ever get round to producing any.' It echoes around the Great Hall and she waits but there is no answer. Fiona, looking out of the drawing room window heard her quite clearly.

That Fiona thinks she's probably gone too far with Jean amuses Nigel, he says it would have done her some good, so Fiona continues with her daily reorganisation and retreats to the kitchen, the only place where Jean never ventures. But Jean still ventures into the newspaper's hatched column and it becomes even more obvious and pointed. Nigel silently hides behind his newspaper and Fiona hits her daily breakfast egg with increasing force.

But there is never a chance for a rapprochement between the women, ten days of escalating mutual attrition and Jean's announcements come to an abrupt end. She doesn't appear for breakfast and her place at table isn't laid for lunch or supper either. A few days later the name MacMuckle does indeed appear in *The Times* - half way down the dispatched column.

Jean died never knowing that Fiona had consulted a gynaecologist eighteen months before and who could find nothing wrong with her. She would never have been told and neither would anyone else except Nigel. He'd listened to what the doctor had told Fiona, that babies sometimes took time to come - she should wait, relax and leave it to Mother Nature who always knew best. He'd asked her questions about Nigel too, had he had mumps as a child? She didn't know, but presumed he had, after all, who hadn't? But the doctor said he should seek advice and she passed that on to him. He'd offered, kindly yet firmly, that he hadn't had mumps, only chicken pox and he thought measles, some sore throats and sometimes swollen glands. His mother didn't talk about illness. In his family it wasn't the done thing. And so, in that same spirit, it appeared not to occur to him that a medical examination of his own function's product might explain the empty cradle. Then the subject was dismissed with something like an adolescent boy's bravado.

The important issue of no issue could be filed under Nigel's credo, what Fiona has come to know as leaving everything alone to come right in its own time.

Those thoughts of the recent past occupy her as she tidies the bedroom Charlie Scott is using. Nigel's cousin, though more like a brother, Jean's beloved nephew and who's staying with them after the funeral. Fiona stops what she's doing to watch the cousins from the window, they laugh, no doubt sharing some memory while they point at something across the loch. And she remembers Jean's spoken thoughts on him when he came home from South Africa nearly eighteen months ago. Fiona had never met him until then and Jean had made him sound like a paragon. Charles Scott, charismatic, moneyed, divorced and back in Edinburgh with his small fortune. And to his aunt that had been unsurprising. He was the confident and clever one - as if by implication Nigel wasn't. And Fiona sniffs at Jean's opinion on Charlie's one misfortune. How it was such a great shame he'd somehow managed to lose his wife to another man and though Jean had never met the girl, she had to be a fool. Did he have one or two children? No matter, they'd only ever be photographs to her, they lived in Capetown with their South African mother. And to Jean that was the price Charlie payed for not marrying his own kind from his own country.

All so easily dismissed, typical of Jean Fiona thinks as she looks at the bed made for the golden boy. His first visit to Glenduir after he came back from South Africa remains clear in her head for many reasons most of which make her uncomfortable still. She remembers that particular day just before he arrived. The tea was fresh in the pot, Nigel was back with the groceries and how she'd startled him when she came into the kitchen.

'Oh it's you,' he said, and you said who else would he have thought it was then poured yourself a cup. He was lost somewhere in his head. You were irritated weren't you and told him you were surprised he wasn't more pleased at seeing Charlie. It had been a long time. And he said he didn't know why you thought that but he was dismissive with it. Then you reminded him he was going to Glasgow for the day on the Friday. Did he really have to go? It was the second time in two weeks, you never went there and he ignored you so you spelled it out. The lawyer, the trustees, the bank - all in Edinburgh? He just replied with one word; business. He was more interested to know if you wanted him to put the groceries away. So

126

while he was in Glasgow you'd have to look after Charlie on your own even if he was going to Inverness to see a man about investing in a fish farm. And remember, you thought that maybe he could find a way to include Nigel in his plan, let his Midas touch gild him too? Then Robbie's rap at the window brought that one-sided conversation to an end. What a production he made of his arrival, huffing, puffing, sucking his teeth until you told him to put his gun down, made him sit and poured him a cup of tea. He stirred it so hard it spun like the Corryvreckan whirlpool. 'At the end of his tether - he'd been up half the night - it was the dog fox' and he'd had enough of 'the biggest, sleekest, boldest, cunning fox' he'd ever known. Marauder of other people's poultry, pet rabbits, the school guinea pigs and the post-mistress's old cat - all lost and now it was his own hen coop which had been cleaned out. He described the carnage graphically and his fury at not being able to 'get the bugger.' You were concerned and said so but Nigel only rolled his eyes and shook his head. Robbie did too, 'well, if that is it, then I will not be going on about it any longer, muckle Nigel, I will be drinking my tea and be getting on my way, so I will. I was thinking you would be wanting to be in the picture, right enough.' That summed it up then he clattered the cup back on its saucer, he made as much noise going as he had coming.

And Nigel? Well, he just sighed with, 'what does he think I can do about it?' So that was that and he took a biscuit, mumbling, 'someone will shoot it sooner or later.' You took him to task over that didn't you? You knew Robbie was upset and needed him to know. He wasn't listening though was he? He was staring out of the window at the mountain so you said he looked like one of his Highland cows chewing the cud.

Fitting for a returning hero, that's what Nigel called Charlie's red MGB while he parked it. He was so self-assured, tanned, fair haired. He had a look of Nigel in his smile - but Charlie's smile dazzled - otherwise there wasn't much to connect them physically though their voices were similar. Nigel appeared genuinely pleased to see him after all, they fell into their old ways and private jokes within minutes. 'You look well, old man - marriage suits you then?' Charlie said that and then took your hand... He called you 'Amy's little sister, no less,' you weren't sure you liked that and he still had hold of you when he asked 'is Mucky keeping you happy?' Yes, you laughed - but wished he wouldn't use that stupid name, Mucky. Then he confessed he hadn't looked after his own wife. She'd gone off with the pool-cleaning man, 'some drongo' he called him with the apt name of Jost de Kok, that was easy to laugh at. He said that's what came of making filthy lucre, it took over and wasn't all she'd wanted. He'd probably have said more if you hadn't been there. Then the pair of them took the stairs two at a time, one powered by practise, the other, you thought, with the ease of a long distance runner. You left them in Charlie's room looking out of the window, sharing memories again, though you heard Charlie call you 'a peach and nothing like old Amy'.

Watched and listened more than you spoke, didn't you? Jean wasn't there to moderate the male-bonded reminiscence, she was still stuck in her friend's spare room at Gallus, she said she had a gippy tummy. Oh yes, Charlie paid attention to you, he asked why you'd want to hear their old tales, you must find them boring. He wanted to know how someone like you was 'snared by old Mucky'. Yes, you blinked, you opened your mouth too, but nothing came out and he apologised for embarrassing you. He was kidding, Mucky was a good sort really, he touched the back of your hand and you saw Nigel glance at that, so you quipped, 'I know he is, he's the very best, I'll have you know.' You did mock primness well.

That had to be an offer made out of family affection more than confidence when he asked Nigel to go with him to the fish farm and give his opinion on it. He couldn't have forgotten about Nigel's trout going AWOL. That sun-kissed Midas would never have his fish desert him, he'd never lost anything - except his wife perhaps. He was to be a sleeping partner only, his money was all that was wanted and he said he'd be staying with you from time to time if he went ahead with it. But Nigel couldn't go with him, Nigel was going to Glasgow for the day. No regrets were expressed but manners had been served. 'So can I take your wife out to lunch tomorrow, old man?' that came out quickly and they both looked at you. 'If that's what she wants?' and, oh yes, you did. Nigel wanted to get to bed, he waited for Charlie then he led the way but you saw the fire glowing hot, flames leap back into life when you're not looking and that's dangerous at night. You put the fireguard up. Then you stayed to lay the breakfast table. No, you weren't long but Nigel wasn't in bed when you went up - he was asleep in that ancestral bed yet again. His alarm clock set for 5am - that was the reason he was there - well that's what you thought.

She picks up Charlie's towels dropped on the floor thinking he probably forgets there are no South African servants to do it for him. She notices a photograph beside the bed of his two children, happy, little laughing faces in the South African sun sitting together in the back of an open top car.

And that Friday you'd laughed too when the roof was down in Charlie's MGB. Fast, noisy and fun - people in the village stared, you enjoyed that and the drive to Inverness and while you waited for Charlie to come back from the fish farm you did some shopping. A new pair of Wellingtons, a tin opener and after lunch that surprise, that Perspex bracelet. The fish farm was no good but the lunch was - so was the food.

Charlie sat very close to you that evening when you played that duet on the piano - the piece involved crossed hands - you didn't know it as well as he did. He called you Sweetie when you got it wrong and told you to keep your leg against his, you'd feel the beat better that way. Then during the fast passage you looked up and there Nigel was, leaning against the door frame. You stopped playing. Neither of you heard him come in, he looked so tired, so grey, so sad.

Why did Charlie have to say you were quite a player? Why did he have to say such a provocative thing? That he thought you'd got the idea.

She sits on the chair cushions she's just plumped up, her hands on her knees, staring down at the threadbare rug. She knows she said the right things, did the right things, went to Nigel, kissed him and ran her fingers across his brow.

But you complained.

The piano was ropey, it needed tuning, and then you were back on the stool fiddling with the sheet music, running your fingertips down the keys, praising Charlie's mastery of the keyboard, so good at jazz piano too, even saying he was, oh-so clever, such a good teacher and let's have another go tomorrow and he'd laughed in that confidential way. But you chided him for that and wagged your finger, he caught and held on to it and said it was only banter wasn't it? Nigel went to feed his dog in the kitchen, you followed, he gripped the edge of the table, you thought he was in pain. But no, he said it was nothing, pay no attention, he straightened up with a quick pull of the mouth passed off as a smile. You knew something wasn't right, something else you couldn't talk about. But all he said was, 'sorry, been a long day, I'm tired that's all.' And you accepted that because Charlie was at the piano again playing *Misty,* so you just checked the joint, turned the heat up under a pan and left him to cut up cold, cooked ox heart.

There's ox-tail stew for their supper tonight, she clicks her tongue at the irony of it and looks at her watch. She should go downstairs and start preparing things but she can't, she's turning the gold bracelet on her wrist, round and round and round. Because...

That night when you'd finished eating, not that Nigel ate much, Charlie pointed, he'd noticed that jumbled row of coloured Perspex cubes lying in a heap on the table. And Nigel picked it up holding it in his open palm. 'What's this, where did it come from?' he said it so seriously - yet you just trilled, 'it's my new bracelet, Charlie kindly bought it for me today, look it's made of that new stuff - Perspex - the latest thing and all the rage - unusual to find something like this in Inverness.' Nigel looked at it then at Charlie but he was smiling at you, 'you liked it didn't you?' he said, *then* he looked at Nigel. 'It's a thank you for having me, not enough I know, merely a gewgaw. Cheap, that's probably why it fell off,' and he took it from Nigel and stretched across the table to fasten it back on your wrist - next to the gold one Nigel gave you on your wedding day... And Nigel didn't move an inch, did he? He stayed as he was, his upturned palm empty and you lifted your arm and shook it slightly. The two bracelets sounded like dice in a cup... Yes, like two dice in a cup. He slouched back in his chair, his head cocked, his eyes down and with his finger he rolled a piece of bread about the table top and into a small pellet.

She sits upright again and stretches her head back, the detail of her recollection enough to make her shudder slightly.

Didn't Charlie say Nigel looked tired, suggest he shouldn't stay up on his account, didn't he say he should go to bed? It's hazy -

someone outside cracked off three shots in quick succession, close enough for you all to stop and pay attention. And Nigel, weary with it, said it must be the fox and 'let's hope Robbie got it. God knows why he keeps missing the bloody thing,' he held his hand out to you. Yes, he did want to go to bed, he wanted you to go with him, but you wanted to wash up, he wanted you to leave it until morning. But another two shots rang out, they got up that time and left you there. So you washed those dishes, hands in the suds and that Perspex bracelet fell off again - it sank - the clasp was unreliable, what else could you expect from something so cheap, but you'd had some pleasure from it. Then those footsteps and it was left in the water.

Why didn't you see it coming? Maybe you did and were waiting for it, maybe that's what you wanted?

The idea makes her swallow hard as she realises she can clearly recall the conversation.

'I thought you'd both gone to bed.'

And at the kitchen doorway Charlie smiled at you, 'Mucky has, I wanted to take a look outside - see if I could spot the fox. The moon's bright, you know.' Had he seen anyone out there? 'No fox, no gun... But I'd forgotten how romantic this place can be in the moonlight, want to take a look?'

'It can, but ...' he didn't let you finish.

'But one has to be in the right frame of mind, is that it?'

'Well yes, there's that, but I was thinking more along the lines of familiarity breeds...' and he did it again.

'Contempt?'

'Something like that.' You ducked slightly to look out of the window at the sky. 'Yes, you're right, it can be pretty wonderful, stars do actually sparkle don't they?'

132

'Sometimes, and some more than others, Fiona.' And you understood that didn't you?

'Star light, star bright, first star I see tonight, I wish I may, I wish I might have this wish I wish tonight,' it came out automatically. That's right, you were embarrassed, so you kept looking up at the sky.

Yes, he was leaning against the door with his arms folded. 'And what is it you wish for tonight, Fiona - anything I can grant?'

'No, it's nothing, it was just some nursery rhyme thing Amy and I used to say when we were children, that's all.'

'You're sure, nothing at all?' he moved forward slightly and you moved back and looked at your watch.

'Well, it's later than I thought,' but that wasn't true, you knew what time it was. 'Help yourself to whatever you like if you want to stay up, the fire's not quite out. I really should get off to bed, Charlie, and thanks again for everything today.' Had he locked the front door? No he hadn't. You said you'd do it and when you passed him he made no effort to give you more room and his fingers brushed your hand... Yes, you're right, it was deliberate.

'So no star-gazing then?' but you didn't answer. 'Ah well, lucky Mucky. Bonne nuit et fais de beaux rêves, ma cherie,' he said as you went.

You didn't answer, you didn't even turn round. He'd squandered those goodnight words of Nigel's. You felt they weren't his to use, it was as if he'd cheapened them.

Nothing more was said, not by Charlie, not by Nigel nor even any mention of what he'd been doing in Glasgow. You thought it likely to be about money or the increasing lack of it. He'd never admit it, you'd given up trying to encourage him to do so by then. Still don't know, it's best not to think about those things any longer...

But you do know you barely considered Nigel that day, that evening. You know Charlie's admiring distraction left no place for a wifely thought...

And that's such a shabby thought that it makes Fiona take a sharp breath and stand up so quickly she loses her balance for a moment. Gripping the nearest piece of furniture she sees how shabby the room is too and tosses her head at it. It doesn't matter it's Charlie and he's used to it.

They see Charlie off in the morning, it's sunny and so is he. He has a new E Type Jaguar now and he leaves with a cheery wave and a couple of jars of Fiona's marmalade.

'He's right when he said with Ma gone it is the end of an era,' Nigel says as they watch the car avoid the pot holes down the drive. 'Perhaps we can live in the present now,' and he makes a final slow wave at the car disappears.

Fiona takes his arm, 'please let's have casual, relaxed suppers for a start?' and he looks at her.

'Really, do you think so?'

'Yes I do - to please me?'

'Huh, I don't think I do enough of that these days,' he says quietly and kisses the top of her head. She doesn't respond, best to let him think on that and she leaves him there in the sunshine with Luath.

He's still there half an hour later, Fiona sees him from a window and stops to watch him for a moment. He does this sometimes, increasingly so, but today she thinks that with all the obsequies done and time to himself he must be thinking about his mother. There he is leaning on his Chiefs' cromach, a shepherd's crook to other people, staring in an unfocused way at the landscape and he's chewing slowly. Times past made by chocolate covered caramels triggering boyhood memories. Yet for all the pleasure these times give him, Nigel is disciplined about having only one packet of caramels per week. A function of unavoidable Calvinistic conditioning; fat or happy, if you must, but never both together. There's discipline too in his sitting on the local bench as a magistrate and on the Board of Governors at a second rate boys' school some twenty-five miles away. Evident again in his timetable of three meals and tea every day, and nowadays assumed when in short daily bouts he sits at his untidy desk. But most of the time these days Nigel moves as the mood takes him, his lassitude becoming noticeable to all who know him. Often he can be seen by the loch throwing sticks into the water for his reluctant wolfhound. Or it might be a bonfire day - they happen quite frequently - there is always something to burn lying about the place. Or sometimes he can be heard making his way around the castle accompanied by the scratching lope of four paws behind him. And, occasionally he can be seen and heard. In the dilapidated summerhouse beside an ever-growing stretch of grass, once called a lawn, where he snores the afternoon away, his obedient dog sitting to attention and snapping at passing bees. She taps on the window and when he turns round she blows him a kiss. To that his face softens and he smiles a little at her as he nods a couple of times. Then he turns away, angling and planting his cromach in the gravel again hunching over with his hands and chin resting on its handle.

He is with his thoughts but not of his mother. With half-shut eyes he sees his castle and the crennelated top tower with its broken flagpole like a defeated jouster's lance. That same tower platform where every morning Robbie blows air into his pipes and caterwauls, or so everyone tells him. But in his mind's eye it is Robbie's father George up there playing as well as his son plays badly and whose voice warns Nigel the caramels would pull the stoppings out of his teeth. But he's never had fillings then or now.

Mewing buzzards circle above him, the dog stirs and he reaches down to stroke its head. Two ravens hop a dance across the top of the mound where as a small boy, and encouraged by Robbie, he rolled down the steep, grassy slope over and over again. But the ravens fly off across the woods, disappearing in gliding, dark specks above the loch where in the mid-nineteen thirties Robbie rowed him about on summer afternoons. Their pirate games; catching his first trout; beloved, ugly little Pigling tucked at his feet; Chrissie on the shore with a picnic and love... But a car door slams and jolts him out of his nostalgic confection. Georgina MacIntosh approaches him with a generous kiss and hug and says what a good send off Jean had but it's Fiona she's really come to see.

'I'm glad you've come,' Fiona says when she sees her friend. 'We haven't had a chance to talk since it happened.'

'Thought I'd drop in, I was passing, is everything getting back to normal?'

'I don't think I want it to go back to normal, I want it to be different, new, but that's something I can't really say to Nigel at the moment. I think finding Jean dead on her bed like that has probably affected him more than he says.'

'I expect so, a heart attack wasn't it?'

'A massive one. She wasn't that old so it was a shock, but there we are,' and she shrugs her shoulders.

'So, my dear Fiona, now you are the undisputed mistress of Glenduir Castle, I'm pleased for you.'

And Fiona is grateful for Georgina's validation but for her the place hasn't lost its mark of her late mother-in-law. It isn't her lingering must of Sobranie Black Russian cigarettes, the regular dram or the Pug which haunts. It is something less definable yet recognisable and can suddenly catch Fiona out. But it's early days yet - she hopes.

'Georgina, do you want to see where she lived upstairs?' she asks. 'I don't expect you ever did. I have to go up there to collect some of her clothes I've only cleared some of them.'

The door to Jean's rooms has a small, brass knocker and the door needs a push to make it open, Fiona stumbles. The place smells of musty time and past life as they step into the gloom. Heavy curtains on old metal runners hiss on their tracks as they're drawn then the rooms light up with the south east sun and show up the forgotten accoutrements of its last occupant's life.

And Georgina says, 'what a marvellous view - and you'll be able to do these rooms up, you'll be able to do everything up now won't you? You'll enjoy that.'

'You're right, I would...' but Georgina doesn't let her finish.

'Didn't Jean have any sort of kitchenette arrangement?'

'She insisted she didn't need one, she said she could do for herself, so she kept everything in that little fridge in the corridor. She bought a kettle and a toaster but not before she raided the kitchen and took a few bits of cutlery and crockery - but a lot of glasses.'

'Hm, she always ate with you and Nigel though, didn't she?' Georgina says as she looks about the room.

'Oh yes, it wasn't supposed to be like that but Jean, in her interior design, knew perfectly well I could cook - and I knew perfectly well that she did.'

Georgina pulls a face asking, 'it needs airing doesn't it, what do you think that smell is?' and makes a face.

'Pampered Pugs probably, and stale booze, spilt whisky - and fags.'

'Ah yes, booze, the ubiquitous Lemon Barley Water.' Georgina subtly taps the side of her nose.

'You knew? - you knew it was Lemon Barley vodka? I don't know if Nigel realised. I only discovered it when I was clearing out the scullery and I took a swig from her tumbler when she wasn't looking.'

'Archie's mother told me, I think most people knew what it was.'

But Jean's exposed secret gives way to the discovery of a dead raven lying on a pyre of twigs in the fireplace. Soot covers it and the hearth where a pair of desiccated mice languish in the log basket. But next door her bedroom holds the stale scent of freesia talcum powder and it increases with every step they take. Sticking out from a corner into the room the bed looks desolate with the horsehair mattress stripped of all its coverings. The bedside table stained with water marks carries a lamp and two tarnished, silver frames with the images of a handsome husband in one and a bonny, little son in the other and Georgina takes a closer look. But Fiona is at the window and the old-fashioned, draped muslin dressing table with its cluttered glass top. She pulls the stopper out of a bottle of scent and puts it up to her nose.

'Good Lord, Fiona - I can smell Jean, can you?' Georgina says as she wheels round.

'It's this, her scent, Shalimar, powerful isn't it?' and Fiona rams the glass stopper back.

'Ah, Shalimar - The Temple of Love.' Georgina floats the words on one long expressive sigh. 'My mother used it too, but oh dear, not an aptly named scent for Jean when you think about it.' Then she hesitates. 'You know, Archie's mother used to say Jean sacked the factor because he started taking an interest in her after Muckle died. Rather a nice man too by all accounts...'

138

'And the estate went downhill after he left. You'd think she'd have wanted to get married again, particularly as she was only been married to Muckle for a year!'

'Well, there were those rumours...' Georgina stops.

Fiona puts the bottle down and hesitates too. Then, 'what rumours? Nigel's never mentioned anything. You can't not tell me.'

'Archie's mother said Jean didn't like it, she tried to but she just couldn't.'

'Didn't like it?'

'Sex, she didn't like sex and when she was sure her duty was done and a baby safely on the way apparently she told Muckle that would be the only child they would ever have. And of course he fell out of that tree days after Nigel was born.'

'I don't think Nigel knows any of this, Georgina. And you think that's why she never remarried?'

'Well, it's an explanation isn't it?'

'Did Jean tell your mother-in-law herself, I mean...'

'No, Muckle told Archie's father, they were close, they'd always been friends.'

'Well, it's not a rumour then is it? But people talk about Muckle fondly, they say Nigel's like him, he couldn't have been a...'

'Brute? that's what they used to call it. Well who's to know about that really, but you knew Jean, she was a cold fish wasn't she, over fastidious in her way, didn't you think? I'd say she probably found it all "rather distasteful". And Muckle? well - he was probably a lusty lad, that's all.'

'Lusty lad yes, but not a brute.' Fiona picks up one of Jean's silver hairbrushes.

'Will you tell Nigel? I probably shouldn't have said anything,' Georgina asks.

'I'm glad you have, and I don't know if I will or not, it's a bit delicate.'

'You know best,' Georgina says and picks up the other hairbrush. 'Look, Jean's initials are still quite clear, the silver isn't really tarnished either.'

'That would fit, sometimes I think she's still here,' and a shiver passes through Fiona as she notices threads of hair in the bristles. Squeamishness not for herself over a few stray hairs but for Jean's attitude to sex. Is it a family trait and now Nigel's got it too? Is that what's wrong with him? But Georgina points at Jean's slippers, half hidden under the bed.

'They keep the shape of the foot as if she's still in them,' she says and Fiona looks too, they make her feel like a trespasser. Making an excuse she leads her friend out but she senses Jean, the sillage of Shalimar shadows her, she can't shake it off, she doesn't want it and steers them both down the stairs. Georgina's goodbye stalls as she holds her friend's shoulders and says she thinks Fiona has some of the Shalimar scent on her face somewhere, she can smell it.

Nigel outside, near where he was before, pokes his cromach into one of the cracks in the castle's rough-cast walls claiming he's measuring whether they've got any wider, but it is an intellectual exercise. Georgina, like everyone else, knows nothing will be done even if the crack becomes wide enough to hold an international gathering of cromachs.

'Nigel, I've just been in your mother's old rooms, what wonderful views they have, they'll be lovely when Fiona's done them up,' and Georgina makes it sound like an order but it doesn't stop her giving him another generous hug. And he, having finished his half-hearted building survey, goes looking for his lunch and finds Fiona in the cloakroom rubbing her face with a towel and soap.

'What are you doing? You're making your nose look like a clown's,' he laughs.

'I'm trying to get rid of your mother; she got me by the nose but I think it's working, I can only smell coal tar soap now. And I hate the smell of it, I'm going to change that too.'

And then it rains - that's not unusual in the glens, nobody pays much attention but it was unseasonably heavy. So it must have been quiet and sneaky as it slithered down the hill and came to rest in hundreds of tons. Nobody heard it take place but at eight o'clock in the morning Nigel slams on the Land Rover brakes when he sees it. In the downpour he sprints to a landslide of mud and rock now blocking the track like an insolent pile of ordure cutting off the short cut between the two villages of Glenduir and Driech. That historic path in a crease between the undulations of not quite mountains but more than hills and made by generations of human and animal feet, carts and latterly plucky vehicles. And now it is stopping up the direct way to avoid the journey of miles made of unsigned crossroads, anonymous forks and labyrinthine frets, the original routes of warring clans' evasions and entrapments. Routes never intended to be metalled highways. This vital ancient track is on Nigel's land and he looks up at where the slope was and sees a huge, jagged scrape torn away. From that tear and freed from the subsoil, roots dangle like severed arteries and bits of greyed quartz stick out of the wound like broken teeth in an assaulted face. And as he stands there in the rain more mud and rubble slides down the easiest drop. Other vehicles come to a halt; their doors slamming shut and he turns to see people running towards him. No words are needed it is all too obvious what's happened during the night.

With a weary sigh Nigel pushes the wet hair off his brow and acknowledges the practical problem of the landslide, the problem of access and the inconvenience everyone knows it will cause. A gloomy voice calls out that another landslide near Stravaig had been smaller and the road closed for a fortnight. This brings a collective groan and Nigel, like a military commander, climbs on a mound and raises his hands for quiet. He shouts a warning that the pile is too dangerous to get across, even by foot, and nobody should try. And it is assumed that Nigel, the Laird, will see to it that the valuable track is reinstated so no-one wastes words on that. But Robbie, standing apart from everyone else, is shaking his head.

By early winter the track remains stopped up with more mud and the inconvenience it causes remains neglected. People petition Robbie to remind the Laird that he is supposed to do something about it but Robbie knows he won't. Muckle Nigel's faulty stewardship has now extended beyond his personal space. And so that winter with the expectation of inevitable depredations on her home Fiona's firm intention is to monitor them herself.

Glenduir Castle takes on its seasonal scent of paraffin from flickering Aladdin heaters on landings and corridors. Snow falls and falls, sometimes rain and it always freezes - outside of course, but sometimes inside too. She checks every room each day and looks up at another ceiling crazed with stained cracks. Yes, the roof leaks - she's never known it to do otherwise and damp crawls the walls too. Pipes burst again and sprinkle water through the plaster ceiling-roses in pretty patterns but short the electric lights and watered-silk furnishings become a literal description. Not enough extra buckets can be found in any of the local shops and finally a lump of damp plaster hits her on the head. In a rare display of anger she hurls it at the fireplace.

The few repairs since she arrived there continue to be paid for by selling more pictures plucked off walls leaving bright, unfaded patches and nothing of Nigel's to replace them. A large portion of her late parents' legacy have already disappeared under the floors and down the drains in expensive new plumbing, something Jean hadn't objected to. And now Fiona has decided Jean's jewellry can pay for some re-wiring. The huge Raeburn portrait of Colonel

MacMuckle of Glenduir, which hangs in the Great Hall and is the last survivor of a once reasonable artistic patronage, is to go the way of everything else. Now Jean can't object to that and Nigel knows it will bolster his income but Fiona knows the Colonel's earnings will run out too.

She grabs a coat, she thinks a blast of fresh air up on the top tower will cool her hot eyes and clear her headache. Up the winding stone steps worn into curves from centuries of feet and she opens the door just as an unkindness of ravens approach. There's a falcon up there too, free from the falconer's fist, its leather jesses hanging from its legs. She watches it run the gauntlet in a swerved, languid arc then soar high and like a dart stoop to snatch a raven mid-flight. She sees its evasion, its sharp-set independence and the reward.

Resting her elbows on a crumbling parapet, her face in her hands, the wind gets up blowing her hair and roaring past her ears as she stares out across the landscape at the horizon almost lost in mist. Screwing her eyes up she shifts slightly, underfoot feels unstable but is only pieces of loose rendering scattered across the lead roof. Lead roofing which isn't sound and lets in the rain, and it looks as if rain is coming again, lots of it.

She pulls her coat tight around her thinking it was probably not a good idea to see how bad things were outside too, then tells herself it has to be faced. She stumbles on that rendering then kicks it away, it looks so innocent like lumps of stale cake but there's the sight of the expensive, damaged lead. The turret roofs can't be avoided, stuck like dunce's caps in each corner and the gaps where their slates have slipped and shattered in shards on the next surface down. Only in the surviving guttering do they sit like stacked casino chips making costly dams.

It's too much and she changes position to look across the glen at the faint shape of Archie's Driech Castle on its high ground. She envies its sound, solid function over form. She can't help comparing it to Glenduir Castle, which must have looked like it and any other Tower House in Highland Scotland. That was until a Victorian Laird attacked his home himself in 1866 and whose architect had been his own ego. Extensions and ornamentations, wings on each side of the original building with more turrets and towers and everything rendered in the pinkish-ochre of local pigmented earths. But now the cracked, rough-cast walls are streaked and faded wearing the dirty colour of an old trousseau's silk underwear. No amount of sunlight is going to bleach or improve it. She can see how fine he must have thought it looked then. But now the result of his incontinence? A prototype Walt Disney castle - and the fairy dust has run out.

Why doesn't Nigel do something? He knows that cracks like varicose veins have appeared on the exterior and the old ones have widened so much that the underlying stonework has begun to show. It's impossible not to be aware of the pot-holes puncturing the drive. That drive lined with fine, ancient oak trees yet they've had their dignity reduced by a neglect of rose and bramble briars. The stone gate posts badly need repair now and one of those heraldic finials, those wolf-like beasts, lies broken, defeated on the ground. And she's losing patience with tourists and hill walkers who all enthuse that Glenduir Castle looks 'picture-book romantic'. Distance does indeed lend enchantment when viewed from the bottom of that half mile drive or half way up Ben Vernacula. And she knows that the mountain with its white, quartzite crown piercing the sky is indeed 'majestic' and when it's covered in 'bonny, purple heather' it certainly does make 'a fine enough picture to grace a tin of shortbread'. But so what? It is becoming plain to her that Nigel is never going to do anything about those threatening cracks in the Victorian wings; those slates slipping and that lead splitting; time-sealed windows rattling; failed and failing guttering and all the rest.

So maybe it is the wind which makes her eyes water and she wipes them with the end of her scarf as she leans against the shelter of a chimney stack, but she doesn't want to go back inside - not yet. High up in her tower with her discontent simmering, the stable clock jerks its minute hand to the hour and the cracked bell strikes its dead-sounding beats. Above her the falcon rises and soars again circling high, it waits, but the first drops of rain spit at her face and she begins her steep descent down the stone stairs and through the tower door into her home. Nigel's footfall rings out on the stone floor and she calls out to him. He looks up at her to ask what she's been doing, has she been up the tower because it's raining. And as she passes him she says that's why she's come back in, wondering why they bother to say anything when it's so inconsequential. He takes a sharp intake of breath as if he wants to say something, then with a slow shake of his head appears to change his mind. Then she stops and turns to look at him.

'Nigel, as everyone seems to think this place is so bloody picturesque, I'm going to start a dinner, bed and breakfast business, we need their money - and urgently.'

The Tipping Point

Like an overstated cartoon character Nigel becomes a cliché of sucked teeth and knitted brows when he sees the advertisement in *The Clan MacMuckle Society Magazine*. It shows a flattering photograph of Glenduir Castle - proving photographs can and do lie - and Fiona's invitation to stay from next year with the Clan Chief and his wife at reasonable rates. She ignores his disapproval and doesn't care about the scandalised chorus of tuttings at the Laird's wife taking in paying guests. But she does care about Robbie's daily morning reveille and with that in mind she chooses the guest rooms carefully. For once it's a relief that the castle windows are stuck fast and that the curtains are heavily lined. With luck they won't be startled awake by Robbie's noise launched into the opposite direction.

Standing in the doorway of one of the newly designated bedrooms Nigel questions if what she's doing is really necessary. He doesn't think there is anything wrong with the rooms, to him they're comfortable enough and points out that she's never complained before. Neither is he pleased that she's taken the old pictures down and put up Naval prints. He knows they were her father's and remarks that Glenduir has no connection with anything sea-faring.

'But I have - and a connection with Glenduir too - don't I?' she's sharp with her words. 'And I want these; I think at least they're interesting, the others were grim. Who wants to look at dead things when they're in bed?'

'And new beds at that, aren't you moving on with this too fast, you said you aren't going to open until next year.'

'I'm pushing on with it and spreading the cost too. And beds? Oh please don't tell me again that if your own bed was good enough for Bonnie Prince Charlie before, or was it after, running away from Culloden, it's certainly good enough for you.'

But Nigel isn't finished, 'it's that twit Inspector from the Tourist Board putting ideas in your head - what does he know about beds?' He looks at his feet. 'Come on, you know how I feel about this, I wish you wouldn't do it, things are not that bad.'

'Not bad? Things are that bad, very bad, Nigel.' At last she's said it. 'We may have just about enough to live on but this place is falling down all about us, isn't it? Maintenance just isn't a priority and I know, even if you won't admit it, that things are getting desperate.'

'Oh Fiona, stop being so dramatic.' He half turns to leave then swings round again. 'Quite simply, I just don't like what you're doing, I never knew you minded so much, aren't you used to it yet? It's not as if this place is a prefab, it has stood for centuries so why would it fall down now? The bottom line is I don't want strangers here, you don't really want that either, do you?'

'What *I* want? All I want is some comfort and peace of mind, Nigel. Is that really too much to ask? I don't want us to be anywhere else but I don't think I can live like this much longer. Look, Nigel, look - don't you see it? Cracks, some very deep, inside and out, there's splitting, there's rot, leaks, ice and you know I mean ice on the inside. And what about outside too? Why can't someone - you even - do something about having all those bramble briars cut back? And another thing - how long do I have to go on apologising, making excuses for why you haven't done anything about having the landslide cleared? All of it, everything, it just gets worse. I can't go on ignoring it any longer, Nigel - I can't.' She thinks she might cry.

'You really mean it don't you?' And he watches her picking up the discarded packaging from the floor. 'Well, I still think this is unnecessary expense. I expect those cost a fortune too,' he points at an unwrapped duvet. 'What's supposed to be wrong with the blankets we have?'

She nods at the pile of blankets on the floor, 'Nigel please - look at those old things? They're only fit for your dog, they are threadbare there's no warmth left in any of them, anyway everyone has duvets these days,' and she strokes it.

'Well, I have those old things - as you call them - on my own bed...'

'Your bed - yes *your bed*? That bed is a tropical island, don't laugh, Nigel - it is. Even without the hangings closed you and your dog raise the heat. That must compensate for your stupid, old blankets I'd say.' His mouth twitches in amusement at her description but she hasn't finished either. 'And something else, none of this has cost you anything; I'll have you know I paid for all this, I'm allowed to spend that how I want, aren't I - alright?'

'Of course you are - sorry Fluff, of course you are.'

His tone and her pet name touch like an unexpected caress and she looks up but he doesn't see, he and his wolfhound have left her to her beds and duvets.

With Nigel's verbal stroke spent and without giving him something in return, she sits down heavily on one of the beds and beneath her the new duvet seems to expire. She can hear the clicking tread of his armoured brogues and soft patter of Luath's feet fading clean away. Holding the other duvet against her like a comfort blanket she lies back on the bed and knows if she stays there for too long she'll fall asleep, she feels tired - she's felt tired for too long. Through clean windows the sun shines and she shuts her eyes, the red of her closed lids burn the colour of fire. But the warmth on her face and the soft embrace of duck down feels like a seduction too rare to resist and all she can hear is the shallow, staccato rhythm of her every breath. She gathers more of the quilt in her arms and curls up but discontent lunges like a rapier, she buries her head into a new pillow and the burning red turns to black blankness. Then she tries to breathe slowly and deeply and questions crowd in. What is it, shame, anger, disappointment? 'I'm so tired of this,' she whispers.

Clouds cover the sun when she opens her eyes, she sits up slouching over and idly fiddles with a piece of discarded blue ribbon. Then through the window she can see Nigel with his dog at the bottom of the grassy slope. Irritated by his criticism of her initiative she picks up the discarded cellophane wrapping and crushes it up in a resisting, crackling bundle only to throw it aside as she drops back on the bed. Why was it so dramatic to worry about the future? Why couldn't he see she was trying to do her best for them - why couldn't he? Why was it so wrong to want - so bad to need? That anger drives her to the window as if she might open it and shout her questions directly at him but it has to be only a gesture, she knows very well that the windows won't open.

The bed entices again and she lies on it face down, breathing in the scent of the bedding's newness, its defiant softness springing back and stifling her. She rolls on her back and lies there with her palms upward and open. Eyes wide, she looks up at the ceiling, it badly needs a coat of white paint. She sighs at the thought of so much to be done, and knows she's doing it all in the wrong order too. There are pieces missing from the egg and dart plaster cornice with its symbolic darts of death and eggs of life and that taunts her with Nigel absent from their bed so much. And he won't be drawn on that either, he seems to be settling into the MacMuckle habit of separate bedrooms despite her enticing efforts. The thought of it spreads like a pain from her very centre. It has become too frequent a visitor and now it hammers at her defences with its shout of - if, if, if. If what? The answer verges on treachery but this time it isn't to be ignored.

If only Tim Robinson had written her more than that one letter. If he'd written again while he was at sea confirming his words would she have been less taken with Nigel? And, if she had married Tim instead she wouldn't be trying to make ends meet in a house of crumbling picturesqueness stuck in a remote glen. It would have been so simple for a Naval daughter to segue into a Naval wife. And she might have had Malta, Singapore, anywhere but Glenduir and Driech to call her backyard. And, if she had married Tim would she have a child by now. But that is one question too many and it can't be played with so comfortably. In it she recognises disappointment, the core emotion never properly addressed and which lurks unfed in happy times but comes out to scavenge in the quiet times, the night times, the lonely times. But, out of synchrony, clocks strike twelve all over the house and pitch her back into reality. Too much the product of her time and place Fiona MacMuckle knows she has to impose more positive thoughts - she's practised enough lately. Lying on a feather bed dreaming a rose-tinted fantasy is not what she should indulge, but the gold bracelet she always wears catches on the duvet's label. She unfastens it and it falls open revealing its engraved words on the inside:

Yesterday, today, tomorrow and forever N&F ~ May 28th 1961. A bracelet of linking lover's knots, Nigel's present to her, delivered on the morning of their wedding day by one of his ushers and pressed into her hand along with his letter. His single letter too, never apart for long enough and only a telephone call away. That one letter safely kept in the bracelet box. She hasn't read it for some time and now she wants it, she needs it. Folded neatly to fit the box she flattens out the creased grid of squares and lies back on the pillows.

My Darling,
        So here it is, our wedding day, and I wanted to bring my present to you myself but I've just been told that to see the bride today <u>before</u> the wedding will bring bad luck. This, I thought, was an impossible outcome for you and me, what possible harm could ever come to us? But the matter has been insisted on by all those detailed to keep me in order!

This bracelet comes with all my love. Never doubt it. I loved you yesterday, I love you today, I will love you tomorrow and forever, just like the eternal circle it will make on your wrist.

I am so proud of you and so happy you want to spend the rest of your life with me. Later today when I gladly promise to love, cherish and keep you, know that I will for all our years to come - together and then with the additions we can look forward to. Always remember this.

I hope you aren't feeling too nervous, Darling - try sipping brandy through a sugar lump, that seems to calm the nerves and later just hang on tight to my arm. Now I must find my sporran, I have a wedding to go to this afternoon!

Yours forever with all my love, N.

Reading it again does what she hoped, it releases a wave of emotion at Nigel's tenderness, his imagination, his loving concern, but she re-folds the letter and puts it back in the box. Her hand shakes so much that she struggles to put the bracelet on again, once fixed it slides down her arm cold in its signal of repossession. She twists it round once, all that is needed to warm and forget it again.

Standing up she drops the duvet, pushes her hair back and straightens one of the prints on the wall remembering it from her childhood. That steel engraving of a 19th century Admiral with his arm extended and pointing at something beyond the frame yet resolutely looking in the opposite direction towards the sea. That contradiction amused her father then, now it could be her own personal allegory until she decided to face the same way as the problems within and beyond the frame. Turning away from both image and thought she catches a glimpse outside of the maddening man she knows she loves and watches him coming back up the grassy slope ahead of his dog.

A slight smile crosses her face as a rogue thought slips past her interior gate-keeper. What bright, blue eyes Nigel has - just like Tim Robinson's.

In the kitchen a bunch of flowers, scentless, almost wilting carnations and maidenhair fern lie on the table with a note. Stopping when she sees them Fiona knows they've come from the village shop where that is the only option available. And as she also knows they are from Nigel, she picks up the piece of paper and reads.

Sorry Darling, this is the best I can do. All my love always, N

Sorry for what, sorry for what's happening to them? Sorry for baiting her about the rooms or sorry those are half dead carnations? and she looks up to see him coming in smiling shyly.

'Thank you for these,' she says, picking the flowers up.

'Sorry, Fluff,' staying where he stands.

'Well, it can't be helped, that's all they do in the shop.'

'I know, but that's not what I mean, I shouldn't have been so hard on you earlier, I know you are only doing your best. Will you forgive me?' but he still stays put.

'Yes, but is that all?'

'All what?'

'Is that all you want to say?'

'What else is there?' he sounds irritated and she moves towards him but he takes a step backwards and she stops too.

152

'You're so unapproachable, Nigel, what is it? You don't go anywhere - you don't even shoot or stalk anymore - you don't get mysterious phone calls, otherwise I could think you have somebody else tucked away somewhere...'

'I what? Don't be ridiculous, Fiona, how can you think such a thing - no, don't answer that...'

'You see, that's it again, you won't go there will you? You don't listen and every time you do the withholding thing you make me feel like a tart,' and she slams the flowers down on the table.

'I don't know what you mean, how can you think you're a tart?'

'I've just told you and I'm not going to humiliate myself by spelling it out. There's an elephant in the room, why can't you see it?'

'Elephant - what *are* you talking about?' and shaking his head he begins to laugh. 'Unless you want me to shoot it,' he aims and fires an imaginary gun. 'Ah, saved by the gun indeed,' as Robbie knocks on the window before letting himself in as animated as his reserved manner will allow.

'You will be wanting to know this, muckle Nigel,' he touches his cap to Fiona who wants to leave the room. 'You better be hearing this too, right enough' he says to her. 'I was putting flowers on my mother's grave, so I was, and this man and woman were coming up to me, Americans they were. You are knowing the type, flashy people and a big limousine with a driver waiting for them, right enough. Anyway, looking for the MacMuckle Lairds' graves so they were and he was right full of questions. Friendly-like though for all that. And are you knowing who he was?' Nigel shrugs. 'Well, I will be telling you, he was saying his name is William B MacMuckle the third and he is the man who is to be the next clan chief.' Robbie hesitates and looks sheepishly at Fiona as he pulls a card out of his pocket. 'He is meaning he *will* be - after your own children - and I was telling him that, so I was.' He hands Nigel the card.

'Obviously I know of him, Robbie, he's a big cattleman I think, but I've never met him - and never wanted to for that matter,' Nigel says as he looks at it.

'Well, you are going to now, that is why I am being here. They are going to The Haggis Hunt in Driech for their dinner and then he says they are going to be coming here to introduce themselves, so they are. And I was thinking you would be wanting to know that, right enough.'

'Thanks Robbie, you're right to warn us, I wonder what's brought them out of the blue like this?'

'Ach, did I not say? He says he was seeing your advertisement in the Clan magazine, Fiona.'

'But I'm not open for business yet,' said with some alarm.

'Don't you be worrying about that, they are not wanting to be staying here, they are at that new hotel that used to be Cranachan House.'

'Mm, well I wouldn't be too sure about that,' Fiona says. 'Perhaps they hope I'll ask them to stay here instead, after all he is a distant relative isn't he, Nigel?'

'Yep, some sort of cousin, the sennachie will know the exact kinship. I don't know what to think about this,' he says and hands Fiona the card.

'Ach, it is nosiness, muckle Nigel,' Robbie says and pats him on the shoulder as he goes. Fiona looks at him pressed against the table lost in thought then at the card.

WILLIAM B MACMUCKLE III

GLENDUIR RANCH

DOUGLAS COUNTY

KANSAS

How pertinent this man's visit is in the light of all that has happened that day - and under those circumstances as welcome as Banquo's ghost, she thinks. A man about to arrive at his ancestral home who will inherit it and everything else Nigel is and has if she doesn't have her baby. How can Nigel not be thinking that too as he stands there saying nothing, staring out of the window at his beloved loch.

A chauffeur-driven limousine creeps up the drive so slowly that neither of them hears it coming. The first they know of the Americans' arrival is the clunk and whoosh of the heavy oak door opening, the ancient iron knocker has been ignored. Fiona pulls Nigel by the hand and they are greeted by the sight of a slight, balding and wiry man wearing a Burberry Mac, tightly belted, with a MacMuckle tartan tie poking out at the neck. Otherwise, he has no physical features to mark him as a MacMuckle. His wife is as polished and groomed in the best American tradition with her blonde hair carefully fixed in place, expensive diamonds on her fingers and expensive dentistry in her smile. Nigel introduces himself and Fiona with the minimum of ceremony but she adds some extra warm words and behind her back pinches Nigel's thigh.

'So how're y'doing Chief and how are you doing ma'am? I'm Will and this is Cynthia, we sure are pleased to be here at Glenduir Castle and to make your acquaintance, isn't that right, Cynthia?' who nods a bright smile. Will wrings Nigel's hand, slaps him on the back and Nigel replies.

'Well, I must say this is unexpected, if you'd given us more notice - let us know you were coming we...'

Fiona talks over him. 'Well, it's very good to meet you both too - isn't it Nigel? We've just been told you were coming, you met Robbie MacMuckle at the graveyard didn't you, he told us.'

'We came up to Glenduir on spec. We're playing golf at Saint Andrews...'

'Are you indeed,' Nigel says.

'Sure we are, Chief, but couldn't see the ball yesterday, the caddy called it the haar,' and Cynthia nods agreement again.

'Palm Beach is better,' she says and Nigel looks at the ceiling. 'Some place you've got here,' she says and the Kansas kinsfolks' eyes are everywhere.

Fiona offers to show them round after tea and leads them to the drawing room with Nigel behind, dawdling like a boy. But Will is eager to inspect the Great Hall in detail and he questions Nigel who answers as briefly as he can get away with. Then when they finally sit down, tea and cake distract Will so Nigel picks up *The Times* crosses his legs and appears to settle into the day's news. But his kinsman is undeterred.

'So Chief...' Will says to the visor of open newspaper but it doesn't move.

'Please don't call me that,' Nigel looks out from the side of the paper, then ducks back behind it. 'My name's Nigel.'

'OK, I'm out in the left field here, didn't want to get it wrong. So when do they call you Chief MacMuckle?' and the paper barricade remains in place.

'Never, I think you are confusing me with Chief Sitting Bull. I am not a Red Indian,' and he drops the paper on his lap like the challenge of a thrown down gauntlet. Cynthia shoots a glance at Will then like the grade teacher she used to be, she educates.

'Oh my, Nigel, you must never call them that, you must call them Native Americans now.'

'I see, well I'll try to remember that when next I meet one,' and with the snap of the paper up and opened again he turns to the TV listings page.

Lines of concern spread across Cynthia's brow, Fiona reads them as fear of having given offence and knows she has. But she also knows people love to talk about themselves and while they do Nigel might thaw. Pouring more tea she asks if they'd been to Scotland before. Will has, though it's Cynthia's first visit and she wants to come back. His first visit had been in nineteen fifty-three, 'the year of your Queen Elizabeth's coronation and mighty cold and wet it was. Daddy was not interested in the family history but Mom was, she thought the royalty and Lords were the cat's pyjamas. We did some sightseeing, Edinburgh Castle and Hollywood Palace. We motored on up here but we'd gotten lost off the highways, so we headed back because we had a flight back home from Prestwick the next day. We've been to London - we stay at The Savoy - but this is the first time I've been back to Scotland.' Cynthia adds how much she likes the politeness and reserve of the British and Nigel behind his paper makes a small grunt and again Fiona covers him.

'Yes, so this time - so this time what brings you to Scotland, golf was it?'

Will puts down his cup and settles in. 'Oh sure - but that Clan Society guy, what's he called - the senn*atchy*? So he didn't tell you folks?' and she gives him a blank look, Nigel does too, but nobody can see him behind *The Times*. 'Y'see it's like this, Daddy passed on in sixty-two and I got all the family papers. I was real interested in the Scottish connection so I joined the Clan MacMuckle Society.' He turns to address the Chief but he remains hidden behind his paper shield. 'You know Nigel, I was raised knowing Daddy was next in line to be Chief MacMuckle if you had no kids.' Will waits for Nigel's confirmation - none comes and the newspaper baffle mutes his sounds of exasperation, Fiona fiddles with a spoonful of sugar so Will carries on. 'The senn*atchy* wrote me Daddy was right about that.' Then with a grin, 'he said the castle was like Walt Disney's and it sure is. My second boy, Don, is a Disney executive, he's real interested. The magazine photographs of the old place does not do it justice and I have my camera with me to take some shots for him. He looks across at Fiona, 'and so - here we are, alrighty?'

The awkward silence is filled by Fiona's inconsequential, 'yes - well, there we are - jolly good.' She wills Nigel to come out of hiding and help her but he holds fast so she offers more cake and points out of the window at 'the loch down there and the mountain up there.' This seems to be of some significance to the two Americans and Will grins at Cynthia nodding like a Chinaman automaton.

'Disneyland,' he says, his non sequitur failing to alert Nigel who's never heard of the place so Will fills the silence. 'I'm talking about a Scottish theme park out there in the heather, a real life Brigadoon that's what you should be doing here.' *The Times* crackles slightly. 'That mountain there's potential there, I just thought of that, don't let me forget to tell Don,' he says to Cynthia, 'get a model monster for that loch. Disney's prop makers could do that.' Then lifts his hands up and looks around. 'He thinks this should be a haunted castle, he's on the money with that one. A souvenir shop for marketing the brand, that kinda thing? Dollars for doughnuts eh?'

Nigel cuts across the American dream. 'What *are* you talking about?'

'Hey - you'd call them money-spinners. Great ideas Don has for bringing folks in, you need a business plan for a place like this. And respect to you and Fiona there, but you sure need to throw some money at this beauty.'

'Your son said this? It's outrageous, no-one is going to turn my home into a cheap, kitsch theme park, as you call it. Let that be fully understood.' Nigel leans well forward in his chair, his legs apart, pages slipping off his lap to the floor.

158

'Hell, Nigel, don't get mad I'm just telling you what my boy said, he knows what he is talking about, sure he does.' But Nigel is up and away before he's finished.

It would be reasonable to think that anyone on the receiving end of Nigel's froideur would know to make a polite exit or at least go outside and pretend to look at the loch or the mountain. But William MacMuckle and his wife are made of something tougher and sit it out. With little choice but to fulfill her promise of showing them around the house, Fiona starts with the Great Hall again where they find Robbie looking for Nigel. He's brought from the butcher in Stravaig the weekly blooded package of liver and lights for the dog. He has a big bag of seed too, for the new bird table he's made for Fiona, and leaves a silent scattering of it in his wake as he opens all the doors in his search. While Fiona points out the armoury on the walls, Will watches tall, red- haired Robbie with his ease about the house. Then his and Nigel's voices and footsteps get closer and with a small nod at the Americans, Robbie is gone.

That Great Hall, the hub of MacMuckle history, depicted and arrayed on the walls, in their very fabric too, drain Nigel's fading echo - and Will faces him.

'Who was that guy who just left?'

Nigel looks at the door, 'You mean Robbie MacMuckle? You talked to him at the graveyard.'

'Sure I did, he said that was his name, the guy we saw at the cemetery, now I see you two together, I see it. Is he your brother? The senn*atchy* said you have no kids and no close relations - you didn't say. Am I here under false pretences?'

'I didn't ask you here, nobody forced you to come.' Nigel catches Fiona's eye and she lowers her head.

'So the senn*atchy's* gotten it wrong, you've got no kids but you've got a brother?'

Nigel's hands tighten behind his back, he moves towards his inquisitor towering over him and indignation escapes dressed as pedantry. 'It's *senn*achie not senn*atchy* – it's *senn*achie, right?'

'Yeah, yeah, got it - sennachie. Hell, Nigel, take it easy,' Will puts his hand up. 'Like I said, I'm new to this game.' Then he scratches his balding head and tries again. 'So let's get this straight, you've got no kids, OK? So who is that guy, Robbie?' Again there is no answer. The confused American stands, he looks at Nigel's turned back and he looks at Fiona still with her head lowered, her foot rolling stray bird seed around. Holding his palms upwards he asks, 'am I missing something, did the sennachie guy leave something out, he does not *know* about, Robbie?' He pauses yet there is no reply, nothing but his own faint echo, then he insists, 'will I be Chief or not?' He waits, watching the very much extant and even more exasperated Chief sit down on an ancient, oak chair with his hound beside him. A face-off, there can be no other description, and Nigel's knuckles are white as he grips the carved arms and his heel drums the stone floor.

And it is Fiona, small-voiced and from near the staircase, who replies. 'What the sennachie told you, Will, was right, we don't have any children. And Robbie is a MacMuckle but he isn't Nigel's brother, he is...'

'OK, OK, so straight up, I will be the next Chief.'

'Yes, you will be the next Chief,' Fiona whispers at his flourish of triumph.

The 24th Chief of the Clan MacMuckle glances at the heir presumptive casting a proprietorial eye all around him but Cynthia reaches out to touch Fiona.

'Oh my, Fiona, Honey, let me say my heart goes out to you, a real shame for you. Not to have children is the biggest sadness for a woman. What was wrong?'

'We've only been married a few years for God's sake,' Nigel cuts across her.'

'Sure, sure - but your Robbie guy said and Fiona just said...'

'And I say again, we've only been married a few years,' but Cynthia persists.

'You'll want a son, what man doesn't especially in your position?'

'Son, daughter, it doesn't matter either can inherit.'

'We raised two boys and two girls and they have been my life, now we have grandchildren too. I can't think what life would be like with no children, I don't know what I would have done if we hadn't had any. Isn't that right, Will,' and Fiona is patted like a pet dog.

But it is Luath who growls as Nigel rises from his chair as if anticipating his master's real intentions. Nigel might have belligerent thoughts but his action is a protective arm around his wife. From some store of ingrained politesse he finds the words to lie that he and Fiona are expected somewhere else very soon. Perhaps Will and Cynthia would, after all, like to take a walk round the loch, or climb the mountain. Though his words go some way to imitate goodwill his mental images of the proposed expedition for the heir certainly do not.

The Americans appear to understand Nigel's bogus urgency and Will's thanks are genuine enough with Cynthia nodding her agreement with everything he says. Then with great pleasure in her voice she warns that they will return and next time she plans to bring all the family to stay at the Castle - after Fiona opens for business of course. Fiona's fixed grin doesn't alter even though she hears Nigel's whispered oath.

'Here, take this, Chief, give it to Robbie,' and Will hands him a £10 note, 'he was mighty helpful at the cemetery. Maybe you and me did get off on the wrong foot, so for old time's sake and family connections I want to make a contribution to this fine place?' and he puts his hand in his pocket again to pull out a fat wad of notes. 'Mend the driveway on me, get some close carpeting laid, anything - you name it, go on take it,' and he proffers the money.

The Chief gives it the briefest of glances and puts his hands behind his back. But he also takes a deep breath and appears to grow in height then bends forward and coolly advises his relative, 'keep your money, I do not want it.'

'Hell, no offence meant, Nigel, I thought it would help, we're all family. Go on take it. Like I say - do what you like with it - OK?'

But Nigel stands firm, his hands still behind his back and Fiona grasps them. With barely concealed contempt Nigel MacMuckle, The MacMuckle and Laird of Glenduir looks down on William B MacMuckle the third.

'Enough, you insult me. Let me be quite clear. I - do - not - want - your - money. I advise you to leave now,' and spins round in his metal-tacked shoes making an ignition of small sparks on the stone floor. He strides off with Fiona trotting behind him unable to extricate her hand from his grip and leaving their guests to see themselves out. Only the chauffeur hears Cynthia call Nigel ungrateful and Will say he thinks him crazy.

Watching from behind a curtain Fiona holds herself in a tight embrace as she waits for the limousine to take the interlopers away. Only then does she look for Nigel. She finds him in the derelict summerhouse with his dog, he sits slumped on a broken wicker chair and his eyes are pink. Without words she puts a large whisky in his shaky hand then sits on a torn deck chair clutching her knees to her chest.

'God, those people are so brash, Fiona, eh? Hides like elephants, why do they keep banging on? Pick, picking away just like that carrion crow over there. Why don't they just belt up, it's none of their bloody business, it's personal, private. Did you see him, did you? Eye-ing everything up, offering me his money - me, Fiona, me,' and he stabs at his chest. 'Bloody cheek, is nothing sacred? A Brigadoon - for fuck's sake - Brigadoon? Looting my life, that's what he thinks he can do, is it?' Fiona's hushes, her calming hands ignored. 'He thinks this will be his does he? It's my home and I love it.' Nigel gets up and points. 'Walt Disney castle, what does he think this is, what does he think *I* am, Mickey Mouse - me? Look at it, look at it, Fiona, it's been there since 1489 and *we've* been here in a direct line of descent ever since... '

She reaches out to him. 'Yes, but the fact is...' He isn't listening.

'For centuries those walls took assaults and raids and generations of us have defended it - we've bred and died there *and* we survived.' Then he turns to look at her, 'now that pip-squeak, that Kansas cowboy turns up to press his claim - well he can take a running jump. I'll defend it too.'

'Yes, yes but, Nigel, don't you see, if we don't have any...'

'See? I see an opportunist, that's what I see - a bloody, impertinent opportunist and his cut-out, cardboard wife with her questions, presumptions. Tell me what I must call a Red Indian, would she?' He sits down again, and gulps his drink noisily like a child.

'Oh Nigel, now you're sounding just like Archie.'

'Well, he's not wrong all the time you know,' and he wipes his face with his hanky for no apparent reason. She can't remember when he's been roused to such an emotional pitch, it distresses her and she rubs his hand but neither looks at the other.

'I think they meant well, they don't set out to be crass that's just the way they are - try not to mind so much. I don't expect we will ever see them again after this, I am going to say we are booked up if they ever try to visit again.'

'Well don't ever forget you said that.' He finishes his whisky and Fiona pulls him out of his creaking chair to take him and his dog off for a walk down to the loch. She takes his hand; he holds hers tight.

They take their usual route, the mossed path through the woods, remnants of the ancient Caledonian Forest, and they don't speak. This is a place close to Nigel's heart, this is a place which will settle him down, but once through it with the loch in sight, the atmosphere and colours change. She sees it, though it never affects him. Today little movement stirs the surface of Loch Duir, the water the colour of brown bottle-glass. Littering the shore bleached sticks lie like bones on a charnel house floor. In other places grey banded pebbles and stones sparkle dimly as if pricked with small, rusty nail-heads pimpling their surface. But a hefty hit, one stone against another, springs trapped garnets and Fiona has match boxes full of them. And all you can hear is your every breath, the clatter of stones and crack of breaking sticks beneath your tread.

And as they walk together Nigel slips Fiona's hand and puts his arm around her. She doesn't look at him, she knows he's hurt but she can feel it too and it creates a curious tension between them. His grip on her almost hurts. They reach the loch shore and she stops to pick up a piece of garnet embedded stone.

'Why do you like it here so much?' she says.

'Because Robbie used to bring me down here when I was a very, wee boy - you know that - he was always real hero of mine, I wanted to be like him when I grew up.' He pauses and looks around at the dismal surroundings. 'I remember the sun shone,' and lets go of Fiona.

'Happy memories are always sun-lit, I think,' she says but he isn't listening.

'It was Robbie who first showed me how to do this,' and he picks up some flat pebbles, skimming them across the still water in an

164

impressive number of skips. 'I used to call them bouncing bombs. I should have patented the name as it turned out.' Then she tries but it fails in a single, wide-rippled descent into the loch.

'Did you miss having a father when you were young?' and she gathers more skimming stones.

'Not so much when I was wee, but I did when I was in my teens and later. I probably needed an older man's influence though there'd been some of that at school. George and Robbie started being deferential you see.' He takes the stones from her and skims them too.

'Sad... sad George died quite so young, makes you think you should always seize the moment, you never know what's going to happen tomorrow, do you?' she says with a shiver. 'Thank God we can't see into the future....'

'I don't know about that, I think it might help.' Together but apart they watch Nigel's many ripples spread and link across the water. Then, without looking at her, he says he loves her stressing the words as if he's never said them before.

'I know,' said as if it is no surprise to her, 'I love you too,' and still they face the loch.

Then he takes her hand again. 'You shouldn't have had to listen to all that personal, invasive stuff that dreadful American woman spouted. Blaming you...'

'I'm not sure that she did, it was sort of ambiguous wasn't it, let's forget it all shall we?'

But Nigel scuffs up the shingle with his foot. 'No, Fluff - sit down here with me.' He gently pulls her on to a beached tree trunk then tries to look at her, it makes her uneasy. 'I'm right aren't I, this bed and breakfast thing is something you *want* to do?'

'Yes, why are you asking me I thought we'd sorted that out? I know you don't really like the idea but I'll try not to involve you with all the guests. And we really do need the money, Nigel.'

'Shh - no - no, I just wanted to be sure,' he purses his lips with a sigh, and looking down at her hands, 'promise me you won't get angry, though God knows you have every right to, there's something important I have to tell you, it's been a terrific burden. I should have told you before.' He turns his face away. There's effort in his every word; the confiding intimacy alarms her too.

'What is, what burden, Nigel?'

'The children thing - what that woman said - you know - no children and all that, well there's something important I should tell you - should have...'

'Yes, you said that, what are you trying to say, Nigel?' and she pulls her hands away from his. 'That you have a secret love child somewhere?' There's an end note of hysteria, it seems a reasonable guess.

'No, for God's sake Fiona. No - how can you think that?'

'Easily, can't you see that? You don't seem to be interested in me much these days,' she shrugs and he grips both her hands in his again as if to pinion her.

'Anyway that's the point - it's not possible, you see it's me, it's my fault. It's my fault that we don't have children. Please will you forgive me?' and he bows his head.

She wrenches her hands back and in a rising pitch, 'what - what did you say - it's your fault? You never told me. Why didn't you tell me - you let me think - when did you know, did you marry me knowing that? Her eyes begin to smart and he tries to touch her face but she brushes him off.

'This is so hard for me, please be patient,' he asks and fixes his gaze on the ground.

'Don't look away, look at me Nigel,' and she lifts his face up. 'Hard for *you* - you ask *me* to be patient, how long have you known? Talk to me, Nigel.'

166

'I swear I didn't know before we were married, I would never have done that to you. I found out after you had the all-clear from your medical man in Edinburgh. I did, in fact, see a specialist in Glasgow a little while after. I'm sorry, I should have told you, I know I..'

'That's over eighteen months ago, for God's sake,' and she hits him. Hard on the shoulder first then lashes out everywhere with her palms and fists. Without any resistance he lets her. 'You bastard, why didn't you tell me, you've known that long how - could - you - do - that - to - me?' each word marked with a blow. 'How could you - what did that Cynthia woman say that made you have to tell me now, what's stirred your conscience now?' She starts lashing out again and he catches her arms, holding them steady.

'Hush - listen, Fiona listen to me, please. You can beat me again when I've explained. Believe me I've tried to tell you before now, sorry. I couldn't do it and the longer I left it the more difficult it became. But she was invading everything that is precious and dear to me. I didn't like that she assumed it was your fault, I know my mother did too but she only ever - oh never mind about her. That American woman couldn't have been more pointed, she had no bloody right to mention such things, they're private and ours, not theirs to discuss and ....'

'So private even we couldn't discuss it,' she pulls her arms free from him, 'and don't ever think your mother didn't hurt me, she did and you knew that, yet you said nothing. How could you let me go through that?' She stops to consider it. 'That's not the man I thought I knew, that was cowardly, MacMuckle. Coward, cheat,' she cuffs him once more across his shoulder then buries her face in her hands which sting. She can't look at him, 'why didn't you tell me, why didn't you tell me?' over and over again like a paternoster.

'Because I thought you wouldn't want me anymore,' he snaps back, 'I didn't want to lose you, I was afraid you would leave me, that's why. I never meant to hurt you. Please forgive me, please?' He looks away from her again and closes his eyes against his own tears saying, 'no, why should you.'

'You are asking too much,' she whispers, her throat hurts. He nods agreement but she adds, 'Go on then, tell me. Why is it your fault, so what happened, why - how did you find out?'

He sighs, he flexes his fingers, he swallows, he fidgets and she feels like hitting him hard on the back as if to dislodge something stuck in his throat. Hesitantly he manages to form an answer from willfully neglected words. 'I have an almost non-existent sperm count. The Doc said the chances of fathering a child were very remote - but not impossible, though I thought he was clutching at straws, humouring me, softening the blow.'

And she makes a choking noise in the back of her throat so he holds her shoulders. Pressing her fingers hard against the sides of her head she repeats the word, remote, as if she needs to fix the reality for herself. And looking up at him again she insists, 'don't stop there, go on finish it - why, what's wrong?'

'Who knows, it could even have been mumps, well that's the best he could come up with.' Before she could remind him he'd told her he hadn't had mumps he hurries on. 'I wasn't keeping that from you, I didn't know but the Doc thought perhaps I'd had mumps orchitis - more straw clutching I thought. But I did have sore throats, swollen glands and so on when I was a boy, maybe on one occasion it was mumps. I can't remember. You knew Ma, she paid no attention to illness and hardly ever called a doctor, school wasn't much better, one just rotted in the San...'

'That's neglect, and a mother should take better care of her child too,' she curls over and holds herself as if to contain her conflicting emotions.

'I know, oh Fluff, you wouldn't be like that, but no good will come of finding someone to blame, it's probably better to think I was just born this way.' And she starts weeping into the folds of her skirt and he touches her lightly but he can feel his own tears and has a mundane thought; which one of them needs his hanky first. As he fumbles for it with one hand and pats her back with the other she sits up into a skewed position and wipes her face with her hand. With barely any voice, 'I'm sorry, so sorry,' he says.

'For what, that you didn't tell me? That's as near to unforgivable as I have ever known - and the other. Well, you couldn't help it.' And with anger at him rising again she thinks of his deliberate silence, of how much that hurt and hears herself say, 'I think you might have broken my heart.' But nothing is clear to her, the quick, alternating pattern of her emotions repeat and intertwine like an aerial dog-fight in her head leaving her disorientated. When she faces him again he looks desolate and even his dog whimpers, pawing at his knee. But pity can chase rage away, calmly she says, 'I wouldn't have left you, how could you have thought that?'

'And why wouldn't I think it?' defiance in his voice. 'I never thought somebody like you would ever want somebody like me. You could have had your pick yet you seemed to find me to your liking; me - a great, useless Highlander. What did I have to offer apart from a rundown house in the middle of nowhere and limited funds? I thought I was the luckiest man in Scotland. I am such a shambling failure, Fiona, I know I am. Take that trout farm, there's an example for you - the trout disappeared. Then the quarry and the transport disaster when the council road was never built. You see? Everything I touch fails and the biggest one is my total failure to give you a child.' He hesitates and his voice softens. 'My Darling, Darling Fluff, you say you wouldn't leave me but I see how other men look at you, and you are young. You could have the life, the children you expected from me, I see that... I really do see that.'

And she can see it too, that alternative flashes in front of her and she looks at him with his head in his hand. Was he replaying the image once more, this time with more certainty that he is going to lose her? She lays her head across his shoulder.

He asks, 'what can I do to make things right, is there anything – anything at all?' She makes slow, indistinct movements of her head, which he interprets negatively. 'I'm sorry, it must have been hellish for you and I know - I knew - I should have stopped my mother but I didn't want to open the whole wretched subject up. You're right, I was a coward, I flunked all of it.'

'Maybe I was a coward too, I could have said something to her myself, but it was difficult, I felt we should discuss it first, and you...'

'Wouldn't discuss it,' he says. 'I know - I should have done lots of things differently but as time went on it just became more difficult. I meant to tell you when I came home from Glasgow that night - d'you remember? I'd thought it better not to mention anything until I had a diagnosis one way or the other, you see.'

'When - what night?'

'When Charlie stayed with us, when he came back from South Africa, remember?'

'That first time I met him?' she murmurs and then remembers it well.

'Mm - I couldn't say anything while he was there, as I said, then I was afraid - please try to see that.'

'But after he left, you could have told me then, what stopped you?'

'He stopped me,' and she's puzzled. 'Don't tell me you didn't notice the concentrated attention he was giving you, he always competed when it came to girls and he always won - most of the time...'

'But that's not what people say, they say you had lots of girlfriends...'

'Look, perhaps they weren't the ones *I* wanted?' and there's truculence in his voice she's never heard before. Anyway, Charlie's always had a way of showing me up - I never minded because I knew there was no contest, Charlie Scott who's got the lot, that's what they used to say about him. He could even charm my mother, inappropriate though that was. Anyway he sparkled as soon as he set eyes on you, he seemed to forget you were actually my wife. Well that's what I thought and I am damned sure if you'd met us both at the same time you would have fallen for him. Put simply, I saw him as a threat.' And she looks down, her throat is tight with emotion. 'Then there was me, I didn't really want to believe the Doc, I wanted to believe it would come right in its own time; after all he hadn't ruled it out completely, - remote, but not impossible. And then as time passed I convinced myself the moment was lost and I should keep quiet, that way there was less risk of your leaving me.' He looks at her and his shoulders drop, holding her hands tighter he speaks quietly, almost apologetically. 'You see, you'd been so restless and yet withdrawn too. Am I making sense to you? But I did think about how you must have felt, I felt ashamed - it shames me now - so I stopped thinking about what it must have looked like - it helped, but when it caught up with me, and believe me it did - I found it almost impossible to look at you without hating myself.' And still he can't look at her; he stands up and turns his back. She tries to speak but he carries on. 'You can't know how much it affected me every month when I could tell by your face and your manner - you didn't need to say anything - that you were disappointed, and I knew it was because of me - grief, it felt like grief.' He falters. 'So you see - I found it difficult, dishonest too.' He turns round to her when he says, 'it's not that I didn't want to - you have to believe that - but it was easier to pretend, to let you think, time, familiarity, that kind of thing. I was between a rock and a hard place, I'll shut up; I can't express myself.'

And there's accusation in her face when she looks up at him and finds her voice. 'But couldn't you have tried to understand why I was restless, wasn't it obvious? And I needed to talk to you about what we were going to do. *I* felt such a failure, Nigel, and there was a barrier of silence between us, which you wouldn't open up. That was what it was about, not about me leaving. I loved you, I wouldn't have...' and she runs out of words.

'I'm the failure - not you,' he says flatly. Then there's silence while she stares ahead focusing on nothing and with a stick he makes small channels in the shingle at his feet.

She can hear his heart and feel his every taken breath when she puts her head against him again. How many years of his pointless bonfires has it taken to infuse the scent of wood smoke in his old tweed jacket? She's never noticed before how all-pervading his smoky aura is but it soothes her a little and he slowly and lightly kisses the back of her neck. His hand lying loosely in his lap and she runs her fingers back and forth across his palm. His strong yet elegant hands, she'd noticed them the first time they'd met. And on the back of her neck she feels his breath slowing down into a steady, gentle pace.

'Why was your mother so - so unsympathetic?' she suddenly asks.

'She thought it bad form to be weak and that included illness. Mind over matter, that's what she used to say and I suppose I have to admit I couldn't help thinking the same, perhaps that played a part in my not telling you.' He smiles slightly and pats Luath.

'Yes, but she fussed over her dog, you do too, don't you?'

'I know, I've often noticed that, particularly in women. Maybe that's allowed - another one of those unspoken rules.' He pauses then throws the stick for the animal.

'Dry your tears and tell me what happens now, what can I do to mend a broken heart?' But she doesn't answer she stares ahead. 'I'll do anything you ask, I know this will take time to get over.'

She'll never get over it, she knows it, she feels bereaved with that visceral emptiness which can't be seen, but will soon reach outward altering bearing and expression which can't be hidden. She tries to stand up but her legs give beneath her but he catches her and she leans on him for a moment.

'Can we leave it for now? I don't think I can talk about it anymore - I need to think.' He doesn't respond to that, just keeps hold of her arm as they walk back slowly towards the track but she senses he wants to say something else.

'This can't wait - you won't leave me now, will you? Say you won't - I don't know what I would do without you,' and he puts his arms around her with something like a needy child's desperation,

'No, of course I won't, I don't want to be anywhere else.' Words which don't quite express what he might want to hear, but then ravens take flight from their tree tops - cawing, grating, raucous like a protest. But together, he with his arm around her, they slip away like fugitives to the castle.

Neither of them eats much lunch, hardly talk or even look at one another too afraid of upsetting their fragile balance. She's wrung out of words and her heart and head hurt. When they finish she leaves the dishes on the table and stands up telling him she's going take a couple of paracetamol and lie down. Does she want him to come too? No she doesn't, she needs to be on her own so he fills a glass with water for her. She gives him a thin smile of thanks wondering if he realises she's rebuffed him for the first time ever. And he watches her leave the room, his dearly loved and wounded Fiona, she moves so slowly. Gently, he says, 'you should try to sleep,' and when she's gone, he weeps.

The Cunning Fox

Nigel MacMuckle dwells on his diagnosis and finds it almost impossible to believe he handled everything so badly, it sears his conscience, it won't leave him alone and it shames him. He sits at the table, fixed and staring at his empty plate, the empty banana skin, his empty glass and he feels cold. Cold and empty. That Friday morning, more than a year and a half ago now, the day he went to Glasgow, was it cold then? He thinks if it wasn't then it should have been.

Did you eat anything for breakfast that day or was it just another banana on the way to the station? You imagined the scene playing out at home, it diverted your thoughts didn't it? Charlie full of bonhomie, Fiona enjoying his MGB and being driven fast - she'd have liked that. And lunch, nothing would have been spared in giving her the best to be had in Inverness. You had Glasgow ahead of you and the engine hit the buffers hard.

Well who would? Who'd want to sit in that doctor's waiting room thinking and thinking until the exact time of the appointment. You walked there, killed time, avoided the ticking clock, dog-eared Readers' Digests, other men making their noises.

It must have been cold because that consulting room was, maybe it had been north facing, or was it because it was painted blue? The leatherette seat squelched and farted, so you sat still, leant forward, that stopped it and that Doctor took so few words to say so much and so many for some sort of explanation. 'I'm sorry Mr MacMuckle, sorry it isn't better news' and you said, 'so you're trying to say as much chance as a snowball in hell - that's it then - nothing else to be done' and he made a polite protest at that, but it was hair splitting, straw clutching and his, 'I don't think that's quite what I said, Mr MacMuckle.' Well, Mr Consultant it may as well have been... And he called you stoic.

Well, yeah, of course you'd be stoic what else could you be? *The* MacMuckle. But you had to go home and tell Fiona - and how was that to be done? How did you start? 'Not impossible' or a 'remote possibility' and each loaded with opposing interpretations of hope. There was no conclusion. As unproductive as you are yourself. And it had nothing to do with virility? Well, that might be so, you understood that, but it's not how it felt.

Back to the station by taxi, fast, and thank God not driven by a garrulous Glaswegian, just one who was as dour as the world thinks us. And don't let there be anyone you know on the train. How could you make yourself invisible cowering in a corner seat? You're bloody unmissable and what does MacMuckle know about cowering anyway? Kept a clear head though, only had one drink against a loose tongue and getting it wrong and then you did anyway.

Closing his eyes Nigel presses his palms against them but he sees too much. He swills his face under the cold tap and lets the water drip down his neck; neither does he dry his hands but wanders through rooms absently anointing furniture and objects. His throat feels tight and his mouth dry, his shoulders ache and he pours himself a large whisky and downs it in one. Idly placing a damp hand on the flat top of the grand piano it leaves a fleeting print and he watches it disappear. Then he flicks through Fiona's sheet music on the closed top. Although the musical notation means nothing to him he recognises the title of one piece, *Misty*. He picks it up and across the top in his cousin Charlie Scott's handwriting he reads.

For dear Fiona. Try this; see how you get along with it. Thanks again for a great weekend. With my love, Charlie.

He's seen it before, it meant nothing, Charlie had backed off quickly, nothing had to be acknowledged though experience had left some suspicion. But he scans the lyrics now. *Look at me, I'm as helpless as a kitten up a tree,* and sniffs at the sentimental image but like disliked scent its unwanted potency lingers ...*the moment you're near, can't you see that you're leading me on? And it's just what I want you to do ...*

Although it isn't Nigel's habit to read into things or over-examine the motives of others, this day with a fevered imagination he wonders if Charlie had meant those words. And, even if he didn't, wasn't it true that the unconscious is often lethally accurate. But speculation increases his insecurity so he puts the music back at the very bottom of the pile; he won't think about it. He lies on the sofa, puts his feet up and ahead of him he sees a familiar sight. The dog fox he'd shot and had stuffed to look as if it were curled up and sleeping. It lies so convincingly on a chair, his joking dupe put there to startle people and amuse him. But that afternoon it haunts him, its demise too connected with his memories... He closes his eyes, tries to relax and clear his head but it fills with impressions and words and feelings and Charlie Scott will not let him go.

Because he said he was going to seduce Fiona into jazz piano and send her the music for *Misty* too. Yes, he said that at breakfast the next day, on the Saturday. And you said maybe Fiona didn't want to play jazz piano, it came out pretty damn quick - but she spoke for herself. She said she wanted to try out some new things, expand her repertoire.

Then gunshot broke - close outside.

A fingernail on a blackboard that's what the chair sounded like, and the window wouldn't budge, of course it wouldn't budge - you should have known that - of course you knew it, but Robbie was outside with his gun and pointing at the thicket. You'd kill the pest, it had gone on long enough. Get the gun, do it, you moved pretty damn quick again - knocked Charlie and his chair over. Bad luck Charlie, couldn't he get up off the floor by himself? But Fiona fussed and handled him - and you saw it.

And there he was outside, standing there in the sun, that big dog fox, well fed, sleek, rusty-coated and as bold as brass with it. A limp but live, blue bantam hen in the trap of his mouth. A face down was it? But then he sat, dropped the bird and flicked his tongue.

Aim - in the centre of the cross wires - fire.

Yeah, you could have done it before now, yeah it would have saved a lot of trouble, but how do you admit you've gone off killing things? It was easier to let Robbie get it but he couldn't and he gave that fox credit too saying, 'the bugger was right cunning, but today it was like he was expecting it'.

And wasn't she a pretty chicken? Soft in your hands but scared and scarred. You told him to find her home roost, she'd be alright. And don't get rid of the carcass, you'd have it stuffed - and without that sneering, teeth-exposing expression on its mask.

Sunk in an undignified squat like that - it was obvious Charlie's back was locked, Fiona didn't need to say so. Of course she couldn't get him upright on her own. You got him on his feet. He staggered then, arms, legs stretched out and face pressed against the wall like that, looking like a saltire cross, and she said he looked pale, that she had something she could rub on his back. No, no she couldn't because you said you'd used up all the wintergreen yourself... Well, as good as. But she's always kind like that. Charlie tried to make light of it, he thought he should go home, but he groaned it. And you joked - or did you? It was sensible, yes go back to Edinburgh, and if he didn't speed round the glens' corners

177

his back should hold and if it seized up again by the time he got home he could crawl out on to the pavement... Your motor isn't much higher than gutter level, that's what you said, and she didn't find that funny. She'd thought of something else and made it sound as if she'd discovered the secret of life. She'd give him a hot water bottle to put at his back for the journey. Yeah, it was a kind thought but he refused it.

Darling Fiona humiliated, her pretty head down, fidgeting with the one bracelet on her wrist, the gold one you gave her on your wedding day. She looked up and her eyes glittered with near tears.

And that is all Nigel wants to remember, the rest is clear but it shames him too much. His eyes are open and he's making noises over which he seems to have little control. Abruptly he swings his legs off the sofa and sinks his face into his meshed fingers. So much harboured and neglected anger is breathed into the cup of his hands in curses and crude blurts of self accusation. He put it out of his mind as best he could after Charlie left. And Charlie never mentioned that visit either, not even in passing. Things carried on very much as they'd always done for them both, but Nigel knows the event represented the major obstacle to honesty and his good intention. And then that fancy French clock hits its impatient, silly strikes telling him the present needs his attention now.

With a cup of tea for Fiona, Nigel heads for the stairs but stops in his tracks at the sight of that curled-up, stuffed fox, eyes shut and mask sealed of its expiring scorn. And grabbing it, he throws it like a skimming stone across the full length of the Great Hall. It smacks so hard against the big gong, it percusses so loudly that it breaks off one of the tusk supports in a lop-sided, jangling valedictory. 'God, that was bloody good,' he says out loud at the noise and damage he's made, but it must have woken Fiona up too. Yet curiously, he finds her asleep. Quietly he closes the bedroom door and drinks the tea himself.

Her eyes open again after he's gone. Why the gong crashed so violently is a question which can wait. Bed makes a safe place from which to let her own thoughts and feelings selfishly wander and it is too soon to make another effort to deal with his. The night Nigel came back from Glasgow plays on her mind too, stirring guilt that she didn't pay him more attention. As she very well knows, Charlie Scott's attention had blunted hers. And she lies there thinking if she didn't see it she should have done... His face was so grey when he came home, he didn't smile, he looked care-worn. Or is that hindsight's lenses?

But he should have told you what the doctor had said - he shouldn't have gone to bed without you. He could have told you when you'd gone up, when he... Instead of hiding it and himself, instead of making love, pointless love, because he damn well knew it was as good as pointless by then. Of course you would have been upset and yes, probably it would have been difficult with Charlie there in the morning. But you would have pretended everything was alright... He could have told you after Charlie left, yes then - after he'd gone and before Jean came back. Why *not*?

And the next time, Nigel creeps upstairs it's with scrambled eggs on toast and a bottle of whisky and she can hear him behind the door. Tentatively, he asks if he can come in and he can because she's finished remembering, there's been enough. Glancing at her watch, she tries to get up but he doesn't let her, he pushes her legs back into the bed and puts the tray down for her.

'I don't think I can eat that, you have it,' she says.

'No, come on, it will do you good, you'll feel better, eat it up, for me?' And his gentle coaxing can't be refused but she feels strangely embarrassed by his careful attention as he sits closer and nervously places his hand on her leg, 'I hope you feel better now - do you?'

'A little, but you look done in, have you had a rest this afternoon?'

'I tried, I had a lie down on a sofa,' and he watches the eggs go from plate to her mouth so she feeds him the next forkful then shares what was left between them.

'You can have a very early night yourself, can't you?' she says.

'Can I sleep here?'

'Do you need to ask?'

'Yes, of course I do, you might refuse.'

'Have you ever known me to do that?'

'No, but things are different now - aren't they?'

She puts her hand up to his face tracing the shadows under his eyes with her finger and touches the red marks she made with her angry blows. Then she pats the bedcovers but that's a vain gesture because he moves away to the corner when she asks, 'Tell me why you kept away so much, sleeping in that old bed of yours?' And he hesitates for a moment.

'Can't you guess - I'm having a drink, do you want one?'

'Nigel, please answer me, I think I know but I want you to tell me. I don't want anything hidden from me; I'm done with all that.'

'Are you angry with me again?' and he hands her a dram she doesn't want.

'No, I just couldn't face it earlier.'

He drinks then swirls the rest round and round watching it lap the sides of the glass. Clearing his throat he stares into his drink. 'This is hellish. I'm sorry, what can I do - tell me?'

She looks at him standing at the end of the bed with his head bowed. 'The missed opportunities, Nigel, all those missed opportunities. After all, your doctor did say there was a remote chance...You cheated me.'

'He jerks his head as if she's struck him and narrows his eyes. 'That's *not* what I meant to do, please, Fiona, please - I felt I had no choice, if you'd known - suspected, you might have gone, left me, in the end I couldn't risk it. I've already said that. It was supposed to make things bearable.'

'*Bearable* - that's a choice word, isn't it? And I can't bear it now, I really can't, you'd have been a wonderful father.' Suddenly she hits the bedcovers with the flat of her hand. 'I hate that bloody bed of yours, Nigel MacMuckle, it's like a big, red, forbidding island and it shut me out.'

'No, I never meant that, I just thought - I thought it would make it easier,' he says quietly.

'For you perhaps, but not for me...'

'Maybe you should have let me get that poodle pup for you...'

'Oh for... I didn't want a poodle, I wanted a baby, but for pity's sake, Nigel, I wanted you too,' her anger rising again and he looks down at the floor as if awaiting sentence.

'I'll get rid of the bed if it upsets you so much. I'll sell it,' he says.

'No don't, it would be like blood money - give it to a museum.' She raises a finger in the air and with a flash of scornful judgement. 'The label would read, The State Bed of Glenduir Castle. The Young Pretender slept here once - before he went into exile. A later *pretender* - old enough to know better, exiled himself here far, far too often,' then there's silence until she flares, 'what did you do to me, Nigel, remember? You turned me on then tuned me in with your pretty spectacular desire, heady stuff, and it always made me feel complete and loved and so wanted. Then you...'

'Stop it. Help me, Fluff, please - what am I to do, what is it you really want me to do,' and now he's angry, 'd'you want me to get in there with you now, d'you want me to make love to you, is that what you want?' and he moves a little closer to the bed.

'Yes - no - stay there - oh for God's sake I don't know, Nigel. I'm angry too. I might even bite you.' She crashes back on the pillows, the tray, glasses and plate slide off the bed and land upside down on the floor. 'No don't. *That,* I know you can do. Leave it alone Nigel, leave it.' Silently, he stands up again and with a tired or is it exasperated sigh he tosses his head back. Is it defiance, is it recoil? 'Oh Hell, Nigel, what am I saying, I shouldn't have said that, I shouldn't have said any of that, forgive me.'

'Yes you should, say what you like it's all fair game. There is nothing for me to forgive.' And she reaches out to him but he turns away. 'Bloody Americans,' he mutters.

Then suddenly her arms are around him, 'I'm glad they said what they did; they've done us a favour, haven't they?' she says.

'I know, I know. Come on, you go back to bed,' and he turns enough to kiss her, she can feel his damp cheek against hers but he moves away when she looks up at him. Then he does something she's never seen before or thought he'd know; puff the pillows and straighten the bed clothes just like her mother had done. Cold and shaky in her underwear and dressing gown she ties its belt tight and widens her eyes against tears as he tucks her in. 'Nigel, can we close this chapter? From now on can we always talk about everything, nothing hidden, no secrets and the truth, never take anything for granted ever again. I want to do that and I promise I will.'

He doesn't answer; he's turned away again and looks out of the window into the prolonged evening of a Highland summer. But in the dim mirror made by that window glass he can see her reflection behind him lying back on the pillows again with her eyes shut and she looks peaceful.

'Please say you understand?' she asks.

182

'Yes I do - and I promise too. So is that it; is there anything else I can do, anything else you want? I think you've let me off lightly.'

'I think you've served enough time in solitary and you've been away too long... What are you doing?'

'Taking my clothes off? It seems a pity to let all this emotion go to waste.' Smiling, she reaches for the knot in her dressing gown belt. 'No wait, Fluff, let me do that.'

And when he has she lies facing him while he wraps his arms around her cold body and tucking her face against his throat, she whispers, 'I can feel the pulse in your neck - your knees are like two warm cricket balls, you always feel warm.'

'And soon you will too, now hush and let me kiss you - and no biting please.'

She pulls him on to her, his weight so suddenly wanted. Clutching at his thighs, his head, his waist, she matches his urgency. Sweet sensations of his breath on her face, his mouth on hers, finding it, losing it and finding it again with the restless energy of impatient new lovers. It isn't enough when his body loosens, hers tightens again and she arches backwards in a push. One stretched gasp with all tension spent and nothing said, only the stresses of exhausted breath.

Then, on a heavy sigh, she says, 'sorry, I'm like a burst dam.'

'Why - what's there to be sorry about? What more could I want,' his hands soothing in calming rhythms.

She wonders what he's thinking. Feelings of regret and gratitude, what else? She feels them too. 'I love you,' she says.

'I don't deserve it... I've always loved you, you know that don't you?' His halting anxiety makes her look into his eyes where a small tear slides over a bruise she made on his fine face. Gently, she brushes it away.

'I'm sorry' he says.

Relations

Fiona looks forward to visiting her sister Amy in Edinburgh every year, she can please herself, do what she wants and shop for the few things she allows herself. But this year she has mixed feelings about leaving Nigel behind because she knows a different setting would be good for them. But he isn't persuaded and keeps to his usual habit saying he wants her to have some time on her own with her sister. She tries once more to persuade him as she leaves but he says he has lots to do, which of course he has.

She has a clear run out of the glens then on to the A9 and the journey south through Invernesshire. Always a short break and snack at the Kenspeckle Tearoom then off again in time to listen to a play on the car radio, a drama beguiling enough for her to stay with it. But with uncanny timing it finishes just as she reaches Fife. There to steal her attention as the rich fields and her richer memories roll out to the horizons where at the southern fringes of the county the road signs point eastwards to her childhood. But she's heading to the very edge of the county and to the ferry which will take her across the Forth. She can't help seeing the motionless ships in Rosyth Naval Dockyard receding into the distance as the ferry reaches the south shore. She can't help thinking of Tim Robinson, but this time his memory doesn't demand as it did before, after all, had he not given up easily? Only a single love letter, for that undeniably is what it was, then nothing.

The mild, mesmeric hiss of rain-glazed tarmac stops sharply as Fiona turns left and east, leaving the remainder of the day behind her. She's crossed a threshold on to the rumbling cobbles of Edinburgh's New Town. She opens the car window to breathe the muskiness of brewing hops, their odour held on the evening's damp air. And though she can't hear the starlings above the car's engine, she sees them wheeling like animated silhouettes and knows well their chattering racket as they return to their fine Georgian roosts of the Rows and Streets. At every visit her cherished collection of sensory vignettes makes Edinburgh her own again.

Her private moment over, she pulls on the hand brake and with their welcomes and embraces done, Fiona passes on Nigel's usual message; his love and apologies for not being able to come as he had other things he had to do. Both Burnets are used to that reason.

The days pass quickly and Fiona with Amy visit Mary and Susie who hardly ever make the long journey to Glenduir. If they do it is always in the warm summer months, but always delighted to see Fiona they fall back into their old accustomed ways.

How lucky they are, she thinks, in their fine Georgian houses. Their lives have almost mirrored her own, except they both have children. They also have husbands in gainful employment and have never needed to earn money themselves. She wonders what it would be like to choose the furnishings and pictures you liked rather than live with other people's taste gathered over the centuries. Two of her older friends of Amy's age had gone out with Nigel before she knew him and though they were married themselves by the time she met him, they both thought she was lucky and said so. Of course for all the right reasons she'd thought so too. But as she sits in their smart, bright and warm rooms she wonders if they'd still think the same way about his castle now. But their esteem had never been for his castle.

A dinner party, informal, warm and reassuring takes her into a parallel existence where everyone drinks too much and she allows herself a little mild flirting. These are friends she has known for so long that there is no risk of judgement there.

She meets Charlie Scott for lunch, he never did go into fish farming, he stuck to property development and rental. He makes more money without even trying, plays his new piano and the field, the first well and the second better - and he shows no intention of changing that. They have lunch at a new expensive restaurant only a few doors away from the flat he shared with Nigel and touches on the same subject when he and Fiona are together. That of Nigel and his reluctance to invest in any of his winning ventures. And she always says the same thing too in her agreement with him. But she doesn't expect him to reach across the table for her hand and squeeze it in consolation and he can't have expected her to say that things are not so bad any longer.

She's booked to have a new hairstyle created by a popular hairdresser and as she walks along George Street she sees herself in shop windows, every confrontation confirming the need to do something about herself. But at the salon's glass door her reflection was backed by the mere glimpse of a man who when she turns to look directly at him is gone.

The stylist runs his fingers through her blonde hair and utters the words, colour and shape. It's an order and she's happy to obey. She watches her transformation with interest, the mirror and lights are unforgiving and having to sit and look at herself for nearly two hours makes it difficult not to notice the small lines and shadows on her face. But the finished result pleases her; the stylist has taken her cut back to how she used to wear it. Looking at her watch she then heads off to Jenner's in Princes' Street and a make-up counter. A flawless faced young woman has time to make Fiona up with what she thinks will suit her from their fashionable colours. Fiona, from the school of less is more, insists she must not look overdone and the result is perfect.

186

Her shopping list has an underlined memo in Nigel's handwriting; <u>collect brogues. NB tacks</u>. As if she could forget? Black brogues, tan brogues, leather soles, just the same as he had always worn, re-soled and always made by Church Shoes. She buys a red cashmere polo neck jumper for him, but she wants clothes for herself. Something else to wear instead of the 'slacks' she'd taken to in 1960, necessary in the cold place that was Glenduir. How Jean had disapproved of ladies wearing trousers, not that she'd said anything, her face did it for her. But Fiona had ignored that and Jean's manners allowed her to keep the trousers on if only in the literal sense. So on that last day Fiona buys dresses and a coat along with shoes, skirts, and in the end more trousers.

Laden with her smart carrier bags, she arrives on time at the Clipe Coffee House for lunch with Amy. The little place is their usual haunt and still as popular as it had ever been.

'Heavens, what have they done to your hair? I didn't think you were going to do anything so... It's like you used to wear it,' Amy says as she ducks and bends round to examine the hairstyle from all angles.

'Oh, don't you like it? I like it.'

'Hm, well let's say it makes you... I liked your hair the way you had it before.' She squints into Fiona's face as they sat down together. 'Have you got more make-up on too?'

'A little. It's not too much is it?'

'I wouldn't say so, it makes you look... Oh, I don't know, it doesn't matter. It's what Nigel thinks that matters,' and she pats Fiona's knee.

The Coffee House owner knows them both well and comes to an unplanned rescue with the diversion of a sad tale and a sob. His wife has burned his childhood teddy bear yesterday and he still hasn't recovered. He doesn't say whether it was a deliberate act of sabotage or not, but Amy's condolences give Fiona time to recover some of the pride she felt until she walked through that door.

Huddled together in its small space with Fiona's shopping taking up too much room, Amy begins the usual litany of, 'do you remembers?' She doesn't really need any contributions from Fiona who idly looks up from her soup and out of the window.

'Amy look,' she points. 'That man outside, I think I recognize him, look.'

'Which man, I see lots.'

'Did you see him - wearing a jacket and flannels? I caught a glimpse of him this morning and I thought I recognized him,' and under her breath, 'it couldn't…'

'I think you've just described quite a lot of men passing by,' Amy laughs, 'anyway I expect you would recognize quite a few people here.'

'I don't know - I don't know why I am so fussed about it.'

'Not to worry, I'm sure you haven't got a stalker, dear. How about going back to Caroline Street after this, we can have a rest this afternoon, before the theatre?'

Both sisters carry the bags and they wander down the hill and along Heriot Row, Amy prattling about nothing much but Fiona doesn't hear her.

There's a mirror in the hall at 62 Caroline Street and Fiona sees herself in it and likes the way she looks all over again. Disappearing to her room for a quick nap, Amy leaves Fiona on her bed, propped up with her new book. She doesn't want to lie down on her new hair-do and flatten it out. The book fails to catch her imagination and eventually she gives it up and looks around what used to be her room. Little has changed only the curtains are new but similar to the originals. She gets up to look at them more closely but the door bell rings and like the good girl and sister she is, she runs downstairs in case it disturbs Amy. In her stockinged feet she opens the door and the low sunlight back-lights the figure of a man. With her hand up to her eyes to block out the sun he still looks indistinct and says nothing.

'Hello, can I help you?' she asks.

'You?'

'Sorry?'

'Fiona?'

'Yes.' She moves to see him better, 'It *is* you, I saw you but I... I think I saw you in George Street this morning and at lunch time.' She feels slightly unsteady.

'I was going to my hotel - I didn't see you.'

'What - why are you here?'

'I didn't expect to see you here either, and not in exactly the same spot I left you. No, you don't still live here do you?' He sounds just as confused as she feels.

'No, no. Sorry, come in Tim, I can't quite believe this,' closing the heavy door behind him shutting out the low sunlight and they stand in the high ceilinged hall while he waits for her to say or do something, but she doesn't.

'Well, well, I can't believe this either, and you haven't changed a bit,' he says.

She points at an open door and leads the way. 'Sorry Tim, you've taken the wind out of my sails,' but, you've taken my breath away, is what she means. She can't tell him about the puzzle his unrealised self had caused her earlier or her recent thoughts about him. But she can look directly at him in the better light and sees his blue eyes are faded and tired, and there's a few grey hairs in his dark hair. But despite the careful grooming there is something worn about his face, she feels sorry for him.

'Oh, I would never want to take the wind out of your sails, I'm the one who should be sorry for giving you such a terrific fright, am I really such an alarming blast from the past?' And he does look perplexed she thinks.

'What brings you here, why are you here?' she says. 'Let's sit down, I think I need to,' but they sit on opposite chairs not together on the sofa. There's a stiltedness, a guarded manner about them, not the relaxed and welcome reconnection of friends.

So, he leans forward, his arms dived down between his knees and says, 'hoping to see Graham and Amy actually, I'm staying at The Hanover Hotel down the road from here, you see. First time I've been in Edinburgh for years. So as I was - well, you saw me near here, I thought I would call round on the off-chance.' He pauses to look at her closely, 'Never in a million years did I ... You look very well.' And that last remark sounds like a cliché, but there has to be a liberating terminus for his confusion. His shoulders drop, she sees that and understands, so gives him quiet thanks. But she knows she doesn't want to share him; she will let a sleeping sister lie. He takes out a cigarette and offers one.

'No, I don't,' but she wishes she did.

'No of course you didn't.'

'Neither did you - a few years ago.' She smiles and thinks about offering him tea, though she suspects he would probably prefer a drink. Yet she offers neither.

He draws hard on his cigarette and she notices his hands. Hands which saved her those years ago. Hands which had held her. He leans slightly more towards her for a moment. 'So why are you here - I knew you were married.'

'How?'

'Well, we did get the newspapers in harbour, somewhat out of date - but someone noticed your engagement, so I knew. When did you get married?'

'Oh... 1961, May 1961?'

190

And he looks down at his hands, 'ah, did you? May 1961, quite quick then.'

'Yes, it was.'

His mouth tightens and he nods a couple of times while he taps the ash off his cigarette. He clears his throat and when he looks at her again a slight smile is in place.

'And so there's children?'

'No, we don't...'

He might not have expected that answer, it wasn't just asked out of good manners. He concentrates on tapping the ash off his cigarette again, easier than judging whether her face asks for further enquiry.

'Remind me again who he is, what's his name?' and he nods at her wedding photograph on a table.

'Nigel, Nigel MacMuckle.' She looks down at her shiny, gold wedding ring and back at him. 'So that's it, married and living way up north. You see, I'm just here to see Amy and Graham and do a bit of shopping, the usual things women do, but I'm going home tomorrow...'

'Ah, I see,' he cuts in. 'And what does Mr MacMuckle do?'

'What does he do? Well - ah - he has a castle,' and Tim slowly repeats the words, a castle, like an uncomprehending foreigner. 'Yes a castle, and a loch, and a mountain too. Don't laugh, it's true and I don't know what else to say. There's a hill farm but it's tenanted so you couldn't really call him a farmer, but he breeds Highland cattle and I suppose being a local magistrate and school governor counts for something. And oh yes, he's a Clan Chief too, though that doesn't involve much if anything really, except sometimes wearing a lot of tartan, feathers, weaponry, that sort of thing - don't laugh.'

'No, hand on heart, I'm not laughing at you Fiona, why would I? You just make it sound funny, that's all. I'm very interested, tell me more, it sounds quite romantic. You know, castle, loch, mountain, like the setting for a Mills and Boon novel,' and he glances at Fiona's wedding photograph again. 'Handsome, Highland hero included, except in your case it isn't a fiction,' and he stretches back on the cushions with his hands behind his head.

'Well it may as well be, because he doesn't really do anything for real, the way you mean it.' It isn't meant to come out sounding disloyal but she doesn't want to talk about Nigel. She's found herself in a parallel universe with Tim where she isn't Mrs MacMuckle, she is Fiona, and it is liberating - she wants it for longer. Then she looks at him with a wry smile. 'Who would have thought someone like you would know even the slightest thing about Mills and Boon romances.'

'Ah well, one picks things up along the way - yes? I had a wife who seemed to read nothing else. Maybe that's why I failed to pass muster in her expectations.'

'Had a wife?'

'Yes, but will be an ex-wife, you see I'm told I'm not good at, married.' He gives a half-hearted laugh. 'You might remember that I have a brother, John. in the Royal Marines, well the irony is she ran off with him. You'd think she'd have known better than to repeat the folly wouldn't you? So that hasn't worked either it won't surprise you to know.' He takes a deep breath, 'but no, Fiona, you see I'm no great shakes, put bluntly I think I'm what's usually called a failure,' and he hangs his head in mock shame.

'I don't believe that for a moment, Tim, go on tell me the truth,' she laughs.

'Well, you should believe me because the truth is, along with marital failure, there was martial failure too, I was passed over as they say, there would be no more promotion for me,' and as if he'd just thought it, 'actually, that about sums me up at all levels! Anyway, I've taken voluntary retirement and things are flexible for the time being, until I decide what I'm going to do with the rest of my life.'

'Oh, Tim don't say that, you've have your life ahead of you, lots of time to...' and she's stuck for the right word.

'There, you see, time to what?' he laughs and lights another cigarette. She tries to cover her stumble with flippancy but he's turned away to look out of the window and doesn't react to her. His teasing tone is dropped when he says, 'things went quite well after Rosyth, everything on track, I re-joined at Gibraltar after my father's funeral. I seemed to be doing it right at that point, - well you might remember that, I certainly was full of it in almost every letter I wrote you but perhaps you've forgotten, after all why should you remember...'

'Wrote to me, you wrote to me? You only ever wrote to me once, Tim, when you had to go off on compassionate leave.'

He frowns. 'Yes, I know. But, Fiona, dear girl - I certainly did write, from Madeira, then Gib and from sea. I wrote to you at this address,' and without hesitation, 'five letters - but of course I stopped once I knew you were engaged.'

'Five?' No, no, not even one.'

'This is 62 Caroline Street isn't it?'

'Yes - but honestly, Tim, there were never any letters from you, but *I* wrote just after you left, to thank you for the oyster shells...'

'Yes, I got that.'

'And sent a Christmas card...'

'Did you? I never got that, but I sent you one too.'

'I didn't get that either.' She looks towards the door and the hall beyond. 'Your letters would have been outside there for me, on that table with the rest of my post, there for me when I came home in the evening. I couldn't understand it, then I just presumed you...'

He looks down at the floor and meshes his fingers making a cracking sound.

'All those letters, Tim, all those letters and a card?' Her words trail off with less insistence as she realizes what has been done. 'Oh, no, ' she says under her breath.

He says nothing, he fiddles with his watch and clears his throat, she sits quite still with her hands pressed together and against her face like a prayer. It's as if they are amidst that magnified silence following close gun fire. The only sound in the room is the little carriage clock ticking its fast time like another excited pulse.

'I think I'll make some tea, Tim,' she says then gets up and stubs her toe.

'Did that hurt?'

'I'll mend,' she answers.

Will they revise the footnotes to their autobiographies after the tea interval - allude to the blindingly obvious? But that's not the sort of hand either of them play. Even if unresolved situations are contrary to his tidy, militarized mind he won't ditch the prescribed script and ad lib and neither will she. He sits back and closes his eyes.

With the clatter of tea cups on a tray he takes it from her, neither speak while they sit together on the sofa now and she pours the tea. But the sound of footsteps on the stairs intrude.

'Oh you're in here,' Amy says before she notices Tim, but he stands up and she looks at him but only for a moment, then enquiringly at Fiona.

'Amy, you remember Tim Robinson from Eddy's ship in 1960?'

Amy hesitates, her eyes widen slightly then narrow, 'what a long time ago that was.' She looks up and down at his jacket, flannels and dark hair. 'Have you seen Eddy lately?'

'Hello Amy? No, can't say I have and we never served together again after *Continent*, he left the ship quite soon after I met you all - if you remember. Rather lost touch I'm afraid. How are you Amy?' She doesn't answer, then they all speak at once and give way with nervous apologies. Silence holds until Amy comes back with a cup. 'How's Graham - well I hope? Tim says but Amy ignores it.

Coolly she asks him, 'so what brings you to Edinburgh?'

'Ah yes that, well it's a fleeting visit to meet up with my brother. I'm staying at The Hanover, we had to sort some family things out, he's a Royal Marine at HMS Condor so he came down from Arbroath this morning. Job more or less done and I go home on tomorrow's train.'

'And where is that?' She asks like an officious form filler.

'Deepest Norfolk for the present,' but Amy just stares ahead though Fiona looks at him encouragingly. 'I've left the Navy, so, as I say, Norfolk, very near Norwich actually - not a place I really knew, Hampshire was my stamping ground. It's out of the way but I quite like it and I get in some sailing too. Anyway, an old Naval chum bought a pub and as I'm not tied at the moment I'm giving him a hand until I sort myself out and decide what I'm going to do next.'

'Norwich? That was a long journey for you and you're taking the train back there tomorrow.' Amy glances at Fiona.

'Yes, that's right,' he says and Amy's eyebrows lift above her teacup. Fiona resents her turning the conversation into something intrusive and one-sided, and what difference does it make how he travelled to Edinburgh. She looks at Tim and for a second he meets her eye, but there is nothing she feels she can do or say in her older sister's house to stop the unsubtle discouragement being meted out to him. He refuses a second cup of tea and a glint of the original young Tim Robinson comes back as he rises to his feet.

'I think I should go now,' he laughs, 'I think I'm getting boring - I'm even boring myself, I'm sure you have better things to do,' and he bobs his head as if an audience were over. Muttering something about going to the theatre, Amy makes no attempt to contradict him. Fiona, angry and embarrassed by her sister thinks she might as well be physically ejecting him. It's hours before they are to go out, but the signal is clear - and it is dismissal. With a stiff farewell given, Amy leaves them alone in the hall. Fiona knows nothing more can be said much as she wants him to stay longer. She feels vulnerable and looks at her shoeless feet as she reaches out to the front door handle but he puts his hand to it first.

'So it's another goodbye, dear girl,' then he puts both his hands on her shoulders, slowly he adds, 'it's been a wonderful surprise; I never thought I'd ever see you again.'

'I know, me neither.'

'A brief encounter… I only wish it could have been for longer.' She doesn't look at him, she wishes it too. 'Be happy,' he says and kisses her on the cheek for just a little longer than it need have taken. Then he opens the door.

'I'm so sorry Tim,' she says, still without looking at him or knowing exactly what she's apologizing for, there seems to be so much.

And he turns on the step. 'Don't be, none of it is your fault, you know it isn't. And I'm sorry too.' She opens her mouth to say more, but with a shrugged sigh of resignation he lowers his voice, *'Oh what a tangled web we weave …'* Then touches her arm and turns away. She watches him for a second then closes the door quickly; she doesn't want to see if he will or won't turn round for one last look.

'…when first we practise to deceive,' she finishes the quote as the closing door's echo fades and their last words die in the space. Of course Tim Robinson would have produced such a perfect words for their shared recognition of the deed done them. She remembers seeing it written in his famous little black book. With a deep breath she saves those words inside her, a small compensation for the contents of his disenfranchised letters. At this moment it would be easy to give way to her gathering tears. She swallows hard against

the tightness in her throat and puts her hand on the door handle, she grips it harder but her wrist doesn't turn and open it. She can't go out can she? Her shoes are still upstairs.

Soundlessly she crosses the stone flagged hall and up the carpeted stairs. Amy in her room doesn't look up through the open door; she's putting clothes away. Fiona stops - she waits.

'Oh you're there, he's gone then has he? So it was him you thought you recognised this morning, did he recognise you and stalk you back here after all?'

'Of course not, he had no idea. He called on the off-chance of seeing you and Graham.'

'Then why didn't you call me?'

'I don't know, it was such a surprise I suppose,' she feels like a scolded child who's eaten all the chocolate biscuits and left the plain ones.

'The pair of you looked very cosy tucked away like that, what were you talking about?' Amy says as she roughly shuts a drawer.

Catching a glimpse of herself in a mirror, Fiona sees it isn't just the new hairstyle which makes her look different, she looks flushed, her eyes are bright and she sees the face of an angry adult emerge - and that anger surges. 'What did you do with all the letters Tim sent me, there were five of them for God's sake, and a Christmas card too. What did you do with them?'

At the demand in her younger sister's voice, Amy looks up as if she's been hit, 'I should think you would be grateful to me now,' she snaps, standing up ram rod straight. Then challenging Fiona with the certainty of a convert, 'you'd have to be blind not to see he's clearly a drinker, lost his driving license I daresay and goodness knows what else,' then flicks her hand dismissively.

'Grateful?' Fiona snaps back. 'I can't believe you said that - how can you? What did you do with his letters? Those letters were for me, not you. Mine, Amy, mine. They were not for you to deal with as you thought fit… God, did you read them?'

'What do you think I am? Of course I didn't read them, I - I just burned them unopened in the boiler. Don't be ridiculous Fiona, remember you were engaged to Nigel anyway.'

'But I might not have been if I had read those letters.' The unchecked words come out like a wail and make Amy flinch. 'How could you? What a despicable thing to do, I was mortified when he told me he'd written. I would never have not answered him. I could tell he realised what must have happened, I think he was hurt and frankly I was furious, I didn't know what to say.' She moves closer to her sister as if she wants to corner her.

'Don't be silly, forget about him. He was a charming wolf and he would have used you. Come on, surely you can see that now - especially today, when you, anyone, can see what he has become.'

'Don't - do *not* call me silly. I think you are being very cruel, I felt sorry for him, I talked to him for longer than you did and he hasn't had much luck…'

'Oh yes, hard luck stories. Grow up Fiona, he was probably looking for a meal tomorrow before he got on his train.'

'That was cheap - and don't tell me to grow up.' She pauses for a moment. 'That's the problem isn't it? You think you know better than me, you always have and it's a handy way for you to hang on to your superiority if I'm the eternal little sister.' Amy tries to stem Fiona's tirade, but she won't not be stopped. 'Were you jealous? Oh yes I get it. You were jealous, Amy. You enjoyed his company yourself didn't you? You couldn't bear for me to have him to myself.' Amy tries again to interrupt. 'No don't, Amy, don't try to tell me what everyone said about him, you and I both know he wasn't like that with me. You couldn't admit you were wrong, you still can't, can you?' Amy tries again to defend herself but Fiona moves closer and puts up a hand to stop her. 'Why were you jealous, Amy? I was the one struggling without Mummy and Daddy. You were the one with a husband, babies, and your own home. You had no right to interfere.' She doesn't mean to finish but Amy pushes past her, beaten by her sister's accusations. 'Don't walk away, answer me, you owe me an explanation, many explanations...'

And at the top of the stairs Amy turns round to her, 'what's happened to you, why are you being like this? I've never seen it before, I can't talk to you about this any longer,'

'You will Amy - I'm not going to let it go until you have.'

The front door closing echoes through the house just as Amy is shouting back that there was nothing more to talk about.

'Halloo! Well, I've got something to talk about,' calls Graham as he runs up the stairs. 'I think I've just seen that Tim - Tim whatsisname - remember? You know, the smooth navigator in *HMS Continent* who was so taken with you, Fiona... Gosh, I must say I like your new look. Anyway, he was waiting to cross the street when I was on the other side. I would have asked him back, but I couldn't be a hundred per cent sure and he looked as if he was in a hurry, didn't recognise me - looked deep in thought and - what's the matter, have I said something wrong?'

'No, Graham, you haven't. Your great visual memory served you well, he's just been here,' says Fiona flatly.

'Well then why the glum faces?' But Fiona moves abruptly to go to her room and he says to Amy, 'what's the matter with Fiona, did he upset her? You look a bit flummoxed yourself.'

'Oh, Graham, what have I done? She's so angry with me,' and pulls him into their bedroom.

But Fiona closes her door, she leans her back against it and hears the low murmur of Amy's voice and then a clear blast of Graham's. 'What? You did what?'And she thinks she hears Amy sob.

Lying in her bath Fiona cries silent tears down her wet face. What does it matter, there's enough water to wash them away and dilute their salt. Like a waveless sea around a flat, barren island the scented water encircles her small, white belly. With her fingers she trickles a pale stream down her torso and it slips away left and right when it reaches the girdle of water at her waist and still her stomach stays dry. Soap bubbles float on the surface, a small collection of different sizes, and she lifts them up in the cup of her hand. Iridescent, fragile, like magical spawn and one by one they silently burst leaving nothing but a slight slick in the lines of her palm.

Tears fall again and she wipes them with that warm, wet hand letting it splash back heavily into the water. Quivering, liquid beads land on her soft, dry flesh then they defiantly disperse too. She places that same hand on the unstretched skin covering an unused vessel. She grieves for the lack of etched scars across her belly, those commemorative badges celebrating maternity. But her firm, unmarked body has never varied in all her adult life - and she resents it. Learning how to lessen then accept her disappointment with every vacant month that passes is as nought. Her childlessness feels like the thrust of a knife, revisiting because of a possibility she never knew had been possible.

Anger with Nigel rises in her again for denying her the right to know she is not at fault. His confession had set off a blaze in her and it is not quite extinguished after all. That morning by the loch his amends and his misery had dampened its intensity but this Edinburgh afternoon fans the embers. And without his presence the flames have reignited and will have to burn themselves out. And she will let them.

She doesn't want to quell the anger she feels for her sister, her indignation is too new and raw, it needs analysis. Amy's betrayal has to be processed and her motives examined more carefully and she fears the eventual outcome will never be more than a repair job, likely to split at the seams whenever any tension arises.

But most of all she's angry with herself for not being more assertive then. She's absorbed Amy's unintentional point when she'd told her to grow up; infuriating, inflammatory, condescending, but that kick's backlash is going to be a voice, her voice, admitted on equal terms with Amy's. And in her maelstrom of emotion something makes her want to disappear, be out of this element. And she sinks down immersing herself completely in the warm water, to let it stop her ears and close her eyes for as long as her breath will let it. Let her, in those moments, indulge the fantasy of a future she might have had. But then with her reverie hardly begun there's the abstract underwater sounds of a door being knocked and a male voice. Coming up in a wash of overspill she hears Graham asking if she wants to take Nigel's telephone call now or later. Later is what she wants, but with that summons into here and now her flight is lost. She pulls at the plug and the water empties in a crude, mocking gurgle. Wrapping herself in towels she notices the cracked nail of her stubbed big toe and thinks it a memento of the day - split.

It had been Amy who wanted to tell her Nigel was on the phone, to carry on as if nothing had happened but Graham insisted he should be the messenger. He'd warned that the sisters' issue must be resolved carefully and properly not cranked back into unsatisfactory service by half-hearted or resentful tinkering at the problem.

He sees his wife smoking one of his cigarettes in angry, red-tipped draws and suggests she should speak to Fiona before the theatre. Her reaction is typically defiant, what is there to say, she only did what she thought was best at the time, what can she do if Fiona won't accept that?

But Graham is wise, Graham knows, and he gently asks her to think about it again, to ask herself if she can honestly say that was her motive. And as she doesn't rail at that he suggests that Tim wasn't a dire threat to Fiona's honour and still she says nothing. So with a hand on hers he says, 'weren't you just a little charmed by Tim yourself, did you really think I hadn't noticed?' and she pulls her hand away.

'Whose side are you on?' she says.

'There shouldn't be sides but you must accept responsibility for causing her this upset and apologise for that - at least.' And hardly has Graham finished before Fiona appears saying she's going to telephone Nigel and Amy asks if she's going to tell him.

'Tell him what, that a man visited today who you think is of little consequence or that through your unwanted interference you turned his visit into something of very great consequence? No, what I say I will keep to myself, it seems to me to be the safest thing to do.' Then she apologises to Graham, who's never seen Fiona be so assertively articulate, his eyes wide as if he finds it uncomfortably thrilling but she doesn't wait for Amy to answer.

Nigel, amiable and as cheerful as he's been every other night too, hopes she's enjoying herself but really wants to know if tacks have been put in the soles of his new brogues. She, with a weariness in her voice, assures him they have and that he'd even underlined the words on her shopping list. She adds that he can safely click clack around in them for the next twenty years. Then there is a small awkward silence until he says she sounds brassed off but she passes it off with a claim of tiredness, which he appears to accept. But she notices the ashtray, the two neatly bent over cigarette stubs in a ring of ash and she wants to go. She sits back for a moment looking at it and is about to throw them in the grate when Amy closes the door behind her, she thinks they should talk, though she sounds unusually tentative.

'I don't know, certainly you should talk,' Fiona says.

'Look, I am sorry I seem to have caused you so much distress today, will you at least accept that?'

'Yes... But?'

'Please Fiona before I go on will you stop being so haughty, I find it difficult to deal with.'

'Huh, that's rich coming from someone who put on a master class in hauteur this afternoon in this very room, wouldn't you say? I would.' She looks away. 'Anyway go on, what were you going to say?'

'I genuinely thought I was doing the right thing in not encouraging you and Tim, I tried to think what Mummy would have wanted. Then there was Nigel, he was Graham's friend, he was a known quantity, if you like, and he adored you from the start,' Fiona looks startled at her awareness. 'Yes, he told Graham. It seemed so obvious to encourage Nigel than chance it with Tim and lose you to Portsmouth or Plymouth - or any other place the Navy gathers...'

'And Tim Robinson was a wolf, that's what you said, Amy, he was not to be trusted, yet you saw for yourself what he was actually like with me... What's so wrong with Portsmouth or Plymouth anyway? I shouldn't have listened to you, I should have trusted my own judgement, I should have written...'

'Because you were too young.'

'No, Amy, I was not too young, you were younger when you chose Graham. And, I think my judgement is sound, so far in life it hasn't let me down. You're wrong and you know it.' Then she fixes Amy with a hard look. 'Have you forgotten you burned all his letters, what does that say? Can't you see you should have allowed me to make up my own mind, why should you or anyone have been so - presumptuous?'

Amy sits as if she's been pushed into the chair. She pulls a cushion out from behind her and holds it tightly on her lap. 'Yes - I suppose you're probably right, Graham said that too.' Fiona thinks she's scored a surprisingly quick victory but Amy straightens slightly and looks at her. 'Are you sorry you married Nigel? Graham wondered, so do I. Is that why Tim Robinson has made such a wave today?'

'You are being disingenuous, Amy, you know you are. You knew he meant something to me, you knew how hurt I was. No, I'm not sorry I married Nigel,' she hesitates at that, but she mustn't betray, mustn't betray anything. 'Life hasn't always been easy but I see Tim in a different light now, finding out that he had been keen enough to write so many times and I already knew he wanted to see me when he got back...'

'Alright, so he was keen, anyone could see that. I think it was what's called a passion - for him anyway and even I could see that.'

'What do you mean it was a passion, do you mean sex? He didn't...'

'For your years, sometimes you can be surprisingly naïve, Fiona.' Amy sighs then rattles off 'a man like that, who had sown his wild oats with such care-free abandon...'

'Randy, you mean.'

'Uh - yes, if you like. And who then becomes patient and attentive as he did, well of course it meant he must be serious...'

'Well, well, you've changed your tune, at the time you attributed that to - let me think - ah yes, playing a long game, you said?'

'Oh for heaven's sake Fiona, stop being sarcastic it doesn't suit you. I am trying, you know.'

'I will, if you stop patronizing me.'

204

'He was exciting and attractive, but that made him dangerous I thought then.' Amy slowly runs her palm up and down her shin and clearly giving herself away. Then with a great unmoderated sigh asks, 'anyway, what is passion? It doesn't last, compared to the durability of affection.' And Fiona thinks her sister probably read that somewhere.

So she cuts in with 'you were attracted to him yourself, that's it, isn't it?' And you didn't want me to have that, so-called passion. Tell me, Amy, have you known passion?' And Amy visibly bridles at Fiona's impudence, but Fiona persists, 'have you?'

With shoulders dropped, Amy sinks back again into the chair, 'Probably not,' then she closes her eyes as if to concentrate. 'I did what was expected I suppose, I married Graham, I never had the chance to test myself, did I?' Her eyes open again but she hesitates. 'You were the pretty one, that was valued, and I was never known for my looks was I? Remember Daddy and his Samuel Johnson quote? "A man is better placed with a good meal before him than a wife speaking Greek". I think that's damn well seared on my heart,' and she sets her mouth hard. 'Mummy agreed with him, didn't she?' Fiona nods. 'You knew I would have liked to go to university, you've always known that, but they laughed at it, I was told not to be so foolish. But you trained for something and you loved it.'

'Hardly the same thing, it was only cooking for heaven's sake.'

'A good meal before him is better than speaking Greek? There you are, see what I mean?'

'But if they'd been alive I expect I wouldn't have been allowed to do the professional certificate...'

'The fact remains that you did.' Then there was Tim and then there was Nigel too. You had choice, Fiona - I didn't.' She pauses again and squashes the cushion against herself. 'Graham was always there and I was fond of him - but no, I don't think it was passion for either of us.' But Amy nervously leaning towards her says quietly. 'Passion, sex, call it what you want - is that what you think you've missed too, is that why you asked me?'

'No, what I miss is children - I might have had them with Tim,' a verbal clout that makes Amy wince. 'You denied me a choice which might have brought them. So, you might say that makes us even, doesn't it?'

Amy doesn't rebel at Fiona's charge, 'so it's Nigel's fault?' she says hardly hiding her keenness.

'Poor Nigel, hardly his fault, who knows what's exactly to blame, but it's only a remote possibility,' and Fiona has lost her defensiveness.

And Amy picks up the baton. 'He didn't tell you before you got married? That's outrageous,' she says.

'Nigel would never do something so underhand, Amy,' indignation returning to Fiona's voice again even if she'd thought it herself once. 'He didn't know and didn't find out until recently. That's it, that's all there is to know, please don't tell anyone.' She stands up to go but Amy reaches out to her.

'I am so sorry, you poor thing, what's wrong? We wondered why it seems to be taking so long,' she says then waits but Fiona doesn't want to give her more. 'So, you probably wouldn't have chosen Tim Robinson given the choice…'

'Oh, I don't know, I think I might have preferred Mrs. Robinson rather than this ridiculous name, MacMuckle.' The subject chased off with a quip, yet Fiona's delivery is dead pan and warns against further attempts at either information gathering or restoring their relationship.

The scraping noise of breakfast toast being buttered and newsprint crackling sums up the atmosphere on Fiona's last morning at 62 Caroline Street. With an edge of irritation in her voice, Amy tries to crank dialogues into being and Graham hangs about saying he'll

206

wait to see Fiona off. Her departure is uneasy yet civilised enough with Graham overcompensating in both bright chat and physical affection. Relieved to be on her way, Fiona drives out of the New Town's strict grids into The Queensferry Road then looks at her watch and turns back again. She drives to The Hanover Hotel.

The old receptionist looks at Fiona's wedding finger when she asks if Mr Robinson is in his room and as far as that person knows he must be as his key isn't in its pigeon hole. With the room number given Fiona runs up the stairs before she can change her mind then stops on the landing, she pushes her hair back and takes a deep breath. Three light knocks on the door and she hears his voice but not what he says, then there's a shout of 'wait - with you in a moment,' and when Tim opens the door he's in his dressing gown.

'Fiona? You, I...'

'I had to come, Tim. Is it alright?'

'Of course it is,' and his arm gathers her into the room. 'I've been on the telephone for ages - talking to my brother, John. I thought you were going home this morning,' he says looking at her closely.

'I am - I mean I was on my way but I had to see you...'

'Look, let me get dressed, you sit down,' and he slaps his forehead with the heel of his palm. 'Aah - haven't we been in a similar situation once before?' he laughs as he takes her hand, but she doesn't sit, she holds on to him and he doesn't resist. 'Fiona you're... '

'Don't say I'm vulnerable, please don't say it.'

'I wasn't, but you are,' and he pulls her tight against him. 'What do you want or do I know the answer?' whispered this time.

'Yes you know, I can feel you do,' she says.

'Pity to let it go to waste then isn't it?' he says as he kisses her lips, her face, her neck then in one easy sequence pulls her clothes off while leading her to the bed.

Like deep hunger, they pay heed to nothing except sating it. The tenderness can wait until the untangling of limbs. But her intensity and physicality is so surprising even to her, as if there's an edge of anger in it. And when they are still and quiet he looks at her flushed and spent, with her eyes closed, her head back and neck arched. The pearl necklace round it makes an expensive noose. Gently, he pulls it forward to loosen it and feels her small gasp more than he hears it.

And he says, 'I can't leave it like this, after that what am I supposed to do? How do I let you go now? I'll do anything you ask but know that I don't want to lose you again...I love you.'

'Did you say that in your letters?'

'Yes... many times.'

'I was *so* hurt, Tim,' she says and puts his head against her. A warm pearl presses against his mouth. He all but spits it away.

'Did you have it out with Amy?'

'You guessed?'

'So what exactly happened to all my letters?'

'She burned them unopened.'

'Well it had to be something like that didn't it, and I thought you'd had a change of heart,' he says, 'and as it turns out - you did.'

'Tim no, don't say that. If I'd known... As God is my witness I don't think I'll ever be able to forget it or forgive her.'

'It matters that much?' he says and strokes her face but she can't look at him, he's asked a question which answers it all. Then he lies beside her and lifts her left hand rubbing his thumb across her fingers. 'So a sapphire not an emerald,' he says looking at her engagement ring.

'Tim, don't. I've still got the two oyster shells.'

'And I've still got that piece of sea glass you let me keep... I've often thought of you.'

'Have you?' And then she looks at him. 'I've thought of you too.'

208

'So what's to be done, tell me.'

'I don't know, I can't think straight, I'm here and that's all that matters. I don't want to think, everything's been turned upside down. I have to go home, don't I?'

'You do, then what are you going to do? You know what I want, but what do you want?'

Her hold tightens on him, 'I don't know, not now.'

'Is this only unfinished business, Fiona?' The hurt in his voice barely hidden in its light-heartedness.

'No - no don't say that, it's not that simple is it?'

'For you it isn't, I know that. You won't say it so I will, he loves you doesn't he and you - well, I won't presume anything there, but I've been on the receiving end myself and I know it's messy.'

'And you loved your wife...'

'Lusted - both of us, it was only meant to be a fling and then - well we had to get married, as they say...'

'You didn't say you had a child.'

'I don't, she miscarried a month later, so...' He doesn't need to say anything else she is thinking it was bad luck too, though for a different reason. 'Anyway it didn't surprise me when she started looking elsewhere after that, I was at sea a lot.' He gives a short laugh. 'It was that she picked my brother, that's what surprised me...'

'It isn't really surprising is it? A clean slate, but from the same quarry?'

'No, not her. It was more about paying me back for not coming up to scratch. Anyway that's all in the past, I can please myself now but can I - d'you think I could ever please you?'

'I know you could, but I need some time and I don't want to hurt him.'

'You will, it's inevitable, you won't be able to avoid it, dear girl.'

She has no answer and they lie together quietly, arms bound around one another. She sees his half eaten breakfast on a table, paper work spread out on it too and on a chair, his suitcase half packed.

'Did you see your father before he died, Tim?' she says.

'Yes, he died three days after I got to Madeira, I had to arrange everything, I should have telephoned you...'

'Why would you not think a letter would be enough,' and at the image of Amy pushing it into the boiler she squeezes her eyes shut and clenches her teeth.

'Well, I thought you'd changed your mind about me, distance doesn't always lend enchantment. I thought you'd probably heard the bad press and I wasn't around to put that right. There was that and of course when I knew you were engaged - well, obviously you'd met someone else and of course I knew I shouldn't write again after that.'

'Bad press? There was bad press from Amy, but I never paid any attention to it.'

'No, I always felt she didn't really approve of me.'

'She was jealous - though I didn't see it at the time.'

A slight smile crosses his face. 'Ah well - but I did play the field, Fiona, I wouldn't say any more than anyone else and I hope I didn't take advantage, but I probably did sometimes.

'Di Reid's flatmate, that tall girl - Jenny?'

'Yes, I can see why that's what was thought, but she read too much into it, I didn't lead her on. Look, this isn't very gallant of me is it? But because it's you, and, I want you to know I'm not quite the Lothario I was made out to be.'

'Well I think Lothario could learn a few things from you,' he starts kissing her again before she can say more. She doesn't want him to stop and this time everything is less urgent but time presses; Tim doesn't, she sees his alarm clock and knows she should go. Getting out of that bed seems to her to be one of the most difficult things she has ever made herself do. He doesn't get up, with the

210

half smile in place he lies there with his legs crossed, his hands behind his head and watches her dress. And once she puts her shoes on he's up like an animal out of a trap and his arms are around her. 'How are we going to keep in contact? I'll come to you wherever you want that to be, but phone calls?'

And she sighs, 'risky, he's around a lot and if I phone you, Norwich will appear on the bill. He takes his dog out in the morning, around nine o'clock and evening, about five thirty, for an hour or so. You could try then. 'Oh Tim, this has been wonderful,' she says as she writes her address and telephone number for him and he gives her his.

'Will you think about us together, the future - is there one?' he says quietly. Let me know, put me out of my misery?'

'I won't be able to think of anything else, Tim. I'll write.'

'And send me a photograph - please?'

His nakedness and the intensity of their farewell kiss lingers enough to make her want to abandon leaving and to hell with the consequences. But he's serious when he straightens her collar, pushes her hair back and touches her lips with his finger. 'I know - that's what I want too but we can't, you must get home,' he says, reminding her of his paternal side in the Seatoun Hotel. 'It'll only make it worse if you don't get back in time. I shouldn't see you out, sorry - you shouldn't be seen coming out of an hotel with a man.' And he reaches for his Paisley-silk dressing gown.

'Certainly not one with a dressing gown on in the middle of the day, have you done this before, Tim?' Her flippancy because she doesn't know how to leave.

'Except for that soaking interlude in the Seatoun Hotel? No I haven't, I've never had an affair with a married woman - before,' and he's still serious. 'Now you must go, this time remember I love you, I won't let you down, I give you my solemn promise,' and he drops her hand.

She doesn't answer, not because she doesn't have one but because her throat is tight and her lips pressed tight together against a surge of emotion threatening to break. So she nods once, looks down and turns away. And when she looks back from the stairs to blow him a kiss, he mouths, 'I love you' and sends a kiss back.

The car indicator clicks, she looks in the rear mirror, changes gear and looks again in case he's there even though she knows he couldn't be. She gives way to the tears, more of anger than sorrow and the urge to turn round and go back is so strong that she draws up by the kerb once she's in the next street. And she sits there biting her lip trying to pull herself together. She's going to be late home so what does it matter if she waits there for a while and she looks at her watch. Had it only been just over a snatched hour and a half - was that all she'd had of Tim? Snatched, he'd used that word in the Seatoun Hotel. Snatched, what Amy did with his letters. Snatched, a future she might have had with him. And, he isn't 'him' - he is Tim. Him, had been Nigel and Tim's wife had remained nameless too, depersonalized as if it would minimize their relevance.

There is a choice set out in her head of each man's pros and cons, it's like form in a race card. And difficult as it is to concentrate on such a hard-headed comparison it is the only way she can keep her emotions in check if she is to drive home now. And she pulls away from the kerb without looking in the rear mirror. Once on the ferry crossing she sits very still in her car and goes over the list in her head.

With Tim she can have children. With Nigel it's remote and how long should she wait to see if it happens. With both she's wanted but one has deceived her. (She knows she's deceived too, but that's brushed aside.) One offers a life continuing in a crumbling castle stuck up a glen, the other doesn't. Happiness with both? No, it will be altered and hindered by her guilt about one. (That might not be felt in the moment but she knows it will catch up.) Then there's love; one in the present tense - that was made quite clear. And the other? Is it really in the past?

She feels distaste at her forensic calculations yet something has been learned in the priority of her self-imposed questions and their immediate answers. And there are hours to go, hours to ponder the details, the thrill of it and being wanted so much, but there's also Tim's reasonable suggestion that for her it's only unfinished business. There's time to consider this, so has she magnified his effect due to her disenchantment with who and what she's got? Is the paragon Tim has become in her mind unrealistic through lack of testing over time? How can anything be decided without that, at such a distance, in secret? Then the word, cheated, insinuates itself claiming the place that, snatched, had taken earlier. Resentment rises when she thinks how she was cheated out of Tim, Amy cheated her, she'd cheated them both. Nigel cheated her of the truth and now she's cheated on him. But a decision about what to do remains elusive and is no clearer hours later as she turns into the twisting roads of the glens.

Holding Lightly

Ahead of Fiona there is the faint but familiar smoke of a bonfire rising in an idle curl. It comes from a place she knows to be near the castle not any of the usual sites Nigel uses. But she gives it no more thought until she steps out of her car and smells the scent of wood smoke but overlaid with that of singed wool. Calling out to Nigel she looks in the usual places and doesn't find him, she calls his name again but there is no reply. From a window she sees nothing, only the overgrown lawn, but nearby the remains of the bonfire in a great patch of grey ash and embers. And she turns away yet is drawn to look again. Not at the burnt wood, the scorched mattress ticking and blankets, some springs or the pieces of smouldering, red fabric. There amidst cracks, spits and flying sparks, lying on the soft bed of ash she sees myriad thread-like streaks of glittering gold - and she knows.

Up the stairs she runs and along the corridor to their rooms. Through Nigel's open door and revealed in the middle of the floor is a large, empty rectangle of unfaded oriental carpet. Sawdust lies scattered across the rest. She calls his name again but only the ticking clock replies and looking through the adjoining door to their bedroom she sees a new bed where the old one had been. It's been made up with new bed linen and a duvet and it makes her cry. Then his voice shouts her name and Luath bounds ahead of him into the room.

'I thought you would be back earlier,' he says before he sees her face, and when he does, 'oh God, have I done the wrong thing again, I thought you'd like it?'

214

And it is she who reaches out to him as he stands apart like a child trying to figure out what to think. 'No, it's fine, it's wonderful,' she says,

'So I've done the right thing,' he says with relief and she nods as she blows her nose. 'I chose it carefully and it's bigger than the old bed too. I burned the old one - on the bonfire outside - it went up like a tinder box.' Then he hesitates. 'You've noticed *the* bed has gone, have you? I decided to burn that too, so that's the end of it. I thought it best, but I'd hoped it would have burned out by now.' He clears his throat and looks down. 'I didn't want you to see the immolation scene - so to speak.'

There's a half laughed sniff and she says, 'so touching, what you've done, and there too.' She points at his bedless room. 'I fear you've cremated a piece of history, you might be thought a vandal.'

He puts an arm around her, 'don't worry, only Robbie knows, he helped me dismantle it. It was much more difficult than I thought, he had to take a chain saw to it in situ, he didn't ask and he won't sneak.'

'But he must be wondering why... Oh dear, it was probably worth a decent sum too, maybe I was a bit rash about that - I never thought you'd burn it. Did you see all the gold thread there is amongst the ash?' He hadn't and they look down from a window to see the circus of cinders littered with a warp and weft of glints.

'Well, stone the crows, look at that! I never thought that stuff was gold,' he says, 'never thought about it at all - isn't it just glistering gilt or something?'

'That wouldn't have survived the fire, would it?'

'Quite right, it wouldn't, so what are we going to do with our bullion then, we can't just throw it away can we?'

'Rake it up - it will have some value, won't it?'

'Well, we'll see about that - what about seeing if this new bed's fit for purpose then?' and he pulls her towards it.

'No, please not now?'

'Why not?' but she won't move.

'Well, you know...'

'No - I don't,' he laughs.

'The time of day, I mean I've been travelling haven't I? I'm grubby...'

'Aw, come on - none of that would have stopped you in the past, it wouldn't have stopped you a week ago before you left - now would it?'

'Please Nigel don't push me, I'm sure the bed's a lovely bed, but let's leave it for the moment, please.'

'Well if that's what you want, far be it from me to make you do something you don't want. I'll go and get your luggage, shall I - is that what you want, eh?'

It isn't until she undresses for her bath that night that she notices. Her hand at her neck and it isn't there. As if she doesn't believe it she clasps at her throat and looks in the mirror, then with her hand still in place she searches the floor and all about.

'What's the matter?' Nigel says from the new bed.

'Erm, I've... Doesn't matter.'

'Well it doesn't look like it - dropped your necklace somewhere have you?'

'Think I must have done.'

'Look for it tomorrow, I want you in here,' and he pats the covers.

'I must have a bath, Nigel, and I want a long soak.'

'I know, I'll wait.'

She starts taking her clothes off carefully in case the necklace hides in the folds. 'You don't have to, I mean, if you're tired...'

'Aren't we going to..?' She doesn't answer or dare look at him, the disappointment in his voice is almost painful to her. She doesn't take all her clothes off either, she knows he's watching. It feels as if he'll see the map of Tim's touch on her skin and she puts her dressing gown on over her underwear. Glancing at him in the mirror his head is slightly cocked and there's questioning in his eyes.

He appears to be asleep when she comes back from her long soak. His bedside light is out but lying with her back turned to him she knows his breathing is awake. Rigid, on the far edge of the bed, without any relaxed curve in her body, she wishes she wasn't there and realizes just how ironic that is. His tentative hand encloses her shoulder and he moves closer.

'Don't you like it?' he says softly.

'I'm a bit tired, you know how it is,' and she pats his hand still touching her.

'No, I meant the bed, Fluff, you don't seem to be very comfortable.'

'Oh, no it is - much more than the old one, isn't it?' Then a sensuous kiss on her shoulder makes her catch her breath. She'd missed that sensuality but now it was like a taunt and any further intimacy would be exquisitely cruel to him even if he doesn't know that only hours before another man left himself physically and spiritually inside her.

'Relax, Fluff,' he says as he draws her to him. 'You think I'm annoyed with you because you've lost the necklace, don't you?' and her tears well up like a gift from the gods.

'Come along don't cry about it, you'll find it, you can phone Amy tomorrow and see if it's there. It'll turn up. How silly to think I'd be angry.'

'But they were so precious and sentimental, sorry.'

'Shh, doesn't matter, just go to sleep, you're tired it always makes things worse.'

Only when she hears the change in his breathing and feels the drop in his grip does she turn away. Lying there with her eyes open, scanning the dimly lit room, listening to the wind outside and wondering how she was exactly going to explain the pearls' loss if they didn't turn up. It is so difficult to lie, she never realised how much it needs imagination and a good memory. A feeling of sick panic rises in her when she thinks about her pact of honesty made with him in that very room so little time before. Yet, though there's guilt about that, there's none for what she's done with Tim. She sits up and drinks some water, looking at the comfortable shape Nigel makes next to her. So pleased is he with his sacrificial bonfire and his new bed for her, yet all she can really appreciate is the memory spooling back and forward of herself with Tim in another bed.

She doesn't see Nigel watching her search her car the following morning. 'No luck, didn't find them?' he says when she comes back inside.

'Uh, you gave me a fright, no not there.'

'Better telephone Amy then,' and he kisses her forehead. But of course Amy hasn't found them, in fact Amy remembers her wearing them when she left. She says she's always admired the necklace, she even admits she envies it. With her hope that they'd turn up the sisters' conversation comes to an abrupt end.

'Not there either?' he asks, only to be rewarded with a shake of her head. 'Try the tearoom you always stop at,' but for the first time ever she hadn't stopped, she had to make up time and drove home in one fast but distracted run. She sees him reading the paper and thinks if he had a proper job to go to she could pretend she'd telephoned when he came back at the end of the day. Instead for his exclusive benefit she has to put on a charade with the Kenspeckle Tearoom. And without giving her name she asks the manager and is told what she already knows.

218

'Don't worry it'll turn up,' Nigel says. 'It's dropped off somewhere if Amy saw it on you when you left Caroline Street, so it can't be far can it? You'll see.'

The next morning, as if following a stage direction, Fiona approaches the Glenduir phone box like a spy. She dials Tim's number and the tone rings and rings to her impatient, 'come on, oh come on.'

'Hello...'

She presses the button and the money chinks into the box 'Tim it's me, I've lost my pearl necklace, I can't find it, did I?...'

'Fiona, Fiona it's alright, I've sent it, I sent it recorded delivery when I got home...'

'Thank God, where was it?'

'In the bed, I spotted it just before I left. You sound the other side of frantic?'

'It was noticed last night and I didn't know how to explain it and I'm in the village telephone box and someone might see me and wonder why.'

'Don't worry. Look here, can't I can safely phone you? Things have changed, a couple of friends have asked to take a yacht up to Montrose with them...'

'You know I never know where he will be or when he - oh God I must go, I think Robbie's waiting to use the phone, I can see him behind me in the mirror, he peered at me as he passed - try Monday evening, six-ish,' and she slams the receiver down.

Hurrying to her car, Robbie calls her name but she ignores him, and drives off in the wrong direction to the village shop in neighbouring Driech. Ahead of her the sight of the church reproaches her with its harsh, grey stone angles full of Presbyterian rectitude but all that passes in a flash. She's planning. She'll make sure she answers the door to sign for the recorded delivery parcel herself. But with that done how is she to explain the necklace's reappearance? Deception and more lies and her stomach turns. It makes her think of Amy but Nigel is in that cohort too, though that doesn't make her feel any better about her own loss of moral ground. But there's respite in Tim going away, out of any contact and at least she will have time to think without his pressure to know what she's decided. So, she lingers in Dreich Post Office over an unnecessary loaf of sliced white bread while the shopkeeper wonders why she's buying there instead of the Glenduir but he's brushed off. Fiona's mind is on only one other thing.

But Robbie has now gone to the castle with the butcher's weekly bag of bones and offal for Luath.

'Ach, I was nearly forgetting,' he says to Nigel and puts his hand in his pocket. 'Have you got something wrong with your telephone then?'

'No, why?' and Robbie puts a handful of change and a small folded piece of paper into his palm.

'There is nearly seven bob there, so there is. I was finding it in the telephone box after Fiona was using it before me. Mind, I am thinking she was in a hurry, right enough. I will not be stopping, I am needing to be on my way.'

Nigel doesn't answer, he's looking at the collection of coins in his hand as Robbie leaves. But the piece of paper is of greater interest and in Fiona's writing there's a series of numbers marked on it. Emptying his palm into his pocket he moves quickly inside and with the bloodied bag of offal in the fridge he unfolds the small scrap of paper. It reveals the word Norwich and a telephone number and it makes no sense to him that she should use a public phone box or that she has any need to be in touch with someone in Norwich. But the main door opens and the paper is put back in his pocket.

220

'Oh, you gave me a fright, Nigel,' she says with her hand up at her chest when she sees him.

'I didn't, you did it to me this time, where have you been?' he says and picks up the kettle.

'Just an errand, to get this sliced loaf,' and she twirls it in her hand. 'Do you want a piece of fruit cake, I made one before I went to Edinburgh? I'll get it.' Without looking at him she crosses the kitchen and bangs about in the larder with tins and plates. 'I'd better take my coat off and light the fire in the sitting room too, hadn't I?' she mutters.

'I've done it, here let me take your coat, relax, sit down and have a coffee.'

'No, I need to go to the lav first,' and she leaves him without even a glance in his direction.

And he waits, he can hear she hasn't gone to the cloakroom, the Victorian staircase's creaks betray her and once he can no longer hear her footfall he follows. Through their slightly open bedroom door he sees her sitting on the bed he is so pleased with that he made it himself that morning - and abruptly she turns to see him.

'Now don't tell me I've given you another fright, will you?' he says as he sits down beside her. 'Are you alright? You seem a little agitated.'

'Am I? I don't think so.'

He rests his hand on her back. 'You haven't told me much about Edinburgh yet, have you, was Amy being particularly bossy?'

'Well, you could say that - one way or another, I suppose. You know what she can be like.'

'And?' he gently pulls her to him.

'Oh it's nothing, nothing that would interest you,' and she manages to look at him.

'No, probably not. But you did enjoy yourself despite that didn't you. You saw friends?' he asks with an edge of defiance in his voice and she gives a very slight nod.

'Ah, that's good then and you're home now, mistress of your own domain and *you* call the shots, don't you?' He lifts her face, looks into her eyes for a moment then kisses her, and again with his intention made perfectly clear. But it is she who lies back and pulls him with her, she who urgently unbuttons his shirt while never letting his mouth stray far from hers. And she who tears at her own clothes, removing only as much as is needed to let him in. His urgency matches hers, each set on their own needs. But after, her hands and mouth don't stop and he feels the light rasp of her nails running through his hair and her kisses hot on his neck.

'Where are you, Fiona?' he breathes as he stops her hand and rolls them both over to face one other.

'Kiss me again,' she says with a petulant child's voice. He holds her head in the curve of his neck.

'I love you, you know that, don't you?' he says and her body relaxes in a throaty sigh but an answer doesn't come. Yet her touch is soft now in its run up and down his back under his shirt. Then she notices the neat, new bedclothes upset and skewed.

'You made the bed didn't you?' she says.

'And you lay in it,' he says amongst his kiss.

He doesn't move then falls asleep so she gently moves away from him. Looking at him almost naked, the beat of desire stirs her again. But she thinks she's been cruel, selfish to let him think that's what she wanted when it was what she had to do to stop any more worried questioning from him. And she flicks her fingers as if to scatter its contamination. Yet, she does desire him and now she's confused. And she thinks what everyone in her position thinks, that nobody has felt like she does and nobody can understand either.

Gathering her clothes together he opens his eyes and reaches out towards her. 'Why don't you come back, we don't have to be doing anything else do we?' It would be very easy, his desirability isn't in question.

She says, 'I think I should get on...'

'Do you? Please don't turn off like a tap, Fluff, that's not like you,' and he catches her hand before she can move. 'I am trying to make it up to you.'

'I know you are, it's just that it's still a little difficult.'

'Why?' accusation like the flash on a blade. 'It didn't look like that to me,' He drops her hand. 'No forget I said that - you're entitled to your anger.'

Anger? He might well think that after what he did and now it's convenient that he does, but that she lets him think it and suffer makes her feel shoddy and dirty, in fact it makes her feel quite sick for a moment. She bites the side of her lip as she looks at him lying back with his arm over his closed eyes. It is as if the vigour has drained out of him, and remorse clutches her for the first time since she's come home. In consolation her arms wrap him but to stay there means lingering intimacy, more quick gratification can't be staged. And for her neither can the closeness they'd almost re-established before she went away. Even the words to reassure him won't marshal themselves but he removes her arms anyway.

'No, it's alright, we'll take it at your pace,' he says. You go and do whatever it is you have to do, I'd better do the same,' and he grabs at his clothes without looking at her.

'Nigel.'

'No, off you go, I'll see you at lunch,' he says as he picks up his trousers and the silver coins that have fallen out of the pocket.

Now there's an atmosphere and she knows she has to remedy it but the idea of making small talk together at lunchtime is more than she thinks she can bear because she questions her ability for more deception, more cunning. She has no appetite for it. So leaving him alone, as he so clearly wants her to do, she shuts herself in the bathroom and runs a bath to immerse herself in a different physical element.

The cast iron bath is old and very long, long enough for her to lie flat out in the peaty, brown water and she lies there, her head back with her face clear, her hair fanned out, her arms outstretched, hands open like floating starfish, her legs lifting and swaying slightly on the surface. She opens her eyes when she hears the telephone ring out once then again but Nigel's voice doesn't call for her. The water isn't very hot, it never is, but she shuts her eyes again and only gets out once it's too cool and her fingers tips look like pink prunes.

From the stairs she can hear him in the kitchen and the smell of cooking offal fills the air with its reek. Nigel never notices but Fiona loathes it and there's a sort of mockery in a cauldron full of boiling hearts. She wrinkles her nose and snorts.

'That's better, you nearly laughed,' he says and takes the pan off the heat.

'Who phoned earlier?' she says.

'Nobody, it went dead... Why is your hair wet?'

'I had a bath.'

'You had a bath at this time of day?' and she nods but he turns to the pan prodding the contents with a knife and says something quietly to himself. Did he really say, 'trying to wash me away?'

The Games People Play

Fiona has something to do today, even if she doesn't feel like it. Nigel was up early and already at Dreer Field supervising everything for the annual Glenduir and Driech Highland Games. Something that's expected of him and he's surprisingly good at it. She wishes he could apply that skill to other aspects of his life. But there's no more time to think about that. This day Nigel gets into his full Highland fig to play the Laird and Clan Chief and she is expected to present the prizes and trophies.

From the back of her wardrobe she takes out her neatly tailored MacMuckle tartan skirt and tweed jacket, the ladies brogue shoes, and in case it rains, a felt hat and waterproof cape. This is exactly what her mother-in-law had worn too, but Fiona had drawn the line at having Jean's clothes altered to fit her. But she does wear Jean's magnificent, gold brooch of the MacMuckle crest, the wolf-like attack dog with ruby eyes. She looks in the mirror and sighs at the sight of herself, she feels like an imposter.

Dreer Field is green and lush, the turf shimmers in the slight breeze. It won't last; soon it will be flattened and muddied from the tread of hundreds of feet, but the arena looks festive decorated with buntings and flags. The Driech Distillery Pipe Band, rousing and accomplished, plays all the way to the field. When it stops Willie MacVicar, the Minister of Glenduir Church and the better for a dram or three, blares out of the crackling, whining loudspeaker system.

'Ladies and gentlemen, welcome to the one hundred and twenty-first Glenduir and Driech Highland Games,' he says. 'May you enjoy this fine day of friendly competition, the many stalls and stands and the refreshments too. And now I will ask The MacMuckle to do us the honour of opening the proceedings for us.'

Nigel strides across the field, kilt swinging, tweed jacket'd with his plaid slung over his shoulder, his cromach in his hand and his Chief's eagle feathers standing high in his bonnet. The extra height makes him even easier to spot wherever he is on the field. Whistling and applause accompanies him while he makes his way to the small cannon, one of a pair which for the rest of the year stands impressively on either side of Archie MacIntosh's front door. It has been used to open The Games for so long now that almost everyone assumes it saw battle in historic service of Scotland. But Archie knows his grandmother bought the pair at a country house roup in Northumberland, and of course that's never admitted. Robbie's proud duty is to hand the Chief a lighted taper and with a deft movement Nigel applies the flame and the cannon lets out a cloud of smoke and a great bang echoes round the hills and mountains.

'And with our thanks to The MacMuckle, the Glenduir and Driech Highland Games are well and truly open,' says the Minister through the loud speakers and losing out to renewed applause as the distillery pipers play MacMuckle's Rant perfectly.

Fiona, standing outside the Stewards' tent, fails to feel any pride this year, in fact she wonders how she came to find herself in this ridiculous time-slip, up a glen, almost in fancy dress pretending to be some sort of leaderene. And bearing down on her, Nigel, like an illustration from *The Clans of the Scottish Highlands* says, 'enjoying yourself? I didn't see you arrive, I didn't want to wake you this morning, I thought as you've been rather tired...'

'No - I'm alright,' she sighs and he pays no attention because the whistle has blown for the tug o' war between Driech and Glenduir.

'Come and watch the inter-glen rivalry with me, that always gets people going.'

'Do I have to? I don't want to be - got going.'

'But you always like the tug o' war?' and he takes her hand but she thinks to herself if he only knew how she was having a tug o' war of sorts herself he'd understand her disenchantment. But aware of the persona that is expected of her she goes to watch, if not cheer, Glenduir's efforts.

But crossing the arena the cacophony from all quarters of the field assaults her. The piping competition clashing with pipe music for the Highland dancing, cheers for the hammer throwing and caber tossing, starting guns, whistles, loud speaker, generators, dogs barking, there's a nightmare-ish quality about it and she pulls her hand away from his and covers her ears.

'Look, what *is* it, Fiona?' he says and stands close up in front of her. 'Are you ill?'

She shakes her head and looks away, 'no, I'm sorry, it's just the noise, I've never really noticed it before.'

'Well, go back to the Stewards' tent and have a cup of coffee or something. Will you be able to present the prizes later? I'll have to ask Georgina if she'll do it if you can't, so tell me,' and she can feel his noisy breath on her.

'Of course I'll do it.'

'Good.' And he leaves her there to go and cheer on the Glenduir tuggers.

'Hello old girl, not going to watch the tug then? ' Archie says to her then laughs, 'has Mucky abandoned you? Are you under the weather - do you want me to go and get him back for you?'

'Please don't, Archie, I'll be alright,' she sniffs. 'I was just going to the tent for a cup of...'

'As you wish, Georgina was there but she'll want to see Driech win, she's bet Mucky they will.' Fiona hears him but she's turned her back and on her way to the tent.

Mucky, Mucky, what a horrible name, she thinks. MacMuckle is nearly as bad and it's definitely very silly even if it's accurate. And what about Driech and Duir? That's so accurate too, it *is* dreich and dour in the glens and even the field is called drear. Perhaps centuries ago, up there on Ben Vernacula, some antique Highland barbarians had a sense of humour as they lay in their dents of wet heather for beds with their plaids wound round them for bedclothes, their teeth chattering, trying keep their spirits up in the absence of any for a dram. She wonders if they glimpsed the glens through the mist and literally named them. And as she reaches the tent she thinks of Georgina earlier on making matey bets with Nigel over the din and guffaws of Glaykit MacLummie and his like, all of them gathered together like a tribal herd in this exclusive enclave. And none of them notice how archaic and entitled they appear, they're all so inured to it that they think it normal...

'Eh, hello you, are you alright, Fiona?'

'What?'

'I thought I heard you say, what am I doing here?' Georgina says. 'Are you supposed to be at the tug o' war? It's started, I'm on my way?'

'Did I? I don't know. I was going to get a cup of something, I'll do that,' Fiona ignores her friend and walks away, so Georgina does the same.

The tent is deserted except for Lord and Lady Stravaig, too frail to do anything else except sit, she in her tartan get-up much like Fiona's but old, neatly mended and carefully cared for. Ossian Stravaig again in his over-sized, moth-eaten kilt, lame but still making a valiant effort to stand on his skinny shanks when he sees Fiona.

228

'They've all gone to watch the tug o' war, Fiona dear,' Lady Stravaig tells her, 'why don't you come and sit over here with Ossian and me, you can tell us all the news, we don't get many visitors at home these days, they're all either dead or ga-ga and of course we don't get out much ourselves, this is such a great treat to be here today. Nigel, that dear boy of yours is such a duck, he saw to it that we have everything we might need. He even had them put a chemical lavatory just outside the tent for us. He's so like his darling father,' and she sighs, 'isn't he Ossian? It was such a loss you know, Fiona dear.' But Ossian's chin is on his chest, he's now snoozing and gently dribbling a half chewed toffee down his Highland Line Club tie.

'Yes I'll sit with you, thank you very much,' Fiona says and there's something touching about this dear, old pair so pleased to be there, though they must have endured The Games for half a century at least. So down on their uppers these days, so grateful for so little and always counting their blessings. 'Can I pour the coffee for you?' she says when she notices how much Grizel Stravaig's hand shakes.

'Don't mind Ossian, we'll let him sleep, he's had a good go at the whisky Nigel gave us. But, Fiona, you must have a piece of this plum cake your dear boy got at the tombola and gave us, he says we can take it home. Perhaps you would cut it for us too.'

And the coffee is as weak and tepid as poor, old Lord Stravaig and the cake as sweet as his wife and when it is handed to her, her gratitude begins all over again. Fiona looks at the snoring Ossian knowing him only as a diminished old man, not the man of once legendary appetites. The peer who sat in The House of Lords but lay with their wives whenever the opportunity offered. And his wife looks at him affectionately, she pats his thin veined hand with her own gnarled fingers.

'He sleeps a lot these days. He deserves to, he had a very tiring life in the Lords, you know, he was back and forth, back and forth you see.' And Fiona smiles at the appropriateness of her words as she looks at Nigel in the distance through a gap in the tent's side. You can't miss him done up as he is and he's laughing - laughing a lot. Georgina is hanging on to his arm obviously heckling him as the heaving Glenduir team, red-faced and almost horizontal appears to be winning. And there's Archie unsurprisingly standing apart as emotionless and static as that caber on the ground waiting to be tossed...

'Where's that pretty, little wife of young Nigel's gone, Grizel?' Ossian says coming to with a snort, half-opened eyes and a wipe of his mouth. 'Oh, you're still here. Coffee and cake now is it - can I have some?' And with the old man set up, Fiona excuses herself and heads off back to the field just as the Glenduir team wins and collapses on the ground like a line of dominoes.

'Oh boo hoo. I owe you a fiver, Nigel, don't I? Georgina says, 'Archie can you give him the money, I was so sure Dreich was going to do it. Did you see that, Fiona?'

'Yes, just caught the winning moment, well done Glenduir,' and she looks at Nigel who is looking at her but then he looks away.

'Nigel?'

'Yes, what is it?' he says as Archie puts five pound notes in his hand and tells him not to spend it all on sweets - that raises a laugh. 'What were you going to say, I hope it's not that you won't do the prizes.'

'No, I said I would didn't I? So I will. It's the old Stravaigs in the tent, I had coffee with them, I hadn't realised how frail they are now. She spoke kindly of you, she was so grateful to you,...'

'Well, I'm glad someone is. Anyway, I'm off to talk to those Canadian clansmen now, you'll find me in the Clan Society tent.'

230

'Can't I come too?' and he turns round to look at her, his shoulders drop and he cocks his head with a sigh.

'Oh come on, Fluff, take my arm,' they haven't walked far when he says, 'Poor old Stravaigs, eh? He led her a merry dance and he wasn't discreet about it either, she must have loved him...' Fiona doesn't answer.

How men like Archie and Nigel manage to consume so much whisky and barely show it has always been a mystery to Fiona. The MacIntoshes arrive for supper and Archie looks as neat as he did when he set out for the Games in the morning. He steers Georgina in who admits she's giggly and everyone else would consider tiddly. But Archie is full of indignation over the, 'bogus Lord Johnny Come-Lately of Thane who's converted that cottage into a gin palace, and now he's written a so-called novel about life the Highlands. Did you see him trying to get into our tent to flog it? The brass neck of the man, what does he know about Highland life? Well, I bought his tawdry penny-dreadful and I'll...'

'Hark at him and his penny-dreadful,' Georgina cuts across Archie's rant. 'I wonder you know what that is. It will be the first book you've ever read,' and she laughs at that though the others don't appear to understand. 'Well, Archie's never read a book, have you, Archie, you old fool?'

'What rot you speak, of course I've read a book.'

'Archie, you've never read a novel!'

'Novels - quite right, never read one since school, don't need stories, I just want to see what rubbish the idiot has written. Give me information every time,' he says with a self-satisfied sniff. And I haven't seen a play since our honeymoon either when I had to endure some mystifying production called, *Look Back in Anger.*' He nods at Georgina, 'she described it as a bathroom sink drama - God knows why - she said it was thought-provoking, I thought it was pointless and dire, but I didn't say so because I was playing the amorous groom at that point.' At this Georgina rolls her eyes.

Fiona wonders if Archie could ever have been amorous and that he even knows the word but then she remembers his rumoured collection of Japanese erotic prints, except that Nigel had told her it wasn't a rumour, he'd seen them.

'Did you ever read *Lady Chatterley's Lover*, Mucky?' Archie says and Fiona nearly chokes.

'I have - but I thought you said you didn't read novels,' he replies not missing a beat.

'That doesn't count.'

'Remember what the lawyer said in Court?' Nigel warns. 'Would you let your wife or your servants read it?' I gave Robbie my copy...'

'Ah, but has Fiona read it?' Georgina asks.

And sharply Fiona says, 'no - no I haven't.'

'Rumpy pumpy with the hired help?' Fiona has never seen Georgina like this before and she cuts her off.

'Yes I know, I know what it's about - it really isn't Lawrence's best work though, that's what people said.'

'I don't think it was honestly read for its literary merit, Fiona,' and Georgina might be laughing but that's patronising too.

'No, I know that, I mean... Oh I don't know what I mean, we've all had too much to drink.'

'You're quite safe, Fiona,' says Archie, 'it won't put ideas in your head, Mucky isn't incapacitated like Lady C's old man is he? Anyway, Robbie is a dead ringer for Mucky - you probably wouldn't notice.'

'Thanks very much old chum,' says Nigel.

'Oh, a reputation to keep, is that it? So are you the one responsible for all the red-heads in your glen?' and Archie laughs his honking laugh.

232

'Don't be ridiculous, Archie, that's the small gene pool, it's a clan MacMuckle thing, lots of them have red hair,' Fiona says and he pays no attention to her, he's too amused by his own supposed wit. With her head down Georgina is trying not to laugh and Nigel seems to be trying to keep a straight face too, though he manages to give Fiona a knowing glance.

But Georgina says she thinks Archie's gone too far but she's still keeping her laughter in check. Not unsympathetic to Fiona, Archie tells her to pay no attention to him though he's far from convincing and Nigel seems to find that funny too. So she looks at him as he shakes his head in a meaningless way as far as she can see. What else can he do? Then she laughs with them for fear of looking humourless. She knows the MacIntoshes think she's being priggish, she knows that's what Archie wants to say, she knows that's what she sounded like and she knows that's not what she meant at all. And just as the improbability of other people's sex lives flashes through her head, Nigel gets back at Archie by mocking his teenage admiration for Katy MacDonald's legs in fishnet tights. The single reason he could be persuaded to take part in a local war effort pantomime in 1944. Georgina has a good excuse now to let her laughter rip especially at Nigel's description of Archie's insistence that he should be the front end of the pantomime horse because that was the best place from where he could ogle the girl. And Archie replies Nigel ogled Margaret Robertson's chest just as much.

Georgina's giggles calm down only enough to say, 'well, Nigel, when I was sixteen I couldn't take my eyes off your chest and your legs when you rowed the loch - and when you went swimming with Archie and Glay,' then she hiccups.

'I never knew that,' says Archie quite seriously now. 'That must have been an eyeful for you,' and he looks at Fiona, 'we swam in the buff like Spartan youths, you see.'

'Spartan youths you say?' Georgina taunts. 'Well, I saw only one,' and she looks at Nigel while she does a sideways slump back into her chair. 'Fiona, I didn't plan it, I used to walk my dog there and anyway everyone knew all the girls in the Distillery office used to watch them too. So there, Archie.'

'Did you know that, Mucky?' Archie snorts.

'Nope, I did not, quite flattering though!' and it's clear he's enjoying it.

'Oh dear, I shouldn't have said that,' Georgina says with another punctuating hiccup. 'I have a very low booze threshold you know,' and everybody does know it but she reaches for her wine anyway, leans towards Nigel and twiddles his hair. 'Oh what the Hell, in for a penny in for a pound, I like your glorious thatch too and I always have,' and hiccups again.

'Drink some water, Georgina, cool down, you are getting frisky,' Archie commands and she sticks her tongue out at him and calls him a buffer.

'I'll have to find myself a gamekeeper then won't I?' she says. 'I don't care for ours, I think I'll have Robbie...' and hiccups again before she can finish.

Now Archie cuts across her, 'Georgina, calm down will you,' he says, tapping the table and Nigel is very clearly enjoying this.

'Fat chance,' Georgina giggles even more and drinks water - for her hiccups.

But Fiona can get away, she can clear the plates while they compare their stories of local 'hanky-panky' which she'd usually want to hear. But in passing, she ruffles the top of Nigel's admirable head of hair. His hand reaches out behind him and holds hers for a moment.

Of course Fiona knows what's going on, she's seen it before, the truth of Georgina's domestic situation playing out in drink. But Nigel could have had her and didn't. Did Archie - does Archie realise he was second best? Second best, the idea is too painful to explore. But the subject of infidelity had taken second place, it hadn't affected Fiona at all. It's her possessiveness which is paramount and she feels how she did when Mary had tried to take Nigel over - only now she feels it more, much more. Fiona doesn't think herself possessive - she isn't - and she understands Georgina's admiration. Does the priority of her possession tell her something she thinks she doesn't want to know she wonders.

When the MacIntoshes leave, Archie about to drive well under the influence and saying his Bentley knows the way home, it is then that Nigel beckons her to him.

He takes a deep breath and says, 'Flashers didn't know what he was saying, how could he? Of course you were right, it's the gene pool...'

'Yes, but were you really putting it about on your own doorstep?'

And he laughs as he asks, 'where on earth did you learn to say something like that? He lifts an eyebrow as if he is expecting her to reply but she doesn't.

All she offers is, 'Georgina has a thing for you.'

'She always did, you know that don't you?' and she just shakes her head as meaninglessly as he had earlier. And then it isn't difficult to do what he wants, the fire still glows and there's a satiny tiger skin rug in front of it. The brush of five o'clock shadow mixed with whiskey-ed breath in hot kisses and caresses unwinds her. Something of yesterday morning's fervour blooms, but this time it's undressed and unselfish and Fiona thinks herself very fickle.

Damage limitation

Robbie drives slowly up to the castle, he always does, his exhaust pipe is broken by the pot holes and never mended. The post van follows him at a short distance and just as carefully. Shuggie, the postman, complains about the state of the drive and Robbie tells him nothing will be done about it and he should know that by now. Under his breath he adds that he thinks things are going from bad to worse, but Shuggie should be keeping that to himself - right enough. And he takes the post from him, signing for the recorded delivery parcel.

Robbie never uses the huge iron knocker on the castle's main door, like all previous generations of his family he comes and goes as he pleases. He puts the post down on the oak table along with two hares he promised Fiona for the pot. When Nigel appears he's told that someone has dumped a large quantity of bottles down by the loch and Robbie will deal with it tomorrow.

After he's gone Nigel picks up the mail, there's a bill in its manila envelope, a letter from his cousin Charlie Scott - and for Fiona, a recorded delivery packet. It feels soft underneath its outer wrapping, like tissue paper covering what? He presses it and feels something identifiable in the small, hard spheres. Fingering them like a rosary in a pouch, he counts ten in a loose huddle and the slight grating movement of their chain. Turning the packet over he looks at the postmark - Norwich - and puts it and his own post back on the table again. His tread is more like a kick as he goes to grab his old coat and scarf then roughly he orders his dog to come to him.

236

Fiona doesn't hear him, cream whipping in the Kenwood Chef blots him out. She's aware of the time, she's expecting the post van, and when the cream is whipped to peaks she looks at the clock then her watch, both tell the same time so Shuggy must be late today. But even though she knows that, she can't resist going to look down the drive in case he's coming but there's no sign of anyone or anything. Leaning against the main door when she comes in again the oak table is straight in her sight-line and her stomach flips. She almost skids across the stone floor to grab the parcel.

Swallowing hard when she picks it up, she handles the promise of her pearls, she sees the Norwich postmark stamped quite clearly. 'Oh for God's sake,' she says out loud - very loud - and then thinks, Nigel signed for it, he's going to ask. But clarity cuts across her guilty reasoning as she sees the other post, both envelopes are for him and he would have taken them and left hers on the table, that's what he always does. Then there's the two dead-eyed hares tied together at the feet and she knows Robbie said yesterday that he'd bring them. And it all falls into place, Robbie and Shuggie always gossip if they find each other there so it had to be Robbie who signed for it, who brought the post in, who put everything down together. Nigel isn't about, his coat and cromach aren't there, he's out with Luath, he must be. There's a sigh of relief as she puts the packet in her pocket. And there's a flash of inspiration born of desperate necessity. She is going to go outside to her car and push the necklace down the back of the driver's seat. But the charade of finding it would have to wait until she next drives the car and Nigel is there to see the find, as if not articulating the lie lessens it.

She's sticking meringues together with the cream, praying to be forgiven for her deception when Nigel comes in. 'What have you done?' she asks and drops a meringue into the cream.

'Cut my hand on a bottle,' he says, his right hand covered in blood and now under the cold tap. She takes it to look at the gash in his palm and asks what he was doing with a bottle.

'A big heap of them down at the loch. I was throwing them in and one of them bloody well broke in my hand then I picked the bits up and cut myself again. Ouch!'

'Sorry, didn't mean to hurt you, it looks deep, stay there and I'll get a bandage, but I think it needs stitches.'

'Don't fuss, it'll be alright all it needs is that Dettol stuff on it,' and he drips blood over to the AGA and winds a tea towel round his hand.

'No, look at it, I'm going to take you down to Fin Livingstone, he can decide what it needs, come on I'll drive you there now. Why on earth were you throwing bottles into the loch anyway?'

'Huh, I don't know - seemed like a good idea. Do I have to go to the Doc's, it'll stop in a minute.'

But Fiona insists, a little blood goes a long way but there seems to be so much that it alarms her. She pushes him to her car and opens the passenger door for him.

He says, 'I've got blood all over the seat,' and bends over to uselessly brush it away making it worse. 'What's that?' he points with his good hand.

'Get in, Nigel.'

'No, that there - down the back of your seat,' and he stretches over to pull at the inch of gold chain peeping up at him. 'How did that...?' he says and holds the rest of the question back while liberating eighteen inches of gold chain strung with ten pearls.

'Oh that's... Nigel, you're bleeding all over the place, get in.'

'Well don't you want it? Take it,' and he shakes it in his closed fist.

'Just put it in the glove box for the moment, I need to get you to the Doctor,' and she drives off in a misjudged lurch.

It wasn't supposed to have been like this and she isn't primed to act surprised gratitude at his discovery, so all she can do is pat his knee hoping he'll take that as her more important concern for his welfare, which at that moment it indeed is. He doesn't speak on their short journey and she pats him again saying she thinks he's had more of a shock than he realises. And he nods at that while staring ahead. Stuck for any other words all she can muster are the sort of blandishments used for a child; 'not long now - nearly there,' and, 'here we are.'

'Anyone would think I'd tried to slit my wrists,' Nigel says to Fin Livingstone after sitting in the waiting room with his arm and blood soaked tea towel up in the air. It was the gasps of the other waiting patients all of them too deferential to ask the Laird what's happened. And Fiona had been right, he does need stitches and antibiotics too. So, Nigel with his bandaged hand in a sling and paler than he'd been before he got in her car makes the return journey as silently as before. But once home he doesn't forget to take the necklace with him.

'Here you are then,' he says handing it to her as they go in.

'Thank you, I...'

'I said it would turn up - didn't I?'

'I'll take better care in future.'

'Will you?' he says as he picks up his two letters from the table. 'Can you open these for me? I'm no use with just my left hand?'

The urge to look after him surfaces easily. He never makes a fuss about illness but his unusual quietness and pallor make her think he is in more pain than he's letting on. And from experience she knows there's no point in saying anything, instead she puts her hand up to his face. Catching her wrist he pulls away slightly. Her surprise registers in a momentary start and all she can think to say is that she'll find some paracetamol for him after she's helped him take off his coat.

'Put your necklace on for me,' he says.

'I will, but I'm taking care of you...'

'Are you?'

'Of course I am, but if it makes you happy,' and she hangs the chain round her neck and fastens it.

'That's better,' he says and arranges it on her throat with a caress.

With great reluctance he takes what he thinks is paracetamol but is something stronger and it makes him fall asleep by the fire. With his dog at his feet and asleep too, Fiona puts an old MacMuckle tartan travelling rug over him and for a moment she stands there looking at him. It's a bad gash yet even so his reaction to it seems disproportionate for him, but it's knocked into place when she tells herself it's guilt talking again and reassures herself that his colour is better now.

It's rare for Nigel not to take Luath out twice a day, but comfortable by the fire with a book and whisky in place, he stays put. There are only two telephones in Glenduir Castle, one near the main outside door thirty feet away from where he sits and another in their bedroom. If Nigel doesn't move somewhere else then Fiona will have to take Tim's call sotto voce with her head down and facing the wall, she can't hang about waiting in the bedroom. In fact she almost wishes he wasn't calling at all. She sits slightly crouched over at the ready as if she were on starting blocks.

'Got a pain?' he asks.

'No, why?'

'Bent over aren't you - or are you cold?' and she sits back. 'I'm going to have to ask you help me with my bath, I think.'

'That's alright, when do you want it?'

'What about now?' and he closes his book.

240

'Right now - don't you want another drink?' she says as the telephone rings out.

'Saved by the bell, can you get that and if it's for me say I'll phone back tomorrow.'

With acted composure and a lack of urgency she doesn't feel, Fiona goes to the door and pulls it to behind her. A deep breath and her heart bumping, head down and facing the wall, sotto voce, she answers. 'I'm sorry but I really can't talk, Nigel's next door. The necklace came today... '

'Hello, we don't have much luck do we? I tried to phone the other day, Nigel answered. Anyway, I thought you said he wouldn't be there?'

'No he shouldn't - but something cropped up, sorry.'

'Pity, but if you can't talk the most important thing is that I'm going to be away, I said didn't I that three of us are delivering a yacht to Montrose? I thought it too good an opportunity to miss...'

'When?'

'I'll be there by Thursday the others are going off on a distillery crawl for a few days but I've said I probably can't. I thought we could meet somewhere?'

'Where?'

'Wherever you like.'

'I don't know, I can't think, this is so difficult.'

'Look, there is a small hotel in Tapselteerie I've found that's out of the way and it's off your patch...'

'I know it, I've passed it in the car. I suppose so but I can't stay, I'll have to get back.'

'I know that, but at least we can talk, plan... well I hope we can plan,' but she doesn't acknowledge that. 'So shall I book myself in for the Thursday night and you'll come down on the Friday?'

'Erm, the Friday, yes. I'll know where to find you, I can't talk, I can hear him moving about. Oh Tim, it's so difficult, so difficult. I mean life just interrupts all the time.'

'I know it does. I miss you, I wish there was some other way, have you given *us* any thought, can you give me anything to hold on to until I see you?' he asks. 'Everything is so frustratingly rushed. You know there's nothing to stop me finding a job in Scotland, I've been thinking about it. Perhaps you could think about that too while I'm away?'

'I can't - I mean I have to go, I really can hear him,' she says as Nigel sneezes and moves about. 'Take care and I hope you enjoy your trip. Thanks for getting my necklace to me...'

'Think of me, won't you. I'll be thinking of you,' he says.

'I will.'

Should she to go back into the sitting room or should she wait and hope any curiosity Nigel might have will have waned. But the close sound of his tacked soles give him away and the door opens.

'Who was that?'

'Amy.'

'I see, you usually have a chin-wag on a Sunday don't you?' and he waits as she fiddles with a pencil.

'I know but, so do you want your bath now?'

'That's what I was going to ask. Come to think of it I'll have to ask you to shave me tomorrow morning too. Quite the nursemaid aren't you?'

'Does it hurt?'

'What do you think?'

Tapselteerie

Bags, boxes and baskets wait at the foot of the stairs to be taken up to Jean's rooms and filled with her leftovers. Fiona wants to get on with this job, it takes her mind off the decision she's promised to consider because with every day that passes it is becoming more difficult.

Nigel, his hand on the mend and out of its sling, is trying to make himself useful and eager to help her. 'I thought I'd give you a hand - get it?' he says waving his uninjured one. He likes his own joke, but she tells him it's poor by his standards. 'I've made a list but it's in my head - I think when we've cleared up Ma's rooms we should tackle the library,' he says. 'Then as you'll have to get the letting bedrooms decorated I thought you'd like to get our bedroom done too. So what do think of that to be going on with?'

'Are you sure?' she asks him though she's really asking herself.

'What? I thought you'd jump at it', and he looks quite peeved. 'You've wanted to do up our bedroom ever since you came here, not to mention...'

'Of course I would...' and she would, but she can't do or say anything else. And every time she thinks about her deceit she's noticed she feels slightly sick. But she puts her arms round him, 'you surprised me, that's all,' she says which is the truth but it's best to get back to the job in hand. 'I'm going to be ruthless about throwing things away, you know,' she says, knowing Nigel won't be comfortable with that; it isn't his habit. But having burned the ancestral bed he set a precedent.

And he pushes his shoulder against Jean's door to open it and comments on the staying power of cigarette smoke. That acrid smell, spilled spirits and sickly freesia talcum powder still incenses the rooms, but to Fiona it is Jean's Shalimar scent which insinuates itself.

'It always amused me that your so correct mother, so polished and groomed, could often be seen in the most unlikely of places with a fag hanging out of her mouth, even if it was a Black Russian. I used to wonder if she smoked in the bath.'

Nigel stops trying to open the sealed window with one hand, 'Never noticed, it was just part of her. I suppose it was the tyranny of addiction, that and the drink killed her I'd say. I tried to smoke; I didn't like it and didn't persevere.' Then with one final yank and push the window miraculously opens and he looks out towards the mountain, 'I'd forgotten how good the views are, you get a quite new perspective,' but Fiona doesn't answer. Nigel has admitted for the first time that he knows his mother drank. To discuss it might chase away his new ease with difficult discussion, that has been so hard won she was not going to scare it off.

Opened drawers reveal packets and boxes containing schoolboy letters from Nigel and hundreds of loose photographs. Under the lining paper of one drawer, wrapped in a piece of thin but unworn, brown paper, Fiona finds a copy of Marie Stopes's *Married Love*; she doesn't mention it and puts it at the bottom of a box. A court cupboard opens with a shriek of stiff hinges, inside they both see the empty vodka and whisky bottles lying on their sides and bundles of yellowing newspaper. In a chest, Nigel finds pieces of his school uniform, moth-eaten and decaying garments now only fit for an exclusively educated scarecrow and he wonders out loud why they've been kept. Fiona has a fair idea of what Jean intended, but doesn't tell him. In the next layer down she finds tissue bundles, opens them and strokes the fine lawn of beautifully made baby gowns. A bigger packet tied with blue ribbon delivers a magnificent christening robe of lace and satin in very good condition. That Nigel ever fitted into it amuses them both and belies the pang she feels. But he's fascinated by his uniform coat and holds it up again examining the moth holes, yet he's perfectly happy to see it dispatched on the next bonfire. But the little garments are too beautiful and precious to throw away, she wants to keep them and she looks at him - after all he'd worn them. She carefully folds them again and absent-mindedly pats them when she put them down on the table. He glances at that and gives her a gentle smile. But she goes back to rummaging in the cupboard and finds a flat, broken box on the other shelf and takes it to the window where Nigel wrestles, one handed, with the dusty curtains. It's a circlet of orange blossom crafted from little, wax flowers, fine gilt wire and green silk leaves, it's Jean's bridal headdress she's seen it in the wedding photograph downstairs. It is beautiful and he puts it on Fiona's head, he wants her to keep it on, it suits her he says, though that feels wrong to her. These concealed personal mementos in Jean's sitting room seem to accuse her of intrusion - even voyeurism. Only the wardrobe and bedroom drawers had been emptied quickly, she hadn't wanted to linger in a place so recently vacated by the woman with whom she'd had such an uncomfortable relationship. Yet as the morning passes with each disclosure from within that room she finds she can take more possession. And so as she slowly pulls at the bundles of old newspaper in a drawer a drinking glass reveals itself.

'Hey, look at this,' she says as she holds up an engraved glass, then another both similar and old.

'I remember those, they're Jacobite glass,' Nigel says looking up from the old photographs.

'Why did she bring them up here? She took more than enough ordinary glasses from downstairs, I had to buy new ones for us.' Fiona says as she huffs on one and polishes it with her sleeve.

'I think they're valuable, I expect she thought I'd sell them and if she couldn't hide paintings she could squirrel glass away quite easily. I suppose we've always had them being Jacobites and all that. I'll ring Graham and ask him about their value, if they're duds we can use them ourselves,' and back he goes to his pile of photographs.

The bags puff up full of cushions, bedding and blankets and with the curtains they will join Nigel's old school clothes on the bonfire. All that is left to deal with is Jean's dressing table and Fiona makes it her own task.

The engraved, silver dressing-table set and the silver mounted cut glass bottles will go to the sale room even though she agrees with Nigel that it doesn't seem right to sell them. But she uses her own mother's and he appears to quietly accept that reason. She seals the Shalimar bottle in paper and drops it in another bag following it with everything from the drawers. With its mirror removed Jean's dressing table stands eyeless in its skirts of shabby, limp muslin. A tug and a rip at the drapery unfrocks it in shreds. A snatch at the top cover leaves a dusty cloud and the bare wood piece revealed of all its trappings.

'Bonfire?' he asks.

'The dressing table? Oh yes, I think so,' and she pushes the muslin rags into the bag then holds it open. 'Can you put that mummified raven in here too, it's in the grate - and the mice there.' She points at the log basket.

'I didn't notice,' he drops them in the bag and a blast of cold air reminds him to close the open window. He insists on carrying the small box of glasses downstairs himself, they've found more in the same drawer. All that is left in the room are contents sentenced by coloured dots. Red for keep, green for go and amber for burning.

Once Fiona has carefully washed and dried the glasses they stand like a display while Nigel telephones Graham. He immediately recognises what they are from the description. Three are different from the others; those are engraved with outlawed Jacobite symbols and an anthem which finishes with the word, Amen. Cautiously, though with barely concealed excitement, Graham adds that if genuine they are known as Amen glasses and are particularly rare and very valuable. The expert will verify and value them if Nigel brings them to Edinburgh and Graham wants that to be soon.

The good news demands a toast but Fiona won't let Nigel use the Amen glasses. A couple of free-gift tumblers from the petrol station are pushed at him and he reaches out to straighten Fiona's bridal circlet. 'Let's go to Edinburgh soon - together? You can have some time with Amy and when we come back we can crack on with the library, yes?'

'Amen to that,' she jokes. 'But I have to go down to Perthshire to look at some second-hand hotel crockery and cutlery for my B and B, it's being sold off. I can get it cheaper than buying new I thought,' she says quietly while playing with a stray thread in her skirt.'

'When's that then?'

'Friday - I'll be away for the day.'

'Why aren't you using what we've got already?'

'Because it's either mis-matched petrol station and Woolworths stuff or rather precious cracked Spode and silver,' and she's still not looking at him.

'Oh right, so where are you going?'

'Perthshire - I said.'

'Yes, but where exactly?'

'Mm? Oh Tapselteerie,' and she pulls the thread clean out.

'Well, it might be worth it I suppose.'

And how sickening it is to have to lie again after some days of not needing to, but she can't risk letting him organise going to Edinburgh on that Friday. That was much more important than second-hand crockery even if her story were true. But with a guilty heart beating hard and her stomach in a knot she sits down heavily and sees Nigel struggling to open a bottle with one hand. She sees herself in a mirror on the wall too, the bridal head-dress askew again and thinks about marriage vows. *Love, honour... Forsaking all others and holding only unto him...* Him, Nigel, doing his best, trying so hard, and she finds it hurts so she snatches the head-dress off. He asks her why she did that and with a barely concealed scowl she says it's irritating her head. Now she's getting slick and quick with her lies, how quickly one becomes practised in these things and she goes to squirt the soda water from the syphon into his drink for him.

'What time do you think you'll get back?' Nigel asks at breakfast and from behind the newspaper Fiona says she can't be sure - six or seven o'clock probably.

'You say it's hotel stuff - hope it's suitable, it's a long way to go otherwise. Anyway, take care won't you, this rain is pretty heavy you know. I'll see you off then the vet's coming to look at the old bull.'

It takes two hours in that pouring rain to reach Tapselteerie and Fiona parks, or is it hides, her car round the back of the small hotel thinking one mustn't take anything for granted. With her hat pulled down against the wind and rain she runs for the door feeling excitement now she is away from home. The small reception area is warm with a fire in the grate and taking her hat off she shakes her hair free.

'A dirty day, so it is,' a neat, small woman says as she appears from the office. 'Can I help you?'

'Ah, thank you, yes,' Fiona puffs, 'I'm here to see Mr Robinson, he's a guest here.'

'Mr Robinson?' the woman says turning the register round to look at the residents' names. 'Nooo, we do not appear to have a gentleman of that name staying with us.'

'He arrived yesterday?'

'No, sorry - see for yourself there is nobody with that name staying here,' and she turns the book round for Fiona to read for herself.

'But, I don't... Is there another hotel in Tapselteerie perhaps?'

'Oh no, just us. Tapselteerie's a wee place, and we only have the six bedrooms. There is not even a public house, people use the bar here.'

'Maybe he's expected today? Maybe I've made a mistake.'

'Well I can go and ask Bruce, he's in the office. It's a Mr Robinson you say.'

'Yes, Mr Timothy Robinson - but it's possible he might have booked under Lieutenant-Commander Robinson,' Fiona calls after her not leaving anything to chance. She can hear two voices then a tall, dapper man appears with the receptionist.

'Good morning to you Madam, now maybe I can help you,' he says, 'I took a booking from a Mr Robinson - that was Tuesday - he booked for arrival yesterday and expected to be here over the weekend. Well, I have to tell you he has not turned up and we have been given no notification of either a cancellation or a change of plan. I'm not saying he will not arrive today, but he has not informed us of that fact. He'll have to pay for last night, mind. He asked for our best room, it is very vexing when people do that sort of thing. So, Madam, if you want to contact the gentleman you are welcome to use our telephone here.'

'Did he give you a telephone number?' she asks.

'No, Madam, he said that wasn't possible.'

'So you have not got a contact number for Mr Robinson then?' the receptionist asks tracking Fiona's every movement with her curious eyes.

'No, he's travelling. Do you think I could have some coffee and biscuits, I think I'll wait.'

'As you wish, Madam, and anything else we can do please do not hesitate to ask,' and under his breath to the fascinated receptionist, 'come on Morag - the coffee tray.'

Sitting by the fire and Fiona cannot believe there isn't a reasonable explanation for Tim's non-appearance. He has to come today, he just has to, something must have held him up, maybe this rain has caused flooding further east and he will telephone as soon as he can find a telephone box.

Two hours later she is still there reading an out of date copy of *The Scottish Field* and with another coffee tray. Morag keeps finding things to do at the reception desk and every time the telephone rings Fiona listens hopefully to the one-sided conversation, Tim is bound to be in touch. Every time the door opens she looks up and every time it is someone she's never seen before in her life all of them commenting on the state of the weather, and her heart sinks. Then without asking, Morag brings her a round of ham sandwiches with the compliments of the hotel. She's thanked, though Fiona has lost her appetite. So Morag waits, she warms her hands by the fire and asks if Fiona has come far.

'Further north,' she replies with a half-hearted smile and a small bite of the sandwich.

'Well, the weather is creating havoc on the roads you know, we've got the wireless on in the office and there's flooding, vehicles overturned, so maybe you better keep that in mind for your journey home?' But Fiona will not be drawn, she won't give anything away. 'Your sandwiches OK then?'

'Yes thank you.'

'Are you wanting more mustard, I can get it for you?'

'No thank you they are very good as they are.'

'Well what about more coffee, would you like that?'

'Really this is just fine,' and she takes another bite to avoid having to speak.

Moving to a window, Morag peers out. 'Och look at that, old MacLachlan's fallen off his bike, he shouldn't be out in this weather and he'll be the worse for drink too,' and she grabs an umbrella to go and rescue the old man. Fiona is thankful for the old man's accident, she puts out money for the coffee and leaves as discreetly as she can. But Morag in the rain, umbrella turned inside out, and struggling to get the old man on his feet sees Fiona drive off and from the office window so does Bruce.

With windscreen wipers on fast and skimming through the wet like a water-ski she drives to the nearest town and spends time in a bigger more anonymous hotel there. She hasn't given up hope, she plans to go back to the Tapselteerie later, Tim must come, he will be there, she's so sure of it.

Back home at Glenduir chaos reigns because it rains, the river Duir has broken its banks and the roads flooded. Telephone lines from the main road are in peril of failing and Nigel in his castle high on a bluff is about the only person who can be sure the water's ingress will only happen through the roof. The telephone rings.

'Muckle Nigel, you will be wanting to know there is a cattle truck capsized at the Burn End corner and flooding too, so you cannot be using that road, you will have to be taking the long way round if you are needing to get out, so you will.' Robbie says, always so clear with his instructions. 'What a bourach so it is, electricity cables hanging so I would not be counting on having power for much longer, right enough.' You will need to be going to check on the bull soon.'

'The bull is fine, Robbie, but Fiona is coming back from Tapselteerie, I'll have to get a message to her not to try to come by Burn End. I'll do that now, thanks.' And what Nigel has in mind is that she should leave her car in a safe place before the worst of the flooding in Glenduir and he will pick her up from there.

'Good afternoon this is the Tapselteerie Hotel?' Morag says into the telephone with her best Morningside elocution.

Nigel replies with, 'ah - I would like to talk to the lady who's looking to buy some of your second hand crockery,' and there is a pause.

'I am sorry Sir you must be making a mistake we are not selling anything like that, we need all the crockery we've got.'

'You're sure are you? This line sounds like frying bacon, did you hear me right?'

'That's the rain making it do that. Yes Sir I'm sure, my husband and myself are the proprietors, I'd know if we were selling the plates, wouldn't I?'

'Well then is there another hotel in Tapselteerie?'

'No Sir, there is not and you are the second person to ask that today as it happens.'

'Right, is there a blonde lady in her twenties with you by any chance? She's pretty, wearing a checked skirt and blue jumper, a beige coloured Macintosh, she drives a red...'

'Oooh right, so are you Lieutenant-Commander Timothy Robinson who was booked for last night because she was expecting to see you, if that's the same lady, though she didn't say anything about crockery. And she had a wee, red mini minor car too, she's gone now. Anyway are we to expect you Sir or are you cancelling?'

252

'There's been a mix-up. Do you know where she was going?'

'No, the line is not good. Well these things happen, no, I don't know where she's gone.'

'I'm not making myself clear. My name isn't Robinson and I've obviously got the wrong hotel.'

Morag speaks up and slowly, 'I said the line's bad, can you hear me clearly now? You've...'

'I *can* hear you. I said my name *isn't* Robinson...'

'Aw that's a shame for sure, I see on the booking form Mr Robinson is from Norwich, I've got a sister living there you see...'

'Well, jolly good for her, but I am not Robinson. Good day to you.' Nigel slams the telephone down and in a rising crescendo he spits, 'Norwich, Norwich, fucking Norwich,' and the lights go out. 'Oh bugger, that's great, that is.' Like a rat out of a trap he gets up only to stumble over Luath, bang his bad hand against the table and nearly kick the dog. 'Fuck it, fuck the fucking lot,' he hisses and sits down again in the gloom with his head bent over, his hand throbbing and Luath barking at the commotion. There is nothing else he can do but go now and wait for Fiona. Doing something is better than ruminating any further.

The Hunting Stewart Hotel at Lippen has a better selection of reading material and Fiona sits by their fire and progresses to tea and scones. Nobody there is interested in quizzing her intentions and her mind keeps drifting to all the reasons why Tim has let her down, except she can't bring herself to accept that he has. She tells herself it has to be a mishap, it has to be connected with the weather. People within earshot say lines are down and roads are flooded so why should they be any different on the journey from Montrose. It's easy to tell herself that Tim is holed up somewhere since yesterday with complete loss of communication. But just in

253

case - she will go back to the Tapselteerie Hotel now, they might have heard from him or he might even have arrived.

'Back again, Madam? You're brave to be out in your wee car in this.' It's Bruce from the office who's at the reception desk this time.

'Has Mr Robinson...?'

'Neither sight nor sound, I cannot keep the room for him,' and Fiona thinks there can't be any other potential takers in this weather or at this time of year anyway, so it's a stupid thing to say.

'Could you ask your receptionist?'

'Morag? No she's not here, she's gone to the hospital with an old man who fell off his bike outside. I don't know how far you have to go, Madam, but take my advice and think about getting home, this is not going to be a night to be out and about.' And Fiona looks down at her wet shoes and feels like crying.

'Thank you, I think I should go home too.'

'Now take care there,' he says.

The proprietor of the Tapselteerie Hotel is right, the weather is atrocious and Fiona has many hold ups and detours on her journey. It takes an extra hour before she turns into the glens but the time passes quickly because all she can think about is her disappointment. Disappointment that Tim wasn't there, disappointment again when she'd trusted him to keep his word. And on that journey the idea that he's holed up and incommunicado becomes a tiny glimmer of unreasonable hope the closer she gets to home but the hurt she feels is almost overwhelming. Then from a field entrance ahead of her, and like a pair of animal eyes, headlights flash through the grey rain and mist and she recognises the registration of Nigel's Land Rover and pulls up beside him.

254

'What's happened, why are you here?' she says, confused enough to half expect him to have some message from Tim to turn back to Tapselteerie.

'It's dangerous, I'm taking you home. Leave your car here, the telephone and electricity lines are down, the Duir's burst its banks, Burn End road's flooded and a cattle truck's overturned and you'd have gone straight into that. You have to go round the long way to get to Glenduir,' and he hasn't got out of the driver's seat. 'So come along and we'll get going shall we?' She, without a word, gets out of her car and has only taken a few steps in the pouring rain when he says, 'haven't you forgotten something?'

'Forgotten?' and she stops, the rain flattening her hair and getting in her eyes.

'Yes, forgotten.'

'What?' she says and looks around her,' I didn't take anything with me, I've got my bag...'

'The crockery, the cutlery, don't you need a hand with it?'

'Oh yes, that. No. I made a mistake,' and she stands there, rain running down her neck and face and even into her mouth.

'A wasted journey then wasn't it?' but she doesn't answer him. 'Come on, get in you're getting soaked.' And in the passenger seat she straightens herself out as he drives off and for no good reason stays in a low gear, growling along the wet road, water hissing up from the road and rain slashing at the windscreen. 'So what do you mean, you made a mistake, what was wrong?'

'With what?' she says.

'The second-hand stuff.'

'Ah, just that there wasn't enough of it...'

'How much do you need? You took a long time to make up your mind didn't you? I'd have thought in weather like this you'd have come home without delay.' She says nothing, he's making her feel like the dishonest woman she knows herself to be, but then she finds some truth to offer.

'I had a couple of coffees and it took longer to get home than it should because of the weather,' and he says nothing.

Near Glenduir and some ten minutes later it's now dark and he says, 'don't expect the power will be on again for some time.'

'Did you get the tilly lamps and candles out?'

'Nope, it wasn't as dark as this when I left.'

And she imagines their benighted stumblings while trying to find them because she knows he hasn't replaced the battery in the torch. She says nothing, she can't chide him after what she's done today.

In the cold, fizzing light of the tilly lamps she says she can make them something to eat and then they may as well go to bed. All he does is make noises of agreement. Bed is cold, the electric blanket can't be used and almost in unison they turn their backs to one another and lie there awake, each preoccupied with doubt.

And sleep comes as sleep will to them both but bringing dreams for Fiona. Vivid, bad dreams. Sights and sounds of an outlandish menagerie gone mad, eyes glowing in the dark, leopards, wolves, goats, all howling, hissing, taunting and she's drowning in dark swirling water pulled under by a tugging hand. Then she breaks free and she fights for the surface into the noise and chaos again but the hand grabs her foot pulling her under and further from the shore of a place she knows but can't place. The scene repeats and repeats until something underneath her raises her body to the surface and sleeks through the water with her lying on its back, her arms round its neck, her head against its head, a creature something like Luath and taking her... Then she slurs something and brings a floppy arm down on Nigel's flank. Loosely, he holds on to her hand with his good one.

256

'Only a bad dream,' he says half awake and she comes to with a guttural gasp, her heart pounding and a need for air. She throws her bedclothes back. He blurs the words, 'what were you dreaming?' into the pillow.

'Drowning, a zoo, animals.'

'The floods, Noah's ark...'

'No, a wolf was - laughing at me.' With a slight snore Nigel lets go of her hand and gets back into the rhythm of sleep. But her heart is still beating too fast and the images take a long time to fade before she too sleeps.

She doesn't feel like getting up in the morning, she feels very tired. But Nigel is already up, he has to be at an event at the school where he is a governor. She can hear him through the open door in his old bedroom and watches him put on his clothes, he's become quite dexterous at doing things with one and a half hands. And once dressed in a three- piece tweed suit, his father's very slightly altered to fit him, and finally the new brogues, he brushes his hair. There's the shrug of the shoulders, the stretch of the neck and he turns to look at her. With a twitch of his mouth he says, 'watching?'

'Am I not allowed to? You watch me.' He doesn't answer that.

You had a nightmare didn't you?' he says.

'Don't remind me, it was horrible.'

'A wolf laughing at you? Sounds more like a children's story to me.'

'And leopards, goats too.'

'Ah well, it's probably all very Freudian, symbolic.' But he doesn't finish, he passes the bed with, 'don't get up, I'll grab something and be on my way. Should be back by six,' and he blows a kiss.

And she pulls the bedclothes over her head once he's gone. Now what? She wants to telephone the Tapselteerie Hotel but remembers all the lines are down and the telephone doesn't work. Could she drive there and be back before Nigel is home? No she can't, the rain beating against the window reminds her of the flooding and Nigel's got the Land Rover - and her mini is parked miles away. Is it divine intervention? Is it human intervention? Whichever it is she's trapped.

It's a coal-fired AGA so there's coffee and toast and hot water to wash with. There's a fire in the grate and books to read and there's a battery in her portable radio but she can't concentrate. She tries playing the piano but each piece becomes louder and angrier as she lets her mind wander to what she is beginning to feel is another rejection. Just as she's murdering a Rachmaninov finale the door opens and a very dishevelled Nigel brings a gust of cold air in with him.

'Why are you back now? It's only one o'clock,' she says.

'The bloody thing was cancelled because of the weather but they couldn't get through to here. I noticed Stravaig seems to be relatively unaffected though.'

'Can we get my car then?'

'What do you want it for - you're not going anywhere are you? We'll get it when all this dies down.' There is no questioning his reasonable decision.

While he changes his clothes she finds something for him to eat and there is only just enough butter, eggs, milk and bread. And there indeed is divine intervention, she can genuinely claim she'll have to take the Land Rover to Stravaig Supermarket and stock up. There's a public telephone box near it and she is going to telephone the Tapselteerie Hotel and Tim's home number too. 'Nigel, I'll have to take the Land Rover to Stravaig, we're going to need basic groceries, I've run out and we don't know how much longer we are going to be under siege, do we?'

'Under siege? that's a good one. Well you'll have to then, won't you? I'll check on old Murdo,' Nigel means the Highland bull. 'See if he's alright, I'll take Luath with me for a walk.'

It feels like a very long time before Nigel finally gets going and Fiona is on her way - the long way round out of the glens then on to the main road to Stravaig. But she's ready, the telephone numbers taken from her diary and she drives far too fast through flood and mud. Yet once there it's as if she wants to delay disappointment or perhaps it's to assuage her conscience - so she shops for what she needs before making her calls.

Bluntly and briefly she asks the Tapselteerie Hotel for Mr Robinson and once she's told he isn't there, she knows he never will be. The call to Norfolk is more difficult, this is loaded with the full gamut of emotion from disappointment to delight. She dials but her hand shakes and she makes a mistake, so she does it again, puts the money in the slot and clears her throat while it rings out.

'Hello?' a woman's voice answers and Fiona's nerve almost fails. 'Hello, who's that?' but Fiona makes herself press the button and is connected.

'Can I speak to Mr Robinson please?' and there's a shake in her voice.

'What's that?'

'Mr Robinson, Tim Robinson please?'

'No, I mean it isn't possible - you can't. Look, this is his wife speaking, who is that?' and Fiona slams the receiver down on the proprietorial voice.

Disappointment is far too dilute for what Fiona feels now and she leans against the grubby coin box. She sees herself in the smeared mirror and sees a fool.

'What's it like?' Nigel asks when she comes back with her groceries.

'What's what like?' she replies and dumps her basket down heavily.

'The roads, everything - you know.'

'Bad, but not as bad over at Stravaig, just like you said.'

'I've had an idea,' and she looks at him. 'Instead of staying here without modern conveniences why don't we take the Amen glasses to Edinburgh? Graham's desperate for them, we could stay at Caroline Street.

'Like refugees,' she says slowly. 'Oh I suppose so, anything's better than this.'

'And maybe you can find some inexpensive china while you're there?'

'Why? Oh yes, I suppose so.'

'Cheer up, Fluff, it might never happen. Or maybe it has?' And she shoots him a glance. 'The deluge?' he says with his hands upturned.

'Huh, après moi le déluge,' she replies automatically.

'Well, I hope not,' but she doesn't understand what he means and she doesn't care either.

Worse things happen at sea

The cobble-stoned hill from Caroline Street to George Street means Fiona must drive slowly with Nigel keeping a firm grip on the box of Jacobite glass with his good hand. At Graham's Auction House the verification of the Amen glasses delivers the prospect of at least £60,000 if not nearer £80,000 for the three and another £10,000 for the rest.

A short distance away, sitting in the bar of the George Hotel, Charlie Scott looks out of the window at the street. Expecting both MacMuckles he looks at his watch and swallowing the last of his drink he sees over the top of his glass a woman go to the bar and order a vodka tonic. As a connoisseur of good looking females he notices her long legs are made for the mini-dress she wears then she turns round and he looks away.

'Charlie - is that you?' The woman at the bar moves closer to him. 'It is, isn't it - Charlie Scott?' an open, pink-lipped smile lights her face.

Unusually Charlie Scott is lost for words for a moment then it's 'Diana isn't it? I recognise your voice and that smile, who could forget that, how are you?'

'All the better for seeing an old friend, Edinburgh's a ghost town to me these days.'

He leans on the bar listening to her reminiscing, watching her expressive, darting hands and her thrown-back head with every gurgling laugh. She hasn't changed a bit. Diana Hunter, the unconventional girl with favours to give and who did the choosing too. In 1956 it was Nigel she'd chosen for some months until she

261

returned to the bigger pool that was London. Fancying his own chances, Charlie had asked her to one of their parties but once she'd set eyes on Nigel it was he alone she chose to the exclusion of Charlie and the many others - and Diana Hunter was known for her multiple choices.

'And Nigel, what became of him?' she says. 'Of course, you're his cousin aren't you - does he live in that Highland castle of his now?'

'Well, if you turn round you can ask him yourself.'

'Ha! if it isn't The Magnificent MacMuckle himself,' and she tosses her head again.

'Diana - is that you?' Nigel says and they make a small collision as they meet. Reaching up to rest her hand along the length of his tie she presses the other hard against his arm and kisses him warmly on both cheeks. 'So - what brings you here?' Nigel says with an edge of false bonhomie while he widens the space between them.

'Up from the Big Smoke via Norwich and I'm here for a couple of days, I've got to do some boring paperwork with - well I don't know quite what to call him,' she laughs again, head thrown back.

Fiona, across the lobby and forty-five feet away, stops to figure out why she's seeing her husband clutched in conversation with an attractive, lively woman. Charlie might be organising the drinks but the central theme is a female whose familiarity now extends to brushing something off the knot of Nigel's tie and rubbing her lip print off his face. And - she laughs too much Fiona thinks as she crosses the floor. Charlie, the redundant sidekick, spots her first and his greeting warm but seeing his wife Nigel holds out a hand to gather her in.

'Fiona, this is Diana - Diana Hunter, we... Diana this is my wife.'

Shooting glances first at Charlie then back at Nigel, to Fiona she laughs, 'oh I see. Sorry, I thought you belonged to Charlie,' and laughs again. Taking Fiona's offered hand with a friendly, how d'you do, she then takes a half step backwards for a quick squint from foot to head at Nigel MacMuckle's wife. Fiona understands and Charlie catches her eye.

'Sherry, Fiona?' he asks.

'No thank you, I think I'll have a Bloody Mary, today.'

'So where's *your* wife, Charlie?' Diana laughs.

'South Africa and she's an ex-wife.'

'Ah - so we've something in common,' she sighs and drains her glass. I haven't been back here since I left, no reason to. Not much changes does it?' She looks around her, 'we used to come here sometimes if we weren't raising the roof at your flat. What a hoot to bump into you both again at our old watering hole, isn't it?' And she nods at Charlie's signalled enquiry, 'yes please - it's a vodka tonic, I think I might need a double now.' She takes out a cigarette, Nigel lights it for her and she steadies his unshaking hand. 'Oh, your poor paw, what did you do?' and she holds on to it examining the bandage crossing his palm.

But he pulls it away saying, 'it's nothing, a mistake, that's all.'

'Mistake? Never, you don't make mistakes, Nigel. Are you here for lunch?'

'No, they're not - I'm whisking them away,' Charlie says before Nigel can say they are.

'Oh shame, we've so much more catching up to do - but we mustn't lose touch again, this is such a bonus. I'll give you my business card and when you're in London all of you must look me up. I expect you come down sometimes, Nigel, don't you? You went to The Army and Navy Match, and Henley wasn't it? And you, Fenella, you must come down to shop, don't you?'

'No, I don't,' Fiona says quite sweetly and Nigel seems to choke slightly on his gin. Because the tonic hasn't been added? That's what it looks like. Diana pats his back while trying to find the cards in her bag and all the contents fall on the floor. She gurgles like a drain while the men bend down to gather them up and Fiona notices keys and the garish cover of a Mills and Boon romance in Nigel's poor paw.

And Diana laughs, 'such a butterfingers - thanks you two, gallant as ever. I have a very nice, bijou B and B,' she carries on, 'very central so you need never be stuck. It would be such a hoot,' and she hands each man her card.

And as Fiona turns away from Diana Hunter's obviousness her eyes stray towards the hotel's main entrance. A man with dark hair opens the glass door then stands still against the light. Scanning the lobby and beyond he then moves forward slowly, his dark-browed, blue eyes checking the people around him. Fiona's shoulders jerk slightly. Catching her breath she knocks her teeth against her glass as she drinks.

And through a cloud of smoke, 'ah, there he is,' Diana says waving at that man who gives an attractive half smile of recognition and raises his arm in greeting.

'Sorry I'm late, unexpected flooding,' he says then, with his very blue eyes, he prolongs his glance at Fiona.

'It doesn't matter; I've just bumped into some of my long lost friends. Nigel, Charlie, Fenella, this is John Robinson.'

His mouth curls slightly, formally and with the slight head nod of the military he shakes hands with each of them. Fiona can hardly look at him when he takes hers and then she holds her glass up against her mouth as if masking her reaction to him. The polite round of inconsequential questions and answers gives her time to compose herself until John Robinson verifies his looks and bearing.

'Home is in Hampshire... Yes, I've been here a few times now... I'm a Royal Marine serving at HMS Condor in Arbroath but my late brother...' Nobody notices Fiona's catch of breath, 'served in a frigate at Rosyth some years back.' He stalls for a moment. 'And we met here a few weeks ago. Tim - my brother - he came up to see me on family business...' But Diana rests her hand on his arm to stop him.

'Actually, his late brother was my late husband, you see...' And nobody notices Fiona reach for the back of the nearest chair.

'Oh you're a widow, I thought...' Charlie's blurt trails off.

'Don't worry, you weren't so wrong, Tim and I were separated - divorcing and that's why I've been at his place in Norwich, I had to pack some of his things up. Sad but...'

Averted glances, murmurings of regret and shifting feet divert attention. Nobody sees Fiona gripping the back of that chair with both hands. Then Diana starts to tell but John takes it from her and his words wash in and out of Fiona's understanding.

'Drowned... Hit by the boom... Delivering a yacht to Montrose... Made a detour to the Island of May... The haar in the Forth... Couldn't see...'

And Fiona can't see, it's as if she's behind a waterfall and it's pulling her down with it too. She wants to get away and can't. Her heart beats so hard she thinks they must hear it. Her legs so unsteady that the red carpet fogs as it comes up to meet her, but she rights her stumble and grabs the chair again. Then with hair-trigger response the familiar brush of Nigel's tweed is against her, the sound of his anxious voice is near her ear and he's holding her steady. Is everyone watching - can they see her struggling against the grip of emotion seizing her? But now Nigel's quiet words begin to mean something, his face is close to hers, his breath tracks across her brow and he's taking her out of this place. But she can't speak, it will release the sob in her throat at the engulfing sorrow of it, the horrible, inescapable irony of it. But it's alright, he's guiding her into a private place in the darkened ballroom. There she stumbles again and he steadies her again yet she can't help pulling away from him as if she's found the strength to escape. But he holds on to the limp sleeve of her coat as she uncoils herself from it and his grip.

'Fiona? Let me, please at least...' He reels her in and holds on to her as she stifles her distress into his embrace and tries to say something honest. It comes out in barely a whisper.

'Sorry, sorry, I can't, I'm...'

'Hush, it's alright now,' and he hands her his handkerchief. She doesn't dare lift her head to look at him. But if she does, she'll see he could use it himself. She waits for him to ask what's wrong and doesn't know how she's going to answer. Yet all she hears again is, 'it's alright, it's alright now' with a slight stroke of her head. She lets him settle her on a gilt chair where he sits beside her and neither speaks. She's hunched up, pressing her knees and feet together, pulling and stretching the handkerchief between her thumbs, she waits saying nothing, waits for him to say something. But he's hunched over, head down, staring at the floor, his hands dangling between his thighs, his tacked heel on the wood floor beating a slow, faint pulse. This is unreal, even in the midst of the overwhelming claim on her emotions at this moment there should be questions, not just from him but from her too.

If he thinks she's upset about Diana Hunter he would say so, and yet he doesn't ask. For her part she'd normally be asking about her, teasing him about her, quoting her, drawing out that boyish embarrassment of his which is so appealing. This, she knows he'd expect too. So why he has no curiosity, why does he leave the situation unpacked? But something has to fill the unnatural void, someone has to suggest the content without showing the true context. She will.

'Was she your...?'

266

'Girlfriend,' and he says it like an oath then stands up abruptly catching the flimsy chair before it topples. And there is Charlie in the doorway bringing deliverance. He asks if he can do anything and though Nigel says there isn't, the truth shows on his face while he asks if the others are still in the bar.

'They're about to go in for lunch,' Charlie says this slowly, he's concentrating on Fiona. 'What about getting something to eat for you, not in here somewhere more congenial and private, I'll see to it if you like?' But it is Nigel who appears to go and deal with it and beckons Charlie to keep her company sitting there tensed up and pale. So, he takes her hand then eventually asks if she's alright.

'I felt faint, that's all.'

'Oh I see, so it's that?' he sounds pleased, but then it's, 'no, I shouldn't pry,' and they sit together in silence until she takes a quick breath, swallows noisily and asks.

'Who exactly is she, Charlie?'

'Diana Hunter? A girl-about-town in the old days.'

'She was very familiar with Nigel.'

'Ah, don't worry about that - he'll tell you himself, she was a girlfriend, that's all.'

'Yes, he said she was. Serious?'

'No, no not as far as he was concerned anyway.'

'Did you know - did Nigel know she'd got married?'

'Nah, she left here and that was the last we ever saw or heard of her,' and he stifles amusement, but not quite well enough.'

'What's funny?' she says.

'Well, her old man must have been quite something to keep her in harness even for the short time he did, poor bloke.' He clicks his tongue and shakes his head. 'I mean - she had an appetite. Hey, look - I shouldn't be telling you things like that should I,' and she manages to pass it off with a half-hearted shrug. 'Listen, she was always over the top. Forget it Fiona.'

'Did they say anything when I left?'

'Don't bother about them,' he says now with some irritation. 'No they didn't, she wanted to talk to the brother about the drowned one's spoils. It doesn't seem morally right.'

'Why?' Fiona asks without looking at him.

'Because she made it sound like pillage.' Charlie slaps his hands on his knees and snorts. 'What a shower eh? Though it was over between them she was still his wife and so she's been to his place in Norwich because she has the legal right to his things. But the brother seems a decent type, he's the executor. Anyway I was superfluous one way or another...'

'You're being unusually sanctimonious aren't you?' Nigel says without a trace of humour and hands Fiona a brandy, which she doesn't want.

'Well, people astonish me sometimes,' Charlie says in his defence, but undeterred, 'can you believe it? She left her old man for brother John - and now that's over too,' he laughs.

'So, you're a gossipy old woman too,' Nigel says. 'Are we really interested in the doings of those people? There's a heartlessness about Diana, there always was.'

'Quite right old man, I agree - and I'm not an old gossip if y'don't mind. Fiona - or is it indeed, Fenella, eh? That she's feeling better, that's what's important,' Charlie says, pleased with his josh.

'Call Fiona by her own name, will you - give it all a rest, Charlie.' This is a clear order from Nigel and she looks up to give him a weak smile while reaching for her handbag, which she doesn't need. Then still standing over her he says, 'well, they're still in the bar, John Robinson hopes you are feeling better - so let that be the end of it, shall we?' Then she looks at him properly, into his steady, blue eyes - and it feels utterly brazen.

'And Diana?' Charlie asks.

'Too busy putting on more lipstick so her mouth was otherwise engaged,' his sarcasm sharp. Then with a weary sigh he takes Charlie aside. 'I think I should take Fiona to Caroline Street, Amy will give us some lunch then we'll get off home. Sorry about today, some other time, you know how it is.'

And Charlie does think he knows how it is. 'Yeah, I think I get your drift. It doesn't last long, take it from me. Look after her,' said quietly, his head turned away, but he wants to know something else. 'Where did Diana and her discarded lover go?'

'Don't ask me, lunch I suppose.'

Lunch with Amy doesn't take long, she doesn't notice the MacMuckles' subdued manner because all she wants to talk about is the play she saw last night. Nigel will drive even if it does hurts his hand and Fiona is relieved at that and her sister's lack of interest.

The journey home is fast and without conversation. Nigel's manner has changed from active concern a couple of hours ago to what now looks close to indifference and Fiona is acutely aware of it. Keeping her self-control intact needs supreme effort and the idea of that Diana, that casual, careless woman who'd had Tim to herself yet threw him away, is making the journey inches away from Nigel almost unbearable. But not as unbearable as the thought that she will never see Tim Robinson again. And when his memory hunts her too hard she finds her bag and fiddles with its contents until Nigel finally asks her what it is she can't find. The word, composure, would be the truth but she passes her fumblings off with excuses. She pretends to sleep on and off when it gets too much for her and she makes Nigel stop saying she's feeling slightly queasy - which she is - and retreats to any available ladies toilets. And every time she comes back he reaches over to open the door for her without expression or word and she cannot ask him what's wrong because he might ask her the same question. But she's had time to think, maybe she didn't make as obvious a scene in the hotel as she thought she had. He must have believed her when she said she felt faint - or did she say that to Charlie? It isn't clear. What is clear are John Robinson's stark words when he called Tim his, late brother. After that everything hazed except what she absorbed in the description of what befell his, late brother. Now all she wants is to be at home again in a place she can hide her grief and where she feels most comfortable. The significance of that thought will occur to her but for now she's only just surviving the journey.

Darkness has fallen when they get home. The power is restored and the lights are on again and makes the castle look welcoming, as if someone is in. Fiona wishes someone was, someone to break the tension between herself and Nigel, someone to treat her like a child and put her to bed with a hot water bottle. Then as they come to a halt Nigel finds his voice and stirrings of a smile, he says she should go ahead and take it easy for a while. He's going to check on his cows then pick up Luath from Robbie. All in place, the usual routine, only the suggestion of what he thinks she should do makes their home-coming any different. But he's given her a timetable, she knows how long he'll take and once she's inside with arms crossed over her waist she folds as if in pain. But then she sees him from the window, he's sitting in the Land Rover, stock still, staring blankly ahead. When he does drive off it's in a noisy spray of gravel and only then does she sit down, hugging her knees, letting Tim Robinson's image form in her head.

And it's Tim Robinson's head she sees - the boom striking it hard enough to knock him out - he lets go and over into the swelling, fogged Forth. He doesn't know he's drowning - nobody knows he's drowning - nobody's missed him - not yet. And in her imaginings that unconcerned boom swings like an indolent hinge while the May Island foghorn booms its doleful note. But he can't hear it now, he can't hear anything, floating, drifting on the surface like a five-point star. Is he face down, is he facing skyward, are his unseeing eyes open? How long - how long before they missed him? How long was he alone? Then into her vivid grief there's a sudden flare of anger that he should have taken greater care, that he should have known better. But the sob she's denying breaks out like a final choking fight for air. She uncurls herself only to mesh her hands hard behind her neck then around her shoulders gripping and pressing her fingers into them until it hurts and hurts again that she is not allowed to mourn, or know his grave. She can have nothing more of him now, not even a photograph - only two oyster shells, one letter and memory.

She has to let go too.

Two sides of the same blanket

Before, and it seems a very long time ago, when Tim disappeared from Fiona's life she almost held on to her disappointment but now all hope is gone she wonders if it accelerates healing. What can she do except silently contain the grief, the memory triggers, the absent moments but not be able to speak of it to anyone. She wishes the Minister of Glenduir Church, Willie MacVicar, were a more sympathetic man and she'd confide in him. But his Old Testament, finger-wagging denunciations are legendary and she's sure he'd make her feel like a Jezebel. There's nothing else except the tried and tested method of filling time and head with as many distractions as she can find. She's quiet, she can't make herself be anything else, but Nigel is preoccupied and he's also found a new energy, he is at ease again, he doesn't notice she thinks - so she's grateful for that.

Her step is purposeful as she hears him in the library but she stops when she sees him pulling out drawers, all the cupboard doors are open too. He's only doing what he said he would but she goes into the room marvelling at the speed with which he's tackling it. Black japanned boxes on the desk tower in an unsteady pile and he sits down to go through them. Feeling she has no place in the ordering of that room she runs a finger across the dusty photograph frames but stops at the faded image of Nigel's parents on their wedding day. Jean wears the orange blossom headdress and is almost unrecognisable compared to the middle-aged mother-in-law she had known and Muckle looks so pleased and proud and so like his son. But until then it's held no more interest to Fiona than any other photograph in that room, yet that morning Fiona feels sorry with all her heart for Jean and Muckle.

She picks the image up to look more closely. What had Muckle hoped for? He probably hadn't, he would have expected, people like him always do, she thinks. It is just the way things are or certainly were in 1929 when that photograph was taken. She knows the history that in his family the long line of one adult male per generation had been the situation either by chance or the more likely reap of war and disease. She imagines he'd have expected to rear a brood of boys with a couple of girls somewhere in the head count and that his expected family was never a subject he'd have discussed with his fiancée - it would have been presumed. And little did he know. And little did Jean know, because Fiona thinks that too could be presumed. What Georgina had told her about Jean's distaste must have shocked her 'lusty lad' though it occurred to Fiona that Jean's delicate sensibilities probably prevailed more than people realised in a world where a girl knew her duty and submitted to it. At this Fiona looks at Nigel poring over a box lost to the world in its contents. Nigel, the product of submission, and she hopes Jean thought he'd been worth it.

'Nigel, were you a big baby when you were born?' she says.

'What's that?'

'How much did you weigh when you were born?' and he looks up perplexed.

'Don't know, but I was big, I do know that. I think it was what you call a difficult birth.

'What made you think of that?' and he returns to his boxes. He doesn't really need an answer and he snaps one box shut and reaches for the next. Its label, written in his father's hand, reads; THE BIRDS OF GLENDUIR Winter/Spring 1929/30. This is of little interest to him but today he is nothing if not thorough. And Fiona watching him sees how he suddenly bends closer to the piece of paper in his hand as if he can't read it properly, then he mouths something as he rakes his fingers through his hair.

'What is it?' she says, 'you look winded,' and he says nothing, just sits back and holds out the piece of paper towards her. 'What?'

'See for yourself - look at it,' and she takes the clear and elegantly written piece of headed writing paper dated 12th April 1930. The day of Nigel's birth.

I, Muckle MacMuckle make this codicil to my last will and testament of 2nd May 1929. In the event of my death without legitimate heirs I leave to my natural son, Robert George MacMuckle of Keeper's Cottage, Glenduir, his heirs and successors....

'What - what is this?' she says.

'A codicil to his will.'

'Yes I can see that, what does it mean?'

'If I've got it right it means Robbie is my half brother, doesn't it?' And he's biting the edge of his thumbnail then takes the paper back from her, brushing it flat with his hand as if to sweep those words away or perhaps make them clearer. 'I can't make sense of this, Fiona. I mean it's written on the day I was born, why, what happened?' and there's irritation there. She shakes her head, how should she know? 'Did you know what was in this box, have you seen this before?' accusation hardly hidden in his voice now.

'Of course I haven't, what makes you say that?'

'You've just asked me about the day I was born, did you know what I was going to find?'

'No, it just came into my head, I - I was thinking about something else. Look let's calm down and think about this clearly,' and she sits beside him patting the back of his hand.

'Well then, come on what do you think?' he asks as if she's being deliberately obstructive.

'Hush, Nigel, listen. Do you think your father was told you might not survive, you said it was a difficult birth and, God knows being stuck up this glen wasn't exactly the place for specialist midwifery...'

'But Ma would have had more children so what was the problem?' He sounds petulant. 'He must have been told she might not survive either.'

'Didn't Robbie's mother die when he was born?'

'Yes, yes, she was a housemaid here I think - before she married George. Anyway, my father would have married again wouldn't he?'

'Nigel please calm down,' and she waits until he does. 'Look, I think I know something which might cast some light on this.' He opens his mouth to speak and she puts her finger up to his lips to stop him. 'Georgina told me that your father told Archie's father that Jean refused to have any more children...' Nigel opens his mouth again and is stopped, 'once she was expecting you. She found sex difficult,' and he grabs her finger before she can put it against his mouth.

'Difficult? What do you mean, difficult?'

'She didn't like it.'

'And how long have you known that, eh? Huh, where did that promise of no more secrets go, tell me that, we had a pact didn't we?' and he pushes back hard in his chair. Then he looks at her with her head down avoiding the accusation. 'Right, so you mean all the glens knew my mother was frigid and my father made to look a fool? For Christ's sake, Fiona, didn't I have a right to know?' She won't look up, she fiddles with her wedding ring but she can see his hands gripping the edge of the desk.

'I haven't known for long, it was just after her funeral,' then she looks at him, he's positioned as if he's going to pounce. 'I didn't know how to tell you, I didn't want to hurt you. I mean, if you hadn't discovered this about Robbie would it have been so important?'

'Important? Of course it's important, it's important to me, you said you wouldn't keep anything...'

'The MacIntoshes kept it to themselves, I'm sure they did, you know they were good friends.'

He tightens his mouth making a muffled growling sound and sinks his face into his palms. But his foot starts tapping the floor and she knows that sign.

'Nigel, I've said I'm sorry, truly I am,' and she strokes the back of his neck. 'Look, what about Robbie?'

'What about Robbie, he's my half brother isn't he? No wonder people mistake him for me, why the hell did I not know this?'

She's relieved she's managed to shift his focus and quickly she asks, 'do you think he knows, do you think his father, I mean George, did he know? Gosh, do you think your mother knew?'

'Well, *she* wouldn't have said anything if she did, would she? She'd brush that disgrace under the carpet - if we had any to speak of. No, it would have come out wouldn't it if George or Robbie knew, you know what this place is like?' Then he starts doodling on the blotter, 'perhaps Robbie's mother told old George he was the father, he worshipped her memory - he probably wanted to believe her. There was no way my father would have married her, and anyway, he must have been only about twenty when Robbie was born. One of those back stairs opportunities - a one-off even.'

Fiona swallows very hard, 'droit de signeur' she says under her breath and instantly wishes she hadn't.

'Who knows, these things happened. But the cuckoo's nest had to be Keeper's Cottage not the castle - that's the way it was.'

'Will you tell Robbie, I mean can we be absolutely sure he's your father's son. Shouldn't he do a blood test?'

'What, the big man who looks like me, looks like my father, unmusical like me, can't play the pipes, and neither could my father - unlike George? What need would you have for any test? It's bloody obvious I'd say.' He stops to bite the edge of his thumbnail again, then narrowing his eyes, 'why is it things are so obvious after you know? Like perspective, you can't understand why they couldn't see what to do, how to make it look real...'

'You've lost me.'

'Painting, everything was flat, no sense of distance.' She shrugs. 'You know, until they discovered perspective? Drawing lines, point of view? That makes it convincing, and to us - well to me anyway - it seems an obvious thing to do.'

'And that's because you know, is that what you're saying?'

'Yeah, same with fakes, once you know, you see it,' then he lightly slaps the blotter with his hand. 'Anyway, back to Robbie. If he could inherit there might be some point in a test, but the poor bugger's on the wrong side of the blanket! Pity though, it would put the Kansas cowboy back in his place.' Then he sighs as he looks away, 'so you see it's pointless, I can't do any more for him than I do already and to think I've always said he was the older brother I never had when I was a little boy. Ironic, isn't it?' and he stops to look straight at her. 'I couldn't be fonder of him and I hope he knows that.'

'I know it, I'm sure he does too,' she says, gently touching his face, thinking how many emotions he's run in so few minutes.

'I don't think I could take any more Fluff,' and now she turns her head away at what she thinks sounds like mild reproach.

'So we'll just leave things as they are then, is that what you want to do? And we'll always keep it to ourselves,' she says.

'I think so, isn't that for the best? What's to be gained by robbing him of who he thinks he is, he worshipped George, and George was so proud of him and his bravery in the war too, rear gunners weren't expected to make it, I'll see him right.'

'I know you will, you always do,' she says, but thinks it best not to ask him if their honesty policy shouldn't have a wider application.

That same evening, after the morning's shock revelation has more-or-less taken root and settled down with her Fiona opens her diary. It is no more than a record, perhaps with occasional thoughts, but not a confessional. There's nothing in it she's ashamed or embarrassed to own, but it would be wise to be cryptic about Robbie's paternity.

She hasn't written it up since before she and Nigel went to Edinburgh and the renewed memory of that visit's revelations make her close it again. She can't commit to paper the names of those two people she met in The George Hotel. She sits with her hand on the cover and thinks of the intimate circle made by Nigel, Diana, Tim and herself, she doesn't want the thought so she'll make a record only of the success of the Amen glasses. She opens the diary again to start at those vacant blanks and bring it up to date. There are the empty, white spaces except for one - three days ago - its date ringed twenty-eight days after the last ringed date, twenty-eight days after the ringed date before that. An invariable and reliable cycle which is entered in every diary she's kept since she was thirteen and a half. She scrapes the pages backwards, she counts the weeks forward again but there's no mistake the circle marks the right date - three days ago. Lightly her hands land at her neck, she fingers her necklace as she closes her eyes remembering. Then into the diary again flicking the pages back to the week she was in Edinburgh alone. The day she meant to come straight home but turned back because she and Tim weren't finished. Was it really the risky twelfth day out of her trustworthy twenty-eight? Her

278

calculation is correct. Slumping forward, she rests her brow on the open pages as she thinks of Nigel and their quick satisfaction the next day - the thirteenth day and she didn't refuse him on the tiger skin rug the day after that. It's not impossible, remote but not impossible, so she can lift her head and breathe again. But she closes the diary, leaves it unwritten because in her chest something flutters, it makes her catch her breath in little skips and it's not unpleasant. Her hand settles on her stomach in an unconscious gesture that makes her smile. Even the echo of Robbie's true parentage, revealed so few hours before, fails to cast a shadow. But she must wait longer, a little longer, but how long is that? It might be a false hope connived at by stress, she knows these things but has no experience, it's never happened before.

Time drags in a way it has never done since Fiona was a child at school longing for the holidays. After ten days and getting too used to the idea of what might be, something over which she has no control, she begins to feel decidedly sick in the morning. Not the occasional queasiness which before she'd put down to her guilty thoughts. It has to be time to tell Nigel and she wants to very much, but she worries she's tempting fate. She worries that if she goes to the doctor for a test it will come back negative and her fears about stress will be right. She even wonders if feeling sick is only wishful thinking and isn't it true that women can have phantom pregnancies like Georgina MacIntosh's dog. And as she sits there on a new bed in one of the soon to be decorated B and B bedrooms she looks around the room wondering if she's going to be able to manage a new baby and a new business, wondering if she really wants to run a bed and breakfast at all.

'Where are you?' Nigel shouts from downstairs and when he finds her he rants about the impatience - or is it impertinence - of the people in Glenduir and Driech wanting him to get on and have the landslide cleared off the old track. Soon he'll have money from the sale of the Jacobite glass, he knows he could have it done then, but what really 'gets his goat' is that he's not used to being told what he should do. Fiona listens but couldn't care less, not now, and all she can find to say is that times are changing.

'And I'd better get used to it, is that what you mean?' he says, arms folded with his back to her and looking out of the window, but she asks him to come and sit beside her.

He turns to her, a puzzled look across his face, 'why? I didn't think you were supposed to sit on beds.'

'Oh come on, it's not like you to quibble,' and that raises a smile from him as he sits near her. 'I have something I want to tell you.' Quietly, as if not to frighten the augury away she says, 'I think... I think I'm having a baby.' He doesn't look up or say anything. 'Nigel, did you hear me? I think I'm having a baby - say something,' and he slumps forward his hands on his knees and still he doesn't answer. So she gets up and drops down in front of him. 'Haven't you anything to say?'

'What?'

'Nigel what is it?' and then she wishes she hadn't asked but she tells herself he must be overwhelmed and puts her arms round him like comforting a child. 'Nigel, it's happened - well I think so, I'm ten days late now and that's never happened before and sometimes I feel sick in the mornings,' facts babble out of her.

'When was it?'

'When was what?'

'When did it get on board?'

'It doesn't matter does it? It happened, whenever it was.'

'So what's that - ten days add fourteen, is that how you calculate it? I only know about livestock,' but he does a quick bit of mental arithmetic. 'Was it before you went to Edinburgh or when you came back, was it then?'

'Must have been.'

'So...uh... at The George you were...'

She cuts in, 'Oh Nigel, you see, not impossible, please be pleased.'

'No, not impossible, that's what the Doc said,' and he makes a noise like a grudged laugh as he says, 'you try so hard for so long and then when you're not paying attention - Bingo! It's great news, but I'll have to let it sink in.'

He's pleased, she can tell he is, for the rest of the day she catches him looking at her, especially when he thinks she's not aware of it. In bed he lies flat on his back and she imagines his eyes are open. And when she curves into him, her face against his shoulder, her hand on his chest, he puts his hand over hers and turns his head to kiss the hair on the top of her head. Nothing is said, and that's alright, she's heard about men who treat their pregnant wives like china dolls. But it will pass.

Her pregnancy test comes back positive and now it is no surprise. Being sick at the start of every day must go beyond the influence of wishful thinking. Nigel, brought up on mind over matter regarding illness, loses his indoctrination to sympathy when he hears her daily retch. And no matter how often she tells him she isn't ill, he can't help behaving as if she is. Treating her like a china doll lasts longer than she thought it would, though he now tucks and encloses her against him at night as if he's protecting her against the big bad wolf. And she blooms again, then once she's past the three month mark she tells everyone there's a baby on the way - and he likes to tell people himself if he thinks she might have missed someone.

People remark on Nigel's mood, it's a long time since he was so comfortable in his skin, though he doesn't really understand that allusion. But now there's even greater energy about him and so he has the castle roof and the walls surveyed. The potholes in the drive are filled with gravel and at the entrance the broken stone hound is mended and once more sits on its own gatepost matching its pair. Then the rhododendrons and briars are cut back and give a clear sightline up to the castle. With gusto he tackles this job himself and, as might be expected, there is a fine bonfire at the end of the week long job. Though Robbie says it's a shame he didn't leave it until the baby is born as if he's forgotten Nigel will always find things to burn. But he agrees that it all looks better, everything looks better - less ravaged.

Yet there is something which troubles Nigel and it isn't money this time. He doesn't want Fiona to go ahead with her B&B, she's going to have other demands on her time and he sounds serious. She thinks it's too late, she has her first guests coming soon, but he says there's enough time to cancel and she must. But money's been spent on doing up those rooms and he calmly replies that they needed doing up anyway. And then there's her all important point that they need the money and his reply is that there will be the profit from the Jacobite glass. But he delivers the coup de grâce.

'Maybe I just need to get a job.'

'What - what are you going to do?' Fiona says in disbelief. 'Put your third class geography degree to use and be a geography teacher?' She doesn't mean to sound sarcastic but he just cocks an eyebrow and purses his lips.

'Hey, that's not such a bad idea, I'd have the same holidays as young MacMuckle,' and he sounds perfectly serious again.

Due to unforeseen circumstances I have to cancel your booking for... is the neat and honest explanation in Fiona's letters to her expected paying guests. She also adds that she won't open for business in the future either, though she pauses before she writes that wondering if she might be tempting fate again. But Nigel's

282

declared intention of finding a job must take priority, he should be allowed to fulfill his words.

Her next task is to strip the new beds and put their duvets away in the linen cupboard and while she does this she can't help thinking how only months ago she had lain on the new bed angry with Nigel and fantasising about Tim. Suddenly her eyes fill with tears and her hand covers her belly, she feels the baby distinctly move for the first time, but it's not just the wonder of that which moves her, it's Tim's memory too. The grief and the sadness she feels for him cannot be avoided but there's something else which makes her burn with shame. Something which is hard to acknowledge. Her sense of relief that she didn't have to decide between him and Nigel, it would have been inevitable once she knew she was pregnant. The right decision only God knew, so how on His good earth could she have chosen?

And she wants to get out of that room, the print on the wall of the Admiral pointing inland but looking out to sea has lost its comedy. Now she sees it was a portent. The egg and dart cornice now relates to her in both its symbolic intentions. And when she hurriedly picks up the two empty water glasses they clink against each other like a ringing bell. The unlucky sound you have to immediately stop with your hand because, in her family at least, it meant a sailor dead. She drops the glasses on the pillows, cheap tumblers Jean had collected with coupons from the petrol station and that mundane recollection breaks the room's spell. With a sigh she picks the glasses up again grateful that she avoided having to buy a pile of unnecessary crockery and cutlery in Edinburgh.

Mrs MacMuckle's having a baby. The Laird's wife is in the family way. Fiona's pregnant. She's expecting. In whatever form the news was delivered the response had been the same, best described as delight though sometimes qualified with remarks such as, muckle

Nigel had taken his time over it - or what was she waiting for. And over the following months, if you listened carefully around Glenduir, the sound of clicking needles might be heard. Enough little woollen garments are produced to clothe a dozen babies, all of which are gratefully received. Robbie offers to make a cradle but Nigel knows there's one in the attic and Fiona wants to use that. So instead Robbie makes both an exquisite dolls' house and a robust toy fort. Nigel wheels out the MacMuckle coach built pram with pride, something Fiona has never seen before and he has been careful to keep hidden. Her reaction to it might not be the one he might expect. The hood needs to be mended but the maroon paintwork with a gold coach-line along the side is still in good condition. But it is the small MacMuckle crest painted midway along the line which makes her point.

'What is it?' Nigel asks looking at her and the pram in turn.

'I'm not going to push it around with that on it,' she says.

'What?'

'That crest, I don't want that snarling wolf head on my baby's pram - and anyway it's pretentious.'

'Well, can't you forget it's there?'

'No I can't, it's horrible,' and she rubs some dust off the hood rather than look at him.

'Very well then,' he says, 'as there will be no doubt whose baby is in this pram then there's no point in keeping such an outmoded signifier on the bodywork is there? It can be removed. Is that what you want?' and she doesn't answer, he is making her feel very small. 'Do you?' he presses.

'If you really don't mind?' she replies still fiddling with the hood.

'Only because you do so much. So that's settled then... Now you can give me a kiss,' and that makes her look up at the slight smile on his lips.

284

He made it sound like his reward but it feels as if he's toying with her.

But there's an undisputed reward when the Amen glasses sell for nearly £80,000. Their sale appears in the national press as it's such a rare event to discover three glasses and, as part of Scotland's national heritage, worthy of comment. Locally, nobody but Robbie knows their provenance and he uses his knowledge to nudge Nigel about clearing the landslide. He expects resistance judging from Nigel's bad temper the last time the subject was aired, and then there had been safety in numbers too.

'Are you not knowing how inconvenient it is for folk having to be going round by the road?' he says.

'Is it?'

'Ach, come on now, just you be thinking about it. Five miles and a half it is and if you are being on foot, like a lot of folk, Glenduir cannot get to Driech and vicey versy. Have you not thought that if Fiona is wanting to take the wee one out in its pram and be going over to see Mrs MacIntosh in Driech - well she cannot, right enough.' Robbie thinks he'll let Nigel think about that and he'll push it further tomorrow when he'll dare to remind him that £80,000 is an awful lot of money, so it is.

And Nigel, a smirk fighting a smile on his face, says, 'I've booked a digger and other equipment for next weekend, so how does that suit you? You'll have to arrange the workforce but if they're all so keen to have the track opened up again then I don't think you'll find willing helpers difficult to recruit, will you? I was going to get Willie MacVicar to announce it in church this Sunday, but you can pass it around too.'

Robbie's face has grown a full-sized grin and he knocks Nigel's shoulder with his fist. 'Ach, I was knowing fine well you would be doing the right thing, so I was.'

Nigel isn't so sure about that but says, 'I try to Robbie.'

Prickles in Luath's paws delay Nigel and it's nearly mid-day by the time he sets off to see the earthworks. He turns the sharp bend and ahead of him tens of cars are parked along the verges. Tens of people from Glenduir and Driech move about energetically with shovels, spades and wheelbarrows, even Archie MacIntosh is there though as might be expected, he's only an observer.

Established birches keel over from the scoop of the digger's bucket and the Minister of Driech church shouts, 'hullo there, Nigel, so what do you think about all these good people turning up?' But Nigel cannot hear him, there's too much noise from the digger and Robbie's enthusiastic whistle blowing. The lanky school teacher, who is there for the crack not the labouring silently offers his hip flask and as the groups of volunteers notice Nigel he raises his hands high and applauds them. To his surprise and pleasure they put down their implements and return the gesture.

'What brings you, Flashers, hardly your sort of thing is it?' Nigel calls out as he approaches the groomed, tweedy Archie perched on a shooting stick beside his Bentley shooting brake and rubber-necking like the hoi polloi.

'Good show, Mucky, it's a fine turnout, we'll be back to our old ways soon. I was passing and stopped to watch. This is the way we used nip back and forth to each other's on our bicycles?'

Nigel would dwell on those memories but he's curious about Archie's interest. 'Yes, but that was then,' he says, 'you never use the track nowadays do you?'

And Archie shows a rare awkwardness when he says, 'well you know - that stand of pines over there,' and points to where the digger is clearing away trees felled by the landslide. 'You're changing the landscape and those pines - well, you know.' Nigel looks across following Archie gaze.

'No, I don't know. What about them?'

'Oh don't mind me...'

'Come on spit it out.'

But Archie reaches for his hip flask and hands it to Nigel and slowly says, 'do you remember I liked nature study when I was a young?' Nigel does, he says he remembers Archie's jars of frog spawn and his attempt to tame a pine marten. 'Well I found a dribble of resin stuck on the bark of a pine tree - it looked like a cinnamon ball.' He stops to point at the very tree, toppled sideways. 'That fascinated me, you know. I pulled it off and there was a dead insect caught inside. I had nightmares - always have. You see, I can't get away, the ground turns to treacle and I am stuck fast, fixed, can't run, just like that insect in the pine resin. I've never liked this place since then - and I don't suppose you do either?'

'Me, why should I not like it?'

'Well, it was the same pine your Pa fell out of.' Nigel turns sharply to look at Archie.

'As it happens, I didn't.'

'No, I was beginning to realise that,' and Archie grips his friend's shoulder for a moment then passes him his flask again but Nigel's eyes narrow as he looks at the pine. 'Probably better that you didn't know which tree it was, my mother always said she'd have had it felled. Maybe Jean didn't know either, you see old Tommy, the postman, saw it happen and came to get my Pa to deal with it. I see you obviously didn't know that either did you?' and Nigel shakes his head.

'So is there something else I don't know?' he asks, but Archie only purses his lips and looks at his feet. 'Oh come on, there must have been talk, there always is, didn't your Pa ever mention it to you?'

'Well, can't say I rightly remember anything much,' and Archie gives him a quick sidelong glance but concentrates on breaking a stick with his foot.

'Look, I know Georgina told Fiona about my mother's dislike of old Adam, I know she kicked my father out of her bed, I mean people talk, things grow legs and run.'

'And you've made a connection have you?' Archie's surprise at Nigel's remark clear in his tone.

'Maybe. I'm aware of something which... Well let's just leave it at that.'

'Very well then, every so often the subject came up. In fact when I was in my early twenties, I think it was then, they said most people put it down to a straightforward accident,' and he hesitates. 'Well you know how it is, some didn't, they said it was the Fuath that made him fall.' Nigel rolls his eyes at that and Archie knows better than to press it any further. But my father said he'd never been able to believe Muckle could have slipped, he was careful, he was as agile as a monkey when climbing trees for those birds' eggs he was so keen on.'

'So did he think he *jumped*?' Nigel says

'No, not exactly.' Archie puts a hand on Nigel's shoulder. 'Look, what good it will do you, I don't know and it's only my family's speculation, mainly my mother's and you can't trust that, she held a great flaming torch for your father. Maybe she was jealous of your mother, you know how women can be.'

'No wait, hang on, Flashers, what do you mean?' Nigel's irritation clear.

'This MacIntosh female weakness for MacMuckle men?'

'No, not that. What speculation, what did your parents speculate for God's sake?'

'That it must have been a great blow to the old boy's pride to be rebuffed by Jean like that. You know he was popular with all the women don't you? and Nigel shrugs. 'Anyway, poor bugger, no way out, just had to accept it. Quite why he couldn't have found something suitable somewhere...'

'So they *did* think it was intentional.'

'Well, my mother would have said that. I don't know, but it seems an inefficient way, wouldn't you use a gun?'

'Too obvious. People would have speculated on what had driven him to do it especially when he had a newborn son. And - It would have cast an inevitable shadow over my mother too.'

'You don't really believe it was intentional do you, Mucky? It was an accident and my mother was just playing with a fanciful idea that's all. If I were you I'd forget it. Nothing can be done can it?'

Nigel doesn't answer, he's hunched over, shaking his head with his hands in his pockets and Archie doesn't add anything, he just pats Nigel again. Then suddenly he says, 'speculation, speculation,' dragging the words out. 'If you did but know quite how much of that is swilling around in my life... Anyway, there we are,' and straightens himself up. 'And I'd rather this conversation didn't get back to Fiona, I don't want her thinking about such things while she's expecting, you know what I mean.'

'No I don't actually, but it's safe with me, I'm off now,' and with that Archie snaps his shooting stick shut. 'What's this rot about your becoming a geography teacher, I told Georgina that she can't have heard Fiona right.'

'No, she did, I'm thinking about it, Flashers, an honest living and I need the income more than ever now, don't I?' But Archie is stumped for an answer to such heretical talk.

A shout goes up, what does the Laird want done with all the fallen trees and brushwood? It's a courtesy, everyone knows he'll tell them to build a bonfire and he doesn't disappoint. The digger moves off with its load from Muckle MacMuckle's place of misadventure and Nigel turns away from it. He waits there until the evening when most of the major blockage has been removed and standing on the top of the remaining obstruction he can almost see the path falling away to Driech. It's reckoned to be another two days work and clearing the rest of the track will be easy. Only when the digger stops does Nigel make to leave, but the driver gets out to call over to him. He thinks there should be a grand opening of the track and the bonfire lit only then. And as expected Nigel agrees to that.

So, a carnival atmosphere descends on the old track the following weekend. Archie provides fireworks and whisky, Nigel sends a barrel of beer and Fiona opens the track with all the impersonated aplomb of a junior Royal tape-cutter. A scratch band forms itself from all the fiddlers and accordion players with the addition of pipers, except Robbie, who can't keep up. The English owners of The Haggis Hunt Hotel fry sausages and serve their surprisingly popular haggis pizzas. Georgina MacIntosh makes people dance by the light of the bonfire whether they want to or not. She has Nigel all to herself because he won't let Fiona do anything so energetic now the baby is expected soon. She and Robbie sit on a couple of big boulders sharing one of the famous Macpizzas and watch Nigel whirling Georgina round and lifting her off her feet and how she happily collapses into his arms at the finish of each reel.

'Muckle Nigel is surely a great dancer, just like the old Laird too and Mrs MacIntosh is having a right good time, so she is,' says Robbie. 'She is getting a better dance than she can get off her own man, I am thinking,' and the pair look at Archie dancing like a well-oiled automaton, sedate and measured in every clockwork step. 'You are knowing what they say about the dancing, sure enough,' Robbie says with a twinkle.'

'That it's a vertical expression of a horizontal desire?' that's what Nigel says,' Fiona giggles.'

'Ach well, there you go, he's right enough about that, so he is,' and still smiling they keep their gaze fixed on Archie. 'No, if you are good at the dancing you are good in the sack too, so maybe this is being the best Mrs MacIntosh can get.' At that Fiona laughs out loud but manages to say that she thinks Archie might be the exception to the rule though Robbie refuses to believe it. And then she finds it impossible not to silently judge everyone's potential as they dance and begins to think Robbie is probably right. She's going to enjoy telling Nigel.

With that reel finished the band demands some liquid refreshment so the fireworks are to be let off and Robbie volunteers. Bringing a rug for Fiona, Nigel takes his place beside her putting his arm round her to keep her warm. She knows she doesn't need this level of care and attention but his concern is so touching that she lets him.

A series of bangs and cracks explode in the sky erupting in fountains and cascades of gold, red and green. Squeals of corkscrewing colour ascend and burst into huge dandelion clocks followed by threatening fizzes firing off upward then screaming like banshees. The spectacle is over too soon and when the silence returns a great cheer goes up.

'What a happy evening,' Fiona says and stretches her legs out.

'And are you happy, my Darling?' Nigel asks.

She looks at him, his face lit by the bonfire's flames. 'Of course I am, how could I not be?' and she pats her belly lightly.

'With me, are you happy with me?'

'Oh Nigel, how can you ask that? You know I am,' and she takes his hand, the one with a long, jagged scar on the palm and kisses the mark. 'Silly boy,' she says. 'You've made a lot of people happy tonight. Shall we go home or are we going to sit here until dawn?'

But Nigel points at all the people leaving, their torch lights darting in all directions, he says it looks like lost fireflies and she calls him an old romantic.

'You must promise you'll always tell me if you aren't happy,' he says and kisses her before she can answer. It's a long kiss and only ends when Archie joshes that they're gathering an audience. And he's right, the Laird and his lady publicly snogging wouldn't have been believed if it hadn't been seen.

'Well done, Mucky,' he says while struggling with a droopy piece of haggis pizza, 'I mean this very good evening, not your kissing skill. I'd say this place is much better for being opened up. Right we're off, what do I do with this insulting marriage of an I-tie pancake covered in haggis then? It's beyond me that anyone would want to eat it. Here dog,' and he drops the pizza in Luath's mouth.

When he's gone, Fiona whispers, 'Robbie thinks you can tell what people are like at sex by the way they dance. And you are "surely a great dancer, like the old Laird too" so he says, and as for Archie - well he's a no-hoper!'

'And what do you say?' Nigel replies.

'Oo, I think he's right.'

'Poor old Georgina' Nigel groans.

Renaissance

And something strange happens after the track opens again. The loch path through the ancient woodland comes alive. High in the trees red squirrels chase and chide in chirps and chucks making the only dissonance in a harmony made of bird song. Birch trees hazy with acid green buds and those old, lichen-clad Oaks offer their new leaves. All promise renewal. And the loch? It shivers in the light breeze, the sun makes it sparkle and the pebble beach sheeny. Fiona wonders at it but Nigel says it's the same as usual. Taking Fiona's hand to steady her he points at some corpses on the shore. Ravens - their black beaks and feet pointing upwards in barbs and hooks. Then, high above them a hawk's high-strung shrieks scrapes the air and he looks up.

'A falcon, d'you see it?'

'Aaah - yes. I saw one some time ago, from the tower, but it wasn't free it had jesses on its feet. Look there's another one too.' Shading their eyes, they watch the falcons' twining soar, their glide, their grace, their ease, their ownership of the sky, then they curve and bank away out of sight. Picking up a stick he throws it into the water for Luath to swim for it. He spots a pair of swans, something he says he's never seen there before.

And she says, 'beautiful things aren't they, they move so effortlessly on the water. I hope they stay,' and points at the cygnet settled on the pen's back and its brothers and sisters in the water keeping close behind. But Nigel sharply draws breath.

'That's Robbie out there in his boat,' he says slowly. 'For a moment I thought it was George, maybe I need glasses,' and he throws the stick again for the waiting dog.

Closing her eyes Fiona stretches her head back to face the sun and tells him it's just happy memories playing tricks on him. But he just waves a slow, wide arc at Robbie who rows closer towards them and stands up, cupping his hands around his mouth.

'You should be seeing this, there is an awful lot of trout out here, right enough,' he shouts, 'I have never been seeing anything like it,' and Nigel says he's pleased to hear it and wants him to catch a few for supper.

'Will you fry them in oatmeal for us, like Robbie and I used to have when I was a wee boy?' Of course she will, and she hands him some flat pebbles for skimming. Together they watch the ripples grow and merge into one another then fade away as the breeze picks up and naps the water. Robbie casts and catches one, casts again and catches another, three, four trout - it is as easy as that.

But Fiona looks down at a patch of wet, 'Nigel, my waters have broken, look.'

'What, are you sure?'

'Yes, we'd better go back.'

'Oh, bugger it! I'd better carry you, are you going to be alright? Then he shouts to Robbie but he has his back to them catching the fish. 'Robbie,' he roars as he holds on to Fiona, who feels like laughing. Robbie turns round and cups his hand to his ear. 'Come back, come here, Fiona's having the baby, we'll have to carry her back to the castle, hurry for Christ's sake.' And Robbie drops the rod and begins to row as if *his* life depended on it with the fishing line playing out behind him. Fiona bent over and feeling some pain but trying not to show it tells Nigel to stop panicking, she's never seen him panic before. And then Robbie is there, almost falling out of the boat and gets tangled up in the fishing line as he does.

'Come along lass, we will be getting you home, so we will, don't you be panicking,' he says.

'It's not me, it's Nigel who's panicking. I think I can walk,' she says but it comes out in gasps.

Both men join hands and make a cradle for her to sit on and with her arms round their shoulders her transport moves off with the speed and efficiency of a pair of sherpas. Now there is enough pain for her to keep her head down trying to suppress her moans.

'I don't know anything about this sort of thing,' Nigel says sounding slightly hysterical as they gather speed. 'I only know about lambing and calving. I hope you know what to do, Robbie?'

'You are being in luck, so you are. In the war I was with my friend and we were helping a WAAF have a baby behind the mess,' he puffs. 'Nobody was knowing she was even expecting, right enough. Anyway, himself was Australian Air Force, he was coming from the outback, so he was, and they were having to be doing everything for themselves like, so he was knowing what to do and I can remember fine. Anyhow, I will be telephoning Dr Livingstone for you - or the district nurse, Fiona'll not be lasting long enough to be getting to the Cottage Hospital, I am thinking. Your pains are coming fast, Fiona?' and she nods only managing the single word, 'very.'

The next time she looks up from her jogged journey and their heavy breathing, she sees they are nearly at the castle door and lets herself release a full-throated groan. Nigel presses his head against hers uselessly telling her to hang on as they're nearly there.

'Don't take me upstairs, put me down here, I'll be alright,' and now she sounds irritated.

'Don't we need hot water,' Nigel says as she bends over clearly in pain and Robbie grabs the telephone.

'That's only in filmmms - oooh,' and she lies down awkwardly on an old sofa. Nigel tries to settle her but she resists with angry hands. 'Oooh, leave me alone,' comes out in a strangulated breath.

'The Doctor is coming, Fiona,' says Robbie. 'Be taking her shoes and stockings off, muckle Nigel - and her - and her underpinnings too. I am thinking you should be putting cushions behind her and I will be getting a blanket and towels.'

All she can do is concentrate on trying to manage the pain which is now almost constant while Nigel, on his knees, pulls at her clothes. If she looked at him she'd see he's biting his lip, his brow is knitted but she can hear him muttering, 'I hate seeing you like this - I never knew - I wish I could take it away,' and if she could she would say she wished that too.

'Uh, aaargh, I need to push now, I want to push. Nigel, I want to push,' and he looks at Robbie, who's waiting at the open door for the doctor.

'I cannot be helping there.'

'For Christ's sake you said you knew what to do, Robbie!' Nigel snaps back at him.

'That I do, but I cannot be looking at Fiona like that,' he says. 'You look.'

'At what?' Nigel says, all his animal husbandry deserting him.

'Look... You look between her legs, is the baby's head showing yet?'

Fiona gasps, 'Bloody hell, Nigel, look will you, I can't hold on,' and Robbie's eyes widen at her outburst.

But the sound of a car coming to a halt and Fin Livingstone's reassuring voice brings audible relief from the men, mostly from Robbie who hadn't anticipated being so embarrassed by the birthing procedure when it wasn't somebody he didn't know. Now was the time for him to boil a kettle for a pot of tea, if nothing else, and unwind the remnants of fishing line still attached to him.

296

Fin has calming words when he says, 'what's all this then, Fiona, catching us out like this, somebody wants to make a fast entrance I think,' as he sees the baby's head. 'Nigel, do you want to leave us to it now?' but Nigel doesn't, Nigel isn't squeamish and he's on his knees again holding Fiona's hand. 'Right, Fiona, you push now,' Fin says as he lays a hand on her to feel each contraction. The noise of her efforts alarms Nigel so much that with each push he squeezes her hand and declines the invitation to watch the birth itself.

'Well done, Fiona,' Fin says from the end of the sofa. 'There's the head, not long now - a big push, the biggest push you've ever pushed.' And with her chin hard against her chest she does just that and Nigel now squeezes her hand with as much force as she is using to expel the baby. And enter the world the baby does with a lusty cry into the Great Hall of Glenduir Castle. Nigel's grip drops as he feels Fiona's body relax and he watches the infant being lifted up.

'Look Fluff, look, a baby.'

'I know, I've been expecting it,' she says with a tired laugh.

'You've got a fine girl she's a good size,' the cord is cut and she's wrapped in a towel.

'You clever girl, are you alright?' Nigel whispers and drops Fiona's hand to go and take the baby from him. 'Hello baby, here you are at last - hey, look what she's done,' he says as the baby grips his finger. 'She opened her eyes for a second, they're very blue, Fluff.'

'They would be. What colour is her hair?'

'Blonde - like yours,' and he gently strokes the wet curls with a finger.

And from Fiona, softly said, 'aah good,' and she lies back on the cushions.

'You will be like your beautiful ma-ma, won't you, baby?' Nigel coos as he sits on the sofa to put her into Fiona's arms. 'She really is beautiful, Fluff, thank you,' and he kisses her hand. Then there's an amused edge to his voice when he says, 'you know, it strikes me my mother's choice of name for me has well and truly come right,' she isn't looking at him, she's entranced by her longed-for baby, but she does hear him say, *'The Fortunes of Nigel* have indeed delivered, I think.'

Within hours, and sitting in his now tidy library, Nigel is at his old typewriter humming something out of tune and banging out a notice for the editor of *The Clan MacMuckle Magazine.*

PLEASE INCLUDE THIS NOTICE IN THE NEXT EDITION OF THE CLAN NEWSLETTER.
N.B. <u>Do not forget</u> to send this edition to;
William B MacMuckle, Glenduir Ranch, Douglas County, Kansas etc.

It is important that the following is printed in bold type on the first page of said magazine.

On June 17th 1965 at Glenduir Castle to Madam MacMuckle the wife of The MacMuckle, a daughter.

Three Gifts

Amy is lost for words when Fiona says Nigel was present at the birth. Nigel must have kept the details to himself and Fiona doesn't tell her the baby was not born in her bed but on the old sofa in the Great Hall and that Robbie had offered but failed to be the midwife. Instead the sisters chat about how fast the baby arrived, how Nigel dotes on her and how Fiona has never seen Robbie so excited as if she were his own. That he's going to be her Godfather has pleased him even more. To that Amy replies quickly, surprised they haven't asked Charlie Scott or Archie MacIntosh. But Fiona knows what her sister implies and insists Robbie is the right man and he'll do it well with, 'so there!' unsaid. Amy supposes her sister will know best, which must be the first time she's ever allowed her that. Then she confirms that the baby is to be called Dorothea after their mother. But only officially, Nigel and Fiona want her to be known as Dodie, it's less formal. And yes, Fiona does know Dorothea means gift, adding it couldn't be more appropriate. Then Amy's curiosity passes as an afterthought. The parcel she forwarded for Fiona, has it arrived yet? It has, it's there on the chair with the rest of the day's post, but she hasn't opened anything yet, Amy's call interrupted her. So, with the savour of superior knowledge colouring her voice, Amy tells her sister that not only did the sender use the wrong address but used Fiona's maiden name too. 'Somebody is very behind the times aren't they?' she laughs, her eagerness to know who that somebody is can be assumed. But it's not to be rewarded, Fiona must go, Nigel has come in bringing with him the MacMuckle christening gown. But he's really there waiting for an opportunity to pick Dodie up. Since she was born she's become his sedative, he's often in a chair with her up against him and both of them asleep.

'Thought you'd like to see if this thing is going to fit her,' he says as he puts the garment down then touches the excess of satin and lace. 'Poor, little thing having to wear such a volume of clothing.'

Stroking the smooth satin, Fiona says, 'if it fitted you then she'll get into it, you said you were a very big baby, she isn't, is she?'

'Nah, she's a little sweetheart,' he says never taking his eyes off her. 'Oh, that reminds me, I have something for you, Fluff, something to be going on with, I've just collected it,' and he pulls something out of his pocket.

And in his hand she sees a small gold heart, it's flat and thick as a coin, engraved on it is the name, Dodie, with her date of birth.

'I had it made from all the gold left in the bonfire after I burned the bed,' he says proudly. I had to wait until she was born to have it engraved but they did it quickly for me and I thought you could put it on a chain and wear it?' She kisses him, then takes it, holding it in the well of her palm.

'It's symbolic, did you mean it to be?' and he nods. 'It's a very clever thing to have done with the gold, I love it, I really do. I had forgotten all about it,' and this time she hugs him hard while he picks up all the post from the chair.

'You've got a lot today, I signed for that parcel too,' and he rattles it.

'Amy forwarded it,' she says, 'it was sent to Caroline Street, under my maiden name.'

And he looks at it more closely, then he sees the postmark. 'Uh - huh. Norwich - how's..?' his voice fading to nothing but she's more interested in dressing the baby in the christening gown. He clears his throat and louder this time, 'from Norwich, aren't you curious to open it?' And the clench of Fiona's stomach is understandable but her head tells her ghosts can't send parcels - but even so - anxiety delays her. 'Here take it, Fluff, give Dodie to me,' and he swaps the parcel for the baby.

'What is it?' she says as if playing for time is going to make any difference.

'I don't know, you'll have to open it won't you.'

Slowly she unwraps a flat, oval-shaped box. There's an envelope too, again addressed to Miss Fiona Lindsay, but she opens the box first. A crack of the hinge and it reveals a necklace. Two rows of graduated pearls with an emerald and diamond clasp. Genuinely bewildered she looks up at Nigel but there's a small card in the box too. She glances at it, all that's needed to read what's written.

'Show me,' he says and she holds the box for him to see. 'Pearls... Yes, and the card?' he picks it up and reads it out. 'As promised, pearls for Darling Fiona. Yours until hell freezes over, Tim. And there's one kiss.' He doesn't comment, hands it back to her and settles into the chair with the baby against him, lace and satin spilling down over him like an avalanche. Then it's, 'well, why don't you see what the letter says,' and he starts patting Dodie's back as he watches Fiona. It doesn't take long to read and she swallows hard, pressing it against her chest as she looks at him, then she looks at the letter again. 'Read it out,' he says but she doesn't answer she keeps looking at the letter. 'Read it out, Fluff, go on - who's it from?'

'It's from John Robinson, remember...'

'John Robinson? Yes, I remember who he is, go on.'

'Well - it says...'

'Just read it out, Fluff, let it do the explaining.'

Dear Miss Lindsay,

We haven't met but I am John Robinson and I believe you must have known my brother Tim. I very much regret I have to tell you that Tim died last year in a sailing accident. He drowned after he hit his head and fell from a boat which he was sailing in the Firth of Forth. Sadly none of the others on board missed him until it was too late.

Naturally this must come as a shock to you if you were not aware of this until now and for that I am sorry to be the bearer of such news. However, as the executor of Tim's will I enclose his bequest to you of this pearl necklace. I have included the sales invoice should you need it for insurance purposes.

May I ask that you sign and return to me the attached receipt in the enclosed stamped addressed envelope.

I do hope you will be pleased with the pearls knowing that was what Tim wanted and something you can remember him by...

She can't read any more and folds the letter against her chest, 'I can't, I can't take it,' she says and holds the box in her other hand as if it were a burning ember.

'Why not - what else are you going to do with it, you can't send it back can you? It's yours.' The confusion in Fiona's head is close to jamming all the filters and she drops the box and letter back on the chair and he puts the baby down to pick up all she's tried to discard. He asks, 'so who was this, Tim Robinson, to you?'

'He was a boyfriend - a long time ago.'

Slowly he says, 'I see,' and she hopes he doesn't. 'He obviously thought a lot of you didn't he?' as he looks at the sales invoice. 'Hm, bought in Madeira, December 1960 - interesting. So was he the one who was so keen on you when I first met you?'

'You've never said...'

'Neither did you...'

'How did you know that?'

'Graham, he told me in passing, he didn't give him a name, said there'd been a sailor in the picture, that's all.'

'When? when did he tell you?'

'Oh, after we got engaged. They're very fine pearls, you've seen that have you?'

'Don't Nigel, I can't take them and they're not as beautiful as yours,' and she puts her hand up to her neck.

'Oh they are, Fluff. Different though, I'll give you that.'

And her recall is jumbled and failing, she mutters, 'he hasn't made the connection...'

'Who hasn't?' Nigel says, picking the baby up again to cradle her.

'John Robinson hasn't connected me with the bequest.'

'Why would he? The woman he met in the George Hotel was introduced as Fenella MacMuckle. Your sailor obviously made his will some time ago, wouldn't you say?'

But he doesn't need an answer to that and running her hand into her hair she freezes like a statue while she tries to figure out what is for him to know and what isn't. And what comes out is, 'but you didn't say anything to me at The George.'

'And neither did you to me... Why would I, what did you expect me to say?' He gently rocks the baby, crooning, '*Oh, what a tangled web we weave...* isn't that right my little one?' But Fiona doesn't hear that and maybe it's just as well. She's turned away to sort her thoughts out, she's made a mistake and she's sure Nigel is going to ask her more now, he's going to make the connection, he must realise now why she was so upset at The George, of course he does. So she'll shift the emphasis and turns to see him cooing at Dodie, happily playing with her little hand. 'Nigel, I'll have to explain who I am, won't I?' and he looks up, the baby hanging on to his finger, 'to John Robinson, I mean - about my name and he's going to wonder why I didn't say anything in The George - and he'll tell Diana and she'll think it *such* a hoot won't she?' But now Nigel is looking at the invoice again and she thinks he's going to ask what happened between her and Tim that he hadn't given her the pearls in December 1960... And Amy, she's going to ask too, who was the parcel from and what was in it - and Nigel's going to tell her - and Graham - then they're going to tell him that Tim called at Caroline Street when she was staying with them. And at best Nigel is going to wonder why she didn't tell him that - even if he can't possibly know what she did with Tim at The Hanover Hotel... The links of deception are unravelling with the speed of chain dropping from a great height as her heart thumps and her mouth goes dry. She has to turn away again.

'Pursued by pearls,' he says and she swings round wanting to ask what he means and expecting the very worst. 'And you're overwhelmed aren't you? Can't say I blame you - quite some gift, but you're stuck with it,' and he kisses Dodie's head. 'But,' he makes that little word last so long, 'some might say such a love token from another man compromises a husband,' and he's sharing his steady, very, blue-eyed smile with her and the baby, 'so, perhaps we should keep this to ourselves.' And with Dodie's face close against his, and the necklace in his hand, he settles back comfortably on that chair again. 'And, I have an idea,' he pauses for a moment but Fiona isn't going to ask, yet in that instant her gestures, her expression, her posture betray her discomfort. But his manner doesn't alter, his warmth is unaffected as he says, 'and I think it's a good idea. Give these pearls to your daughter, put them away until she's grown up and can appreciate them...'

'Nigel, I can't do this.' She stops and it stops him too. Her head is bowed now, her hands in a tight knot as she struggles with tense, 'I should - I mean I should have...'

'Shh, look she's nearly dropped off,' he whispers. 'No need to say anything, nobody need know. Your sailor isn't here to mind is he? And anyway I don't imagine he would, after all it is a very romantic story isn't it?'